HOPE SPRINGS ON MAIN STREET

Book 3
in the Briar Creek Series

OLIVIA MILES

FOREVER

NEW YORK   BOSTON

Forever
Hachette Book Group
1290 Avenue of the Americas
New York, NY 10104

www.HachetteBookGroup.com

Printed in the United States of America

First Edition: October 2015
10 9 8 7 6 5 4 3 2 1

OPM

Forever is an imprint of Grand Central Publishing.
The Forever name and logo are trademarks of Hachette Book Group, Inc.

The Hachette Speakers Bureau provides a wide range of authors for speaking events. To find out more, go to www.hachettespeakersbureau.com or call (866) 376-6591.

The publisher is not responsible for websites (or their content) that are not owned by the publisher.

ATTENTION CORPORATIONS AND ORGANIZATIONS:
Most HACHETTE BOOK GROUP books are available
at quantity discounts with bulk purchase for educational,
business, or sales promotional use. For information,
please call or write:

Special Markets Department, Hachette Book Group
1290 Avenue of the Americas, New York, NY 10104
Telephone: 1-800-222-6747 Fax: 1-800-477-5925

For my beautiful daughter.
And for Dad, who loves Vermont.

Acknowledgments

I'd like to thank my editor, Michele Bidelspach, for her spot-on feedback, her support and guidance, and the careful attention she gives to understanding the heart of each of my stories.

Thank you to my copy editor, Lori Paximadis; my publicist, Julie Paulauski; my production editor, Carolyn Kurek; the brilliant art department for creating such a gorgeous cover; and everyone else at Grand Central who has had a hand in bringing this story from a manuscript to the shelves.

I'm so grateful to my family and friends who, after five books, haven't tired of cheering me on. Special thanks to Natalie Charles, for the brainstorming sessions, support, and a sprinkle of humor.

And last but certainly not least, thank you to all the readers who have taken a visit to Briar Creek and brought this fictional town to life.

HOPE
SPRINGS ON
MAIN STREET

CHAPTER
1

I have something to tell you, Mommy." The words were whispered, almost shyly. "I'm in love."

The light ahead turned yellow, and Jane Madison hit the brakes a little harder than she'd intended. Looking up, she caught her five-year-old daughter's reflection in the rearview mirror and tried not to show her amusement. "Oh really? What's his name?"

"I don't know," Sophie replied simply. "But we're in love."

"I see." Was it already starting? Trading in dolls for boys? Jane glanced into the mirror once more, noticing the multiple strands of pink princess jewelry roped around her daughter's neck and the clip-on plastic earrings that had been part of a set from her birthday last month. Sophie was still her sweet little girl, albeit a slightly boy-crazy one. Perhaps they watched too many cartoon movies where the prince swept the peasant girl off her feet, whisking her away to the castle where they would live happily ever after...

As much as she hated to rob her child of such a beautiful fantasy, it might be time to introduce a new message, one where the girl goes to college, finds a career, and doesn't pin her entire life on one man. A man who could just leave her in the end.

Well, at least she had some good things to count on, like ice cream for dinner when Sophie wasn't home, trash TV when the evenings became too quiet, and the twisted comfort of knowing she didn't have to bother taking the time to shave her legs anymore, unless the urge struck— and more and more often, it didn't. And she had Sophie, of course. That was all that really mattered.

Jane waited for the light to switch and then eased down the winding roads, slick from three days of rain. The leaves had started to turn, and the strong winds from the past week had blown them in her path, dotting the pavement with bursts of orange and gold. It was a gray day, a dreary day, some might say, but not for Jane. It was the perfect night to curl up with a bowl of homemade soup and catch up with her daughter. Though Sophie had been at her father's house for only one night in the last week, Jane had spent all of the hours last night when she wasn't watching reality television or scraping the bottom of the ice cream container counting the hours until the house was again filled with endless chatter and peals of laughter.

"So tell me, Sophie. How do you know you're in love?"

"He pushed me on the swings at recess today," Sophie explained. "That's called true love."

If only it were that simple. She pulled onto their street, waved at the neighbors she'd come to know in the six years she'd lived on the block, and felt the same sense

of calm she always did when her house came into view. The orange-and-white berry wreath she and Sophie had picked out last weekend hung from the hunter-green front door, secured by a twine ribbon, and the colorful red, purple, and orange mums they'd sprinkled throughout the landscaping were downright cheerful; there was no denying that. But just as she began to perk up at how nice the fall decorations looked, she felt the familiar dull heaviness settle over her chest—it was still happening, nine months after her husband had moved out.

"Well, he sounds like a very special young man," Jane said with a grin, and then stopped with a start as she considered something. The new music teacher at Briar Creek Elementary was pretty cute, and Sophie had developed a fierce crush on her seventeen-year-old camp counselor over the summer—Jane had barely been able to keep from gasping the time Sophie had tried to tickle poor Andrew, giggling the entire time. Yes, her daughter was a natural flirt. Where'd she get that from? *Her father*, Jane thought ruefully. "Is he…as tall as you?" she ventured.

Sophie nodded eagerly as Jane released her from the booster seat and grabbed her sparkly unicorn backpack. "Although, actually." Sophie froze and put a finger to her mouth. "He might be just a little bit shorter."

Jane laughed. "Come on," she said, pulling the overnight bag from the trunk. "I made you some chocolate chip cookies last night. Your favorite!"

"Oh, yummy! Kristy made me some, too."

Jane flinched, but said nothing. She took her time opening the door, trying not to think of the woman her husband had left her for as she turned the lock and flicked on the light. The soup she'd left simmering in the slow

cooker all afternoon filled the house with warmth and spices, but it did little to touch the emptiness that lingered in her heart.

Sophie made a mad dash for the kitchen, ignoring Jane's cries to take off her rain boots first. Jane sighed as she hung her coat on the hook in the mudroom. She could already hear Sophie peeling the foil off the plate of cookies. Next she'd be telling her how much better Kristy's cookies were. It wasn't enough for the woman to steal her husband. Now she was trying to win over her daughter's affections, too.

Sophie looked up as Jane entered the kitchen. "These are a lot better than Kristy's cookies. Hers are all burned around the edges, and they stick to the inside of your mouth. She uses applesauce instead of butter. Aunt Anna made a face when I told her that."

Jane turned to her daughter with interest, a slow smile creeping over her face. "You don't say," she murmured as she pulled a gallon of milk from the fridge, her spirits lifted all at once.

"I told her I liked them, but when she wasn't looking, I fed my cookie to the cat. You're not mad, are you, Mommy?"

Joyful might be a better word. Jane pressed her lips firmly shut as she handed the glass of milk to her daughter. "You did the polite thing, Sophie, but as for feeding the cat, it's probably better to stuff the cookie in your pocket next time." *Or flush it down the toilet.* "Chocolate isn't good for animals. Now, why don't you go upstairs and unpack your bag while I finish getting dinner ready?"

"Can we have a pajama party tonight?" Sophie asked excitedly as she hopped off the counter stool.

Jane glanced at the clock to see it was only ten past five. On the days she didn't work, the party sometimes started as early as four. "That sounds like a *great* idea." She sighed at the mere thought of removing the ballet tights that clung to her waist under the yoga pants, leaving an unflattering imprint on her skin. Fall session had started today after a three-week break since summer boot camp—in less than a month she had forgotten how confining and itchy a leotard could be.

She thought of the two empty ice cream containers buried deep in the trash can. Maybe she should start baking her cookies with applesauce, too.

Taking her daughter's hand, they raced up the stairs, quickly changing into their comfy cozies, as Sophie called them. While Sophie busied herself with a coloring book at the art table in her bedroom, Jane started a load of laundry, humming under her breath, until the doorbell rang and everything stopped.

Her heart began to pound. Who the heck would drop by at this hour? But right, it wasn't even five thirty. And she was robed in pink and purple plaid pants, a long-sleeved T-shirt, and—God help her—no bra. Hot faced with embarrassment, Jane ran through her mental list of possible visitors. A Girl Scout selling cookies, perhaps? Or a door-to-door salesman? She could claim she was under the weather; that would explain her choice of late afternoon attire, though not Sophie's nightgown…She bit on her nail. The worst scenario would be her ex-husband—actually, no, the worst would be his girlfriend—dropping off something that Sophie had forgotten. The bell rang again, and Jane began frantically rifling through the laundry basket, looking for something

that wasn't stained or wrinkled or didn't smell, anything that was more appropriate than what she was wearing. The bell rang a third time. Jane stepped away from the laundry pile. She was a mess either way, but at least this way she was clean.

Anxiety tightened its grip as she rounded the corner, and she chastised herself for not holding out for at least another hour—six was a far more acceptable time for pajamas, sort of... She edged to the door, holding her breath, and then sighed in relief when she saw her older sister through the glass panel.

"Grace! Come on in!" She smiled, ignoring the way Grace's expression folded in confusion as she swept her eyes down to Jane's feet, cozily covered in oversized bunny slippers. Jane felt the heat in her cheeks rise. She'd forgotten about those.

"Off to bed already?" Grace laughed, but the insinuation stung, and Jane told herself that this particular part of her weekday routine really needed to stop. And it would. Soon. Sure, it was more comfortable to live in pajamas, but the day was still young enough for people to stop by—people who were fully clothed and, unlike her, willing to go out in public.

"It's a dreary day," she explained good-naturedly, taking Grace's umbrella from her hand. "I have homemade minestrone soup if you'd like to stay for dinner."

Grace nodded and followed her into the kitchen. "Luke has a board of education meeting tonight," she explained as she set her bag on the floor and slid onto a counter stool. From above them there was a thump and a scamper of feet. Grace laughed and pointed to the ceiling. "Is she dancing?"

"I love my daughter, but I don't think the Moscow Ballet is in her future," Jane said with a rueful grin.

"How was class today?"

"Good," Jane said pensively. It had actually been very quiet compared to previous sessions. She should probably view that as a good thing, considering how rambunctious the girls in one of her summer classes had been. Between the squealing and jumping, she'd had to start carrying a bottle of ibuprofen in her dance bag.

Grace raised an eyebrow. "You don't seem very sure about that. Has Rosemary been trying to set you up on more dates?"

"Jeez, no." Jane laughed. She'd allowed her boss to set her up on a series of eye-opening dates last spring, all of which confirmed her belief that she was better off alone. One of her dates hadn't liked children and had consumed so much booze she'd had to tell the hostess to take his keys. Then there had been Brian. She had pinned so much hope on the man pitched as a bespectacled doctor. He *was* sweet, even if he had turned out to be a male nurse instead of a surgeon, but he didn't make her heart flutter, and besides, he had now been in a long-term relationship since about a week after their dinner date. She'd tried to tell herself that was for the best, that she hadn't felt that spark, but she couldn't deny the part of her that felt the sting of rejection. The lack of attraction had clearly been mutual.

So, yes, she was alone. Not by choice, but she would embrace it. What other choice did she have?

"Rosemary thankfully hung up her matchmaking hat after she finally got Anna and Mark back together," Jane said, smiling at the thought of her sister and Rosemary's

nephew living so happily together after years of stubborn silence. "If my little string of dates taught me anything, it's that dating is no fun at all."

"You just haven't found the right guy yet," Grace encouraged.

"Show me someone who is uncomplicated, committed, emotionally available, and crazy in love with me and my daughter, and then I'll reconsider. Until then, I'm happy right here."

"At home in your pajamas." Grace held her gaze.

"That's right." Jane nodded. "I've had enough dating for one lifetime, thank you very much."

Grace gave her a stern look. "You know how I feel about that."

Yes, Jane did, and she wasn't about to continue this conversation. Now that Grace was getting married and Anna was equally in love, it seemed both sisters were more focused than ever on seeing their younger sister settled down and happy.

"Yes, well, my classes were fine today," Jane said briskly. She paused, wondering why she felt so bothered by the day. Enrollment capped at ten students per class, but her three forty-five Intro to Pointe class had just four students, and Rosemary had been unusually quiet when she'd left for the day.

Oh, well, the session was just beginning, and seasonal colds were already going around. Perhaps a few of the girls had been sick or would be late joiners. Surely they'd want to audition for *The Nutcracker*.

"It was very calm. Very...stress-free."

"With Rosemary?" Grace didn't look convinced, and Jane had to laugh at that. Her boss could be demand-

ing, but Jane was too grateful for the work to complain. If Rosemary hadn't stepped in and offered her a teaching position at the studio last winter, she wasn't sure she would have had the nerve to confront Adam about the affair. It was just the ray of hope she needed to prove to herself that she could stand on her own two feet. She'd given up any hope of a ballet career—not to mention a college education—to get married and settle down. Her husband had been her life, and now she had to live one without him in it.

Jane took a loaf of sourdough bread from a bag and set the oven to preheat. "So, to what do I owe the honor of your visit?"

Grace's eyes twinkled as she gave a slow smile. "I found Sophie's flower girl dress."

"For real this time?" Grace had already changed her mind on her own wedding gown six times, and she was yet to commit to the flower arrangements, even with the big event only a few weeks away.

"I just want it to be perfect."

"I know." Jane felt bad for giving her sister a hard time. She'd been a bride herself once, caught up in all the little details that seemed so trivial now. She should have spent less time worrying about flowers and more time worrying about her future husband and the little voice that kept warning her to walk away... "Let me see what you picked out."

Jane hurried to the island and leaned in as Grace rummaged through a glossy bridal magazine, stopping at a picture of a little girl wearing a deep crimson ball gown in raw silk, with a thick ivory bow at the waist. After the chocolate brown option Grace had proposed last week,

Jane knew that Sophie would be thrilled with the idea of wearing this dress.

"Should we get Sophie?" she asked, grinning.

"She had better like it," Grace said. "These dresses take at least three weeks to arrive. I'm really cutting it close."

Jane grinned. "Sophie! Sophie, come on downstairs. Aunt Grace has something to show you!"

Soon there was a thump, heavy enough to make the sisters wince and then giggle, followed by a pounding of small feet down the wooden stairs.

"What is it, what is it?" Sophie announced breathlessly as she scampered into the kitchen.

"You're in your pajamas, too, I see," Grace remarked, taking in the pink nightgown with the ruffle trim. She gave Jane a pointed look, and Jane pulled in a deep breath, telling herself not to let it get to her. So, yes, she had become a bit of a hermit in the months since Adam had moved in with his girlfriend, but could anyone blame her? Her husband had cheated on her, lied to her, and then proceeded to move in with his mistress just three miles across town. Briar Creek was small and word traveled fast. Even if she was the wronged party, and even if she did have the support of many, she didn't need the sympathy. Or the reminder. She just wanted… She popped the bread into the oven and set the timer. She just wanted to feel safe, she supposed. And what better way to feel that way than to stay home, surrounded only by those you let in?

"Sophie, look at this dress," Jane said. "Do you want to wear that when you're a flower girl?"

Sophie jutted her chin at the picture Grace held up and shook her head. "I'm going to wear a blue flower girl dress."

Jane and Grace exchanged a look of alarm. This was at least the eleventh dress Grace had fallen in love with, usually before finding one she loved even more the next day or, in the case of the chocolate brown gown, having it boycotted by the flower girl herself. Time was running out for further indecision. This dress was going to have to work.

"But honey, Grace and Luke are having fall colors for their wedding. Remember how we looked at those pretty red and orange flowers?" *And the green ones, and the purple ones...*

"But my flower girl dress is blue! Blue velvet! Kristy said so."

Jane slid her eyes to Grace, who stared at her, not blinking.

"What do you mean, Kristy said so?" Grace pressed gently when it became clear Jane was unable to ask.

"Kristy showed me my dress. It's blue velvet with flowers around the neck."

Jane was having trouble breathing. Her chest felt tight, and her heart was pounding. She stared at Grace, willing her oldest sister to make this right, to clear this up. Grace bit down on her lip, studying her niece, confusion knitting her brow.

"Kristy said you're going to wear a blue dress for my wedding?"

"No! For *her* wedding!" Sophie cried, frustration causing her plump little cheeks to grow pink. "When she marries Daddy!"

Jane felt the blood rush from her face, and for a moment she thought she might be sick. Or faint. She slumped into a chair, listening to Grace make cheerful

conversation with Sophie in a blatant attempt to smooth over the situation, but her mind was spinning. Adam was getting married—to the woman he had left her for! He had strayed from their marriage, ripped apart their family, and yet he was ready to settle down with a new wife, live the life they should have shared and could have—if he'd loved her.

Tears prickled the back of her eyes, but she blinked quickly, refusing to let them fall in front of Sophie. There would be plenty of time to cry tonight—God knew she wouldn't get any sleep now, ultrasoft flannel pajama pants or not.

It was so easy for Adam. He'd gotten bored of one wife and quickly found another. He didn't have to live with an emptiness in his heart, or think of something funny that had happened that day and find there was no one in the bedroom to tell it to—and that it was too late to pick up the phone and call someone. He didn't have to stand at the playground on a Saturday afternoon and watch other smiling couples push their children on the swings, feeling like his heart was twisting with each breath—because Adam was actually one of those happy couples!

He'd moved on. He'd found someone. He didn't have to go on dates, try on new people, see if they fit. While she…she was still trying—in vain, it would seem—to make sense of her new life, the life she hadn't chosen, and to forget the one that had been taken from her.

"Jane?" Grace's voice was overly bright, her smile bared, her green eyes electric. "Why don't we have some of that delicious soup?"

"I'll set the table!" Sophie volunteered. She took three placemats from the basket on the counter and began

arranging them on the pedestal table. "Daddy said it's important for me to help, so I can show a good example."

What was she talking about? Jane moved slowly to the slow cooker and lifted the lid, feeling her stomach stir from the aroma. She couldn't eat if she tried. Adam was living the easy life, wasn't he? No harm done, on he went. No regard for her, or the damage he had caused. No glance back. Must be nice. Must be nice indeed.

"Daddy said I'll have lots of responsibility when the new baby comes."

The glass lid fell from Jane's hand, shattering in the ceramic sink. Grace's hands were on hers instantly, but she wasn't cut. Not physically at least.

"What did you just say, Sophie?" she managed, even though she didn't want to know. She didn't want to know anything.

"There's going to be a baby, Mommy!" Sophie's eyes danced with excitement. "I get to be a flower girl! *And* a big sister!"

Jane swallowed the lump in her throat, trying to process everything, waiting for the wounds to seal shut again. She'd told herself she was better off alone, that she preferred it that way. If she didn't give her heart away, it couldn't be broken. This was a fresh reminder.

Grace's hand was still tight on hers. "You sure you don't want to give dating another try?" she asked halfheartedly, but concern darkened her eyes.

Jane nodded firmly, but the tug in her heart said otherwise.

CHAPTER
2

Henry Birch stood in the middle of the perfectly land-scaped town square, his travel-sized umbrella hanging at his side despite the light drizzle that filtered through the golden oak leaves. He roved his eyes over Main Street, up around Cedar Lane, and down Chestnut, past the fat pumpkins squatting at the base of each shop door, and the corn-stalks wrapped around every iron lamppost, considering how he might summarize his hometown of Briar Creek.

With its quaint shops and cobblestone streets, it is easy to be lured in by the charm of this small Vermont town, but do plan on limiting your visit to a three-day weekend, lest the locals get too friendly...

He rolled back on his heels, lips thinning, and popped open his umbrella. Just ahead, smack in the center of the square, was the white gazebo, freshly painted last spring, no doubt just like it was every year. Wet leaves stuck to its wide stairs, where he'd sat many a day watching a festi-val, chatting with friends. Back then, his gaze was always off in the distance, his attention only half present as anxi-

ety churned in his gut, looking for a hint of a problem, an issue he'd have to deal with or hide, until inevitably it presented itself and he'd have to leave. It always ended the same way—his face burning with shame as the curious stares followed him until he was safely out of sight.

He tightened his grip on the plastic umbrella handle and turned back to Main Street, trying to ignore the acid that burned his stomach. There was no sense wasting time on memory lane.

He crossed the street and headed deeper into town, scanning for a quiet place to work on his latest assignment. Most of the shops had turned over since he'd moved away more than six years ago, reminding him that even in Briar Creek, things did grow and change. He frowned as he caught his reflection in the window of a new restaurant called Rosemary and Thyme. The travel writer in him forced to admit it looked half decent, at least from the outside, with its tall paned windows and a hint of thick velvet curtains and dark wood. He scanned the menu behind a glass case, impressed, and then glanced away before he invited trouble. That was just the problem with Briar Creek: If you stood still long enough, you were bound to run into someone who knew you way back when, someone who would want to know how you'd been and what you'd been up to—*Didn't you get married?*—someone wanting to offer condolences, who would lower their tone when they mentioned why...

Well, he didn't need their damn pity any more than he needed their inquisitions. He dodged through the rain, ducking under awnings, falling back on the few places he knew. Quickly deciding his options were Hastings, the local diner, or an armchair at Main Street Books,

he decided on the latter. Hastings would no doubt be filled with locals wanting to chat, and he wasn't here to catch up.

The door to the bookstore jingled when he pushed it open, and he set his umbrella in the overflowing stand, wiping his feet on the coir mat before walking over to a display table to peruse the new releases. The smell of coffee and sweet cinnamon pulled at his attention, and he glanced to the right, grinning as he ventured into the adjacent café. His sister had mentioned that the Madison girls had recently spruced up the place, but this was a complete renovation. A bakery counter lined the far wall, filled with scones, pastries, and muffins, and clusters of farm tables filled the space near the large paned window. Despite the addition being new, the floorboards were wide and stained a rich mahogany to match those of the bookstore, and instead of modern track lighting, wrought iron chandeliers and sconces lit the room they called the Annex.

It was just the kind of local gem he liked to highlight in his articles. *If* he was writing an article on Briar Creek, that was. And he wasn't. Most definitely not.

Henry grinned as he dropped his bag from his shoulder with a thud. This was officially home for the next few weeks he was stuck in this damn town.

A few people he mercifully didn't recognize sipped cappuccinos and read books or chatted in low voices. Henry walked to the counter, glancing around for someone who worked there, and waited with growing impatience. The last thing he needed was to be standing around when someone came in and recognized him. Then he'd be forced through the usual song and dance, the one he'd already been through just about every time he dared

to leave the Main Street Bed and Breakfast, when all he wanted to do was get in and out and on with his day. Alone.

He gritted his teeth and looked around the café. He was just about to step into the bookstore itself when a flush-faced and frazzled-looking woman came through a back door, tying an apron at her waist. The color in her cheeks rose when she met his steady gaze, and after a beat, she gave a genuine smile, but it did little to mask the trepidation in her eyes.

"Henry! This is a surprise!"

He felt his grin widen as he scanned her shocked expression. With her flushed face and bright smile, Jane Madison looked just as beautiful as she had on her wedding day. He remembered the day clearly; couldn't forget it if he tried. And oh, had he.

"Jane! Wow...Jane!" He shook himself back to the present, pushing back the thumping of his chest, and he took in that smile. He reached out awkwardly to embrace her, but the counter was wide, and the opening was a few feet down. After they shared a laugh, he stuck out his hand, holding hers in both of his. "It's so good to see you! You working here now?"

She nodded, then glanced down at her hand—he hadn't let it go yet, and he still didn't want to. He felt his grin turn rueful as he loosened his grip and shoved his hands into his pockets, but Jane just blinked and bit her lip, watching him expectantly. Of all the people in Briar Creek, she was one he was at least glad to see. She'd married his best friend, after all.

"I work here part time. I teach ballet at the studio, too," she added quickly.

How could he forget the long legs, the dance bag she toted around when she'd dated Adam...the scholarship to that academy she'd given up when he proposed? Henry let his eyes pass over her face, wondering if that was regret he sensed in her expression. Her hazel eyes were wide, and rimmed with long, black lashes. She'd filled out a bit since he'd last seen her—no longer so gangly. The soft curves suited her, he decided at once, lingering on her hips. He swallowed hard.

"You keep busy," he remarked.

"That I do. So...what brings you to town?" Her eyes darkened as she held his stare.

"Ivy," he said, referring to his sister.

Jane's shoulders seemed to relax. "Ah. Well, what can I get for you? Coffee?"

"Black," he said, reaching into his back pocket for his wallet. "The biggest size you've got. I have some work to catch up on."

"Travel writing, right?" She slid the mug to him, holding up her hand in refusal when he held out a five-dollar bill. Her smile was shy, hesitant almost, and she looked away every time they made eye contact.

Guilt rested heavily on his shoulders. He'd been away too long. But then, what part of coming back was ever supposed to feel easy?

"I insist." He grinned, dropping the money into the tip jar.

Her lashes fluttered as she sighed. "Well, then at least take a muffin. Wild blueberry, freshly baked this morning." From a basket she took an enormous, crumble-topped muffin. Blueberries the size of nickels burst from the moist cake, and Henry's stomach rumbled at the sweet scent. "They'll sell out quickly," she pressed, grinning.

"Did you make these yourself?" he asked, accepting the plate.

"God, no." Jane laughed and the pink in her cheeks grew higher. "My sister Anna makes them. She runs a restaurant and café in town—Rosemary and Thyme? You may have passed it."

"The nice-looking place on the corner of Second." Henry nodded, impressed.

"She and Mark Hastings opened it this summer. It was a café called Fireside before that, but when they joined forces, she expanded."

"Mark Hastings!" Henry grinned. He hadn't thought of the Hastings guys in years. "My sister and I don't chat as much as I would like, but I feel like Ivy mentioned something about Luke and Grace getting back together." He shook his head. "I must be more out of touch than I thought. I didn't even know they'd broken up."

Jane's eyes widened at this. "Oh, there's a lot you don't know, then. You've stayed away too long."

He locked her gaze, ignoring the truth in her statement. "Why don't you fill me in, then? We could have a coffee, catch up a bit." He motioned to the empty table near the window. Work could wait. "What do you say?"

She seemed to stiffen. "Oh. I have to watch the counter."

He glanced around the room. Everyone was engrossed in a book or a conversation, or huddled over a laptop, deep in concentration. A quick scan beyond some bookshelves to the front door revealed it empty.

"If a customer comes in, I'll understand. I have an article to finish, so I'll be here for a while."

She gave him a long look, and he soaked in the pleasure

of looking into her pretty face, without excuse. "You're not going to take no for an answer, are you?"

He arched a brow. "Should I?" But even as he said it, he knew he should. He should go to the corner, open his laptop, and get on with his life. His work kept him busy, kept his mind from running down paths it should resist. From lingering on people like Jane Madison and everything she represented, everything she'd once meant.

She hesitated. "Coffee it is, then. I could use another cup, honestly."

Smiling easier now, she reached for another mug, and that was when he saw it. The engagement ring he'd personally helped Adam select at a jeweler in the neighboring town of Forest Ridge was missing, as was the plain silver wedding band he'd held in his breast pocket at their wedding, retrieving it on cue, watching as his best friend slid it onto her slender finger. She'd been smiling then, her eyes glistening with tears behind the soft sheen of her veil, and he remembered thinking Adam was the luckiest guy in the world.

Now, her fingers were bare, and it suddenly clicked. That sorry bastard had lost the best thing that had ever come into his life. And now here he was, reminding Jane of a time in her life she probably just wanted to forget.

He of all people could relate to that.

CHAPTER 3

Why was she being so defensive? There was no reason to be. Henry Birch was a nice guy. Ivy's brother. Decent guy. Honest guy. Sometimes a little too honest, if she dared say so, but still an all-around good guy. So what if he once was Adam's closest friend and best man in her wedding? That was years ago. He hadn't even really kept in touch...

But something told her that her trepidation had something to do with more than the fact that Henry and Adam were as close as brothers growing up—it was that Henry looked...different. Better. Downright...handsome.

"I'm sorry about you and Adam," Henry said as soon as she sat down at the table. He ran a hand through his dark brown hair, his sky-blue eyes locking hers. Had she never noticed those eyes?

She held his stare for a moment, dismissing the flutter that zipped through her stomach, and waved off his concern with a simple shrug. "It's been almost a year."

She experienced a little jolt at the realization. A year... already? It was an alarming thought. Nine months had

somehow passed since that terrible Christmas week when she'd finally voiced her suspicions about the affair. Nine months was all it had taken for Adam to start over, to put everything they'd shared permanently in his past, while she was still living in the home they had chosen together, raising their only daughter, stuck in the remnants of their life together. It was so unfair. So terribly unfair. It should have been her moving on first—her finding triumph in the wake of his betrayal, her finding happiness again…

Across the table, Henry was watching her carefully, one brow lifted in question, his lips pulled into a frown. Oh, there was that flutter again! Jane took a quick sip of her coffee to steady herself. What was wrong with her? So he was a good-looking guy. He'd always been a good-looking guy. He'd always been nice—quiet and sensitive. But he was also Adam's best friend. And besides, he was just visiting Ivy, so really, there was no point in any of this. He was a good-looking man and that was the sum of it. And clearly her sisters were right: She needed to get out more. But oh, the thought of it…

"I'm fine," she assured Henry, forcing a smile. And she was. She was just wonderful, crawling into an empty bed every night, knowing the only men who ever hugged her anymore were her sisters' significant others, a fact that was, she knew, painfully pathetic. And she was perfectly happy eating cheese right from the block while standing in her kitchen on the nights her daughter wasn't with her. Why dirty a dish? She could think of nothing more depressing than cooking dinner for just herself, and oh, wasn't it a thrill to take that Snickers from the freezer, tear open the wrapper, grab a glass of wine, and know that no one could stop her? So really, there was nothing for any of

them to worry about. Yes, she was a twenty-six-year-old single mother whose cheating husband had impregnated his mistress. Worse things had happened, surely. "I'm just fine," she said again.

She took another sip from her mug, glancing at him over the rim. From the pinch between his brow, he didn't look convinced. It was on the tip of her tongue to ask, the burning question that made her heart speed up and her palms sweat: *Have you talked to him?* But she forced herself to refrain. She didn't want to know the details, didn't want to hear about the wedding or the baby, if they knew the gender, any of it. It made it all too real. Made the life she'd valued feel too replaceable. Disposable, really.

She glanced down and blinked into her mug. *Don't cry.*

"Well, if you ever want to talk about it, I have firsthand experience in failed marriages." Henry took a sip of his coffee and set it down on the saucer, his smile grim.

Jane frowned. "I'm sorry. I should have sent a card."

Henry arched an eyebrow, but his mouth twitched playfully. "A card?"

Jane shifted in her seat, feeling uneasy under the weight of that stare. "That's right."

He leaned into his elbows on the table, his thick brows furrowing, but there was a gleam in his sharp blue eyes that only two people who'd been through a hellish experience could share. "Did people send you cards when you and Adam got divorced?"

"Well, no..." Instead they'd sent casseroles. Desserts. Fudge brownies and cobblers. And she hated cobbler. It seemed every woman over the age of fifty had a desire to plump her up or set her up with their nephew, and every woman under thirty-five could only gape, no doubt

concerned that a wandering eye was somehow contagious. *Don't worry*, she wanted to call out, *just because it happened to me doesn't mean it will happen to you!* And it didn't. They were the lucky ones. But then, they hadn't stupidly married their high school sweetheart at the ripe age of nineteen, either.

"I appreciate the concern, but it's better this way. I'm not exactly marriage material." Henry leaned back in his chair and held up a hand. He brought it down to his mug, clutching it by the handle, and Jane allowed herself a glance at his hand. Sure enough, no ring. His fingers were strong and manly, so capable looking. She idly wondered how they might feel running over her bare skin...She took a quick sip of her coffee. This was getting ridiculous!

"Caroline and I were over before it began," Henry said. "We never even made it to our second anniversary."

"Good thing you didn't have children," Jane noted. "It's easier that way."

Henry's frown deepened, and Jane wondered if she'd hit a nerve. "Yeah. Good thing."

He tore the muffin apart and offered her half. Jane shook her head, but her heart began to race when she glanced into his eyes, catching a hint of amusement. "At least a bite," he said, bringing a small piece close to her mouth. His fingers scanned her lips, and she twitched on reflex. Panicked, she brought her mug to her mouth and downed the rest of her coffee. Her stomach was flipping and twisting, and being fed by a handsome man, in the window of the Annex, where all of Briar Creek would see, was...not an option, no matter how tempting. People would talk, and it would get back to Adam, and he would learn it had been Henry, and no good would come from

that. The last thing she needed was to look like she was trying to make her ex-husband jealous.

"Have you met anyone else?" Jane tipped her head, wondering why a hard knot had just formed in her abdomen. It was a natural follow-up question, and besides, she was genuinely curious how long was customary to move on after a marriage ended. Really, she told herself, that's all it was.

Henry shook his head. "Nah. No time. My works keep me bouncing from one place to another."

"Sounds amazing." Jane smiled. She'd only been out of Vermont twice in her life—once for her honeymoon in Florida and the other time to visit Grace when she was living in New York. She'd had the opportunity to leave a long time ago, but then Henry knew that already.

Henry shrugged again. "I like it. Can't say Caroline did, though."

He looked down at his mug, growing quiet, and Jane instantly regretted broaching the topic. She hated when people asked her anything about the divorce, or even how she was doing. Was there anything worse than being stopped in the supermarket by a gentle hand on her arm and kind eyes accompanying the "How are you holding up, dear?" when all she wanted to do was buy a gallon of milk?

"I suppose you've heard that Adam is getting remarried?" There, it was out. She may as well be the one to bring it up. From the startled look in Henry's expression, she realized he hadn't known, and she felt her earlier wariness begin to fade.

"Already?" Henry looked downright bewildered, and something about that made Jane laugh.

"It is soon, isn't it?" She leaned across the table, happy for the chance to confide the thoughts that were leaving her sleepless and exhausted. Enjoying the moment, she reached across the table and broke of a piece of the muffin Henry had been so willing to share. Oh, it was good. Anna certainly didn't disappoint. But then, her sisters never did.

"Very!" Henry shuddered, then flashed her a wicked grin that made her stomach roll over. "But then, I'm not eager to repeat the process."

She dismissed the twinge of disappointment she felt and focused instead on his lingering smile. She'd forgotten about that hint of a dimple on his left cheek. Caroline, whoever she was, was probably mighty disappointed when things didn't work out with Henry. It was hard enough to lose a husband, but to lose a quiet, sensitive, funny guy like him? Jane couldn't imagine, and luckily, she wouldn't have to. Henry wasn't looking to get married, and since when had she started looking at Henry like this in the first place?

She shifted in her chair and forced her attention back to more sobering thoughts.

"It doesn't stop there, actually," Jane admitted, and she was rewarded by Henry eagerly leaning into the table, until she caught a waft of his musky scent. "They're having a baby."

Henry frowned at this and pulled back in his chair. "Aw, Jane. That can't be easy."

"No." Jane blinked quickly, feeling the familiar prickle at the back of her eyes. She cursed to herself, wishing she hadn't brought it up. But Henry had always been such a good listener...

He's a writer, she told herself firmly, thinking of her sister Grace. Writers were always good listeners. They observed life. They recorded it. They embraced it. It was nothing more than that.

And she was just a lonely divorcée, and before that she'd been a lonely wife, with a husband who couldn't be bothered to ask about how she spent her time when he wasn't around, much less how she was feeling.

Across the table, Henry was still frowning at her, and she hated the concern that shadowed his clear blue eyes, but worse, the lack of surprise.

"I'm sorry, Jane. Adam and I haven't kept in touch much over the years. I liked your family Christmas cards, though."

She spared a wry grin. "I suppose you received last year's?"

"In March, when I got back from Asia, but yes. Why?"

"Most people received them around the same day they learned he had moved in with his mistress. A few people even asked me if they should return the card!"

Henry's expression darkened. "People in this town talk too much."

Jane studied him as he rubbed the back of his neck, then turned back to the window. His jaw was set, and a day's worth of stubble had collected over it. It made a soft sound when he ran his hand over his chin.

"Well, small-town life does have some drawbacks," Jane agreed vaguely, deciding against asking about his mother. Ivy rarely spoke of Mrs. Birch, even after her death this summer, and Henry had never wanted to, either. There had been talk, gossip when Jane was younger, about Mrs. Birch's reputation, but Jane had tried not to pay any attention. She could sense the way it affected Henry, the

way he could seem so withdrawn at times, the way he seemed to enjoy getting out and joining her and Adam for a pizza, even if he didn't talk much, just listened instead.

She understood not wanting to talk about things that hurt. Now, more than ever.

Henry took another sip from his mug. "Sure does."

"Well," Jane sighed. "I should probably get back to work." She gave him a small smile and stood, feeling a little sad that their conversation had been so short.

"I'll see you again," Henry said, his voice clear and firm, as if the topic wasn't open for discussion.

Jane felt herself waver, thinking of Adam, of how happy he'd be to see Henry again, how the two would fall back into old patterns, and the likelihood of Henry talking to her without feeling awkward or torn would be unlikely.

"You know where to find me," she said simply.

She walked back around the counter, started a new pot of coffee, and glanced at the clock. In two hours, school would be out, and life would get back to normal. Sophie would be tired, no doubt in need of a snack, then there would be the kindergarten ballet class, and Tiny Tappers for Sophie while she taught the ten-year-old group, then home to make dinner, get to bed, and prepare for tomorrow. That was her life. Full, busy, and it would be enough.

And the man sitting over at the near window, staring at the rain collecting on the pavement instead of the laptop he'd just set up in front of him? He was part of her life with Adam. And that life was long gone.

"Jane, do you have a moment?"

Jane glanced up to see Rosemary Hastings, or Madame

Hastings as she liked to be called at the studio, standing in the doorway of studio 1. Her graying hair was tied back in a low bun, and a long white chiffon dance skirt was tied at the waist of her long-sleeved black leotard.

"Of course." Jane smiled brightly as the last of her five-year-olds trailed from the classroom, leaving just Sophie behind. "Change into your tap shoes, honey. Class starts in fifteen minutes. When that's over, we'll go home and have dinner."

"That's what I wanted to talk to you about, Jane." Rosemary came into the room and closed the glass door behind her. "There isn't going to be a tap class today."

Jane looked up from helping Sophie with her shoes. "Oh no? Are you feeling sick?"

"There isn't going to be a Tiny Tappers class this session, Jane. I've had to cancel it."

"Cancel it? But why?" She had depended on Sophie taking that class while she taught Ballet Three. Surely Rosemary knew that.

"Low enrollment." Rosemary raised her palms. "Only four children were signed up for the class."

"I only have three girls in my four forty-five today." Jane frowned, realizing where this conversation was headed.

"I'm afraid we won't be able to offer that class either this session, Jane. I'm offering it with Ballet Four instead. I'm sorry, but I don't know what else to do other than combine a few classes. The art school down the road needs extra studio space, and I'm considering entering into a schedule with them a few days a week."

Jane looked around the studio, from the gleaming oak floors, to the walls of mirrors, to the skylights that let in

natural light. "But...you don't even let anyone walk in here with street shoes!"

Rosemary closed her eyes and shuddered. "I know, believe me I know. I'm getting older, though, and I'm on a fixed income. Now, don't get me wrong. I've lived comfortably off what my late husband left me, but I've put three children through college with it, paid off my house, and used most of it toward investments around town, this place included. This business supports me; it's not just a hobby."

Jane nodded, knowing just how much money Rosemary had given to not just her children, but also her sister-in-law by marriage, Sharon Hastings, and her nephews Mark and Brett. Rosemary had been widowed twenty years ago, and while she lived well, she also lived generously. Too generously, it now seemed.

"Please don't say anything. I'm sure this is just a temporary problem, and I don't want my son worrying. Luke was given an inheritance—all my children were—but that is their money, not mine. I want Luke to use his share toward his new life with Grace, toward their children." She waggled her eyebrows at this, and Jane gave a watery smile.

"Maybe it will pick up soon. Kids are busy with the start of school," she offered, even though the excuse sounded lame, even to her own ears.

"Maybe." Rosemary didn't seem to believe it either. "Whatever the reason, I don't see much choice. I only wish I could have given you more notice."

Jane chewed on her lip, thinking of the position this left her in and knowing she had no right to voice her complaint right now. This studio meant a great deal

to Rosemary—it had gotten her through the loss of her husband—and Jane knew too well how important it was to have a purpose to help get through the rough patches. She looked over at Sophie, who was struggling to tie the bow on her tap shoes, and smiled.

"How many classes do you still need me for?" Jane hedged.

Rosemary winced. "Four?"

Jane tried to mask her shock. This essentially cut her income in half, and even with Adam's child support there was already little left after she paid the mortgage and monthly bills, despite the strict budget she adhered to. There was hardly anything left over for little luxuries, and Christmas was only a few months away...

"Perhaps you could ask Grace if she needs more help at the bookstore," Rosemary suggested eagerly. "Or maybe Anna needs someone at the restaurant? A hostess perhaps?"

Jane gave a brave smile, but her heart was beginning to pound. Working at the studio had been perfect for a single mother with a young child—Sophie could take lessons while she taught. Grace and Anna might be her sisters, but there was no way she could bring Sophie to work with her at either establishment. And the cost of childcare would wipe out anything she earned by the hour... Her mother was sometimes available to help, but more often than not, Kathleen was overbooked with her interior design business.

She supposed she could always sell the house and move in with her mother to save on bills. The old Victorian she'd grown up in was certainly big enough, but it wasn't home anymore, and Sophie had experienced

enough change in the past year already. Jane had poured so much of herself into decorating Sophie's room, envisioning it even before Sophie was born. That was the room where she'd held her baby, rocked her to sleep, read her stories, and tucked her into bed each night. She couldn't bear the thought of closing the door on it forever. So much had already been lost.

She squared her shoulders. "Well, I'll see you tomorrow, then?" Jane tried to smile, but her tone was a bit tinny.

"Monday," Rosemary corrected, her eyes kind as she set a hand on Jane's wrist. "I've cancelled the Friday and Saturday classes."

Jane struggled to recover from her error. "Oh. Sure. Monday." She usually worked at the Annex on the weekends Sophie was with Adam anyway. Maybe she could ask for an extra shift to make up for the lost class time.

She remembered what Rosemary said about not worrying Luke and stopped herself. Grace was getting married in a matter of weeks. This was, Jane knew from firsthand experience, the happiest time in her life. She didn't need to worry her sister now. She'd worried Grace enough already last year, dragging her back from New York and confiding in her about Adam and his little fling at the office.

Jane pressed her hand to her forehead and closed her eyes. She was getting a headache. She couldn't think about this right now.

Sophie was staring at her when she opened her eyes again, a look of worry creasing her small face. Jane had worked so hard to hide her struggles from her daughter. No five-year-old should have to see their mother fall apart.

"Change of plans, Soph." She smiled, bending down

to undo the knot Sophie had formed with the black shoe-laces. "We get to head home early tonight."

"Yeah!" Sophie cried, and then paused. "But I love tap."

"If only other little girls did," Rosemary tutted from the edge of the room. "Tell me, Sophie, what do the kids in your class like to do after school?"

"I don't know." Sophie shrugged. "Watch TV?"

Jane heard Rosemary snort, and she had to smile. Leave it to Sophie to always take her away from her troubles, even for just a minute.

"Ready, honey?" Jane stood and shrugged Sophie's ivory button-down sweater over her shoulders, then gripped the little girl's hand tight. She had her daughter, and that's what mattered. *Focus on that, Jane.*

"Jane, I'm here, if you need to talk more." Rosemary looked pained as she watched them go. "And next session might be better. I . . . hope so, at least. *The Nutcracker* auditions are in two weeks, and I might need extra help with rehearsals . . ."

They both knew *The Nutcracker* was Rosemary's show. She'd lie awake at nights choreographing it, then drink pots of coffee all through November and December to stay sharp. She obsessed over every detail, her biggest fear that the performance would get stale, too similar to last year's, and ticket sales would plummet. By the third week in December, you could hear her humming the opening number under her breath, and her blue eyes would go wild if any of the girls dared to cough or even suggest they might have a cold coming on. The best Jane could hope for was to fill in for a few of her boss's ordinary classes as the opening night approached.

"It's okay, Rosemary. Besides, you're probably right. Next session will be busy, and with the holidays coming anyway...it will be nice to have more free time. Don't worry about me. I'll land on my feet."

And if she had anything to do with it, the dance studio would, too. It had to.

For now, she would just have to ask Grace for more hours at Main Street Books. Surely Grace might need some time off in the coming weeks to plan her wedding. She was admittedly overwhelmed with all the details. Some time to focus on her upcoming nuptials might help...both of them.

Jane let a sigh roll through her shoulders. That was exactly how she would frame it. Not as a favor, not a cause for alarm, but as a suggestion that she take some of the burden off her older sister...while helping herself in the meantime. After all, as Rosemary had pointed out, the winter dance session might fare better than fall, and there was still the hope that an opportunity to perform in *The Nutcracker* would lure the children back to the studio. It was a temporary setback, and if not... Her heart began to pound. She'd cross that bridge when she got to it. She'd learned over the past year not to get ahead of herself when she could avoid it; it only led to more stress, and she had enough to deal with at the moment.

Like Adam getting remarried, and Sophie being his flower girl and sister to his mistress's baby.

Jane closed her eyes and leaned back against the smooth leather headrest. She'd been sitting in the car outside Rosemary and Thyme for a good ten minutes, strumming up the energy to put on a smile and join the girls for more wedding planning fun, wanting more than anything to know her heart was in it. She was happy for Grace—of course she was—but now, she couldn't stop thinking that Kristy and Adam must be excitedly planning their wedding, too. No doubt Kristy was thumbing through bridal magazines, shopping for her dress, contemplating lace or satin. She didn't even want to know what the ring looked like. To think of Adam—her husband!—going to a store and selecting a ring for another woman... Well, it was downright inconceivable. Jane was certain he'd gone with something bigger and showier this time around, not like the chip of a diamond she had sitting at the bottom of her nightstand drawer at home.

Before she could continue down this path of self-destruction, which would soon end with a pajama party, a spoon, a half gallon of vanilla ice cream, and a jar of peanut butter, Jane opened the door and hurried to the set of heavy double iron doors. It was Saturday night, and she'd already spent enough time worrying over things that were out of her control.

Inside, the restaurant was warm and lively—a sharp contrast to Main Street at this hour. An inviting fire crackled in the hearth, and groups of women and a few couples sipped wine on the sofas and club chairs Anna had arranged in the lobby. Jane craned her neck deeper into the dining room looking for her sisters and friends,

breathing in the smells of warm fresh bread and garlic. Already the buzz was having an effect on her mood, and she chastised herself for sitting in the car feeling sorry for herself when she could have been inside, enjoying the fun and forgetting about her troubles.

Ivy Birch, Grace's best friend, spotted her first and waved her over to where Grace, Ivy, and Kara Hastings, Luke's middle sister, were already through the better part of a bottle of wine. Grace happily poured the rest in a glass for Jane as she dropped into an empty chair and began unwrapping her scarf.

"Thanks," she said, taking a sip. "Is Anna able to join us?" She glanced toward the kitchen, hoping their middle sister would be able to get a break for a night. She'd thought Anna had worked hard running Fireside back when she was all on her own, but the success of her café was nothing compared to the popularity of the new establishment. They had a wait list two weeks out, but that didn't stop people from lining up for a spot at the bar night after night, hoping for a chance to try the chef's special.

"I'm right here," Anna said, pulling out the chair beside her. Her cheeks were flushed, her blue eyes bright, and her smile positively radiant. Hard work had always suited Anna, but Jane suspected being back together with Mark had more than a little something to do with her sister's sudden glow.

"Busy night," Jane commented.

Anna shook her blond hair from its ponytail and took a long sip of water. "Which is why unfortunately I can't stay for long. We have another round of reservations in an hour. I'm sorry, Grace," she said, as she reached for the bread basket.

"Don't worry about it. We'll have plenty of time to catch up more at the cake tasting next week."

Anna grinned and sat a little straighter. "I hope you'll like what I came up with."

"And I hope you like the bridesmaid dresses." Grace laughed, but her brow furrowed as she glanced around the table. They'd all seen the first four dresses, each later frantically calling the others to question the off-the-shoulder number with the enormous bow on the left hip, or, the following week, the empire waist cocktail frock cut in such an unfortunate way that they'd all appeared to be at least five months pregnant.

From under the table Jane felt Anna take her hand and squeeze it tight as Grace flipped through a magazine and stopped at her page marker. She turned the spread to them, and looked up.

Silence stretched as the four women stared at the dress they would most likely be wearing down the aisle, for most of Briar Creek to see.

"Well?"

Jane's shoulders relaxed as she studied the simple, strapless crimson taffeta gown with the A-line skirt to the ankle.

"It will look stunning with the bouquet we decided on," Ivy said.

"Oh…about that." Grace bit down on a nail as Ivy's mouth gaped.

"Don't tell me you're changing your mind again."

"No," Grace said hesitantly. "I just…thought maybe we could add some purple in there, too. I still go back and forth on whether I should do a plum-colored dress for Sophie."

"So long as it's not blue, and velvet, I don't care what color the flower girl dress is," Jane remarked. She reached for her wineglass and took a long sip. It was only once she'd set it down that she realized all eyes had shifted to her.

Darn it. She hadn't wanted to make this night about her. There would be plenty of time to fill the women in about Adam's latest blow, but not now. Tonight was supposed to be about Grace, about her wedding. About escaping reality and focusing on the fantasy. Wasn't that what a wedding was? It was the fairy-tale moment. It was hardly the same as a happily ever after.

"Long story," she said, forcing a laugh. Grace's smile turned sad, and Jane yanked open the menu with a newfound sense of purpose. She decided on one of Mark's seasonal specials—butternut squash gnocchi in a sage butter sauce—which she knew was paired with Anna's apple crisp cheesecake for dessert. Normally, and especially now that she was back in the dance studio, she watched her figure, but tonight she was too exhausted to bother, and something about being here, in a bustling restaurant with some of her favorite people in Briar Creek, helped put things in perspective again. Had thin thighs and a tight waist kept her husband from wandering astray? Nope!

"So, how was class today?" Anna sipped her wine, looking at her expectantly.

"Oh . . . I didn't have any classes today." Jane was happy for the darkness of the room. If her sister saw the heat in her cheeks, she'd be onto her in a second. As it was, Jane struggled to make eye contact. She reached for another slice of bread.

As expected, Anna frowned. "But it's Saturday. You always have classes on Saturday."

"Rosemary isn't offering the same classes this session," Jane replied in what she hoped was a breezy tone. "By the way, your scones were a big hit today."

Anna did a poor job of masking how pleased this made her. Though she now exclusively ran Rosemary and Thyme and provided pastries for the bookstore, she remained a financially invested partner in the family's business.

"Henry commented on them, actually," Jane said. He'd been back again that morning, causing her to almost spill a pot of coffee when he slipped her a smile from across the room.

"Henry Birch? Adam's—" Anna stopped herself, then leaned across the table. "Ivy, you didn't tell us your brother was in town."

Ivy looked up from her conversation with Kara and Grace, a strange expression darkening her features. "Oh. We've all been so busy with Grace's wedding. I guess I forgot."

"How long is he in town?" Anna pressed.

Yes, Ivy, how long? Jane held her breath, wondering why she suddenly felt so nervous. What did she care how long Henry stuck around? Because he was hot, she admitted. And because somehow she hadn't noticed how hot before.

"I don't know, really." Ivy shrugged, and Jane felt her heart skip a beat. That was hardly the same as tomorrow or next week. "He's rarely in one place for long," Ivy finished.

Of course. He was a travel writer. And he hadn't made it back to Briar Creek in years, not even for his mother's

burial this past summer. There hadn't been a service, and Ivy claimed she was fine handling things on her own, given everything, but Jane still wondered how Henry could have stayed away.

Well, it was none of her business. He was back now, maybe because he had been kept away over the summer. And soon, he'd be gone again. There was no sense in wishing he would stick around for longer, and it didn't matter if he did. He was Adam's friend at the end of the day, and like so many things, their divorce had split more than just the two of them.

A waiter appeared with another bottle of wine and a cheer went up at the table. Soon, Jane was caught up in the chatter again, and she didn't even give Henry another thought until they'd stood to leave and she heard the rich, booming laugh that always brought a smile to her lips. She scanned the room looking for him, anticipating going up to him, maybe saying hello, perhaps having a drink... He was sitting on a bar stool, his back slightly hunched, his broad, strong shoulders defined by the thin material of his green sweater. He turned slightly, his gaze drifting in her direction, and she was just lifting her hand to wave in case he caught her eye when her smile froze.

He wasn't alone. And the person he was laughing with was her ex-husband.

The bartender cleared the half-empty glasses from the end of the gleaming mahogany bar and lifted his chin at Henry. "What will it be?"

"Just a club soda," he replied evenly.

"Still drinking those, I see," Adam said, taking a long sip of his beer.

Henry took his drink and plucked the cocktail straw from the glass. "Yep. Some things don't change."

"But some things do," Adam countered. He looked at Henry squarely. "I don't know if you heard that Jane and I split up."

"Ivy mentioned it." He decided to leave out the part about running into Jane, or learning about the remarriage. If Adam wanted to tell him, he would.

"Marriage is hard," Adam said.

"You don't need to tell me that," Henry remarked, taking a sip of his soda. He shook his head, thinking of the brief time in his life he'd spent with Caroline: their whirlwind courtship, their wedding day—everything felt possible then.

"I can't really believe I'm about to do it again," Adam said, meeting Henry's gaze from the corner of his eye. His jaw pulsed. "Kristy's pregnant. She wanted to get married. Insisted, actually." He took another sip of his beer.

"Ah." So there it was. He wondered if Jane knew this part—if it would matter to her if she did. She'd seemed a little down during their conversation the other day, and Henry had left the bookstore a few hours later with half a mind to go over to Adam's house, grab him by the collar, and give him a piece of his mind, the way he'd wanted to so many times before.

He pushed aside the guilt he felt for reaching out to Adam. Adam's relationship with Jane aside, there was a bond between them that couldn't be overlooked.

Their meals arrived, and Henry eagerly bit into his burger. "It's hard to picture you as a father of two," he mused aloud. The Adam he knew liked to have a good time. Henry had told himself that Adam was getting it

out of his system before the wedding day—after all, who couldn't love Jane Madison with her bright eyes and that sweet smile?—but he'd clearly overestimated his friend's intentions.

"I love being a father," Adam said, suddenly smiling. "It's probably the reason I stuck things out with Jane as long as I did." He studied the beer in his glass, then tipped it back.

"You married young." Henry could give him that much. Hell, he could make the same poor excuse for himself. He'd met and married Caroline within the span of ten months. Proposed to her after only three. Looking back, he wondered if he would have latched on to anyone who'd passed through his life at the time. He was looking for a life raft. Looking for an escape. For a sense of simplicity and security he'd never known.

He was looking for what his best friend had found.

And then thrown away.

He took another sip of his soda, thinking of the way Jane looked at the bookstore this morning. Her ash brown hair had been pulled up in a ponytail, revealing that long, graceful dancer's neck. She'd come over to his table, given his mug a refill, and asked politely about his work, but she was still guarded. Her eyes were hesitant, her smile a little less warm than the one she gave the other patrons. She didn't linger. And damn it if he hadn't wished she had.

Sitting here with the man who'd cheated on her, he supposed he couldn't blame her.

"Well, live and learn. I'm determined to do it right this time," Adam said. "I owe my kids that much."

A part of Henry didn't want to hear this. He wanted to give Adam a good punch in the face instead for not giving

Jane the fair chance he was giving Kristy. But the other part of him understood, or was trying to at least.

Good people could do bad things, he told himself. It was a mantra he'd repeated many times over the years. Then it was about his mother. Lately, it was about himself.

"So when's the wedding?" Henry asked. It was just meant to be idle conversation, but the look in Adam's face told him he'd hit a nerve.

"Four weeks from now. If you're in town, I'd love you to be there. Kristy didn't want to wait or do it over the holidays and... there's a chance I might be taking a job out of state."

"Anywhere interesting?"

"Denver," Adam replied.

"Good city. Good skiing, too, if you can handle the powder instead of the ice." Henry grinned.

Adam hesitated, seeming to want to tell Henry something, but finished the last of his beer instead. The white froth coated the glass, pooling at the bottom when he slid it across the smooth bar. "Do me a favor and keep it to yourself, just until everything's settled. There are still... a few details to work out."

"Not a problem. You know me. I hate gossip." If he closed his eyes, he could almost hear the voices over the din of the restaurant, the gossip that trailed in his mother's wake. There was no escaping it in Briar Creek.

He turned away, back to his food. Soon enough, this would be over. He'd be gone. And all these people would fade away again. The way he needed them to.

CHAPTER 5

Petals on Main was having an unusually busy start to the fall season, Ivy noted with a pleased smile as the bell on the door chimed for the sixth time in only half an hour. She finished jotting down a phone order—three dozen pink roses for a third wedding anniversary, how sweet was that?—and set the handset down with a sigh. She had promised Henry she would take it easy, but that wasn't exactly possible when the store was bustling with customers, each needing her undivided attention. She'd planned on eating one of the granola bars she kept on hand, but every time she broke away, another customer pushed through the door, smiling in expectation, waiting for assistance.

Her hands began to shake as she typed in the order. She couldn't put it off much longer.

"Hey there, Ivy." Mark Hastings grinned at her over the antique farm table she used as a counter. She'd had the antique shop down the road refit it with higher legs, so she could use it as both a workspace and a checkout area

without compromising the design of her space. So much thought, time, and energy had gone into this little shop. It was her own private jewel box, bursting with a rainbow of colors, no matter how gloomy the weather outside. It was her happy place. Her sanctuary. Why couldn't Henry see that?

If it were up to her brother, she'd close up shop tomorrow and book the next flight to San Francisco. But then, if it were up to him, she never would have opened it in the first place...

"Mark! Hello!" She wiped at the beads of sweat that had formed at her hairline and shed her pale blue wool cardigan, leaving it to drape on the chair she hadn't managed to sit in since the store opened. "Picking up for the restaurant already? I don't have the order filled yet, but if you give me an hour, I can drop it off." Normally she hand-delivered the flowers to Rosemary and Thyme, and, if she had a few minutes to spare, she stuck around to chat with Anna while she went around to each table and swapped out the old stems for new and cleaned up the bigger arrangements she maintained in the bar and lobby.

"Nah, I thought I'd surprise Anna with a bouquet, actually." Mark looked uncomfortable as he shoved his hands in his pockets and darted his gaze around the room, and Ivy tried to hide her smile. Once the most eligible bachelor in town, Mark was still a little out of his element when it came to a committed relationship.

"Well, aren't you sweet!" Ivy grinned, and was rewarded by Mark's visible expression of relief.

"I didn't know if girls really liked that type of thing," he admitted, grinning bashfully.

Ivy arched a brow, internally rolling her eyes to the

ceiling. *Men.* "I earn my living selling flowers, so I can assure you that yes, women like flowers. A lot. In fact, an entire holiday is built around them. Well, and chocolate of course."

"Good." Mark's smile widened. "So, what do you recommend?"

"Oh…" A wave of nausea moved through her and her heart began to race now. She gripped the counter a little tighter, hoping her voice didn't sound as desperate as she felt. She should have taken the medicine as soon as she picked it up. Instead, she'd put it off, gotten busy… focused on all the work she had to do just to keep this place afloat. "What's Anna's favorite color?"

It was blue, she knew, but she always tried to let the customers be their own guide. She helped where she could, with suggestions instead of persuasion. Flowers were meant to express the giver nearly as much as the recipient, after all.

"Probably… red. Maybe pink." Mark frowned, looking suddenly lost.

Ivy came around the counter. The granola bar would just have to wait. "Why don't I show you a few things and see if anything stands out?"

The wariness in Mark's deep-set brown eyes seemed to fade. "Thanks, Ivy."

"My pleasure." She walked him around the shop, pointing out various roses and gerbera daisies, the blood rushing in her head the entire time. *Don't faint. You can't faint. Just hold on for five more minutes. Five minutes.*

Her diabetes was something she'd kept to herself over the years—only Henry, their mother, and a handful of others in town knew about it. She knew it was nothing

to be ashamed of, that there was really no secret to keep, but she'd learned early in life that the less people knew about you, the easier it was to fit in. The room began to tilt. *Oh, God.*

"Ivy? Are you feeling okay?" Mark's expression turned to one of concern. "You look a little flushed."

"Oh, do I?" Her cheeks were on fire and she was sweating through her cotton blouse. Her vision was going in and out, dimming in the periphery. "It's a little warm in here, isn't it? I've been on my feet for a while."

Mark took her by the elbow and led her to a bench near the front door. "Let me get you some water."

"Juice," she said quickly. "There's, um, some juice in the fridge in the back room." She always kept some on hand for when her blood sugar dipped, and she didn't need to do a reading now to know it had.

He returned a few seconds later with a plastic cup and a granola bar. "I hope you don't mind. I found this in the back room near the sink."

He had no idea how much she did not mind. Her fingers were shaking so hard she could barely peel the wrapper. Frantically, she took a bite, waiting for the sugar to hit her blood. She needed to get her insulin under control. Henry was right. And that's why he couldn't know about this little scare. It would be just the kind of thing he'd use to try to yet again convince her to leave this town, and everyone in Briar Creek, behind her.

"Looks like there are two doctors in your family," Ivy joked when her body temperature finally dropped and her pulse had settled. Her skin felt cool, and she brushed the matted hair off the back of her neck.

"Oh, I could never do what Brett does," Mark said

ruefully, and Ivy's heart skipped a beat at the sound of Mark's younger brother's name. "When my mom was sick, I learned a few things, though."

Ivy nodded. Mark had sacrificed a lot to help his mother through chemo—twice.

"How's Brett doing?" Ivy dared to ask as casually as she could. She peeled the wrapper back on the granola bar, finishing it with one last bite, somehow unable to make eye contact with Mark.

He shrugged. "Good, I suppose. He'll be back for Luke's wedding."

So much for getting her body under control. At this, her stomach flipped, and her heart began to positively thunder. *Is Brett seeing anyone?* she wanted to ask. But the bigger part of her didn't want to know. There was always the chance that he would bring a date to the wedding. Grace, being her best friend, would happily share the guest list if she asked, but Ivy wasn't ready to extinguish the hope just yet that he would come alone, maybe spot her across the room in that beautiful crimson bridesmaid dress, realize what he'd been missing his entire life, and push through the crowd to ask her to dance. He'd hold her all night long, pressing her into his rock-hard chest while he whispered sweet nothings into her ear, and after she caught the bouquet he'd whisk her off to the B&B where he was staying and slam the door shut with his foot while he slowly unzipped the back of her dress and chased kisses down her neck until she groaned, and then...Then again, he might show up with some beautiful blonde on his arm. It was depressing enough to go stag to your best friend's wedding, but if Brett showed up with a date... She simply couldn't bear it.

Briar Creek wasn't exactly the hot spot for the singles scene, and try as she might, she couldn't shake the crush she'd harbored for... practically her entire life!

Ivy stood, feeling slightly better, and tossed the wrapper into the trash under the counter. Turning back to Mark, she said, "So, have you decided?"

"I feel like I've seen this one flower in her apartment before..." He pointed to a bushel of hydrangea. "Maybe I should stick with roses though." His expression turned pleading. "I don't want to mess this up."

Ivy marched over to the bright blue hydrangea and plucked the six best stems. "You're doing just fine, Mark. I happen to know these are Anna's personal favorite."

"Why didn't you tell me?" He laughed.

"Because I'm not the one giving Anna flowers. You are." She flashed him a knowing smile before wrapping the flowers in brown paper and securing the stunning yet simple bouquet with twine. "Go sweep her off her feet."

"Thanks," Mark said, as he turned to leave. He paused after he opened the door, his grin wavering slightly. "Are you sure you're feeling okay? There's nothing I can do?"

Ivy waved him off with a smile she didn't feel. "Never better. Now go give Anna those flowers!"

"You're the best, Ivy."

With one last wave, the door closed behind Mark. Ivy stood in the now empty shop and sighed. If only his brother felt that way.

Ivy was putting together a bright red and orange arrangement when Henry came into the flower shop. He stopped at the front of the store, waiting for her to finish, observing his sister's handiwork and the care she poured into it. Petals on

Main was quaint and charming, thanks to Ivy's artistic eye. Even if his twin sister didn't own the place, he would have been impressed. Reluctantly so, perhaps, but impressed just the same.

The battered wood floorboards were covered in galvanized pots, bursting with sunflowers and colorful arrangements, with small, handwritten cards giving a description. Some, like the roses and lilies, he recognized, but others he had only seen from a distance and never stopped to appreciate. He grinned. Leave it to Ivy to notice the beautiful things in life.

She was always stopping to pick wildflowers on their walks home from school, always careful to hold them by the stems until they were safely inside. She'd climb onto the counter to fetch an old jam jar, placing the makeshift vase on the center of the old kitchen table they almost never sat at. They were nothing more than weeds, really, often dandelions or buttercups, but that didn't stop her from putting the arrangements all over the house. "Maybe they'll cheer up Mama," she'd say, her blue eyes bright with newfound hope. "Maybe they'll make her smile."

Henry swallowed the knot in his throat. Only one thing made their mother smile, and that was the sweet sound of wine filling a glass. She'd rarely given Ivy any notice. Henry was there for that. Until he wasn't.

His jaw tensed as he watched his sister tuck one final stem into the round vase and stand back to survey her work. He was here now. And he was going to be damn sure his sister was taken care of once and for all.

"Did you get your health insurance straightened out?" he asked, as soon as the customer had disappeared

through the door, awkwardly clutching an arrangement that must have weighed a good twenty pounds.

"You don't waste much time," Ivy commented, holding his gaze. She pursed her lips and began brushing some discarded stem and leaf clippings from her work stand. "How are you today, Henry? Pleasant to see you. What have you been up to this fine fall day?"

"You know why I asked." He softened his tone and rolled up his shirtsleeves. "I'm worried."

Ivy handed him a small wicker wastebasket, and he cleaned off the rest of the surface until all that could be seen was the nicked wood. Well used. Well loved, no doubt. She might not have succeeded in turning their mother's life around, but it was obvious she'd made a success of brightening the lives of others in town.

"I told you," Ivy insisted, still refusing to meet his eye. "I'll get on a better health plan after the start of the year. My deductible's high, and I've had a lot of expenses recently. That's all."

He knew what expenses she meant, and his gut twisted so hard he had to remind himself to breathe. He'd sent a check for the burial. A check that was never cashed.

"That's no excuse to be missing appointments and skipping your meds," Henry said. He gave her a hard look, but she just strolled around the store, determined to make light of what was a very grave situation. Bad enough to drag him back to Briar Creek.

"Did you get your prescription filled with the money I gave you?" She hadn't been pleased when he'd insisted on attending her doctor's appointment last Friday, but considering she'd landed herself in the hospital only ten days ago, she'd also known there was no point in arguing.

She sighed heavily. "Yes. I went to Forest Ridge and got it filled this morning."

"Good." His blood still ran cold when he thought of that chilling phone call he'd received from the emergency room doctor, asking if he was Ivy Birch's next of kin. The air had stalled in his lungs for those few paralyzing seconds, and all he could think was, *I've lost her, too.* When he'd shown up at her bedside the next day after catching the red-eye, Ivy had looked startled, then embarrassed. She hadn't wanted to worry him, she'd said, when he questioned the light-headedness and the blood sugar levels. She hadn't thought it was a big deal, she'd had the nerve to say. She'd waited, held off, until it was nearly too late.

He hadn't been able to save their mother, but he'd be damned if he didn't save his sister. She was all he had. All he'd ever had. He closed his eyes, the guilt now twisting deep in his chest like a knife. Maybe he'd been selfish to leave town all those years ago. Maybe he should have sucked it up, stuck it out. The way Ivy had.

"I'm feeling up to starting on the house this week," Ivy said now. "I'll give you a hand with the attic. Maybe we can start with the boxes in the garage."

"No," Henry said firmly. "You're on your feet all day here. You shouldn't be working so hard."

"I can't exactly afford to pay for help right now," Ivy pointed out.

"Maybe not, but I can."

"Henry!" Ivy shook her head until her auburn hair shook. "I told you. I'm not comfortable taking your money. Besides, I'll have plenty of cushion once we're able to get Mom's house sold."

Good luck with that, he couldn't help but think. The old farmhouse had been dilapidated when they'd been growing up in it, and that was thirty years ago. He hated the thought of even going back to that place, but Ivy was right—if they could sell it, be free of it once and for all, they'd be better off for it. Especially Ivy.

"In the meantime, promise me you won't get behind on your meds. Did you take your insulin yet today?"

A strange flush coated Ivy's face. "I'm about to."

Henry balled a fist at his side. "Do it now. Let me watch."

"Henry!" Ivy protested, placing her hands on her hips. "I'm thirty years old!"

"And I'm older by eight minutes." He softened his tone. "Please, Ivy."

She stared at him, then nodded slowly. Silently, she disappeared behind a door, returning with a syringe. Though he'd watched her do it a thousand times growing up, even administering the medicine himself at first, and later teaching her to do it herself, he still winced when the needle went into her thigh.

"There." Ivy glanced at him, her blue eyes bright and determined. She pushed her skirt down, her cheeks flushed. "Satisfied?"

"I'll be satisfied when I know I don't have to worry about you anymore," he said, but he knew that day would never come. He'd been worrying about her since he was old enough to know no one else would, and long before she ended up in the hospital at age seven. Still, it wouldn't stop him from trying. "We'll walk through the house together, but after that, I plan on doing the heavy lifting." When she started to protest, he held up a hand. "Don't make me change the locks on you, Ivy."

She laughed, and he did, too. It was an easy laugh, the way only siblings could so naturally connect. He suddenly missed her so much his heart hurt, even though she was standing right in front of him. Phone conversations weren't enough. He wished she'd taken him up on his invitations to visit him in California.

"How's the inn treating you?" she asked, settling onto a wooden rocking chair. "You know you're welcome to sleep on my couch."

Ivy's apartment above the shop was homey, but smaller than most hotel rooms he frequented. The couch was nothing more than a loveseat, and he doubted his six-foot frame could sleep comfortably there for more than one night, let alone a few weeks.

A few weeks, he reminded himself. A few weeks and then this would all be behind him again. The house would be gone, never to be stepped in again. The memories would be banished. He could leave town knowing that part of his life had been exorcised.

"The accommodations are comfortable. The food's decent. I checked out Rosemary and Thyme last night. Nice place."

Ivy stopped rocking and frowned. "You were there last night? I was, too." She paused. "Who were you with?"

"Adam Brown," Henry said, rolling back on his heels. Given Ivy's closeness with the Madison sisters, he braced himself for her reaction.

"He was a good friend to you growing up," was all she said, however.

The best. Adam was a year younger than him, but they'd been next-door neighbors, and Henry hadn't minded. He loved nothing more than sitting down to dinner at the

Browns' house, eating every last bite of a hot meal, sticking around until he couldn't put it off any longer, and he was hit with the sad reality that the fantasy was over, this wasn't his home, and his time was up. He'd hated nothing more than climbing that hill to the old, rundown farmhouse.

"How about you? Did you have a date?" Henry grinned suggestively, but Ivy pulled a face.

"Fat chance of that." She sighed and pushed herself out of the chair. Reaching for a bunch of roses, she began shucking the leaves from their stems. "No, I was with my girlfriends. A bunch of us are bridesmaids in Grace and Luke's wedding. There's still a lot of planning to go over."

Henry felt the smile fade from his face. "Was Jane there?"

"Yes." Ivy stopped working. "Why do you ask?"

He gritted his teeth, thinking of what she must have thought, if she'd seen. He ran a hand through his hair, cursing to himself. He hoped to God she hadn't.

"Oh, no reason," he managed, giving a shrug to convince himself that it was really no big deal. Adam had been his friend; hell, he'd stood up for the guy at his wedding. It made sense to get together now that he was back in town. "I just can't imagine it's any fun to run into your ex."

"You would know better than I would," Ivy pointed out, resuming her task. "I think Jane's going to be okay, though. She has Sophie, and she's gone back to her dancing. She teaches at the studio, you know. She helps Grace at the bookstore, too."

"The Annex," Henry added, thinking that he had planned to work in the café for a few more hours this afternoon. Now, in light of this conversation, he wasn't so

sure. When he'd been in yesterday Jane had been pleasant, stopping by to chat. If she'd spotted him last night, chances were she'd keep her distance today.

The thought of it disappointed him. More than it should.

"You've been in then?" Ivy seemed pleased by this. "I'm really proud of them all. They really know how to make the best of a rotten deal."

Henry knew she was referring to their father's death and Jane's divorce, but it hit a personal nerve. "So can we," he said, his blood beginning to surge with adrenaline. "We can take that ramshackle house and make a killing on it. Now wouldn't that be sweet?"

Ivy spared him a lazy smile and plucked some roses from a plastic container. "Let's just hope we get the place sold. I'll be happy for that much."

"Who says we can't come out on top?" Henry countered, and he sensed his sister waver. "We deserve to come out on top." And they would this time. He'd make damn sure of it.

Monday mornings were traditionally slow for Main Street Books. People had spent their weekend browsing and buying, and relaxing with a cappuccino and one of Anna's famous pistachio biscotti. Grace was usually able to cover both sides of the shop on her own, but today Jane decided to stop by, just in case...

Hay bales, mums, and an arrangement of heirloom pumpkins flanked the cheerful red shop door Jane had known and loved since she was barely older than Sophie. Grace was creating a new fall-themed window display when Jane turned the knob and entered.

"You're just in time," Grace said breathlessly. "You can help me with this leaf garland. Every time I go to hang one end, the other side comes undone." In her hands was a string of construction paper leaves made by the children at last week's story hour, the name of their favorite book scrawled on one side.

Jane set down her bag and helped her sister drape the

garland over the inside frame of the window. Her stomach was knotting and her heart was beginning to race at the mere thought of asking about extra shifts. It was crazy, she knew—she could tell Grace anything. She just needed to be sure she brought it up in a way that didn't sound the alarm bells. She'd promised Rosemary that much.

"It's quiet in here this morning," Grace remarked. "How about a coffee to get the day started right?"

Jane nodded, deflated by Grace's observation. She scanned the room, seeing just a few customers settled in armchairs or at a café table, and decided to make the most of the opportunity. She waited until Grace had come back to the front counter with their steaming mugs, then asked, "So, any more hints from Luke about the honeymoon destination?"

"No," Grace replied with what Jane knew to be mock annoyance. Her sister had spent the past month trying to get Luke to give her a few hints, but he'd adamantly refused. Even Anna wasn't able to get any information out of Mark—Grace had tried that tactic, as well as nudging Jane to try to pry it out of Rosemary, but if Luke's mother had any idea what her son was planning, she was keeping her ruby-painted lips permanently zipped. "Last week I told him that at the very least, I need to know what to pack. For a moment I thought I had him, then he stopped just as he was about to speak." Grace shrugged, but she was smiling. "Given how cold it's already getting here, I can't see him taking me any farther north. That would just be cruel."

"Not for a honeymoon," Jane said wistfully. She wrapped her arms tighter around her thick sweater. It

certainly would be nice to get away, kick back on the beach somewhere warm, forget about her troubles for a bit.

"Jane, I'm sorry. If you want me to stop talking about all this, I will."

Jane shook her head. "It's fine, really."

Grace looked unconvinced, and Jane sighed as she sunk into a chair at the table nearest the bakery counter. "I've been thinking about it, and I don't think I'm upset that Adam is getting remarried and—" She couldn't bring herself to say it. For years she had longed for more children, but Adam was so distant, coming home late and leaving early, usually passing out on the couch in front of the television most nights instead of coming to bed. "I just thought that I would be the one getting on with my life first. It felt more...fair that way." She gave a watery smile, feeling suddenly childish. Fair. There was nothing fair about your husband cheating on you. What made her think it would stop there?

"Are you sure you don't want to give dating another try?" Grace urged.

Jane stiffened and took a gulp of her coffee. "No, definitely not." She felt tense at the mere thought of another blind date, the stress of dressing in something slinky and skin-baring, the anxiety of walking into a restaurant and looking around, with no idea what the night had in store. Some women might find that kind of thing exhilarating, but not her. She didn't want excitement and expectation. She just wanted someone to come home to at the end of a long day. She just wanted laughter, and comfort. She just wanted a friend. A friend who told her she was pretty, or lit up when she was around.

Her mind shifted to Henry and the brief laugh they'd had his first day here, how quickly he'd picked up on her feelings. He always had a knack for that. Sometimes when she wished he didn't.

Then just as quickly, she thought of him sitting at the bar with Adam, no doubt hearing her ex's side of things, hearing all the reasons their marriage broke down and why Adam felt justified in moving on.

She took another sip of her coffee. No use thinking about Henry now. But if she could just find another guy like him—one who was not her ex-husband's oldest and closest friend—then maybe—

"You're smiling," Grace observed.

"What?" Jane locked her sister's gaze sternly. "I was just thinking that really, my life is much better like this. I've had enough complications. I just want things to be simple."

"Love is rarely simple," Grace pointed out.

"Exactly." And that was all the more reason to avoid it. "Besides, we know more or less everyone in town, and I don't think there's really anyone here for me or it would have happened before."

"Before?" Grace snorted. "When? You dated Adam all through high school and you've only been divorced for a matter of months."

"You know what I mean," Jane said. "Any of the single guys left are just friends by now. There's no . . . spark." At least not like the one that ripped down her spine every time she thought of Henry.

"Do Mom and Anna know yet?" Grace hedged.

Jane slumped her shoulders. "I know I have to tell them before Sophie blurts it out, but I just haven't found the

time yet. Soon. I don't want to worry them." Jane rubbed the spot between her eyebrows. Of course her mother would worry. Her face turned all red and her lips got all pinched every time Adam's name was even mentioned. It would be no consolation that Jane's marriage had been destroyed not by a casual fling but by, it would now seem, true love, as Sophie would say. "So, did Luke at least say how long the honeymoon would be?" Jane asked.

Grace smiled. "Two weeks. That's all he would give me."

"Don't worry about the shop," Jane said, seizing her chance. "I can cover for you."

"What about your dance classes?" Grace frowned. "I figured I'd hang a sign while I'm away. People would understand."

"Nonsense! Besides, I have fewer classes this session."

Darn it. Grace immediately looked panicked. "Fewer classes? Why?"

Jane waved her hand through the air and gave what she hoped to be a reassuring smile. "It's usually slower at the start of the school year. Things pick up during recital season, which is why Rosemary brought me on last winter. So, I'd be happy to help with the store," Jane reiterated. "We don't want to miss out on any holiday shoppers, after all."

From the look of realization that swept Grace's face, Jane knew she'd hit her mark. "The wedding is still almost seven weeks away, but thanks. I appreciate it. Speaking of, you should be getting your formal invitation this week."

Jane managed to keep her tone subtle as she pushed her chair back and brought her mug to the sink. "I'm around before then, too. If you get busy with the wedding planning."

Grace came around the counter and stood beside her. "I'll keep that in mind, thanks."

Jane tried not to let her frustration show. She had promised Rosemary not to worry Grace or Luke, but her sister was hardly picking up on the hints. "It helps, you know. Keeping busy. It keeps me from thinking about... everything."

She hadn't even realized how true the words were until she'd said them. Her most difficult nights were the ones spent alone, when Sophie was with Adam, and her sisters were off with Luke or Mark. Sometimes she joined Kara or Ivy for dinner or a movie, but it wasn't the same, and she always felt half-present, wishing for the simple pleasures that domesticity could bring, no matter how nice the restaurant or how gripping the film.

Grace set a hand on her arm. "You free today, then? I wouldn't mind a couple hours to place those dress orders."

"You haven't done it yet?" Jane laughed, but the relief she felt overrode her amusement. "I'm free." Free as a bird. "My first class isn't until four."

My only class, she thought. The hard knot in her stomach returned.

"How about a six-hour shift then?"

Jane reached out and gave her sister a hug. "You're the best."

"Just don't tell Anna that. Don't want her getting jealous." Grace winked.

Jane was still smiling minutes later, after waving her sister off. With a six-hour shift and a class this afternoon, she at least had today squared away. She'd have another chat with Rosemary about her future at the studio, and

then make some decisions from there. After all, there was no sense in getting ahead of herself if she didn't need to. If things at the studio picked up, a few weeks of scrambling wasn't the end of the world. And if they didn't...

She started a fresh pot of coffee. She wasn't going to worry about that. Not yet, anyway.

By eleven, the store was filling up, and her smiles were coming more naturally. As much as she liked the comfort of her home, there was something to be said for being out, surrounded by life and engaging in conversation, even just pleasantries.

She set the last blueberry muffin in the toaster oven to warm and turned to the next person in line. A hot flush spread over her body as her eyes locked with Henry's. A crooked smile broke his face, and she swallowed hard, willing her heart rate to resume at normal speed, and hoping the heat hadn't spread to her cheeks. Unfortunately, she knew it had.

"Hot in here," she exclaimed through a smile, and made a show of fanning herself. *Pull it together, Jane!*

Henry's brow furrowed at this but his deep-set blue eyes were warm as they held hers. "Not outside. I'd forgotten how brutal the weather can be here."

"Just wait until winter," she bantered, and then stopped herself. Chances were Henry wouldn't be around come winter. He might not even be around by next week.

As if she didn't need another reason to keep her distance.

"So, what will it be?" She pinched her lips tight and exhaled slowly through her nose. Henry's brow seemed to furrow, and that smile slipped just enough to reveal the smooth fullness of his lips. His eyes bored through hers.

She decided it was a good time to check on that coffee. Wouldn't want it to overflow or anything.

"Large coffee. Extra large if you've got it." Before she could inquire, he was sure to add, "For here."

She cursed under her breath as her fingers curled around the coffeepot handle. An extra large drip for here meant he didn't plan on leaving anytime soon.

No matter, she told herself, filling a white mug stamped with the Main Street Books logo, careful to leave half an inch for cream. She tried to ignore the fact that she now knew how he took it. It was just part of good customer service, really. Definitely nothing more than that. After all, she'd known Henry for years. She handed him the mug, a jolt zipping up her arm as his fingers brushed hers. A dimple quirked when he grinned, and her heart began to pound again. She blinked at the counter, trying to find some semblance of composure. So, it was a dimple. Big deal. Surely he'd always had it. But then, maybe she'd been too focused on Adam to notice before...

"I'll take one of those cranberry scones today, too." His eyes were already on her when her gaze flickered to him and darted immediately to the basket of scones. She all but grabbed it and dropped it onto a plate, lest he see the way her hand was suddenly shaking. Honestly, if he would just stop staring at her like that, with that lazy grin pulling at the corner of his mouth and those long curly lashes blinking ever so casually, she wouldn't have to be so flustered.

She was just out of practice, holed up in her house most evenings after Sophie had gone to bed. It wasn't like she was checking out the dads at the school—how pathetic would that be?—and there weren't exactly any other men

around town with a strong square jaw and just the right amount of stubble...

Now Henry was eyeing the plate she had been holding in her hand for what she feared had been an alarmingly long period of time.

"Sorry," she gushed, and blinked at the cash register. She handed him the scone and began punching in his order. "Lost in thought for a moment."

Lost in those eyes was more like it. Honestly, this wasn't like her. She didn't check men out. She wasn't looking for a man! But that's all she was doing. Looking. She was hardly shopping for a new boyfriend. Her dating days were over. So were her married ones.

"Quiet in here today," he remarked, slipping a few bills into the tip jar.

"Mondays are usually slow," she agreed. *Please just go. Take your coffee and your scone and go to your seat, preferably with your back to me so I can't be tempted by your square jaw and boyish grin.* She stared at him, waiting for him to go, but he lingered at the counter. He opened his mouth as if to say something and then stopped. The smile he'd sported when he'd first come in was gone, and there was something wary in his expression, something uncertain, as if he had something he wanted to say. She knew that look all too well. She'd come to dread it.

Small talk was about to come to an end.

"I saw you with Adam the other night," she offered conversationally. Really, there was nothing to be upset over.

"I didn't know you'd be there." His jaw set, and his eyes fixed squarely on hers.

She shrugged and brushed some crumbs from the counter. "Funny place to meet, my sister's restaurant."

"You're mad—"

"Mad? Of course not! You and Adam were best friends. I'd be surprised if you didn't get together while you're in town. I just wish you'd gone to Piccolino's or the pub. I mean, maybe Adam doesn't know that Anna would like to fillet him... Good thing she wasn't aware of his presence or he might have gotten a bad piece of fish." She laughed unhappily as she rang up the order. The door jingled and Jane looked over to see a customer coming around the tables of books. She waved and smiled as one of her students' mothers approached. Just what she needed: a friendly face to ground her.

Henry was frowning at her and Jane felt her cheeks grow pink. She'd shown her cards, damn it. She'd tried so hard not to.

"You know, I think I might bring Ivy some coffee. She's busy over there and doesn't break away enough."

Jane nodded. "Sure. One coffee to go?"

"I'll bring mine, too."

A twinge of disappointment tugged at her chest. "Sure. No problem." She smiled through a shaky sigh and transferred his coffee and scone to a paper cup and bag.

Her fingers brushed his as he reached out to take Ivy's coffee cup from her hand, and once again, a tingle shot up her arm. Their eyes locked, and her chest began to pound as his mouth tugged into a bashful grin.

"Jane, I didn't mean to upset you. I'm sorry if I did."

Oh, jeez, was it that obvious? She'd tried so hard not to show her hurt, to reclaim some sense of pride that Adam tried to steal when he'd made a public fool of her, first

cheating on her and then flaunting his mistress all over town. She'd bravely assured concerned neighbors and friends when they inquired about her well-being that she was fine. Just fine. She'd even suffered through kindergarten orientation, all on her own, while Adam and Kristy sat across the room, holding hands. She'd worn her best twinset and an A-line skirt that she'd admittedly spent a good twenty-five hours shopping for online, squared her shoulders, and bared her teeth into a smile that said *Humiliated? Shunned? Scorned? Not me!* She was better off without him—she knew it—they all knew it! She had nothing to be hurt over, no reason to feel hot in the face and let down when his name came up or she spotted him in, say, her sister's restaurant. A place he had no business going to. A place he had clearly chosen, once again, without any regard for her . . .

"Look." She closed her eyes and shook her head. "It's . . . fine. Really. It's always a bit of a . . . shock seeing Adam, that's all." That was a mild word for it, she thought. "I'm glad you got together with him, though. You were good friends. I'd be more surprised if you didn't see him while you're in town."

"You sure?" He looked skeptical, and damn it if that grin didn't spread a little wider.

Jane swallowed hard. So he had a nice smile. Lots of men did. Lots of men who didn't have dinner with her ex-husband. "It's fine," she said a little breathlessly.

Henry took a step backward. "We were all friends, Jane. I'd hate to think me talking with Adam would change anything."

Adam. There it was again. Nothing he said or did could undo the one person they had in common, and the one

person she needed to forget the most. So what if a lock of that rich brown hair had spilled over his forehead and she had a sudden urge to brush it away from those deep-set eyes? So what if he was not just cute, but also kind? None of it mattered when one fact remained. Where there was Henry, there was Adam, and she couldn't have that.

Jane forced a smile. "It doesn't change a thing."

CHAPTER 7

Henry emailed his article to his editor and leaned back in his chair with a sigh. He supposed he should be relieved that he'd met his deadline and had nothing new on his plate, but instead he felt agitated. He needed to keep busy. His job was the perfect distraction, and now, for the next few weeks at least, it was gone.

Henry slid his laptop into its case and slung his bag over his shoulder. Time to call it a day. The B&B was just down the road, and he could unwind there for a few hours, maybe even catch an hour or two of sleep, if he was lucky. Most people he knew struggled to sleep well while traveling, but not him. Hotel beds were meant for sleeping alone. It was only once he was settled, in his stark and spotless apartment, that he noticed something was missing.

The Main Street B&B would score high on his travel wish list. He'd been expecting loud floral wallpaper, a candlewick coverlet, and dusty pink carpeting, but the room was surprisingly fresh and everything about it indicated a pleasant stay. Everything except—

"Mr. Birch!" The innkeeper, Mrs. Griffin, smiled as he entered the lobby a few minutes later. Henry stifled an eye roll and forced a tight smile, trying to steel himself against those eager green eyes and that toothy smile. He glanced into the lobby, looking for a reason to break away and change his path. A woman in her late twenties sat in the floral wingback chair, smiling at him over the pages of her magazine. He vaguely returned the gesture. Sometimes—rarely—he mixed business with pleasure, finding that casual flings abroad, with an end date and time stamp, were the only ones that worked. He'd disappointed enough women for one lifetime.

His gut tightened. He'd be damned if he disappointed his own sister.

"I take it you're having a nice stay in Briar Creek?" Mrs. Griffin pressed as he neared.

Henry did his best to suppress his sigh as he paused at the base of the stairs, his hand tightly gripping the carved banister, left foot already lifted. He was used to the proprietors of local establishments making bold efforts to impress him; it was just part of his job, and often one laced with perks, like room upgrades, or a complimentary bottle of Champagne he'd pass off to a nice-looking couple first chance he had. But his patience was wearing thin today. The exhaustion was hitting him now, so much so that he might actually succeed in dozing off for a bit without his mind beginning to spin.

He gave a tired smile. "It's a very comfortable inn you run." Then, thinking it best to feed into the nervous tick in her eye: "I especially enjoyed the hot chocolate you sent up last night."

She puffed up a bit and patted her hair as a girlish

laugh flitted through the lobby. "Nothing says sweet dreams better than homemade cocoa!"

"Indeed. Well, thank you again."

He turned to go, but she stopped him once more. "And have you been able to walk around town during your stay? Such quaint little shops, don't you think? Many new ones since you've been gone. I tell everyone, there's no state prettier in autumn than Vermont, no sirree, and our little town is just decked in sugar maples. Have you tried the local cider? Made fresh, same day down at the orchard. Briar Creek has so much to offer at this time of year!"

"Mmm," he managed, lips pressed tight in a grimace. "Yes, well, I should really—"

She planted one foot behind his on the stair. "There's the Harvest Fest coming up, but then of course you must remember that." She blinked rapidly.

"When is it?" he asked with dread.

Mrs. Griffin's smile burst with pleasure. "Why this weekend, of course! Last Saturday in September, per tradition."

He knew all about tradition. On the day of the Harvest Fest, he and Ivy climbed into the back of the old station wagon his mother had bought used, years before either of them had been born, and drove them into town, the radio blaring that oldies station she preferred. Despite how cold Vermont could be that time of year, he'd have to crack a window to escape the waft of the floral perfume she used to disguise the liquor on her breath. By the time they arrived at the town square, almost magically transformed for the event, he dared to feel a little hopeful at the sight of other kids running around, bobbing for apples or decorating pumpkins, but then he'd remember that neither he nor Ivy had any money to participate, and the few

times he'd thought ahead and saved up a few bucks from shoveling snow or raking leaves, his mother would find a way to borrow it. She'd nudge him with her elbow, her eyes pleading, and he'd begrudgingly hand it over, hating the way his heart turned over when she ruffled his hair and grinned her thanks. Keeping their mother happy was worth more than any caramel apple.

"Stands open at ten sharp," Mrs. Griffin continued.

"Good to note." *So I can be sure to miss it.* Henry climbed one step higher, eager to get away and be alone.

"Be sure to arrive early for the fresh donuts! And the cider!"

Ah yes. The cider. Mom's favorite, especially with a splash of brandy. By her second she was relaxed; her third, downright happy; by the fourth, he would stop worrying about Ivy and start worrying about her; and by the fifth...People started to talk.

She never did stay happy for long. No matter how hard they tried to keep it that way.

"Yes, well. I've got a few calls to make." He smiled politely and hurried up the stairs to his room on the second floor, locking the door behind him. He marched to the television and flicked it on, hoping it would drive out the noise in his head.

He tossed himself down on the bed, closed his eyes, and listened to the laugh track of the cheesy family sitcom until the noise was finally silenced.

Two hours later, Henry tossed on a sweater and headed back into town. The wind had picked up in the short time since he'd last been out, and the maple leaves rustled above him and crunched under his feet as he turned off

Seventh and onto Main Street. It wasn't even four o'clock, but already the glow from the iron lamps lit the street, and children scurried down the sidewalk bundled in peacoats and wool hats. One little girl just ahead stopped every few feet to pick up a leaf, adding it to a growing bouquet she clutched in her small hand.

Henry smiled sadly. It was something Ivy used to do, once the flowers were gone for the season. He quickened his pace to hold on to the image a moment longer, his attention locked on the child with the long brown hair and small, happy voice, until he noticed the woman beside her.

"Jane."

She turned to him, a pleasant smile on her face fading into one of surprise when she saw him. "Henry. Hello again."

He glanced down at the little girl, studying her more closely. "You must be Sophie." He grinned, and was rewarded with a shy smile in return. The little girl reached up and took her mother's hand, her other maintaining a firm grip on the leaf bouquet at her side. "I was just admiring your pretty leaves. You picked all the best ones."

Sophie beamed. "I like the red ones best. But sometimes orange. And the yellow are pretty."

Jane gave a soft laugh and arched a friendly brow. "We're making a centerpiece," she explained.

"Having a dinner party?"

"A pajama party!" Sophie exclaimed, giggling.

Jane's face flushed pink, and she stammered with her words when he looked at her quizzically. "It's um... something I promised Sophie we would do tonight."

"We do it *every* night, silly! As soon as school's over!" Sophie cajoled, and Jane flashed her a stern look.

"Not *every* night." Jane rolled her eyes at him. "Children. They love to exaggerate."

"But—"

Jane said over Sophie's protest, "So, um... What are you up to now? I mean, we're—well, we're heading to the studio. We have a dance class. I teach. But then, I told you that already." She laughed. Color spread up her cheeks when she met his gaze. "Sorry. I'm a little out of practice talking to men." Her eyes widened in alarm. "I mean, not that you're a man. Well, you are, but..."

He slid her an easy grin. "I know what you mean. I spend a fair bit of time on my own these days, too."

She gave him a grateful smile. "My sisters tell me I need to get out more. I'm working on it."

"I'll walk a bit with you if you don't mind," he said. "I'm on my way to see Ivy."

Jane seemed to perk up at this, he noted. Probably because he'd established he wasn't headed to see her ex-husband instead. He fell into step beside her, wishing their walk was a bit longer.

"I walked by the flower shop on my way to collect Sophie from school and saw your sister through the window. She was hanging some new wreaths. I bought one last month, actually. She's really talented."

"She is," Henry agreed. Turning to Sophie he said, "When my sister was little she was always making bouquets. Just like yours."

Sophie held her bunch of leaves a little tighter to her chest. "Maybe one day I'll be a flower girl, like Ivy!"

Jane glanced at him from the corner of her eye. "That's what she calls Ivy. A flower girl."

"I'm already going to be a flower girl," Sophie continued

happily, and Henry noticed she was actually skipping, her shoes hitting the sidewalk with all her force. Jane kept a tight grip on her and seemed unfazed. "I get to be a flower girl two times," Sophie added in a mock whisper, her eyes dancing.

Jane's expression immediately tensed as the little girl rambled about dress color and flowers, and Kristy and Adam.

She motioned to the next street, and they all turned right. "So, how's your deadline coming along?"

"I sent it to my editor this morning. There will probably be a few changes, but other than that, the assignment's finished."

"I suppose I won't be seeing you and your laptop at the bookstore as much, then," Jane said, and Henry thought he detected a hint of disappointment in her tone. Or maybe he was just wishing he did.

He liked talking with Jane. Liked the ease of her manner, the way she didn't pry. The way she could so easily shift topics when things got awkward. He glanced over at her, detecting a twinge of sadness in her eyes. She was a strong woman, holding things in for the sake of her daughter, no doubt, but she also had a wall up. He knew the feeling.

"You're not getting off that easy," he bantered. "I'm still dreaming about that blueberry muffin. Those are worth writing about."

"Maybe you should, then," she surprised him by saying.

They stopped walking so Sophie could collect a few oak leaves. "Write about Briar Creek?" Henry wondered if his lip had actually curled.

"Why not?" Jane's smile grew with her enthusiasm. "You're a travel writer, and you said you completed your

last assignment. It will give you something to do while you're in town."

He was shaking his head. "Nah."

"We have the Harvest Fest coming up."

As if he needed another reminder. "It's a nice suggestion, but... I don't think my editor would go for it."

Jane was on a roll now, motioning to this place or that as they walked. "You said you like getting a feel of the way of life, highlighting spots only locals usually frequent. This town would be perfect for that! You'd have a real insider perspective."

"Exactly," he said, seeing his opportunity to shut this conversation down. "I write about places I've never been to, not ones I've lived in. I know it too well. I'm not a tourist."

"Oh, but Briar Creek has changed so much. Main Street Books is a great example."

True, and tourists loved independent bookshops, he'd noticed. Still, it wasn't an option. "I just don't think I'm the right person—"

"And then there's Rosemary and Thyme. Piccolino's," she said, referring to a long-standing Italian restaurant. "The B&B. I've heard it's nice. There's a cute little stationery store over on Chestnut, and a new clothing boutique, too."

As much as he disagreed with her, he couldn't help but grin at her passion. She loved this town, felt a connection to it he never would, even if a part of him wished he could... that his time here had been different.

"And then of course Petals on Main. Ivy sells beautiful soaps and candles there, all locally made. It might really help her shop if you featured it!"

He frowned at this. The magazine he worked for had

the highest subscription rate in the industry, and Jane was right—his readers wanted a little local flair, and the gift items Ivy sold along with her flowers would be just the sort of souvenir they'd take home.

His stomach burned when he thought of his sister, struggling to pay her bills, refusing to cash the check for their mother's burial, claiming he'd done enough and it was her turn now. Thinking it would help her grieve, he'd let it go, but now, knowing the sacrifice she'd made, he wished he hadn't. He should have gotten on that plane the day she'd called. But he couldn't. He just...couldn't.

He'd do anything to make sure that Ivy was taken care of, provided for—but Briar Creek? He didn't write fiction, and nothing he had to say about this town would compel tourists to visit.

"I think I'll leave it to someone else," he said tightly. "Besides, I probably won't be in town long enough to do it justice."

"Oh." Jane blinked a few times. "I...didn't realize your stay was so brief."

They had come to the front of the dance studio. Small girls in pink tights wove past them and in the door. Sophie began tugging Jane's hand, insisting they were going to be late.

"I'll let you go. It was very nice meeting you, Sophie," he said. She looked so much like Jane, with those big eyes and sweet smile. He glanced up at Jane, holding her gaze steadily. His mouth felt dry, and he had to force himself from suggesting dinner or finding some other excuse to stay with her a few more minutes.

Jane needed someone stable, someone who could give her everything Adam couldn't. He wasn't that guy.

"So, I'll see you around."

"The Harvest Fest?" She smiled brightly.

He nodded slowly before turning off and sunk his hands into his pockets. He'd been planning on avoiding the town's big event, but now that he knew Jane would be there, suddenly the thought of it was almost appealing.

Ready, girls? Glissade, arabesque, pas de chat." Jane nodded as the last of the girls crossed the room, managing not to wince as a few of her less graceful students nearly shook the walls upon coming down from what should have been a small, delicate jump. "Very nice, girls. Now, for next class, let's work on quiet feet. Quiet as a mouse." She held a finger to her lips and demonstrated a soft, silent landing.

The girls stood in a row, nodding enthusiastically, and then thundered out of the room. Jane sighed. She did her best, and the girls had fun. She supposed that was the most she could expect from a group of seven-year-olds.

"Any rising stars?" Rosemary asked, sailing into the room with her dance skirt swishing at her bare ankles. The opposite of the majority of their students, she moved so lightly that Jane often jumped when she realized her boss had entered the room.

"Maybe in Wednesday's class," Jane mused.

"About that, Jane, I still feel bad about our conversa-

tion last week. I want to believe enrollment will pick up for the next session, but..." She lifted her palms. "There's no guarantee. Enrollment has steadily declined over the past few years. Maybe girls don't like to dance anymore."

"Grace mentioned that Luke commented on the amount of homework going around."

Rosemary folded her arms and assessed Jane over the slope of her nose. "Did she now? Well, I might have to have a talk with my son, then! Children need balanced lives. Have you noticed this with Sophie?"

"She's in kindergarten," Jane replied. When Rosemary's eyes simply widened further, Jane explained, "She doesn't get homework."

Rosemary seemed disappointed at this. "Our five- and six-year-old classes have the lowest enrollment since I opened the studio twenty years ago. There must be another reason for it, then."

"There's that new gymnastics facility in Forest Ridge," Jane said with a shrug. "And I know Sophie's been talking about ice skating lessons." Not that she could afford that right now, even with child support.

She fought through the guilt. Sophie was a happy little girl, amazingly so given all the changes that had happened in the last year. Jane's stomach twisted when she thought of how many more were ahead. Before long, Sophie was going to have a little sister or brother, an entire new family that Jane wouldn't be a part of. For years she had longed to give Sophie a sibling. As much as part of her was happy Sophie would have this new person in her life, the other part of her ached that she couldn't be the one to offer it.

"Are you going to the Harvest Fest this weekend?" Rosemary asked as Jane shrugged on her coat. Already

the air was crisp, and there was talk of a potential snow-fall next week. Normally Jane liked this time of year best, but snow made her think of the holidays, and this year, the holidays would be different.

She swallowed the lump that had formed in her throat. It was one thing to be divided from the person you'd vowed to love for the rest of your life, but to have your child taken from you half the time? That was the worst of it.

"We love the Harvest Fest!" Sophie exclaimed excit-edly. "Mommy and I are entering the punkin' carving contest this year. I draw the face and Mommy carves. And you know what they have there?" She cupped one hand to the side of her cheek and leaned in close to Rosemary. "Caramel apples!" She practically sang the words, and even Jane had to laugh. Cheap thrills, she always said. She was happy such simple things still brought her daugh-ter such joy.

She could learn from that.

"I was thinking I might set up a stand this year," Rose-mary said. "It might draw some attention and remind peo-ple about the classes we offer. I'll hand out fliers for the *Nutcracker* auditions, too."

"Good idea," Jane said. "Maybe we should display some of the costumes from last year's show. Most kids are enticed by a sparkly tutu."

"We can certainly try. It the meantime, I'm still com-ing to terms with renting out the space to those artists. The income would certainly help bridge the gap for now, but when I think of the mess they might make. Paint, Jane! That stains, you know." She shuddered.

Jane was well aware. She still had one of Sophie's murals on her laundry room wall to prove it. She'd been

furious when it had happened, but now, three years later, she couldn't bring herself to paint over it. It was just another memory that made her house a home.

"I was wondering... What will we do about *The Nutcracker* if the cast is small?" It was Rosemary's big event, bigger than even the Spring Gala, which was held every year on a makeshift stage in the center of the town square. While Jane's mother defined the holidays through the annual Holiday House decorating contest, *The Nutcracker* was Rosemary's pride and joy and, for most of Briar Creek, a family tradition. Held on the twenty-third of December each year, Jane could still remember bundling into the backseat with her sisters, the radiator heat on high, watching the lights twinkle through the foggy windows as the family drove through the snow-covered town. Her dad couldn't have enjoyed it as much as his wife and three daughters did, but he always encouraged Jane with her dancing, and he never would have admitted to being bored.

Jane smiled softly. She'd like to think her dad was looking down on her, happy to see that she'd followed her love for ballet in the end.

"*The Nutcracker* is important to people in this town," Jane insisted. "They'll be as let down as we would be if we can't pull it together."

"I can't think about that just yet," Rosemary said quietly.

"Well." Jane tied her scarf around her neck and took Sophie's hand. "One bridge at a time, as they say." It was how she'd lived her life for the past eighteen months, since her father died and then her marriage crumbled. One day at a time.

She managed to smile until they were out of the building, but she was all but grinding her teeth when they got to the car. Jane had left it parked in front of Main Street Books, and for once, the thought of going home and slipping into flannel pajamas felt like anything but an escape.

"Hey, how about we go to Hastings for dinner tonight?" she suggested.

Sophie started jumping up and down. "Can I have a milkshake?"

Jane laughed. "How about we split one?" Drowning herself in ice cream felt like just the solution right now.

They walked up Main Street and pushed through the door of the old establishment across from the town square. There were a few customers at the counter chatting with Sharon Hastings, but other than that, the diner was empty. Jane slid into a red-vinyl booth near the window. She leaned across the Formica table to help Sophie with her coat, but her daughter swatted her away.

"I can do it myself," Sophie insisted, yanking at the fabric.

Jane sat back, smiling even though her heart began to tug as Sophie fumbled with the buttons, her brow pinched in deep concentration. Her little girl was growing up. Already it was becoming an effort to pick her up, but more and more, Jane wanted to. She wanted to hold her, rock her to sleep, breathe into that sweet-smelling hair. Soon, that phase would be over. No more little ones to hold, no more lullabies to sing.

Oh, she knew what Grace and Anna would say—that Jane had only just turned twenty-six and that her entire life was ahead of her. She wished she could share in her sisters' optimism, but a string of bad dates last spring had

made her feel hopeless. She hadn't even found herself attracted to another man until this past week— Her stomach tightened at the image of Henry.

Nonsense. He was just passing through town. And he wasn't marriage material.

She placed their order, deciding at the last second to splurge and order two shakes, and then settled into the booth. A few minutes later, Ivy came through the door. Jane waved and called her over.

"I don't see you in here often," Ivy said with a look of surprise. She sat down next to Sophie and loosened the zipper of her down coat. "I probably come here more than I should. Bad habit."

"It's convenient," Jane commented. Petals on Main was just a few blocks down the road, and Hastings was the closest thing to fast food in Briar Creek now, especially as Anna had turned Fireside Café into Rosemary and Thyme, an upscale full-service restaurant.

"Still, it's probably not the healthiest choice. I just hate cooking for one."

Jane gave a wry smile. "I find that whatever I make lasts half the week, and by then, I'm sick of eating it." She'd gotten into the routine of cooking while she was married to Adam, so much so that she hadn't even thought of giving herself a break and coming here before. It felt illicit and oddly special. Running into Ivy was an extra perk. She decided to make a point of trying it more often.

Ivy ordered a house salad and sipped her water. "I'm meeting my brother tonight to go through my mom's house." She grimaced. "I think I'll need my strength to keep up. That place needs a lot of work. More than he knows."

"Then you should have ordered something heavier."

Ivy looked out the window. "Oh, you know me. I'm always watching my carbs."

"Do you want some of my milkshake?" Sophie inquired, shifting her straw in Ivy's direction.

"No thanks, honey. It's all yours."

"That's nice of you to offer, though," Jane said to her daughter. She glanced at Ivy. "We're still working on sharing. I knew if she and I split a shake, I'd get one sip, and I'd be warned about how big it was."

The women laughed. "I don't remember going through any of that with Henry, but we must have."

"You two always seemed tight," Jane commented, thinking the same could probably be said for herself, Grace, and Anna. They'd had their bumps along the way, particularly Anna and Grace, being older and more strong willed, but for the most part, they relied on each other for everything. Even when they didn't always tell each other everything.

Jane took a long sip of her milkshake. She'd have to tell her mother and Anna about Adam's plans soon. The way news traveled in Briar Creek, they'd find out from someone else before long.

"Henry and I needed each other growing up." Ivy folded her straw wrapper into an accordion. "It was just the two of us most of the time."

Jane gave a sad smile. "How are you holding up?" she asked carefully, glancing at Ivy for a reaction.

"I'm really okay," Ivy said, and something in her tone made Jane know she meant it. Jane wished she could say the same for how she felt about her father's death, but she still felt his absence every single day. "It helps to have Henry here."

"I've talked to him a bit," Jane offered. She glanced over at Ivy, wondering why she was even bringing this up. Why her stomach suddenly felt like it had a dozen butterflies hopping around in it. It was just Henry after all. "He was wrapping up his deadline at the bookstore. I told him he should write about Briar Creek next."

Ivy just shook her head as a waitress brought over their plates and set them down. "He likes to travel to places he's never been before. I can't see him wanting to write about Briar Creek. Though it would be sort of neat, wouldn't it?"

"Maybe I shouldn't have brought it up. It just seemed like a good idea. Briar Creek's come a long way recently. I doubt it's much of a tourist destination, though."

"There's the ski resort just down the road," Ivy countered. "And some people like small towns for romantic weekend getaways. Not that I would know."

Jane slipped her a knowing smile. "Still no luck in the love life department?"

"What love life?" Ivy groaned. She speared a tomato wedge with sudden force. "I haven't been on a date in... over a year. Oh my God, I didn't even realize that until now. The last date I went on was with Sam Logan. I remember because we got to talking at the Fourth of July picnic last year and shared a beer at the pub that night." She paused, then made a face. "That's not even a date, is it?"

Jane tried not to laugh. "It sounds better than my recent experiences."

Ivy tipped her head. "One of your dates was nice, right? The nurse?"

The girls locked eyes and started to giggle. "He was very nice," Jane said when she'd composed herself. "Very, very nice. But..."

"No spark?" Ivy sighed. "I know the feeling. Once you feel the spark, it's hard not to hold out for it."

Jane peered at her, suddenly wondering just how much Ivy was holding back. "Anyone in particular?"

Ivy took great care in shuffling the lettuce on her plate. "No...not really. Just..." She looked up at Jane, her eyes pleading. "You know when you have a connection with someone, don't you? Like, you feel it. You get nervous when they walk in a room, you get excited at the thought of seeing them again, and you miss them even when they've only been gone for like five minutes. Everything they say is somehow fascinating, and everyone else just becomes boring in comparison. And when you talk, it just...clicks. It just feels right."

Jane was nodding, but her cheeks were starting to burn. She knew all right. She experienced every single one of those emotions and then some every time Henry came near. Ivy's own brother! If her friend had any idea...Well, she just wouldn't. Besides, she'd probably be the first one to tell Jane that Henry wasn't the man for her. And he wasn't, Jane knew that, even if her heart didn't. Henry was warm and funny, and he had that way of holding her eyes until she was forced to look away, even though she didn't want to. It was easy with Henry. He seemed to get her in a way that few others did. It felt natural. It felt comfortable. It felt—

Wrong. It was all very, very, very wrong. She needed a reliable man. And what was reliable about a man who traveled for a living and never wanted to marry again? "I'm not sure I can trust my own judgment," Jane admitted. After all, she'd thought Adam was her mate for life, and he'd been sleeping with another woman. What a fool she'd been.

"I know Adam hurt you, and I know he was your husband, but I don't think he was the right guy for you."

Jane snorted. "You don't need to tell me." She glanced at Sophie, who was happily coloring on a paper placemat and sipping her shake, oblivious to the conversation. "I know it's for the best, deep down. It's not about the breakup, really. It's more about... being disillusioned. I can't help but feel like my entire life was snatched out from under me sometimes."

"If you had to describe your ideal mate, what would he be like?" Ivy grinned.

Jane couldn't match her enthusiasm. "I just want someone I can count on, without question."

"But what other traits?" Ivy pressed.

Jane felt her heart begin to race with sudden frustration. She just wanted a guy who loved her, and who she loved back. She wanted someone to laugh with, someone to come home to, someone who was there on the good days and the bad, and someone whose mere presence was a source of comfort, not concern. She wanted someone to make her feel special, someone to make her feel cherished, not taken for granted.

She wanted the impossible. Maybe Grace and Anna and a few others had found their happy ending, but she'd had hers once before, and it didn't meet the same fate. Somewhere along the line, it all fell apart instead.

"What about you?" Jane asked, deflecting the attention. "Describe your ideal man."

Ivy's expression turned dreamy. "Oh, I suppose he'd be tall, with dark hair and deep-set eyes. He'd be smart, a doctor probably. Or, you know, maybe a lawyer," she added quickly. "And he'd have a killer smile and a special

way to make me laugh. He'd be serious, but not uptight. And he'd be family oriented."

Tall, dark, and handsome...and a doctor. Sounded like she was describing Mark Hastings's brother, Brett.

Jane was just about to point this out when Ivy's cell phone rang. She glanced at the screen. "Henry," she explained, pressing it to her ear.

Oh, there was that pulse-racing, stomach-knotting, quiver-down-the-spine feeling again. Jane tucked her hair behind her ears and sat up a little straighter, just in case he was about to drop in.

Nonsense. So what if he did? She might enjoy his company for a few minutes; there was hardly any harm in that.

Ivy muttered a few one-syllable words into the phone and set it back on the table. "I should head out," she said, flagging the waitress. "It's time to face the old homestead."

"Hopefully it sells quickly," Jane said, hating the disappointment she felt. She told herself it couldn't be because Henry wasn't joining them, but rather that a nice, warm chat with a good friend was coming to an end.

"Jeez, I hope so." Ivy zippered her coat and set a ten-dollar bill on the table. "See you later."

Jane waved goodbye and turned to Sophie. "Finish your dinner, honey. Then we'll go home."

She sank back into her seat and finished the rest of her shake. As much as she loved sharing a dinner with her daughter, it wasn't quite the same as adult conversation. It would be nice to have someone to talk to, to share the events of the day. She scrolled through her phone, seeing if one of her sisters had reached out recently, and frowned at the missed call on her display. Her attorney.

With a shaking hand, she dialed the number, willing herself to stay calm.

It answered on the first ring. "Ah, Jane. I'm glad you called."

"Rob? Is everything okay?" She took a calming breath, but her heart was pounding out of her chest.

She ran through a list of potential scenarios, reasons for his call. Maybe she'd forgotten to pay his last bill. But no . . . she was sure she had. Maybe there was another bill, another set of fees. Her gut tightened. Like she could afford to shell out another dime right now.

"Would you be available to stop by my office tomorrow morning?"

Jane felt the blood drain from her face. "What's going on?"

There was a slight pause at the other end of the line. "It's probably best for us to discuss this in person."

Uh-uh. No way. She'd never sleep tonight.

She pushed her plate away. There was no way she could eat now.

"Rob, what is it?"

Her breath came in spurts as she clutched the phone tighter, waiting for the blow. What now? What more could Adam possibly take from her?

"It's about Sophie," her lawyer said gently. "Adam's relocating out of state, and he's petitioned for Sophie to go with him."

CHAPTER
9

The knot in Henry's gut grew tighter with each minute that ticked by on the car dashboard. He shifted in his seat, trying to get comfortable, but it was no use, and Ivy's car wasn't the problem. The radio blared a way too upbeat tune and he reached over and flicked it off.

"Sorry," he said, giving his sister a guilty glance. "I just didn't feel up for it right now."

"We're almost there." Ivy's lips thinned, and Henry knew she was dreading this just as much as he was. They rarely talked about their mother. Even when she was alive, they communicated in silence through meaningful glances that spoke words too painful to voice. The few times they'd had to address a situation, like her failed stint in rehab, the string of arrests, or the numerous times she was passed out on a couch, they did so efficiently, without emotion. Henry knew that deep inside, Ivy ran the gauntlet of emotions like he did, but there was no use in letting it out. It didn't change a damn thing. It was better to try to forget about it for a while.

He heaved a sigh. "The sooner we get started, the sooner it's over, right?"

"A necessary evil," Ivy agreed, her eyes still fixed to the road. It was growing dark, and the old country roads weren't well lit.

Henry clenched his teeth, his shoulders growing tense as Ivy slowed and then pulled the car onto the gravel driveway. It was a Pavlovian response—the tires bumped and the first wave of nausea hit, his chest heavy with dread and a sense of foreboding. If he closed his eyes he could almost hear the bottles crashing, see his mother thrashing about, screaming about something.

He and Ivy had learned to live around their mother, careful not to set her off, sometimes trying to calm her down, to bring her over to the couch and offer up her favorite game show, or sometimes to sit in her wrath, to hear it but not see it. "Don't look her in the eye." He could remember saying that to Ivy when they must have only been four or five. She'd nodded her head, her eyes large and understanding. *Don't look her in the eye, 'cause when you do—*

His back began to cramp. He'd get in and out and he'd never look back. The sooner they got to work, the sooner it would be over.

The house looked smaller than he'd remembered it, barely visible in the shadows of the moonlight cutting through the tree branches. It was a dark night, the sky murky with dense clouds, and an owl hooted in the distance. God, he hated this place. He preferred the bustle of the city, the chaos of the traffic, the way you could just melt in, anonymously, but somehow never be alone. Out here, he was painfully aware of just alone he and Ivy were in the world.

Slowly, he let himself out of the car and followed Ivy

up the path to the front door, careful not to trip on the flat stones that had settled unevenly over time. As Ivy fished out the key and fumbled to find the lock, he peered into the distance. There was Adam's old house, lit up and cheerful in the near distance. He turned his back to it, his heart pounding, resisting the part of himself that wanted to run down that hill, push open the door, breathe in the warm air, sit down at the dinner table, and laugh and talk the way families did this time of night. His jaw tensed. That was never his home, much as he'd wished it could be. This was his reality.

He shoved his hands into his pockets and hunched against the brisk wind. There would be no running away from his problems tonight. He was going to face them, head on, and then hopefully forget them forever.

The lock finally clicked, and his stomach heaved when Ivy pushed open the door. Even over the sound of the rustling leaves, he could hear her sigh. "Here we are." She flicked on a light and the hallway sprung to life around them.

"It's freezing in here," Henry pointed out. He looked to the ceiling for any sign of damage. "We're lucky we came when we did. If we'd held off much longer, a pipe could have burst."

Ivy's forehead creased. "I know I should have stopped by and turned on the heat, but I . . ." She shook her head, and Henry let it drop. She hadn't wanted to come back. Who would?

The hallway itself was sparse and bare. To the left was the living room, where he and Ivy used to sit on the floor around the wood-carved coffee table, playing cards. He always let Ivy win.

"This room's going to take the most work," Ivy was saying from the back of the house.

Turning, Henry marched to the kitchen and then halted in the doorway. The yellowing floral wallpaper was singed above the range, and the countertops were damaged beyond repair with dark stains. The window near the sink was cracked, and the molding around it was warped and peeling, indicating a leak and potential wood rot. The rubber soles of his shoes stuck to the peeling linoleum.

"I'm sorry," Ivy said despairingly. She blinked several times. "I should have come sooner, I just..."

Henry swallowed hard. "Don't apologize—it's not your fault."

They made their way up the dimly lit stairs, poking their heads into rooms instead of entering, and then came back down a few minutes later. Henry paused at the door to the basement and then yanked it open. He flicked the switch; nothing happened, but it didn't matter. They knew these stairs by heart; the creaking of the boards was cemented into their memory from all the times they had hidden down there to get away. Ivy stayed close behind him, the light from the main hall guiding their way.

They reached the cold concrete floor and Henry reached up to pull on a cord. A single lightbulb lit the room. Damp settled over them, and he covered his mouth with his hand. Had it always been this dark and wet down here? It had seemed like their haven at one point, a refuge from the stress unfolding up above. They used to run free down here. He could still picture Ivy in her hand-me-down roller skates, laughing as she wound her way around the room. He crossed over to the back of the room, nearly tripping over something. An empty vodka

bottle rolled to the wall. Several more were collected in the corner.

"Sometimes she couldn't be bothered to throw them away," Ivy said quietly.

Henry rubbed the space between his eyebrows. His mother couldn't be bothered to do anything most days. Couldn't get out of bed. Couldn't go to the store for groceries, much less fix a meal. Their dad was gone before they were even born. Their grandmother had lived with them for the first six years of their life, but when she died, everything had fallen apart.

Henry shuddered to think what might have become of him and his sister had his grandmother not lived as long as she had.

"Sometimes it amazes me we even managed to get to school every day." Or that his mother managed to hold down a job, albeit never for longer than a few weeks at a time. She shuffled around, cleaning houses or waitressing in neighboring towns. The secretary jobs rarely lasted more than a few days, especially when she got too friendly with the boss. He shook his head. He'd blocked so much out, refusing to go back there and think about that time in his life. It was so much easier to run, to keep running, to keep putting distance between him and this place.

Henry had liked school. It had opened a whole new world to him, a life beyond these four walls. He kept to himself mostly, playing with Ivy at recess or spending his free time in the library, until he'd met Adam. Adam was a year behind, but that didn't matter. The Browns lived next door, just down the hill, and they both liked fast cars and baseball. For a first grader, that was enough, but after the first time Henry went to Adam's house, he clung to

his new friend like a life raft, and Adam happily went along with it. Suddenly Henry had a warm, safe place to go every day, and a loving, smiling mother to feed him an after-school snack on the walk home each afternoon. He could still remember Mrs. Brown checking his backpack each morning to see if there was a lunch, often adding an apple or a few slices of cheese or a carton of chocolate milk. "We have extra," she'd say with a casual smile. If Ivy had already gone ahead, wanting to meet up with some of the girls, he'd give her half of his share at the playground.

His lips thinned. He should visit Adam's parents while he was in town. But somehow, the thought of going back there was almost more unbearable than being here. It was just a reminder somehow that they were a family, and even now, all these years later, he was, well... still on the fringes.

"So what should we do with everything?" Ivy asked, when they returned to the main level.

"Get rid of it," Henry said. He shrugged. "I don't see any reason to keep anything, do you? It's not like Mom was one for family photos."

"I guess not," Ivy said sadly. She sighed and wandered back into the living room. Neither of them made any movement toward sitting down.

Henry looked around the room. It was just as dark and uninviting as he had remembered. No pictures hung on the walls, and the mirror that had been hung over the mantel all his life still bore the enormous, jagged crack through the middle from the time their mother had thrown his boots at it. He and Ivy had stood frozen, not daring to speak or even breathe, as she railed about money and

expenses. They waited until after she'd stormed upstairs and slammed her bedroom door shut, and then Henry had quietly picked up the shards of broken glass, thrown them away, and forced his feet into the too-small boots. He'd worn those things all winter, even though his big toe ached, and he never asked for another pair again.

The next Christmas, when his mother was in a "festive" mood, she'd brought them shopping downtown. As much as they preferred this side of her, another part of it terrified them even more. She cranked up the radio in the car and even ran the heater, singing at the top of her lungs as they swerved into town. "Pick anything you want!" she'd cried, laughing and smiling, and taking their hands. He and Ivy had glanced at each other nervously, shrugged, and then decided to enjoy it while it lasted. Ivy wanted a new doll with a pink dress and long and dark silky hair she could brush, but he told her no, first things first. They managed to get a new pair of boots each, gym shoes, and a matching hat and mittens set for Ivy before things turned sour. By the time they'd returned to the toy shop, he could smell the sourness on his mother's breath, and the glint in her eye had returned. When Ivy whined about the doll, their mother ripped it from her hands and slammed it back on the shelf. Ivy began to cry.

"We'll go the library," Henry said, as his mother headed for the car. If she bothered to reply, it was lost in the winter wind.

With his sister at his side, he made a collect call to Adam's mother. She picked them up ten minutes later, giving a forced, bright smile, her forehead wrinkled despite the cheerful tone she tried to maintain.

"You know if you ever need anything, just come next

door," she said when she dropped them off later that night, a warm meal in their stomachs.

Once, when he was playing in Adam's room, he overheard Mr. and Mrs. Brown talking about him, using words he didn't understand, like *authorities*. When he went to the library the next afternoon, he looked it up, and then slammed the book shut.

If the police took his mother away, then he and Ivy would be sent away, possibly split up, forever. He'd read enough books to know how that worked. He couldn't let that happen.

From then on, when Mrs. Brown asked how things were at home, he just shrugged. She suspected things, he was sure, but he wasn't going to give her any proof. His sister needed him. She still did.

"How do you feel?" Ivy asked after she turned the key and checked the knob, ensuring the house was locked behind them.

He looked at her. "Pretty crappy."

She gave a thin smile. "Me, too."

Henry gave her a long look. "I'm sorry I didn't come back sooner."

Ivy just shrugged. "We weren't sure what was going to happen with Mom a year ago. There was no reason for you to come back before now."

He opened his mouth to say something about the burial, to explain, or apologize, but no sound came out. He'd been in a small town about half an hour outside Amsterdam when Ivy called him to tell him that the time had come. It was no surprise, but still it was a punch in the gut. He'd said nothing, just held the phone to his ear for a good half hour, listening to Ivy's breath on the other end.

They didn't discuss the arrangements. Ivy said she wasn't going to have a service, and Henry put a check in the mail for the burial expenses. He couldn't sleep that night, but not because of sadness. No, the only emotion he felt was anger, anger so deep he couldn't contain it, and he cursed his mother and cursed himself for not being able to save her, no matter how hard he'd tried.

The last time he'd spoken with his mother, he'd managed to convince her to go to rehab, only he didn't word it quite like that. He'd found a nice place outside Orange County, where she could relax and regroup. Slowly, she'd come around to the idea, and he paid for the full thirty days, bought her a first-class ticket, and arranged for Ivy to drive her to the airport that night. She had no idea that he'd been saving his money, pinching and scrimping and hoping it would be enough, that maybe, somehow, they could find a way to be a real family.

She checked herself out of the facility forty-four hours after she'd arrived, hit the airport bar, and was stopped by security before she could board the plane. When they called him to pick her up at LAX, he refused.

It was his last effort, but after she died, he wondered what would have happened if he'd tried just one more time… He inhaled sharply. No point in thinking that way.

"I'll call a clean-up crew and see if they can come out this week or next."

"Thanks." Ivy popped the locks on the car and they both slipped inside.

Suddenly in need of a reminder that there was life outside this dreadful place, Henry flicked on the radio. Instantly, an announcer's voice filled the air. Slowly, life went back to normal.

They passed Adam's old house. The light was on in the kitchen, and he strained his eyes to get a glimpse inside. It looked the same. Small. Quaint. The porch light illuminated a perfectly maintained row of hedges along the base of the front window.

"I know it's not easy for you, being back in Briar Creek." Ivy paused. "I want you to know that I appreciate it."

"Then do me a favor," Henry said. "Take the money I offered you and get yourself some better health insurance."

"Henry..." Ivy sighed. "I told you, it will all work out. This year's just been more expensive than usual."

"Because of the burial. Cash the check, Ivy."

"No." Her voice was sharp. "You did enough for her. It was my turn."

He ran a hand through his hair and stared into the dark forest. She was determined to make the arrangements her sole responsibility. Maybe he should let her.

"Besides, that's not the only reason things are tight," she continued. "My rent went up on the shop this year, and my wholesaler raised prices. It adds up."

"I don't like you putting money toward the business that should be going toward your health."

"What's the alternative?" Ivy asked. "If I don't have a business, then I'm really screwed."

"You know I have the money." He wasn't wealthy, not with a journalist's salary, but he lived a comfortable life and had few expenses given how much he traveled for work. "Please let me help."

She said nothing more until they were in town and she pulled to a stop in front of the hotel. He could tell by the look in her eyes that she was tired. He should let her get home to rest.

She stopped him before he could say goodnight. "Jane mentioned to me that you were considering featuring Briar Creek in one of your articles."

His heart sped up. "When did you talk to Jane?"

Her gaze was steady. "I had a quick dinner with her this evening before I met up with you. She and Sophie were at the diner."

He'd been in his room, preparing himself to go to the house. He suddenly wished he'd taken Ivy up on her offer to meet for dinner instead.

"I'm not the best person to write about this town." He arched a brow, giving her a long, knowing look.

"I know." She sighed, then leaned across the armrest to give him a hug. "You're the best, Henry."

He unhooked his seatbelt and crawled out of the car, waving until his sister was out of sight, her words still ringing in his ears. He wasn't the best. Not the best son, not the best brother. Guilt burned in his stomach, leaving him uneasy and agitated when he thought of Ivy's struggles, her bills, what Jane had said about putting Briar Creek on the map.

Ivy was his family. She was all he had. And he'd do anything for her. *Even write an article on this godforsaken town*, he thought ruefully.

CHAPTER
10

Grace and their mother were already gathered in the large, gleaming white kitchen of Rosemary and Thyme when Jane entered, breathless and harried. Everyone was smiling, in good spirits, and Jane tried to muster up the same energy. It was no use. Her thoughts were on one thing, or one person, really. Her daughter.

"There you are!" Kathleen stood and gave Jane a hug. Hot tears immediately threatened, and Jane closed her eyes, holding her mother a little tighter than usual.

Blinking quickly, she pulled back, smiling brightly and grateful she hadn't yet removed her sunglasses. "Sorry I'm late. I had an appointment this morning and traffic was bad."

"An appointment?" Grace frowned at her from the marble-top pastry station. "Everything okay?"

"Oh…" Jane waved a hand through the air and slid onto a stool next to her sister. She shoved her sunglasses into her handbag before setting it at her feet, hoping her eyes weren't red from crying so much. "Just thought I'd

try a new dentist over in Forest Ridge." It was a simple excuse, and one they didn't question. Jane breathed a little easier. Somehow keeping her thoughts to herself made this entire nightmare feel a little less real.

"Well, I hope you brought your appetite." Anna grinned, setting a porcelain plate in front of her. "Now, honesty is important. And remember, Grace, I can create anything you want, so if you like some aspects of a few, let me know."

Jane picked up the heavy fork and eyed the ten round cakes in front of her. Normally her mouth would be salivating by now, but her throat felt scratchy, and her hands were trembling. When she set the fork back on her plate, it clattered. "Sorry," she said, masking her nerves with a smile.

"Mind if we start?" Grace asked. "I skipped breakfast because I knew we were doing this today."

Jane arched a brow. "Luke isn't joining us?"

"He's not a big sweets person. He said as long as I'm happy, he'll be happy." Grace's smile turned a little wistful, and Jane felt her own expression tighten. *Imagine having a guy like that*, she thought, and then she straightened her back, brushing away the sting. This was Grace's special time. She'd had hers. It was just difficult to remember that once she'd been the happy bride-to-be. She'd actually thought she was entering into years of sunshine and roses.

She managed not to snort.

"Besides," Grace continued, "I think he knows that anything Mark and Anna make will be a crowd pleaser."

"I'll second that," their mother said, leaning forward eagerly.

Anna gestured to the first cake in the row, and even Jane felt her mouth begin to water. It was coated in glossy

dark chocolate and wrapped in a stunning cream-colored ribbon of pulled sugar. Anna took a large knife and cut a wedge, revealing three beautiful layers of cake. It was so moist and dense, not a crumb fell as she plated it and passed it to Grace. "This one is the least traditional," she said as she handed Jane and Kathleen their servings. "Here you have a Belgian chocolate cake with a milk-chocolate hazelnut cream center, coated in a dark chocolate ganache. Grace, this might be an option for the groom's cake."

Grace eagerly tucked into her piece, closing her eyes as she swallowed. "Don't even bother with the rest. This is the one."

In the distance, Jane heard Anna and her mother laugh. She tried to join in, but her mind was spinning again, her pulse racing, and for a minute she thought she might be sick. It had all started this way for her—the wedding dress shopping, the flowers, the cake—and somehow it all ended not just with an affair, but with Adam trying to take away the one thing she had left. Sophie. She'd given her daughter life, loved her with every ounce of her being, and now she risked losing her. It was unimaginable.

"Jane?"

Jane looked up to see Anna staring at her quizzically. "Everything okay?" When Jane nodded, her sister tipped her head. "You haven't tried the cake."

"Oh." Jane lifted her fork and brought a small piece to her mouth. Her throat tightened. "It's delicious," she managed.

She went through the motions with the next six cakes, even managing to voice her opinion about the one she liked best—a vanilla sponge cake with layers of raspberry

purée and marzipan—but her heart began to twist in her chest, making it difficult to breathe. Adam was going to take Sophie. Her little girl was going to live somewhere else, somewhere not with her. She wouldn't be there to tuck her into bed at night, to pick out her clothes for school, to make her favorite foods. Instead, *that woman* would be doing it all.

She reached for the pitcher of water Anna had set out, nearly knocking it onto the worktop.

Her mother stared at her for several long seconds, her blue eyes narrowed. With shaking hands, Jane filled her glass and took a long, cool sip. Now wasn't the time to fall apart. Now was the time to take action, to think. To do... something. She just wished she knew what.

Grace tossed up her hands and shrugged. "Well, I can't decide."

Anna chuckled, shaking her head and sending her loose blond ponytail over one shoulder. "I figured that would be the case. So long as you make up your mind by a week before the wedding, it shouldn't be a problem." As Grace began to say something, Anna held up a finger. "But, no changing your mind. The entire town is coming to this wedding, and I can't redo that many tiers on short notice. And once I start decorating—"

"I understand." Grace nodded firmly, but Jane caught the nervous twitch in her brow.

"Once I start the fondant, that's it. That's your cake." Anna stared at Grace, who was now chewing on the corner of her lip, eyeing the crème brûlée cake with the decadent caramel center.

"It's going to be this one or the red velvet. I'm nearly sure of it," she added, giving an apologetic smile.

"Take these samples home and think about it." Anna pulled some pastry boxes from a shelf and began transferring the cakes. "Jane, bring some home to Sophie."

"Tonight's Adam's night," Jane blurted. Quickly, she reached for the box. "Thanks. She'll love them."

"If you store this in the refrigerator, they should keep until tomorrow," Anna said kindly.

Grace checked her watch and stood. "Oh my, I should get back to the store. I need to get it open before lunch hour."

Jane's pulse skipped. "I can cover the rest of the afternoon for you, if you'd like." If she just went home now, she'd wander the rooms, feeling the emptiness.

Grace pulled her chestnut hair from her coat collar and fastened the buttons. "Oh, it's a slow day, but thanks. I'll see you tomorrow?"

Jane swallowed, managing only to nod. Maybe she'd pop into some shops, get some groceries. The thought of keeping up the pretense that everything was okay much longer was exhausting, though. She'd go home. She'd make a list and strategize. With her white pastry box in her hands, she followed Grace and their mother out of the kitchen, nearly bumping into Mark on his way inside.

"Good morning, ladies!" He grinned, but his gaze roamed quickly to Anna. At the sight of her boyfriend, Anna's blue eyes lit up, and the grin she wore was contagious.

"You're late," she bantered, but a pleased flush spread over her cheeks. "But since you were sweet enough to remember my favorite flower, I'll forgive you this once."

It was then that Jane noticed the huge bouquet of blue hydrangeas anchoring the farm table Mark and Anna used as a desk at the back of the kitchen. Recipe boxes

and cutouts from magazines littered the surface, which was nestled near the big paned windows.

Leaving them to the cozy little world they'd created for themselves, Jane felt her heart grow heavy. She'd had a cozy little world of her own once, and she supposed she still did. But for the second time in a year it was being threatened, thanks to the one man who'd once been a part of it. Her heart was beginning to pound again, and she clenched a fist at her side. It had taken every ounce of willpower after leaving her attorney's office not to drive straight to Adam's office and have it out with him, to scream at him, to show him how much he had hurt her, to ask when it would end, when it would be enough, and what she had ever done to deserve it. She thought it was over. She thought that pain was finally behind her. But when she caught the whisper of joy in Grace's voice, or that smile that lit Anna's eyes, she couldn't help gritting her teeth against the sting of loneliness. Not for Adam—he was no good and she knew it—but for that feeling of comfort, stability, and...happiness, she supposed. She hadn't dared to be happy in a long time. And without Sophie... A hard lump wedged in her throat. Without Sophie she didn't stand a chance of ever finding happiness again.

Forcing her shoulders back, Jane heaved an unsteady sigh and pushed through the front doors of the empty restaurant. Outside, Kathleen waited until Grace was a block away before setting a hand on Jane's arm.

"This can't be easy for you, seeing your sisters in love, Grace getting married."

Jane opened her mouth to finally release the horrible, unbearable news. Only Grace even knew that Adam was getting married and having another child. Now, standing

with her mother, staring into her kind, familiar eyes, she felt as if it would burst from her. She couldn't keep the tears back much longer.

But before she could speak, her mother said, "This is harder on me than I expected, too. It's...sad to think that your father won't be here to walk Grace down the aisle. Maybe I'm being silly, but I started wondering, who will I dance with at the reception?"

Kathleen's eyes misted over, and all at once Jane was back in mom mode, as Grace playfully called it, checking her feelings, straightening her back, and pulling it together. It was what she did best, after all.

"Oh, Mom." Jane sighed. "I'm sorry." She knew it was no consolation to mention that she'd wondered the same. She obviously didn't have a date for the wedding, and while maybe Mark or his brother, Brett, would take pity on her and give her a friendly swing around the dance floor, chances were she'd be sitting at the singles table, watching all the fun from a distance.

Adam was never a good dancer, she reminded herself. Even at their wedding, he didn't hold her very close, and the few events they'd gone to that had a band, Adam preferred to sit at a table and watch. Why couldn't he have just spun her around a few times, knowing how much she enjoyed it? You did things like that for people you loved. At least, she did.

"Please don't tell Grace I mentioned any of this." Kathleen's whisper was urgent, and Jane nodded dutifully. Neither of them should be taking anything away from Grace's happiness right now, and if that meant dealing with her problems all on her own, then that's what she would do. It wasn't like she didn't have plenty of practice.

She heaved a sigh. If she didn't tell her mother the partial truth soon, it would come from someone else. "You should know that Adam is getting remarried." She thinned her mouth, waiting for it.

Her mother's expression turned horror-stricken. Her wide eyes didn't blink for several seconds.

"And, he's having a baby."

There. It was out. She exhaled through her nose, bracing for a reaction.

"You don't seem very shaken up about this," Kathleen remarked.

Jane clenched her fist inside her coat pocket. "Nope. Why should I be?" She gritted her teeth into a casual smile. "We all know I'm better off without him."

"That's my girl," her mother said, patting her arm. "You'll find someone else. You're young, and pretty and—" Kathleen frowned and peered over Jane's shoulder. "Is that—"

Jane followed her mother's gaze across the street. Her eyes snapped open as her heart began to pound, the dread she'd felt now replaced with an emotion just as powerful. God help her, it was lust. She turned back to her mother, hoping the heat would fade from her cheeks before Kathleen noticed, but her mother was still focused on Henry. Jane wished she'd swiped on some lipstick or something. Her mascara had probably been cried off. *Please don't let her call out to him!*

"I didn't know Henry Birch was in town," Kathleen mused. A slow smile curved her mouth. Catching herself, her eyes darted to Jane's.

Jane drew a breath as Henry crossed the street. Oh, no. He really was coming over here, and here she was,

downright giddy over...her ex-husband's best friend! What was wrong with her? "I've seen him a few times." What was once more?

"He was always a *nice* boy," Kathleen said. "What he ever saw in Adam, I'll never know..." A guilty flush heated her cheeks. "Sorry, Jane."

"No apology needed," she replied. She wondered the same thing herself most days. Henry and Adam were a mismatch, but then, couldn't the same be said for herself and her ex-husband?

She eyed Henry as he reached the curb, quickly closing the distance between them with his long, confident stride. A grin stretched across his handsome face, crinkling those blue eyes that seemed to pull her into a trance. She shook it off, dropping her gaze to the ground, away from that casual smile and the magnetic effect he had on her. She had a million reasons for not indulging in the skip of her heartbeat every time he came near, but this morning's conversation with her attorney trumped them all.

Adam was lining up his army, preparing for battle. And Henry, being Adam's oldest friend, was someone she'd be best to keep her distance from for now.

Henry felt the smile slip from his face as he approached the Madisons just outside Rosemary and Thyme. Kathleen, with her kind eyes and warm smile, waved heartily as he neared, but Jane seemed to stiffen instead of returning his grin.

Determined not to dwell on the matter, Henry greeted her mother with a brief hug, stepped back, and shoved his hands into his pockets. "It's good to see you Mrs. Madison. I'm sorry to hear about your husband." He knew

through Ivy that Ray Madison had died about eighteen months ago—it couldn't have been easy on any of them. He glanced over at Jane. Especially Jane.

He alone knew the torment she felt over choosing to give up that dance scholarship, the fear she had that she'd somehow let her father down.

"Thank you." Kathleen squeezed his hand once before releasing it. "Well, I have an appointment I'm already late for. Henry, are you in town for long?"

Only as long as I have to be.

He shrugged. "Can't say. I'm helping my sister fix up our old house. We're hoping to sell it soon."

A knowing expression seemed to cloud Kathleen's expression. "Well, then I'm sure we'll see each other again before you leave. Briar Creek is small that way."

Like he needed to be reminded, he thought grimly.

"I'd like that," he told her, and he meant it. The Madisons had been good to his sister, like family to her, really, and for that, he was eternally grateful. The same way he'd always be grateful to the Browns.

He inhaled sharply and turned to Jane, who watched quietly as her mother disappeared down the sidewalk. He shoved his hands in his pockets and rolled back on his heels. He should go, leave Jane be—to heal, to move on and find a guy. The right guy. But for some reason he couldn't. "Ivy said she had dinner with you last night. I was sort of disappointed to miss it."

Her eyes widened slightly. "Oh, well...That would have been...nice." Her gaze darted the second it met his. "I should probably get going, too. I have some stuff to sort out before—"

"I was hoping I'd run into you today, actually," he said,

blocking her path before she had a chance to get away. He scanned her face, noticing the flatness in her eyes, the paleness in her usually rosy skin, and he frowned with sudden concern. Something was wrong, and he was guessing it had nothing to do with his meet-up with Adam the other night.

Divorce was difficult. He knew it firsthand—the sense of loss, of failure. Of hopelessness, at times. For months after he and Caroline separated, he replayed their relationship, trying to pinpoint the exact moment when it all went off path and things fell apart. He told himself he liked his independence, started taking more assignments—longer assignments—to push away the aimlessness that seemed to make his mind spin. Was it doomed before they even walked down the aisle? Probably, he told himself. Caroline, like most women he'd met since her, seemed to want something from him he couldn't give. Not to her. Not to anyone.

They wanted a family man. And what did Henry know about that? He'd tried his best, but it didn't come naturally. Caroline had told him he hadn't given her a full chance—them a full chance. Maybe she was right. Maybe the person he'd let down more than her was himself.

He cleared his throat. "I've decided to take your suggestion. I'm writing a piece on Briar Creek."

Her eyes sparked with interest. "Really? That's wonderful!" She tipped her head. "What made you change your mind?"

"I figured I could help Ivy, plug her flower shop," he said. He glanced down Main Street, where orange leaves danced on store awnings, rustling in the breeze. "I thought I'd start with the festival this weekend."

"Sophie and I will be there," Jane offered, and then

blinked rapidly. Tears welled in her eyes, and she ran a hand over her mouth, waving him back when he stepped toward her. "Sorry. I don't know what's come over me. I'm...fine. Really."

"No, you're not fine," he said, scowling. A rush of adrenaline heated his blood, and he pulled a fist at his side, wanting to undo whatever was causing her so much distress. "What is it, Jane?"

"I can't talk about this with you," she whispered, confirming what he already knew.

"It's something to do with Adam."

She hesitated. "It's...Sophie. He's...he's leaving Vermont and he wants to take Sophie with him."

Henry dragged a hand through his hair, cursing under his breath. He should have known something more was going on. There was shiftiness in Adam's eyes Saturday night that wasn't typical for small talk, or a person with nothing to hide. "I was afraid of something like this."

Jane's eyes turned sharp. "What?"

"When I met up with Adam, he mentioned he might be moving."

"And you didn't tell me?" Jane stared at him, her eyes so full of hurt and confusion that he couldn't form an explanation fast enough. All he wanted to do was take the pain out of her eyes, out of her life. She brought a shaking hand to her forehead and shook her head. "Of course you didn't. You're Adam's friend."

"I'm your friend, too," Henry insisted, but he stopped right there when he saw the look in her face.

"No. You're obviously not."

Is that really what she thought? "He asked me not to say anything—"

She was backing up, shaking her head, and her entire body seemed to be shaking. "And so of course you didn't. It's my daughter, Henry. My *daughter*. She's all I have."

"I didn't know what he meant, Jane—" Henry took a step toward her, but she held up her hands. "Jane, I wasn't getting involved."

"Do me a favor, then. Keep it that way." She turned and ran down the street, her long brown hair swinging behind her. He watched her go, feeling the weight in his chest grow heavier with each step she took.

She had it all wrong.

His loyalty might have seemed like it was with Adam all those years ago, but his heart had always been with her.

CHAPTER 11

The only thing Jane could be grateful for in this moment was that Sophie was spending the night with her father, the rat bastard. She snorted at the bitter irony, and then plucked another tissue from the box. The last, she noted, swiping at her face and then crumbling it into her hand. And she'd promised herself that one box of tissues was all she'd allow. She certainly wasn't going to keep custody of her child by falling apart, was she?

Jane stood and tossed the box into the recycling bin, on top of an empty oatmeal container. It seemed that ensuring Sophie had three balanced meals a day, a bath, freshly laundered clothes, and a bedtime story wasn't enough to make her a fit mother. Another sob burst out when she pictured Kristy waving Sophie off to school each morning...in Denver!

She took the magnetic notepad she kept for grocery lists off the fridge and pulled out a chair from the kitchen table. Grace had always laughed at this habit, but Anna had secretly supported Jane's need for her organizational

skills. Maybe it was silly, admittedly, to jot down things on her to-do list that she had already accomplished that day, like making a bed or getting the dishwasher loaded, just for the sheer sense of validation that came when she then crossed them off seconds later, but it was nice to have credit for something once in a while, and being a housewife had more often than not felt like a thankless job. She had lost count of the number of dinners she cooked that Adam hadn't come home to eat. Though she religiously changed the sheets on the bed once a week, her husband could go for months without noticing, especially since he was sleeping on the couch by the end of things, claiming he'd nodded off watching television.

She should have known then that something was up, that he was pulling back. Instead, she'd trusted him. Too much. She wouldn't be making that mistake again.

Jane sighed and clicked the top of her pen. Her lawyer had told her that as the primary caregiver, she had a strong case, and she should focus on proving that she provided a stable home. Emotional stability was easy, but financial... that would be difficult, and the attorney fees certainly weren't helping.

She put a check mark next to emotional stability and then started on the more distressing points. Four dance classes totaled... She scowled at the sum. Not enough. Ten classes was a solid part-time income, but four made it look like a glorified hobby. If things didn't change quickly at the studio, she'd have no choice but to take full-time employment elsewhere. It wouldn't be the first time she'd had to give up her dancing for Adam.

She moved on to the next point on her list: Main Street Books. She manned the counter at the cafe three days a

week, surely that counted for something, it being a family business and all. Grace had made sure to include her on a small business health insurance plan, and Sophie was covered by Adam's. That part wouldn't be an issue. What would be tricky, though, was proving that Sophie's life would be better here than it would be with her father and new sibling. Adam could provide the ice skating lessons Sophie longed for, not to mention dance, music, and no doubt annual vacations, not that he'd been inclined to take them when they were married, she now thought, narrowing her eyes. On paper, Adam had it all. A happy family unit of four versus a struggling single mother. She didn't care what the lawyer said about her having been the primary caregiver up until now. The nagging thought wouldn't go away: She didn't stand a chance.

She knew she could always pack her bags and move to Colorado, too, but why should she have to? Hadn't she given up enough already? Adam was the one moving, and he had Kristy and a new baby on the way. Her entire family was here, as was his.

How could Adam take Sophie from her grandparents and aunts?

Anger boiled in her blood, quickly replacing the self-pitying tears.

"No," she said aloud, crumbling the list in her hands. No way would she let him take her daughter, her dancing, or her home from her.

She poised her pen over the top line of a fresh sheet of paper and began running through the places in town she might find employment. By the time she had reached the end, her fingers had stopped shaking and she felt like

she might almost be able to get through the night without waking up.

Ivy was always saying how busy she was, especially lately. She'd start with Petals on Main.

Henry pushed through the door of the local diner and made his way up to the counter. He'd avoided Hastings since returning, but he couldn't bear one more morning of Mrs. Griffin's runny eggs, or the way she insisted on pulling up a chair and chatting with him all through breakfast, no doubt curious about his time here and his reasons for staying away. The Main Street B&B, despite its comfortable accommodations, would never suit his needs. What he needed was a place to go where no one knew him and no one bothered him. A place like his condo in San Francisco.

He'd get there soon. But not soon enough.

Henry turned over his mug, and a young woman filled it while he skimmed his options. Same as he remembered. Not that he was surprised. The place was an institution, and from the looks of the crowd, it was a second home to many of Briar Creek's older citizens.

"Henry Birch, isn't it?"

Henry set his menu down and glanced at the man on his left, who was studying him with interest. His gray eyes were clear, his smile more of a smirk. Henry searched his face for recognition and came up empty.

"Yes. Do we . . . did we know each other?" He grinned apologetically. "Sorry, it's been a while since I've been back in town."

"I knew your mother," the older man said with a bit of a smirk.

Henry felt his smile freeze. He ground on his teeth, giving the man a hard stare. "I see." He turned back to the counter, hoping to catch the waitress's attention. He'd leave right now if he wasn't so hungry; his only other option was a muffin at the Annex, and he wasn't sure he should get too attached to that place . . . or the sight of Jane behind the counter.

"I'll have a Western omelet," he told the waitress, and closed his menu shut.

He took a sip of his coffee and stared at the wall. He'd hoped that by keeping his back to the room he'd go unnoticed. So much for that.

"Yeah, good ol' Debbie. She sure was fun."

"Yeah, well, all that fun caught up with her," Henry ground out. His jaw tensed even more. He took another sip of his coffee and pulled out the complimentary newspaper Mrs. Griffin had personally slid under his door that morning.

Eventually the man left, and Henry dared to glance over his shoulder. A group of middle-aged women were sitting at the table closest to him, watching closely. "Debbie's son," one whispered, after he'd turned back to his paper. Another clucked her tongue.

Hastings, Briar Creek's requisite small-town greasy spoon, serves up standard diner fare with a sprinkle of gossip and a dash of speculation. Plan your reading material ahead and nab a seat at the counter, unless having your life story judged over a stack of pancakes is high on your travel wish list.

Henry rubbed a hand over his jaw. He supposed he'd have to change his attitude—and fast—if he expected to sell this town with any conviction. He took a sip of his

coffee, finding it better than expected. Well, there was one thing he could mention in the article. Now, if he could just find a few more...

"Henry Birch!" Mark Hastings boomed through the door, his grin wide as he took long strides to the counter and slapped a heavy hand onto Henry's back. "Long time, no see around these parts!"

Not long enough, Henry thought ruefully, but he matched Mark's enthusiasm. They'd been casual friends growing up, and Mark just had a way of putting those around him in a good mood.

"Eh, thought it was about time." Henry motioned to the empty stool beside him, and Mark slid in.

"I can't seem to leave this place, even though it's all I wanted to do for years." Mark shook his head and pushed the menu aside. "I'll have a Western with rye and a side of bacon, Vince," he called out. The cook glanced at him through the window pass and nodded.

"You own Rosemary and Thyme now, right?" Henry folded his paper and slid it to the side. "I was in there the other night. Nice place. I was impressed."

Mark looked pleased. "It's the restaurant I always wanted to be running. I just took the long road getting there."

"And you and Anna?" Ivy had mentioned they were more than professionally linked.

Mark held up his hands. "What can I say? She's the one." The waitress filled his mug and he took a long gulp. "So how about you? Married? Seeing anyone?"

"Was married. Not seeing anyone, really."

Henry frowned at his choice of words. Why leave the door open like that? He wasn't dating—he didn't date, not seriously, at least—and thinking about Jane Madison

again hardly qualified as seeing her. Jane was off limits—
she always had been. Back then, because of Adam.
Now...for so many reasons. He reached for his coffee
and drank it back.

"How's Ivy doing?" Mark frowned as he shifted in his
seat to face Henry. "When I stopped into the shop on Sunday she seemed a little under the weather."

Henry's hands stilled on his mug. He'd seen his sister the very same day and she'd told him she'd never felt
better. He'd have to have a chat with his sister, and soon.
There was no way he was leaving town again unless he
knew this time that she was able to take care of herself.

Ivy was unloading boxes when Henry pushed through
the shop door half an hour later.

"Here, let me get that for you." He took the giant box
from Ivy's arms and set it on the counter while she signed
for the delivery. "This thing weighs a ton. What's in it?"

"Vases." Ivy motioned to the FRAGILE sign stamped on
the top. "Careful with those."

"I'm always careful," Henry said pointedly. He held
his sister's stare, waiting for her to come clean with him.
To his frustration, she simply turned on the faucet and
began filling a galvanized pitcher with water.

She wasn't leaving him any choice. "I want you take a
break from the store."

"What?" Ivy's eyes shot open in surprise as she turned
off the tap. "Forget it. No way."

"Mark told me about what happened on Sunday,"
Henry said tightly, trying hard not to lose his temper. Ivy
didn't take her condition seriously enough, if skipping her
meds proved anything.

"That's all?" Ivy shook her head and carried a watering can over to some potted plants. "I got a little lightheaded. What's the big deal?"

"The big deal is that you aren't monitoring your blood sugar. What did you eat for breakfast today, Ivy?"

"Stop."

"I'd feel better if you would take the next day or two off."

"I told you, I feel—" But she stopped when she saw the look on his face. "I suppose I don't have any orders today. I just hate to turn away a potential customer, though." She sighed. "What if someone plans to get engaged today, or someone has a baby?"

Henry felt the corner of his mouth begin to twitch. She cared about people, and he loved that about her. "I'll cover for you."

Ivy burst out laughing. "You? You don't even know what a Gerbera daisy is, do you?"

Henry stiffened. "Sure I do."

Ivy arched a brow and folded her thin arms across her chest. "Oh, yeah? Show me."

They locked eyes for a beat before Henry let out a sigh of exasperation. "Okay, so I don't know what a—"

"Gerbera daisy," she offered patiently.

"I don't know what a Gerbera daisy is, fine! But I can take orders and handle a cash register for one or two days." He softened his tone. "Everyone needs a break sometimes, Ivy."

Ivy wavered. "If someone calls for a delivery, can you try to push them off? Unless it's something urgent, like a new baby or—"

"Or an engagement. Fine." He was getting somewhere. He just hated that he had to strong-arm her into it.

It took another half hour of Ivy's excuses before Henry could usher her out the door. Deciding to make himself useful, he found a broom in the back room and swept the shop floor and then the little stoop out front, where leaves had fallen overnight. Afraid to touch the flowers for fear of killing them, he got a rag and dusted the containers and work surfaces, and even washed the windows, inside and out. He was just starting to feel like he had a handle on things when the door jingled.

Shit. A customer. He could only hope it was one who knew what they liked and didn't expect any fancy ribbons.

His stomach heaved with dread, but when he turned to face the door, his pulse quickened with interest. Jane stood frozen in the doorway, staring at him with those big eyes, and he slipped her a grin before he remembered how they'd left things, how mad at him she was.

He took a step forward, letting his gaze drift down to those long legs, his gut twisting with sudden desire. He was eager for the chance to explain himself, to get a second chance.

But that didn't mean he was going to get one.

CHAPTER 12

You have got to be kidding me. Jane glanced around the room, hoping her horror didn't show on her face. "Is Ivy here?" She craned her neck hopefully, even as it became obvious that Ivy wasn't around. She glanced to the door and studied it longingly. Oh, to turn and leave. Or better yet, to have never walked in. It had been a mistake coming here; she should take this as a sign.

Across the room, Henry's smile was friendly, revealing a glimpse of his dimple. His blue eyes gleamed with invitation, and Jane felt her heart turn over. He couldn't make this easy, could he? He couldn't just be a jerk, prove to her that she was right to keep her distance. He had to be the nice guy, the guy he always was. The yin to Adam's yang. Nevertheless, she reminded herself, always at Adam's side.

"She's taking the day off, actually," he said casually.

Ivy taking the day off? The shop closed once a week, and even then Ivy used the day to visit the flower market, or catch up on paperwork. Jane and Grace used to joke

that she gave Anna a run for the biggest workaholic in Briar Creek. Something wasn't right. "Is she okay?"

Henry nodded, but his jaw pulsed, and Jane had a sneaking suspicion he wasn't being completely honest. Ivy had looked so pale lately, but there were often times when she seemed tired and run down. Jane just chalked it up to her being overworked and stressed. Now she wondered if there was more to it.

"I'm covering today. Is there something I can help you with?"

Jane couldn't hide her surprise. "You're...covering. For Ivy. Here?"

Henry folded his arms across his chest and leaned a hip against one of the display tables. "That's right. Is that so hard to believe?"

His hands pulled his navy-striped rugby shirt tight against the curves of his thick biceps. She traced her gaze up the length of them, over the wide span of his shoulders, remembering the way she felt in his arms when he turned her around the dance floor all those years ago. Jane blinked and looked up to lock his hooded gaze. She swallowed. Hard. "Just surprising, that's all."

Henry held her gaze for a second more, then relaxed his stance. "What can I help you with then? We have some pretty Ger-garber-gro...We have some nice daisies over here." He pointed to some potted purple mums.

Jane bit the inside of her cheek. Why was it so impossible to stay mad at Henry? She wanted to turn and run, to yell and scream and blame Henry for not warning her that Adam was dropping hints about his plans, but maybe that wasn't fair of her. No one could have known what Adam was up to, after all.

"I was just stopping in to see Ivy." Jane edged backward, gearing up to make an excuse and then bolt, but the door behind her swung open as she did, causing her to jump.

"Mrs. Griffin." Jane felt her mouth curve into an easier smile at the sight of the local innkeeper. "How nice to see you."

"And you too, dear." The words were spoken with a smile, but immediately the woman's brow pinched, her bright green eyes slanted in concern, and the telltale hand went to Jane's wrist.

Here we go.

"And how are you holding up, dear?"

"I'm fine," Jane said, baring a smile through clenched teeth. *She means well*, she told herself.

"Only fine?" Mrs. Griffin winced.

"I'm fine, really, Mrs. Griffin, just...peachy." Peachy? Why couldn't she have said something like wonderful, great, never better? Because she couldn't lie, that's why, and when she tried, she said things like...peachy.

"That bad, dear?" Mrs. Griffin shook her head, her lips pinching into a tight, almost painful frown. "That man didn't deserve you. A bright, sweet, beautiful thing like you. You had so much to offer, so much ahead of you! You know what you need, don't you?"

Jane stifled a sigh. She may as well get it over with. "What's that?" she managed, bracing herself.

Mrs. Griffin tightened her grip on Jane's arm. "The love of a good, strong man, that's what." Suddenly noticing Henry, Mrs. Griffin's eyes brightened, and her entire face lit up with a smile. "And well, well. What do we have here?"

She waggled her eyebrows, sliding a sly smile to Jane. *Oh, for God's sake.*

"Hello, Mrs. Griffin," Henry said affably. Jane couldn't even meet his eye. Chances were he found all this entirely more amusing than she did. "I'm covering for Ivy today. Can I help you with something? Some nice daisies perhaps?"

As he went to motion to the mums again, Jane intervened, quickly gesturing to the galvanized pot of Gerberas. "Aren't they pretty?" she asked, grinning broadly.

Henry immediately fell silent.

"Oh my, they are. But they're not exactly what I had in mind..." Mrs. Griffin turned her attention back to Henry, who seemed to stiffen. "I was thinking some dahlias might look beautiful on the coffee table in the lobby. Can't you just picture it, in front of the hearth? A really... *romantic* flower, dahlias are. Gerberas are pretty, but they're a bit too...casual for what I have in mind. And right now, I'm feeling inspired." She beamed.

Henry nodded slowly. "O-kay..." He shifted his eyes around the shop, and Jane bit down on the corner of her lip. She tried to subtly point to the bin, then motion dramatically with her eyes, but he didn't catch her hint. "What about sunflowers?" he asked, energetically crossing the room to a huge bucket of the flowers.

Mrs. Griffin pulled a face. "Not elegant enough for my tastes. Hardly screams romance, Henry." She tutted at Jane.

"What about some roses?" Jane suggested, but Mrs. Griffin wrinkled her nose.

"Too expected. No, dahlias will suit me just fine." She crossed her hands in front of her, waiting.

Jane met Henry's bewildered look and squared her

shoulders. She crossed the room and plucked a beautiful peach dahlia stem. "Dahlias really are beautiful."

Henry was quickly at her side, his shirt brushing up against her arm as he began assisting Mrs. Griffin with her order. Jane felt a quiver zip down her spine and she snatched back her hand. Her gaze lingered on his thick forearms, where he'd pushed up his sleeves. The smell of musk was somehow stronger than the perfume from the hundreds of flowers, and more pleasing, too.

She closed her eyes, briefly, imagining what it would be like to lean in, press her body across that hard chest, and feel his arms wrap around her waist.

She jolted herself upright. Safe, she decided quickly. It would feel safe. In . . . a brotherly way.

She roamed her gaze up over that chiseled jaw and her breath caught as he flashed her a smile. Her insides pooled.

There was nothing brotherly about that.

"So . . ." Henry stood behind the farm table, clutching the stems in his fist, blinking at Mrs. Griffin, who seemed prepared to wait for him to say what he had to say, however long it would take. "Did you want these in a vase?"

Mrs. Griffin waved a hand through the air. "Oh, I have plenty of vases at the inn. Crystal," she added, arching a brow and turning to make sure even Jane had taken note.

Jane smiled to acknowledge the fact, then slid a hand over her mouth as she met Henry's wide eyes.

"Okay, so . . . er . . ." Henry's breath seemed to come in spurts as he gingerly set the flowers onto the brown paper Ivy used to wrap her bouquets.

There was no way he would know how to tie a bow

unless it was a shoelace, and Jane would take bets on the fact that he wouldn't angle the paper correctly, either.

Sure enough, he began to roll the paper directly from the side, instead of the corner, and soon the flowers were encased in a paper tube. As Mrs. Griffin's shocked gaze grew wider and wider, Jane blurted, "Is that the phone?"

Both Henry and Mrs. Griffin stopped to gape at her.

"I don't hear anything," Mrs. Griffin remarked.

Jane paused and held up a finger. "There it is again. It's the phone in the back room," she explained to the older woman, then gave a not so subtle glance at Henry. "Ivy keeps that ringer on low, so she doesn't disrupt the customers. It might be important—I'll handle this for you if you need to take it."

Henry stepped back from the flowers as if they were a ticking bomb. "It might be about that um...order of... carnations." Without another word, he disappeared into the back room.

Jane stepped around the corner, tossed the rumpled and torn paper in the bin behind her, and started over.

"Carnations?" Mrs. Griffin wrinkled her nose. "Ivy doesn't sell carnations now, does she?"

Jane just smiled. "I think she's looking for ways to accommodate everyone's taste and budget. After all, it's the thought that counts." She would have been thrilled if Adam had ever bought her carnations, especially the pink ones.

"Carnations," Mrs. Griffin muttered.

Jane wrapped the dahlias, secured the arrangement with twine, and rang up the order. As she held the door for Mrs. Griffin, Henry reappeared. "Thank you for coming in today," he said to the innkeeper.

"And thank you for your assistance." Mrs. Griffin smiled. She paused in the doorway, her eyes darting from Jane to Henry. "These will add such a romantic touch to the lobby. It really is such a cozy place to sit and chat, have a glass of wine…Nothing like snuggling up on a couch in front of a crackling fire to warm these chilly autumn nights, hm?" Her smile was anything but innocent.

Henry shifted on his feet. "You do have a lovely inn," he offered diplomatically.

When Mrs. Griffin was gone, Henry turned to Jane, heaving a sigh and grinning ear to ear. "I owe you."

Jane tossed him rueful smile. "You're right. You do."

"You're still mad at me for not telling you that Adam mentioned he might be moving."

Just hearing the words caused Jane's breath to catch. For a moment she'd been distracted, caught in Henry's presence, in that grin, and the way his hands moved as he gathered the flowers. In the way they might move across her bare skin… Reality crashed down on her like a cold, harsh blast. Adam was moving, and he wanted Sophie to come with him.

"I'm starting to understand why you didn't think to tell me," Jane said. "But I still wish you had."

"I didn't know about his plans for Sophie, Jane. He never mentioned that part."

Jane knew from the crinkle in his blue eyes he was telling the truth. Adam wouldn't have been stupid enough to blurt that out. He let his attorney do his dirty business and handle the majority of his communication.

"Do you…know what you're going to do?" Henry's voice was gentle, and it would be so easy to tell him she hadn't a clue, that she was fighting to hold it together for

even five minutes without bursting into tears, but she couldn't tell him that. She couldn't tell him anything. Anything she said could possibly be mentioned to Adam, and that would be disastrous.

"I'm letting my attorney handle it," she said instead.

Henry nodded. "If you need anything, Jane, I'm here. I hope you believe me."

Her heart wanted to believe him, but she had to think with her head right now. Now wasn't the time to be taking foolish risks, not when one mistake could cost her her daughter. "Well, I'm happy I could help you today. Ivy's put a lot into this store, and I know she thrives on making sure her customers are satisfied."

"You mean, you don't think Mrs. Griffin would have been happy with some mums on her lobby table?"

Jane laughed. "How did you know?"

"I quickly skimmed one of Ivy's flower books while I was hiding in the back room." Henry grinned. "Nice save, by the way."

"As I said, I'm happy to help." Jane let a sigh roll through her shoulders as she glanced around the room. It was probably time to go. She'd stop by another day to see if Ivy was looking for part-time help, but with Henry pitching in while he was in town, she supposed she'd be better trying somewhere else first. She'd move on to the next stop on her list—the stationery shop—or maybe she'd drop by the inn, see if Mrs. Griffin needed seasonal help. There was no use in checking on Main Street Books. When she'd passed by it was clear that Grace had everything under control for the day.

Henry's hooded gaze locked hers, and Jane realized she was lost in thought, and that quite possibly she had

been staring at him this entire time. Heat rushed to her cheeks, and she covered her nervous energy with a small smile.

"Well, I should probably go. Tell Ivy I said hi." She set a hand on the cool brass doorknob, but Henry closed the distance between them with two quick strides.

Jane's entire body went rigid as she looked up into his eyes. Her heart pounded with each breath.

"Wait."

"Yes?" Jane whispered. She could feel the rise and fall of her chest, and she wondered if he sensed it, too. It was hot in here—it wasn't just the flame in her face—and she suddenly wished she had managed to get the door open before he stopped her. The smell of his skin was all-consuming.

Henry raked a hand through his hair, and a lock spilled over his forehead. "I don't suppose...Do you have plans for the day? I mean, you're probably busy, but in case you're not..." He blinked a few times.

Holy *crap*. Was he asking her out? Was he going to suggest lunch? Had nosy Mrs. Griffin managed to plant a few seeds in his mind—or worse, did he think he was doing her some favor after the pity the innkeeper had taken on her?

His jaw twitched as he stared at her. No pity to be found there.

A date. Was it possible? Her mind began to spin. What should she say? Yes, no? No, she would obviously say no. I mean, the man was Adam's friend, and Adam was suing her.

"Why do you ask?" *Smooth, Jane!* Mentally, she fist-pumped, and she licked her lips to cover her smile of victory. She hadn't known she had it in her, and she knew her

sisters certainly didn't think so, either. How many times had they prepped her for the dating scene, begging her to lose the jeans she'd personally thought were rather fashionable and the V-neck sweater that showed just enough cleavage for her comfort zone. She could still remember the look of horror on Grace's face when Jane had shown up to the pub one Saturday night wearing a turtleneck sweater. But this? Grace would be so proud. Jane couldn't wait to tell her.

She stopped herself. She wasn't going to be telling her sisters anything, because there was nothing to tell. Henry was a friend, an old friend, and, okay, maybe a hot friend, too.

"I hate to even ask, but I promised Ivy I'd look after the shop and I'm sort of doing a hack job of it. You were so good with Mrs. Griffin. I just thought maybe you could..."

"Help?" Of course. He'd told her flat out that he wasn't marriage material—what made her think he'd have any interest in a single mom going through a custody dispute with his old buddy? Still, she perked up a bit at the thought of spending more time with him, even though she knew she shouldn't. The smart thing would be to keep her distance, get over this little...crush...and think of Henry as she only ever had. As a friend. That's all they were.

"I'll pay you," Henry added quickly.

As if she needed more incentive. Jane smiled and reached out her hand. "Consider me hired."

CHAPTER 13

She had a job for the day, and who knew, maybe it would lead to something more permanent. She should be happy, she should be elated, she should dig her to-do list out of her handbag and victoriously scratch off the first item. She should not be hiding in the back room of Petals on Main taking deep breaths and frantically swiping cherry ChapStick over her lips in the sad hope that enough layers would create a pop of color. She should not be wishing she had worn something other than these jeans her sisters always frowned at and this sweater, no matter how soft the angora or how cold the temperature. She should not be pinching her cheeks and wondering if Ivy kept mascara on hand.

Jane plucked one of Ivy's aprons from a hook in the stock room and made a quick call to her mother to see if she was available to pick Sophie up from school.

The arrangements made, she cinched her apron strings a little tighter in a vain attempt to make her waist appear a bit slimmer over the sweater, grateful she'd left the

turtleneck at home, and hesitated in the doorway of the shop. It was quiet, though no doubt a customer would arrive at any moment. It couldn't be soon enough, frankly. She needed someone else to focus on, someone other than Henry and that grin that made her stomach flutter.

"Everything situated with Sophie?" Henry asked, coming into the doorway and startling her.

Jane pressed a hand to her chest and laughed to cover her surprise. "My mom's going to take her over to the studio after school. I'll meet her there."

"I'm glad you're pursuing your dance again." His voice was low, his eyes intense, and Jane glanced to the floor. This wasn't something she wanted to talk about, not with Henry. Not when he had been so insistent that she never give up ballet in the first place.

He was there when she was accepted to the dance academy, exactly five weeks after accepting Adam's proposal. She couldn't suppress her shock and joy, but she did a good job of masking her devastation in turning it down. Her heart wrenched as she read the letter aloud to Adam and Henry that night at the pub, a mix of pride and loss. It was her greatest accomplishment, a dream she had held since she first slipped on ballet slippers as a child, and one she relived night after night as she lay in her bedroom, staring at the posters of prima ballerinas that covered her floral wallpaper. She'd actually done it. All that hard work, all the years of training and discipline had paid off.

"That's great, baby, but you're going to tell them no, right?" Adam draped a lazy arm over her shoulder and took a long sip of his beer.

Jane had faltered, and then quickly composed herself. She knew she wouldn't accept the spot, but somehow,

hearing Adam dismiss it so easily, she wanted it more than ever. She glanced up to see Henry staring at her, his eyes crinkled in concern, or maybe disappointment, and she felt a wave of something like anger...or maybe it was shame.

She knew it wasn't common to be engaged at eighteen anymore, but Adam was three years older and they'd been dating for years. Why wait?

"Because you have all the time in the world," Henry had said the moment Adam went to feed the jukebox.

"He proposed to me," Jane said, flipping her palm so her chip of a diamond was on full display. "We're getting married, and I'm not going to break my promise to him."

"Why don't you take some time to consider it?" Henry had pressed. "You just got the letter today. It's what you always wanted, isn't it?"

Jane had to sit on her hands to still their trembling. She didn't want to hear this, not one word. It was painful enough having to turn down the opportunity without him reminding her how much it meant to her. "What I want is to marry Adam." She smiled.

Henry stared at her for a long moment and then finally shrugged. "Whatever makes you happy, Jane."

Something in his eyes, even then, told her he knew how it would all turn out. If only she'd had the same foresight.

Jane pushed past Henry into the flower shop and grabbed a rag from the wash sink. She scrubbed at some soil that had spilled onto Ivy's prep station. "I'm not really pursuing my dance. I'm just teaching a few classes for the kids in town."

Henry wandered over to her, and she caught a hint of his warmth, the soap on his skin. Her stomach tightened. She scrubbed a little harder. Soon, this table would

positively shine. "Either way, I'm glad to see you dancing again. You always enjoyed it."

"I do enjoy it." Meeting his eye, her breath paused at the softness in his deep-set gaze. "It's a wonderful job, really. Things have a real way of working out the way they're meant to." She crossed to the potted mums Henry was so focused on earlier, happy to have an excuse to keep her back to him. They needed a little tending, well, not really, but he wouldn't know the difference.

"That's optimistic even for you," Henry remarked.

Jane's heart was beginning to pound, but she refused to let him get to her. Staying strong was what she did best.

"What's the alternative?" She glanced over her shoulder and forced a smile. "To fall victim to the circumstances of your life? To run away instead of letting the dust settle?"

Something in Henry's expression shifted, and he lowered his gaze to the floor. "Suppose so."

Jane brushed a loose strand of hair from her forehead with the back of her hand and moved on to the left wall of the room, where Ivy kept hundreds of beautifully scented candles, all locally made, stacked on wrought iron baker's racks.

"So, what kind of classes do you teach at the studio? Ballet?"

Jane nodded. "The young ones are fun, but it's rewarding to see the progress some of my older students are making."

"What about adults?"

At this Jane laughed. "No, no adults."

"Why not? There must be some folks around town who are into that type of thing. I took a salsa class when I was in Miami." He winked, and darn it if her stomach didn't roll over.

"You took a salsa class?" She couldn't fight the smile that teased her mouth.

"Hey, I've got moves, Jane." He set his hand on her hip and her heart seized in her chest. She froze, looking up at him in panic, but he just slipped her an easy grin and waited. Her shoulders rose and fell with each breath, until she realized he was trying to get around the counter and she was blocking his path.

She blinked rapidly, then shifted to the right, but he didn't move, not right away. His eyes gleamed as his smile grew a little broader, and as he finally moved past her, his hand lingered on her hip, until it finally slid off.

This was going to be harder than she'd thought.

"Seriously, though," he continued. "You should offer some adult classes. Salsa, ballroom…" He stopped, seeing the look on her face. "Why not?"

Jane tried to picture some of the local residents lining up to learn the tango and cringed. "I don't think people around here would go for that sort of thing."

"You're the one who's been trying to tell me Briar Creek has a lot more to offer than it seems."

He had a point there. "We base our classes on enrollment, so—"

"Perfect. If people sign up, you have the class. Nothing lost in trying, is there?"

"Why, Henry, that's very optimistic of *you*," Jane replied. He matched her grin and held it, his smile boyish and slightly lopsided, and Jane felt a rush of heat spread over her. She wasn't imagining it. There was definitely something there, something in the glint of his eyes that was anything but platonic.

Henry was flirting with her. Or maybe he was just having a little fun.

Whatever it was, she was putting a stop to it. This was nonsense! Her entire world was crashing down on her and here she was, getting caught up in sparkling blue eyes and a friendly grin?

Henry popped the lid on a delivery box and looked her square in the eye. "As a matter of fact, it is optimistic of me. What can I say? Maybe you bring out the best in me."

Jane dismissed the compliment as nothing more than part of their banter, but the flutter in her heart lingered as she began dusting the shelves. Trying out a few new classes at the studio might be just the solution she was looking for.

Leave it to Henry to always unearth the obvious.

The shop picked up shortly afterward, leaving no time for a lunch break, much less conversation. Jane helped some women she knew select fall wreaths and planter fillers, while Henry manned the cash register and took telephone orders. For minutes on end, she could almost forget he was in the room, until she caught his laugh, or worse, his eye, and felt the immediate, involuntary tightening in her stomach. Tonight she'd go home and watch one of her favorite romantic comedies, just to remind herself that other attractive men did exist in this world, even if the actors, like Henry, were untouchable.

"Ivy certainly keeps busy," Henry mused, as Jane untied her apron. She hung it on a hook on the wall and rubbed the back of her neck. A hot bath after class today would be just the thing. She couldn't wait to get off her feet. First, though, she intended to talk to Rosemary about Henry's suggestions.

"Will she be back tomorrow?" Jane inquired, hoping her inquiry sounded more casual than her motive. She hoped to talk to Ivy about part-time employment as soon as possible. Time wasn't on her side, not if she wanted to show the judge she had some financial security in place.

"I'm not sure, honestly. She rarely gets a break, so I wanted to give her one while I'm in town."

Jane tried to hide her disappointment as she reached for her peacoat. "How's the house coming along?" She hadn't been out that way since she and Adam had split last winter, but even then the Birch house was in severe disrepair and would most likely require a lot of work before it would be ready to list. And a lot of time, Jane mused, wondering just how long Henry intended to stick around. The inn couldn't be cheap, and peak foliage was nearing—Briar Creek's busiest tourist time, other than ski season.

Henry's jaw pulsed, and Jane immediately regretted asking. It couldn't be easy to say goodbye to your childhood house, even if you hadn't been home in a while.

"It's going to take a lot of work. I'll be happy when it's over and done with." Henry's voice was gruff. "In the meantime, I'm still forging ahead with the article on Briar Creek. If you can think of anything other than the usual I should feature, I'm all ears." He frowned, seeming to think of something. "Does the dance studio still put on a show?"

Jane finished buttoning her camel coat and took a few deep breaths. If she answered honestly, it could get back to Adam that the studio was in trouble, and so was her job security. Wouldn't that be just the ammunition he needed to make a case that Sophie was better off with him? "Auditions for *The Nutcracker* are next week," she said

diplomatically. Whether or not there would ever be a performance, however... She felt a dull headache come on.

Henry pulled a small spiral notepad from his back pocket and jotted something down. "Good to know. Tourists like that sort of thing." Pausing, he reached back into his pocket and took out his wallet. "Before I forget."

Jane stared at the wad of bills he held out to her and shook her head. She'd done the guy a favor, on behalf of Ivy really, and Ivy was her friend. A steady job was one thing, but this? As much as she could use the money, it felt too awkward. "It's fine. I was happy to help."

Eventually, Henry slid the money back into his wallet. "Let me repay you somehow, then."

Jane's heart lurched at the mere possibility he would suggest dinner or even coffee. She needed to leave, right away, before something was said that couldn't be taken back. "I should go. I'll be late."

"Jane." He reached out and took her arm. She stared at it—the big, thick fingers wrapped around her coat, not flinching, strong and steady in their purpose. She held her breath as she looked up into his eyes, feeling herself relax at the sight of that lazy smile, until he opened his mouth and then closed it, as if he was struggling with what he might say next.

Her heart began to clamor.

"You can feature Main Street Books in your article, if you're really looking for a way to repay me. We're still rebuilding in a way, and... it would probably help the cause."

Henry dropped her arm, and she couldn't help wishing he hadn't. "Are you going to be okay?"

She stared at him, blinking back tears that suddenly prickled the back of her eyes at the warmness of

his tone, and nodded over and over. From the way his mouth quirked downward, she could tell she hadn't been convincing.

"Have you talked to Adam yet? Maybe you guys could work something out. He can't be that unreasonable."

Jane nailed him with a hard look. "Actually, yes, he can." Her heart was beginning to pound with fresh anger and she cursed to herself under her breath. "I'm Sophie's mother. I do everything for her. And he's trying to take her away from me. I call that unreasonable. And cruel."

"Sorry, I just meant—"

Jane held up a hand. She was getting angry with the wrong person. "I'm letting my attorney handle all communication. I don't want to talk about this." *With you*, she finished to herself. Henry was Adam's oldest friend, and that type of history created a loyalty she didn't have.

Henry let out a breath, nodding slightly. "Well, let me know if there's anything I can do to help," he offered, and something in the softness of his eyes made her almost think she could believe him.

"You've already helped," Jane said, thinking of the suggestion for the adult dance classes she planned to run by Rosemary tonight. "With...um, getting my mind off things for the day." *And onto others ...*

"I'll see you at the festival?"

Jane nodded as she opened the door, realizing Henry's question was more a statement. They'd see each other again, and next time, she'd have her emotions in check.

CHAPTER
14

Briar Creek's annual Harvest Fest was, perhaps, Henry's least favorite day of the year, with the exception of his birthday, his mother's birthday, Christmas, and pretty much all of summer break. Holidays brought out the worst in his mother's mood, and parties were for people who could enjoy them without having to worry they were giving more fodder to the gossip circles. There was a time when he envied the carefree way others could look forward to celebratory events, but now he knew those days were no different than any other. You only missed what you wished you had. And what he wished for in that moment was the cool, quiet solitude of his San Francisco high-rise. It was just what he needed to get his head straight.

Henry roamed his narrowed gaze over the town square. He walked along the perimeter, jotting notes as he went along, even snapping a few photos of the pristine white gazebo under the shade of a magnificent sugar maple tree. Red leaves scattered on its roof and stairs,

where hay bales and barrels of red and orange mums had been set up.

Ivy was head of the decorating committee this year, something she admitted she'd been doing for the past three years. She certainly was invested in this town, he admitted.

"The decorations look great," he said, coming up behind her at the donut stand. He eyed the half-eaten cider donut in her hand, about to ask about her sugar levels, but she beat him to it.

"I planned my entire day around this donut, Henry, so please don't ruin it for me. I have it under control."

Henry wanted to believe her, and he knew that he had no other choice. He ordered one for himself and fell into step beside her.

"Anything new with the house?" she asked.

"I called some contractors yesterday," he told her. "They're coming out next week to patch the roof and repaint the siding. They'll start on the interior after that."

Henry tossed the wax paper wrapper into a bin and jammed his hands into his pockets. He didn't want to think about going back to that house. Not today. It would cloud his creativity, and right now he needed to stay on assignment.

Just ahead Jane was helping Rosemary Hastings drape a folding table with a white cloth. Her ash brown hair fell loosely at her shoulders, the morning sun reflecting off the subtle copper highlights. Catching his stare, she looked up at him, and he held his hand up in a wave. After a beat, she returned it, but the wariness in her smile had returned. He hadn't liked the way they'd ended things the other day in the shop. He'd been trying to comfort her, but

she'd left seeming rattled and upset, unable to make eye contact as she hurried away, still smiling. Always smiling. Whenever he thought of Jane, he thought of that smile.

He strode purposefully to the dance studio's stand, noticing the way her eyes flickered in alarm.

"This looks nice," he said, gesturing to one of the costumes they had on display that a couple of girls had stopped to admire, but he was barely noticing the stand. He couldn't take his eyes off Jane, the way the sun brought out the amber flecks in her eyes and the pink in her cheeks.

"Audition for *The Nutcracker* and you can wear it all you'd like," Rosemary remarked to the girls. She handed over a clipboard with a sign-up sheet, but the girls just glanced at each other.

Jane, Henry noticed, was frowning, and the light in her eyes had gone flat. Clicking the top of his ballpoint, Henry said loudly, "What are the performance dates? I want to be sure to feature the show in my article."

The girls elbowed each other and looked at Henry with sudden interest. Pretending he hadn't noticed, he continued. "You never know. Depending on what month the article is featured, I might even be back to cover the show."

The taller of the girls reached for the clipboard and signed her name, and the other one followed suit. Henry watched as they ran off to a group of friends, discussed matters, and then three others added their names to the sheet.

"Well, Henry Birch, I don't suppose you're looking for a new job by any chance? Dance recruiter?"

Henry grinned. "I think I'll stick with travel writing, if you don't mind."

Rosemary set her hands on her hips, but her blue eyes twinkled when she said, "What? Briar Creek not interesting enough for you?"

Henry shifted his gaze to Jane, who was helping a few other kids with the sign-up sheet. "Oh, it's interesting all right. I'm actually writing an article on the town while I'm here."

"Well, isn't that exciting! It isn't often someone puts Briar Creek on the map. Tell me when it comes out; I'll be sure to buy a few copies."

Henry nodded. "I'll let Ivy know."

"Oh." Rosemary pinched her lips tight. "Not in town for long, then?"

Henry shifted his gaze to Jane. She quickly looked down and began straightening some fliers. "I have places to be, Mrs. Hastings. It's not personal." But it was. It was very personal.

"Well, what is it then?" Rosemary asked. "We haven't seen you around these parts since—"

"It was six years this past June," Jane said, before the words formed on his lips. He stared at her, but she blinked and looked at Rosemary. "The last time we saw Henry was the night of my wedding. It's an easy date to remember."

And it was one she probably wanted to forget. Almost as much as he did.

Henry met Jane's cool gaze, feeling his heart kick with each second that ticked by. Her eyes were clear, free of the emotion he'd seen in them at the flower shop, as if challenging him to call her out on it, to remind her that he'd warned her, that he knew this is how it would end. That Adam, good friend that he was, wasn't the man for her.

"Oh, look, here come a few more girls. Henry, work your magic." Rosemary wiggled her eyebrows. She waited until the girls were in earshot to loudly exclaim, "Oh, yes, Henry, we do *indeed* offer a number of classes, and of course we are *thrilled* that you're going to be featuring *The Nutcracker* in your article on Briar Creek! It's not every day a little girl has a chance to see her picture in a *nationally* distributed magazine."

Henry nodded his agreement. "With these costumes, you never know. The show might just make the front cover of the magazine."

Rosemary smiled serenely as she handed the clipboard over to a few girls. "Auditions this Wednesday. Every dancer gets a part." She slid her eyes to Henry and mouthed, "Thank you."

Henry folded one of their glossy fliers into his notebook and held up a hand, his gaze steady on Jane, who was still determined to avoid eye contact. A heaviness settled over his chest as he took a step backward. "Always a pleasure, ladies. Good luck."

Rosemary clucked her tongue as he turned. "Now, that's the one you should have married, Jane," he heard her mutter, followed immediately by Jane's urgent whisper to let it drop.

Henry flicked his collar and moved quickly to the other end of the festival, hoping to ward off the fresh sting of regret. For months after Jane and Adam's wedding, he'd tried to block out the image of her standing there in that simple white dress, all frothy and feminine. They said every woman was beautiful on her wedding day, but he'd never believed it until he saw Jane. Her hair was swept back below the transparent gauze of her veil, and her eyes

shone with such joy that he instantly wished he could let it drop. But he couldn't.

Within seconds of seeing her in the doorway of her dressing room, her smile had faltered. "Don't tell me Adam's got cold feet," she gushed, and Henry felt like the wind had been knocked out of him, until he realized she was only joking, and he swallowed back the concern that up until that moment had plagued him, leaving him guilt-ridden and agitated. Was he really going to warn her? Tell her she was being foolish, that Adam wasn't the man for her? He'd seen firsthand the way Adam flirted with the women at college—was he responsible for making Jane aware? And what kind of friend would that make him to Adam?

It was too late, he told himself. Jane wanted to marry Adam, and now all he could do was stand by and watch her make the biggest mistake of her life and hope to hell his friend honored his vows and took good care of her. For the hundredth time that day, he told himself: *Say nothing.*

"You look beautiful, Jane," he said instead, and his heart began to thump as if he'd just told everything else he'd been holding inside.

"Do I?" She'd been so young then, so fresh faced and eager almost, and the hopefulness in her eyes when she'd posed the question nearly tore him in half. Jane was the most beautiful girl he'd ever met, and by her reaction it was clear the man she was marrying didn't bother to tell her so often enough.

Her father arrived then, looking nervous and proud, and clearly struggling to keep his emotions from getting the best of him. "My baby's getting married," he said, swallowing hard. "You ready, sweetheart?"

Jane nodded then, leaning in to give her father a hug,

and over his shoulder she looked up and smiled at Henry, and it was that smile he could never forget. It was that smile that twisted his gut as he walked down the aisle and stood beside Adam, his best friend since he was six years old. There were the Browns in the front row, glancing at him almost as much as Adam, reminding him that he was one of them, that they'd taken him in, given him a home, given him love. They were his family in a way, and now Jane would be, too, and he'd just keep looking after her, keep subtly nudging Adam to walk a straight line.

He'd handed over the rings and listened to Jane recite the words they'd rehearsed. For better. For worse. He'd kept his mouth shut in a firm, thin line when the priest asked if there were any reasons why these two should not be bound in matrimony, but he couldn't keep quiet when he saw Adam three hours later, flirting with the daughter of one of his mother's friends.

Jane wasn't ready to hear the truth back then. But he couldn't blame her. The truth hurt.

"Mommy, can we carve punkins now?" Sophie's cheeks were sticky from her caramel apple, and her eyes had taken on that glazed sheen that came with too many sweets.

Jane looked over at Rosemary, who nodded firmly. "I've got this covered. You go show your little one a good time."

Jane flashed a big grin at her daughter and took her hand. The pumpkin carving contest was one of their annual traditions, and this year she and Sophie were ready. They'd done their research, bought a set of special tools, and even traced their design in advance. If they didn't win

(and Jane, never much of an artist, was fairly certain they wouldn't), Sophie was going to take it hard. She'd always been a sensitive child, but the emotions reared high ever since Adam moved out. The littlest thing could bring her to tears, but when it came to discussing anything directly, she seemed completely adjusted. Jane had tried talking to Adam about it a few times, but he just shrugged it off and told her to stop worrying. Oh, her lovely husband. Always the pinnacle of support.

"Now, let's make sure we get a big, round one," Jane called after Sophie as she broke loose from Jane's hand and ran toward the huge display of pumpkins, donated by Finnigan's Farm. Jane stood back and let Sophie inspect the offerings, trying to fight the heaviness in her chest when she considered how much had changed in the span of twelve months. At last year's festival, all three of them had selected the pumpkin, and Jane had tried to fool herself into hoping that maybe the suspicions were all in her head, that she hadn't seen, clear as day, her husband kissing another woman the previous summer. She'd dared to feel some hope as they walked through the festival, the picture of a smiling family, but the distance in Adam's eyes had only confirmed what she already knew, and by the end of the day, she found herself staring at other families—happy families—comparing them with her own, seeing the way a husband would whisper something in his wife's ear to make her laugh, or the way he would idly take her hand as they left the cider stand.

She steadied herself with a breath. Strange as it was to say, last year's festival had almost been a lonelier experience than this year's. At least she wasn't pretending anymore.

"You girls entering the pumpkin contest?" a voice

behind her asked, and Jane felt every hair on the back of her neck stand to attention.

She turned ever so slowly, until her eyes latched squarely on Henry's. A warm tingle spread over her body as his mouth pulled into a grin. So much for getting control of herself.

"We are!" Sophie called out, doing her best to carry a pumpkin at least her half her body weight in size. Jane laughed and went to help her, but Henry beat her to it.

"Do you mind if I take some photos? It's for the article," Henry explained.

"Oh, I see. I suggested the article and now I'm being called on for favors." Jane couldn't help but grin when she saw the way Sophie lit up around him.

"I seem to recall making a few suggestions of my own." Henry fell into step beside her as they moved toward an open picnic table, his body so close she could feel his torso shift with his stride. Her stomach turned over, and she put a hand to it, taking a steadying breath. "Have you given any more thought to the adult dance classes?"

Jane brightened. "As a matter of fact, I discussed the idea with Rosemary and she loved it." Better yet, she'd told Jane to take over the classes, bringing her total for the week to six. It still fell short of her original ten, but whenever the pulse-racing fear woke her late at night, she remembered that things were slightly better than they'd been only a week before. Thanks to Henry. "We're going to do ballroom dancing and adult tap." She slanted a glance at him. "Don't laugh."

"Come on, Mommy, you have to start tracing the picture!" Sophie thrust the pencil drawing of the witch flying across the moon on her broomstick. "Come on!"

Henry eyed the paper with wonder. "Impressive."

She didn't have the heart to tell him she'd traced it from an image they'd downloaded off a craft website. "I doubt the same will be said for the pumpkin."

"You just don't give yourself enough credit." His voice was smooth but firm, and she felt herself blush.

After another wail of impatience from Sophie, Jane set to work scoring the image onto the surface of the pumpkin, wishing she'd thought to bring some tape. The image came out lopsided, and there was no way she was going to be able to cut around that broomstick without the entire section caving in. She should have gone for the nice, easy jack-o'-lantern face. Instead, she'd had to choose the elusive and challenging one. Wasn't that just the story of her life? Even with the most basic task, she had to go and make things difficult for herself.

She was just getting ready to pick up the carving knife, when Henry set down his camera. "Stop there. You forgot to clean out the guts."

"The what?" Jane paled. She turned back to the pumpkin and studied it with a frown. Ah, darn it. Adam usually did this part, and she gladly let him. Barely suppressing a sigh, she cut a hole around the stem and stared into the contents. God help her.

"Come on, Mommy!"

"I'm getting there," Jane told her firmly, as she pushed up the sleeves of her coat. The wool was thick and it didn't stay put. She had just started to roll the hem when she heard Henry's soft chuckle.

"Here." He peeled off his jacket and pushed up his sleeves, revealing those thick, strong, slightly tanned arms. Jane's breath caught as he reached down next to her, his

body close behind her, his chest hunched forward, his skin slightly brushing against her wrists. She swallowed hard.

He took the scoop and reached down into the pumpkin, pausing to flash a devilish smile that made her heart skip a beat. "This is the fun part," he said.

"Ha. No thanks. It's all yours." She laughed.

Henry just shrugged and continued scraping out the pulp, until no seeds remained. He held out a few in his palm to Sophie. "If you take these home and roast them, they make a really good snack."

Sophie made a face of disgust, and Jane and Henry started to laugh. "You clean them first," Henry added, and Sophie grinned up at him before cautiously touching one of the seeds.

"What happens if you plant them instead?"

"Then you can grow your own pumpkin," Jane said, brightening. "Wouldn't that be fun?"

Sophie contemplated this for a moment. "That sounds like a lot of work. I think I'll eat them instead."

"What would you do without me?" Henry winked, and Jane lowered her eyes. Her cheeks flushed and she reached for a tool, but her mind was spinning, and she couldn't even remember where she'd left off or what she should be doing with the darn thing.

It was a rhetorical question, and one they both knew the answer to. Henry had always been a good friend, and lately, he was one of the best she had. Better to leave it that way.

CHAPTER 15

With Sophie's help, Jane carried their crudely carved pumpkin over to the judges' stand and stood back to admire her handiwork. The witch's hat had gotten lost after a sloppy error with the knife—a mistake Jane blamed Henry for. Henry and his deep, penetrating gaze. Fortunately, the broom and the cape had survived, even if they did look like a spoon and a bat wing. Jane glanced at the other entries and sighed. She'd tried.

"It's the best punkin ever!" Sophie shouted, clapping her hands.

Well, it was certainly the most interesting. Jane took Sophie's hand and led her past the expertly carved jack-o'-lanterns. The crowds had picked up in the hour since they'd started their project, and the wind had, too. Jane plucked Sophie's red mittens from her pocket and slid them onto each small hand, then wiggled her matching hat onto her head.

"What should we do next?" She swept her eyes around the square, evaluating their options. Yes, she may have

kept one eye out for Henry while she was at it, but only so she could be sure to lead Sophie in the opposite direction. They were running into each other too much for her comfort, and she didn't like the way she got all nervous when he was around her. The man was off-limits, despite the way a flash of that grin could send an electric bolt down her spine. Now was the time to keep a level head and focus on her custody battle, not go weak in the knees over the friend of the man who was suing her!

She squeezed her daughter's hand tighter, feeling her heart wrench at how uncertain the next few weeks were. Not having someone to love or share her life with was hard enough, but the prospect of day-to-day life without Sophie at her side?

"I want to do the corn maze! Wait, no, the apples. Let's bob for apples!" Sophie pointed to the barrels of water across the grass and tugged Jane's hand.

Jane curled her lip. Sticking her face in a barrel of icy cold water was not what she had planned for her day, but the gleam in Sophie's eyes made her laugh. "If that's what you want to do, okay."

She handed over a few dollars and helped Sophie onto the stepstool, and they laughed as Sophie chased the apples through the water. Just when Jane was beginning to worry that Sophie's mouth was too small to claim one, the little girl lifted her face out of the water, her smile triumphant as her teeth gripped the apple.

"Bravo!" Jane clapped, and wiped the water from her daughter's face with some tissue she always kept in her handbag.

"Now it's your turn, Mommy."

"Oh..." Jane looked desperately around the festival

for something to distract a five-year-old. "What about getting your face painted?"

Sophie's lower lip began to wobble. *Here we go again*, Jane thought, guilt landing squarely in her chest. "You said this was our mommy and daughter day."

"Well, it is," Jane assured her.

"But we're supposed to do everything together!" And just like that, Sophie burst into tears.

Jane cursed her ex under her breath. A year ago, she'd still been able to shield Sophie from the strain of her marriage, but she couldn't protect her child from the sting of reality forever, and too much change had taken its toll. Jane closed her eyes for a beat, and then crouched down to give her daughter a tight hug. Smoothing Sophie's hair with her hand, she pulled back and looked into those big tear-filled eyes. "You *really* want me to bob for an apple?"

Sophie nodded, beaming through her tears, and well, there was no way Jane could say no to that face. She stood, her heart sinking with dread as she handed over a few more dollars and stared into the barrel of water.

Here goes nothing. Pulling in a long breath, she gripped her hair back with one hand and bent down to the apples, attempting as best she could to grab a stem with her teeth for minimal damage.

"You're not going to get it that way!" Sophie was instructing her. "You have to try to bite it! Stick your face in! Your *whole* face."

Obviously, the humiliation was not going to end until she managed to catch an apple, and so, with an internal eye roll, she did as she was told and attempted to bite the side of an apple before it rolled away.

"Oops! Almost!" Sophie giggled.

At least one of them was finding this funny. Jane heaved a breath, and tried again. Minutes seemed to tick by as she tried in vain, and Sophie's cries of delight seemed to grow louder and louder and louder, attracting, Jane suspected with sudden horror, a bit of a crowd. She tried another approach, coming at it from the side, and then reverted to her original plan to pick one up by the stem, and she was just about ready to call the whole thing quits and put up with Sophie's emotional outburst for a bit, when she pinned a Red Delicious against the side of the barrel.

"You did it!" Sophie screamed, jumping up and down. Jane laughed and plucked the apple from her teeth, but her smile immediately faltered when she saw Henry standing a few feet from Sophie, barely suppressing his smirk.

"How long have you been standing there?" she asked, quickly wiping her face with her scarf.

His grin widened. "Long enough."

"She did it, she did it! Did you see me, too?" Sophie ran up to Henry and he bent down to grin at her.

"I sure did! In fact, I even snapped a photo. Do you want to see?"

Sophie jumped up and down, eager to see herself in a moment of fun-filled success, but Jane's heart began to pound harder when she saw the phone in his hand. "Please tell me you didn't take a picture of me, too."

"Of small-town fun at its best?" His blue eyes danced, but for once, her heart didn't flutter at the sight. "You were the one who insisted Briar Creek had so much to offer. It's not every day you get a chance to bob for your apple…"

Every time Jane blinked, the image of her with her

head in that barrel, teeth bared, flashed. "Please delete the photos."

Henry chuckled softly and took a step toward her. With the pad of his thumb, he brushed her cheek until the remains of the cold water were gone, replaced with the warmth of his skin, which set her body on fire. She met his eyes for a beat, surprised at the intensity she saw flash through them and waiting for him to say something, pull back, take his hand from her face. She was breathing hard, but not over concern about a potentially embarrassing photograph. "I didn't take any photos," he reassured her with a slow smile. Dropping his hand to nudge her with his elbow, he added, "Though based on your reaction, I'm sort of wishing I had."

Jane arched a brow up at him. "Blackmail, is it? Though I don't know what you'd be looking to get from me."

"Oh, I could think of a few things…" Henry's smile slipped, and his gaze latched onto her. Jane felt her breath still, and every nerve ending stood on alert. He was standing close, close enough for her to sense the musk on his skin and feel his breath on her face, to see the way his lips were parted ever so slightly. She wondered what it might be like to kiss him. He was probably a very good kisser.

"Mommy! Mommy!"

Jane broke Henry's stare and turned to Sophie, who was pointing to something in the distance. "It's Daddy! Daddy's here!"

Jane felt the blood drain from her face as she watched Sophie take off across the grass and throw herself into Adam's arms. Her heart was beating so fast it felt like it might come out of her, and her mind was spinning with every emotion she'd kept bottled up for too long.

Beside Adam stood Kristy. Jane couldn't resist letting her gaze drop to the other woman's stomach. No noticeable baby bump yet. For a second she dared to think that Sophie had been telling stories, or somehow she'd misunderstood, but as Kristy's cool gaze met hers, she set a proprietary hand to her abdomen.

"Jane." Adam nodded, then glanced behind her, perking up at the sight of his friend. "Henry. I'm surprised to see you here."

"Sophie tells me congratulations are in order." Jane tipped her head, thinning her mouth. "When's the big day?"

"Three weeks," Adam replied.

Jane could barely suppress her shock. "Were you planning on telling me or letting me find out through the local grapevine?"

"I figured I'd tell you eventually."

Something in the casual way he said it, in the lazy way his lids drooped, brought every hurt and every betrayal to the surface. Her heart began to race with adrenaline, fresh anger aching for a release. She couldn't hold back any longer. "That's all you have to say, Adam? You're just going to pretend like everything's okay?" She glared at him, hating the cold set to his gaze as he locked her stare. "Didn't you think I had a right to know? Wouldn't it have been respectful to tell me all this news directly?"

"What do you expect me to say, Jane?"

Sensing something was amiss, Sophie ran back over and took her hand. Jane held it tight before motioning to the face-painting stand. "There's no line. Why don't you run over now and surprise me with what you pick out?" With trembling fingers, she gave Sophie a five-dollar bill. She waited until Sophie was cheerfully seated in front of

the artist before turning back to Adam, who had the nerve to reward her with a condescending smile.

"We had a deal, Adam. You and I agreed that I would stay home, and you would work. That was our deal." She was probably making a scene now, and oh, wouldn't this feed the gossip mill for weeks, but she didn't care. She'd kept quiet for too long, tried to be the bigger person— where had it gotten her? Her voice was shaking, and she took a steadying breath to control it. "I could have gone to college, had a job, but instead I took care of the house, of you, and our daughter. And now you're trying to use your career and financial position as leverage?"

Adam's jaw pulsed but his gaze remained steady. "I'm her parent, too."

"You made your choices, Adam," she said, sliding a pointed glance at Kristy. For once, there was no sting upon seeing the other woman. "There are consequences."

"You can't deny me my daughter."

A bitter laugh escaped from somewhere deep inside her, and she realized with sudden panic that it just as easily could have been a sob. He wasn't going to stop. He really couldn't be reasoned with. "Oh, but you can deny me? I'm the one who bathed her, took her to every doctor's appointment, and registered her for school. I'm the one who checked on her every night before I went to bed. I cooked her dinner. I gave her medicine if she was sick."

"And now I'd like a chance to do that."

"Now?" Jane cried, but the hysteria in her voice was turning to one of desperation. "I'm her mother, Adam," she hissed, willing herself not to cry. Crying would give him more power to hurt her, and it wouldn't solve a damn thing. "How can you justify taking her from me? She *needs* me."

He had the nerve to shrug. To dismiss her efforts, her role, so carelessly. God, she hated him! "And she needs me, too. I don't want to miss out on seeing her grow up."

"Then don't move!" Jane tossed her hands in the air. She gripped them into fists, and brought them down tight at her sides until her nails embedded on her palms. It was her only restraint.

"That's not an option," Adam replied firmly.

Her breath was so heavy, she could barely hear her words over the sound of her blood rushing in her ears. "Adam, think of what you're doing. She needs me. She'll miss me—" Her voice cracked on the last word, and she felt a strong hand on her shoulder. She didn't need to look over to know it was Henry's.

"Don't say anything else," he said quietly, and his voice was thick, so steady and assured, that she nodded. She shouldn't have said anything at all; the lawyer had advised her not to. If there was any part of her ex-husband that still cared for her, she had to try to get through to him. But from the set of his jaw, she was beginning to wonder if he'd ever given a damn about her at all.

Jane let Henry lead her away, keeping her eyes firmly on the ground. If she looked up at the bastard again, she wasn't sure she could hold herself back. Sophie came running up to her, her nose painted black, with whiskers splayed over her cheeks.

"I can't stay here," she whispered aloud, but Henry was already steering them toward the exit.

"But I don't want to leave!" Sophie wailed. "No one will see my kitty face!"

Jane opened her mouth to reason with her, but Henry cut in: "I don't know about you, but I'm pretty hungry. I

don't suppose kitties like pizza and ice cream?" To Jane he said, "That pizza joint's still around, isn't it?"

Jane nodded and motioned to her car up ahead. "You don't have to—" she said, as she popped the locks.

Henry opened the passenger door. "I want to."

"How'd you learn to be so good with kids?" Jane asked, as she rounded the corner into the kitchen. Upstairs, Henry could hear the sounds from a music box winding down, no doubt just in time for Sophie to fall asleep, her stomach full of the roasted pumpkin seeds they'd made together.

He folded the top on the pizza box and tucked in the chairs around the table. "I had a lot of practice. With my sister," he added.

Jane tipped her head. "But Ivy's your twin."

Henry shrugged. There was so much he wanted to say, but couldn't. "I guess I always felt protective of her growing up." Still did.

Jane smiled. "That's sweet." She pulled a bottle of wine from a rack. Turning to him, she asked, "Would you like any?"

Henry stiffened. "No, I, um…" He could make his excuses, call his sister for a ride back to town, but he wasn't ready to leave just yet. Jane's house was cozy and warm, with thoughtful decorations and just enough clutter to make it feel lived in. One of Sophie's dolls lay face-down on the counter, and the fridge was covered with her drawings and school event news. The weight of what Jane must be going through came more alive than ever. Sophie was Jane's life.

"Do you have any soda? Or coffee?"

Jane's gaze narrowed slightly, but she put the bottle back. "Decaf okay? If I have regular now, I'll be up all night."

He stepped back to give her space, watching as she swiftly moved about the kitchen, his gaze traveling down the curves of her tight-fitting jeans and back up to the swell of her breasts under that soft sweater. He swallowed back a surge of desire and glanced around the room, feeling suddenly out of place in the home that until recently had been Adam's. It was like all those nights the three of them would spend together, back when she and Adam were just dating, and he'd feel like a third wheel, but not enough to make him want to leave. From the first time Adam had introduced her, he'd wanted to be near her.

Henry pulled in a breath. Still did. That was one thing that hadn't changed.

Noticing a framed picture of Jane and Sophie at what must be the dance studio, Henry smiled. He used to go to every dance performance he could just to see Jane turn around the floor, her hair pulled back to reveal her long, graceful neck. Jane didn't mind; she liked the support. And Adam wouldn't be caught dead alone at one of those things. The only way Henry could get him not to blow her off was to cajole him into making a group thing of it, and he was always rewarded by the huge smile that lit Jane's face when she spotted them in the audience at the end.

The flowers were his idea, too. Girls like that type of thing, he'd been sure to tell Adam, always purposefully stopping off at the grocery store before the performance, and all but handing Adam the flowers to buy. Early on Jane had remarked she loved peonies best, and so that's what she got.

Sure, Adam wasn't exactly the ideal boyfriend. He

got drunk at college parties and made out with a few girls, and yeah, Henry had sat stone faced when Adam relayed it, barely able to suppress that sloppy grin. When he announced he was going to ask Jane to marry him, Henry experienced a plague of emotions. It was what Jane wanted, but was Adam really the man who could make her happy? Forever?

His doubts were confirmed when Adam bailed on Jane's senior prom—last minute. Though he'd never tell her, Adam had confided there was no way he was spending his Saturday night at a high school dance. Henry hung up the phone and made up his mind to take Jane himself, easing her disappointment by telling her Adam had sent him in his place, knowing damn well that Adam hadn't given her feelings a single thought. Nor did he when he showed up two hours late to her graduation party, or the time he missed her birthday.

Henry stepped away from the photos, turning his back to the happy family, feeling weird and out of place, reminded of everything he didn't have and had never found.

He thought of Caroline, and his jaw set.

"Here you go." Jane handed him a steaming mug, served just the way he liked it. She let out a long sigh as she led him into the living room and sat down on the sofa. Her eyes had lost their earlier glow, and she looked small in her fuzzy sweater.

"You have a lot going on every day," he observed, coming to sit next to her. He set his mug down on a coaster. "The dance classes, and the bookstore. Raising Sophie."

"Oh, it's not too much, really." She gave a weary smile and pulled her feet up under her.

"But you're doing it all on your own. Some women in your position wouldn't handle it so well," he said tightly.

Jane blew on her coffee, clutching the mug with both hands. "There's no real choice, is there?"

"There is, though, and that's why I'm so sorry you're going through this."

Jane smile drooped. "We don't need to talk about this. You're Adam's friend—"

"I'm your friend, too, Jane."

She blinked up at him, her full pink lips pulling into a small smile. His groin tightened and he reached for his coffee before he did anything stupid. Like kiss his buddy's ex-wife.

"I have to admit I get a little tired sometimes. The stress lately ... I haven't been sleeping much."

That made two of them.

"Why don't you try to rest, then?"

"Oh. No...I don't want to kick you out." Her cheeks flushed, and for a second he dared to think she might not want him to go. He considered it, imagining how nice it would be to stay here in this cozy house, with Jane, sweet, loving Jane. He pulled back.

Jane was his friend. He'd told her so and he meant it. And that's all she could ever be.

He reached over and took her mug from her hands and set it down on the end table. "Who said I'm going anywhere? You make some of the best damn coffee around, and I'm going to sit here and finish it while you get some much-needed rest." When she opened her mouth to protest, he said, "I'll call Ivy to give me a lift back into town. Don't worry about me. You have enough to worry about."

Hesitating briefly, she finally leaned back. Her brown

hair spilled over her shoulders as she set her head on the pillow. "That does feel good," she admitted.

Henry pulled a soft blanket off the back of the couch and draped it over her.

"Thanks," she said, and then paused for a beat. "Thanks for everything, Henry."

He stood. "Get some rest. You need it."

Letting her have the full sofa, he sank into an armchair and reached for his coffee. The wind howled outside, and the branches rattled against the windows that framed the hearth. Jane's breathing grew steady within minutes, and he suspected she'd be out for the night. He knew he should really call Ivy and ask for a ride into town. The longer he stayed in this house, the more he didn't want to leave. But at the end of the day, he'd have to. This was her life, her world, and just like with the Browns, and his in-laws, and every hotel he stopped at on the road, he was only passing through.

CHAPTER 16

"Oh, there you are, Mr. Birch!"

Henry closed his eyes, savoring the darkness for a moment, and then glanced over his shoulder. Mrs. Griffin was bustling toward him, her lips curved into a knowing smile.

"Good morning," he said, keeping his tone light.

"Indeed it is! And my, don't you look rested, if I may say." She blinked up at him, but he refused to take the bait.

Yeah, he'd slept well. Better than he had in years, even if it was on an armchair and ottoman. Something about being in Jane's house, with her steady breathing lulling him, had brought a sense of calm and comfort he hadn't had in . . . possibly forever.

"We missed you at turn down last night," Mrs. Griffin continued, giving him a knowing look. "I trust you found the key under the urn and let yourself in? Hmm?"

Henry just gave a mild smile. "It was a late night."

"Well, it must have been! I just happened to be sitting

in the lobby until past midnight—too much excitement from the festival no doubt!—and I didn't see you come in..." She fluttered her eyelashes and folded her hands in front of her blouse, waiting.

"As I said, it was a late night." He smiled again and headed to the door, but Mrs. Griffin hurried to keep up with him, blocking his path.

"But then I saw you after breakfast, and I thought, oh, see, safe and sound. Nothing to worry about. He must have made it back last night after all and I just didn't see him." Her eyes glimmered.

"Safe and sound. Now, if you'll excuse me—"

"But then I remembered that when I was about to unlock the front door this morning I got distracted by the ding of the oven, yet just now I noticed the door has been unlocked since I last checked." She stared at him, not allowing so much as a blink. "Seems that someone was gone *all night* and decided to slip in while the rest of us were enjoying my prize-winning coffee cake. Blueberry streusel, mind you. Only the best for my guests."

Henry locked her twinkling gaze and sunk his hand into his pocket, closed it around the key. "I stayed at my old house if you must know."

Her earlier titillation was replaced with a small gasp. She brought a hand to her mouth to cover her surprise, but it was too late. Not that Henry blamed her; the house was uninhabitable. He should have told a better fib—that he'd camped out on Ivy's couch, or spent time with a friend.

After all, that's all he had done. So why not just say it? Why cover it up? Why make it out to be more than it was?

"Well...I..." Mrs. Griffin chewed her thumbnail, shaking her head with pinched brows as she studied the

key now safely back in her hands. "Well, you must be starving."

"I'm fine, but thank you." He could still taste Jane's rich coffee and homemade waffles with warm maple syrup. She might credit her sister, Anna, for being the chef in the family, but there was no denying that Jane knew her way around the kitchen. "I'm actually headed back to the house now."

"How's it coming along?" Mrs. Griffin seemed to wince.

Henry shrugged. The painters were tackling the wood rot and already the outside was looking more cheerful. The inside, though... it would take more than a fresh coat of paint to brighten that space. "With any luck we'll have it on the market in a few weeks."

"I'm glad you mentioned that. Things tend to pick up around here during the holidays. After all, there's so much to see and do in these parts, and who doesn't love a white Christmas?" When he didn't react she huffed. "Should I assume you'll be leaving before then?"

"Would it be possible to let you know in a week or two? Until more progress has been made on the house, I can't be sure how long I'll be here, and I'm on assignment—" Crap. The innkeeper's eyes immediately sprang open, and her mouth formed a little *o* of surprise.

"An article? Dare I ask if the subject is our charming little town?"

Henry braced himself. "As a matter of fact, it is."

"Oh!" Mrs. Griffin clasped her hands at her breast. "Oh! Well, isn't this wonderful! My, there is just so much to share, so much to highlight, I imagine, what with the shops, the dining. The *accommodations*." She held his stare, her smile pert.

"I'm sure the readers of the magazine will find much to love about Briar Creek," Henry said flatly. *Even if I don't.* "Well, I should get going."

"Oh, well, enjoy your day, Mr. Birch! And, don't worry about rushing your stay. You take all the time you need. The Main Street Bed and Breakfast is always happy to have you."

Henry flicked his collar and exited the building, shaking his head when he passed the urns that flanked the double glass doors. It was the first place a burglar would look, but he suspected Mrs. Griffin's motives in locking the inn at midnight sharp had more to do with her overflowing curiosity about her guests' comings and goings than her concerns about safety. She was harmless, but nosy. Just like so many in this town.

The drive to the house was easier in the light of day, but he was still counting down the days until he never had to see it again. The winding roads were flanked by the forest, now vivid hues of orange, gold, and crimson, and without any traffic, he covered the short distance from town in a matter of minutes. He rounded a bend and turned onto their old country road, his heart beginning to pound when he saw Adam's mother outside her house, raking leaves into piles.

He tightened his grip on the steering wheel. He slanted a glance behind the shield of his sunglasses, taking in the chin-length blond hair, the face edged with laugh lines, and eased off the accelerator. Confusion wrinkled her expression as he turned into her driveway and pulled to a stop, and the joy in her face when he climbed out of the car filled him with guilt.

"Henry! My goodness, Henry!" Dropping the rake,

she jogged across the yard to him, arms spread wide. He let her pull him in for a long, hard hug, and he closed his eyes, hating himself. Hating that his best friend's mom had cared more for him than his own. Hating that he somehow felt he'd let her down just as much as his own mother. He'd turned his back on this town—on the rumors and talk and the glances and whispers. But he'd turned his back on the people who'd cared, too.

"Do you have time?" Her clear blue eyes were hopeful as she looked up at him.

He nodded. He'd find any excuse to put off returning to his childhood home, but this visit was more than a distraction. It was time to face his past. His whole past.

"Come inside. I'll make some coffee." Linking her arm through his, she led him up the path and into the warm, sunlit house. He wiped his feet on the mat in the hall. A radiator hissed and then clanked in the distance. Just ahead was the old grandfather clock that chimed on the hour, and there, to the left, was the winding staircase Henry had slipped and fallen down once, bruising his knee.

She took his coat and hung it on the coatrack next to her own. "Now, isn't this a treat." She smiled, and patted his hand, squeezing it close. "I don't suppose you're hungry? I have some chocolate chip cookies. I always keep them on hand. They're Sophie's favorite," she added.

It was odd to think that she was Sophie's grandmother, that the little girl he'd started to know had been a part of Patty's world for years. She was like Jane in many ways—caring, nurturing, and family oriented. He wondered what she thought about her son's divorce.

The kitchen was bright, if a bit cramped, with shelves

of cookbooks above the desk where Patty used to sit and pay the bills or chat on the phone.

Henry slid into his old spot at the table. "I'm sorry it's been so long."

Patty just shook her head as she filled the teakettle and set it back on the burner. "You're busy!"

"Yes, but…I should have written. Or called." Like Jane, Adam's mother sent a Christmas card every year to his apartment in San Francisco. She sent a birthday card, too, always handwritten with a chatty note, always with an open invitation to visit soon, careful not to pressure. He'd saved them all in a drawer in his kitchen, but he'd never reread them.

Now, he realized he should have written back. But somehow, after he'd left Briar Creek, it was easier to pretend he'd never been there at all, to avoid the reminders, to start fresh. Easier to keep running, keep looking forward. Wake up in a new place, any place, that wasn't in this town.

"You're here now." She smiled as she set a plate of cookies on the center of the table. "So tell me, what have you been up to?"

"Oh…" Henry shrugged, and started telling her about some of his latest trips, making sure to include parts she might enjoy, like the tulips in Holland or the gelato in Italy.

"I wasn't sure if you would come back this summer," Patty finally hedged. "I'm sorry about your mother. I know she had her problems. I always hoped she would find a way to work through them."

Henry set his jaw. He took a bite of his cookie, tasting nothing. The last letter from Patty was the only one he'd never opened. He could tell from the creamy envelope

that it was a condolence card, no doubt meant to offer sympathy. He didn't deserve sympathy. He didn't deserve to grieve, either. His mother had drunk herself to death. And he'd given up on her. "I tried to help her." The cookie lodged somewhere in his throat.

Patty nodded. "I know you did. Ivy, too. We all tried."

Henry nodded. His mother's drinking was no secret, despite his efforts to make it one. Patty had always been careful not to share the gossip she heard, instead choosing to pretend nothing was amiss. How many times had she dropped him off, tried to engage with his mother, befriend her, even. The times things were really out of hand, she gently stepped in, offering to take Henry and Ivy for the night. "Two kids and no help?" she'd say in that friendly way of hers. "I don't know how you do it."

"Adam and I got together last week," Henry volunteered. He hadn't intended to mention this, but it beat continuing down memory lane.

Patty carefully set her cup on its saucer. "Oh? He didn't tell me. So much has been going on lately." She smiled weakly.

Henry drew a breath. "I heard about his new plans."

Patty took a moment. "It's been a very strange year, and a difficult one for me. Jane was . . . well, Jane was like the daughter I never had."

"Do you still see her?"

Patty was quick to shake her head. "I love Jane, but Adam is my son. I suppose that's the sad reality of these situations. When one part of a family isn't working, the rest suffer, too."

Henry bit back on his teeth. He understood more than she knew.

"I just want them to all be happy. And Sophie. Poor thing." She trailed off, shaking her head.

Henry opened his mouth to say something, then paused. It wasn't his business, and she was right. In the end, loyalty fell with one side or the other. Whose side was he going to take? Jane's, or the person who had brought him into this home, shared it with him, given him the closest thing to a real mother he ever had.

"Have you seen Jane since you've been back?"

Henry nodded. "A few times. I ran into her at the bookstore. I stopped in for coffee and there she was."

"The new café." Patty brightened. "I've heard it's lovely. I haven't been in, of course."

They shared a glance, saying nothing more.

He stayed for half an hour, chatting about his job and her involvement in the gardening club. "Promise to visit me before you go," Patty said, her eyes growing misty. "Come for dinner, like old times. I'll make you that chicken stew you always loved so much. Extra carrots."

"I'd like that," Henry said, feeling his gut tighten on the words. He'd like it a lot. Too much, really. And he knew one person who wouldn't like it all.

Birthday bouquets were Ivy's favorite. Get-well flowers were uninspiring, anniversary bouquets consisted of entirely too many roses, and funeral arrangements were obviously depressing as heck. Wedding flowers, however, were the absolute worst! She could spot a bride-to-be from the moment the bell above her door jingled. It was something in their eyes—something wide and darting and frenetic in intensity. She'd take three calming breaths, plaster a smile on her face, and serenely smile as they showed her

their ideas, careful not to take even the slightest offense when they shot down most of hers. She reminded herself to have patience; after all, someday her turn would (hopefully) come, too, and then she'd feel the pressure of creating the perfect event, obsessing over the smallest details, right down to the napkin rings. Of course, Ivy already knew exactly what kind of flowers she'd have for her wedding, but not everyone was as confident when it came to their vision…She'd do well to remind herself of this when the bride-to-be became a little too demanding, or questioned her ability or taste, or called to make sure, yet again, that everything would in fact be delivered on time. She told herself not to take offense; they were simply nervous wrecks and it was her job to soothe them, take one task off their plate, talk them off the ledge, and help create the wedding of their dreams.

But sometimes, when she had three arrangements to finish and a phone that wouldn't stop ringing, she really struggled to remember any of this.

Across the counter, Grace let out a small sigh, jutted her lip, and squinted in thought, then flicked to the next page in a bridal magazine Ivy kept on hand. *For the love of*…Ivy took another deep breath to steady herself.

"Why don't I give you some time to think about this while I—"

"No!" Grace looked up in alarm. "I need your opinion. You know best."

Ivy felt that, all things fair, she probably did know best, but she'd learned early on that the easiest way to take the blame from an unsatisfied bride was to voice too strong an opinion. "It's your wedding, Grace. You have to

be happy with your flowers at the end of the day. Only you can decide what will make you happy."

Grace stared at her. "Is that the spiel you give to all your brides?"

Ivy laughed. "Yes."

"See, I know you too well." Grace smiled and opened a new magazine.

That she did, Ivy thought, but there were a few things about her that Grace didn't know. Things she'd rather keep to herself.

Ivy eyed Grace and started to gather her courage. Her heart was beginning to pound and her palms were growing sweaty, which meant that really, this little crush on Luke's cousin had lingered far, far too long. Like, more than a decade too long. She should just ask if Brett had a plus one and get on with her life. If he had a date, then she could prepare herself instead of experiencing a shock. And if he didn't... A ripple of butterflies zipped through her stomach.

She opened her mouth, but no sound came out. She closed it firmly, smoothed her palms over her starched cotton apron, and tried again. "So, I've been meaning to ask—"

The door behind Grace jingled, and Jane popped her head into the shop. The smile on her face faltered when she saw Grace. "Hey. I didn't expect to see you here. Who's watching Main Street Books?"

"Anna's replenishing the pastries, so she told me she could cover for half an hour. She said it was a nice break from the restaurant."

"Uh-oh. She and Mark aren't having problems, are they?" Mark's reputation as a ladies' man was still

embedded in the town. Reputations were hard to shake around here, Ivy thought, frowning.

"God, no." Grace rolled her eyes. "Those two can barely keep their hands off each other, even though they're together morning, noon, and night."

"Making up for lost time, I suppose." Ivy smiled.

"Speaking of lost time, how's your brother?" Grace set the magazine to the side to give Ivy and Jane her full attention.

"Good, I suppose. He's taking over the bulk of the work on the house so we can finally get it listed. I don't know what I'd do without him, honestly." Wasn't that the truth? Aside from that one little hiccup when she'd announced her plans to open the shop, Henry had been her rock for as long as she could remember. Even though he'd been away these past few years, the bond was still strong, and she focused on that on the days she missed him or wished he was close. Like when their mother died. Henry needed to spread his wings. He needed to go out into the world and put distance between him and this town. She understood. She just wished he understood why she chose to stay. "I keep hoping that he'll decide to stay now that..." She didn't finish the thought, but the look on the Madison sisters' faces told her they understood.

"Well," she said brightly. "Jane, I owe you a big thank-you. Henry told me you helped him out the other day in the shop. I didn't even want to think what was going on in this place with him in charge."

Jane laughed. "It was my pleasure. I really enjoyed the work."

"Well, Henry was singing your praises, so you must have worked some magic." Ivy grinned, noticing the way

a pink flush spread up Jane's cheeks. Interesting. She'd always hoped her brother would have had the nerve to make a move on Jane, and she'd so much as said so years ago, but he'd dismissed the idea with a scowl, reminding her that Adam was his best friend, the Browns were like family, and Jane was too young for him. All very good points back then. But now... "So what brings you into the shop today?"

Jane opened her eyes in surprise and glanced at her sister. "Oh. Um. I was just passing by and thought I'd say hello." She shrugged, but Ivy wasn't buying it. Jane didn't seem to have much to say, so she'd hardly stopped in for a chat.

"How are the wedding flowers coming along? Have you made up your mind yet?" Jane asked Grace, and she was rewarded with a nudge of Grace's elbow.

"It's a big decision," Ivy said diplomatically, and Grace snorted.

"There you go again. You tell all your brides that, don't you?" She laughed. "I'm not like the rest of them, though, right? I mean, it *is* a big decision."

Ivy shared a secret smile with Jane. "Take all the time you need. However, I really do need to finish these arrangements. They're due out in an hour and I'll be lucky to get them finished in time. Sundays are usually quiet, but I'm about ready to take the phone off the hook!"

"Do you need help?" Jane asked.

Ivy waved her off. "You've been a big enough help. I'll manage. It's just tricky sometimes." The phone rang again and Ivy tossed up her hands. "I just need ten good minutes to finish this bouquet."

"Here. Let me." Jane stepped behind the counter and

answered the phone, jotting down notes so Ivy could handle it later. When she hung up, Ivy grinned over her shoulder.

"I should hire you," she laughed, reaching for a handful of baby's breath.

Jane opened her mouth, a hint of a smile teasing the corners of her lips, until Ivy continued, "That's my promise for the new year. As soon as I get that house sold and some bills squared away, I'm going to hire a delivery person and a part-time assistant." She loved making the deliveries herself—seeing the surprise that lit up someone's face when they realized someone had sent them a gift—but Henry was right, and something had to go. She was working too hard, and she struggled to manage her diet. Who had time to eat a balanced meal when most days her lunch was a granola bar at four? She couldn't risk landing in the hospital again.

"The holidays must be a busy time, though," Jane said.

Ivy shrugged. "They are, but I'll just have to get through them. Until that house is sold, I don't have a choice."

Jane fell silent and walked back around the counter. If Ivy didn't know better, she might think Grace's little sister was actually blinking back tears. She stuck another stem in the vase. Impossible. Jane didn't cry, at least not in public. She was stoic and strong. And she didn't reveal too much of herself.

Sounds like someone I know, Ivy thought with an inward grin.

"Well, I should get going. We're offering some new classes at the dance studio tonight. I guess I'll see you there, Grace?"

"Ballroom dancing," Grace explained, grinning. "I'm really getting married!"

Jane barely managed a smile as she turned and left. Ivy stared at the door long after she had disappeared through the paned glass. Something was going on with Jane, and she suspected it unfortunately had little to do with Henry being in town. She'd talk to Grace about it. But first, she'd finalize the plan for Grace and Luke's wedding, once and for all.

Shuffle. Hop. Step. Shuffle. Hop. Step." Jane brushed the toes of her tap shoe against the floor, slowly demonstrating the move, then repeating it again, a bit faster. "See?" She glanced up at the mirror, catching the confused expressions from the row of middle-aged women behind her.

"I think I have it." Mrs. Griffin, frowning with great concentration, brushed the toe of her shoe against the floor, then stepped, then hopped.

"Almost!" Jane smiled in encouragement. "Let's try again, this time with the music." She pointed the remote at the stereo, waited for the cue, and then began shuffle-hop-stepping.

"That's too fast!" Mrs. Griffin cried out. She set her hands on the waist of her hot pink leggings and let out a huff. "Too fast, do you agree, girls?"

The "girls" all nodded in unison, and so, stifling a sigh, Jane turned off the music. So far, even her four-year-old class was easier to handle than this crowd. Announcing they were taking their third water break in half an hour,

the women dropped to the floor and fanned themselves over their Spandex leotards. Mrs. Griffin readjusted her neon leg warmers, smiling demurely when some of the other ladies complimented her on them. Jane stared them down, waiting for them to stand up again, and then looked up at the clock on the wall. Had the minute hand always moved so slowly? She had ten minutes to motivate the group and give them a reason to return next week.

Next time she'd remember to bring some eighties hits with her, but for today, they'd have to stick with jazz.

"Why don't we just shuffle for a while? We'll do eight counts with the right foot, then eight with the left." Jane demonstrated. "Ready?"

In the mirror she saw ten pairs of arms shoot out at a ninety-degree angle, and ten pink-, aqua-, or shiny fuchsia-clad legs poised for position. They shuffled, at their own pace, some moving their arms like helicopters to keep their balance, others stepping down between each shuffle to readjust. One woman, whom Jane recognized from Rosemary's book club, gripped the barre with two hands, as if she might fall over at any moment.

Jane glanced at the door to see Rosemary staring through the window, her blue eyes wide, her mouth agape.

"Don't make me laugh," she said to Rosemary when the class finally finished. Jane sunk into one of the white slipcovered armchairs in Rosemary's office and took a sip of water from her plastic bottle. "They worked really hard."

"Oh, they worked hard all right. Hard at making a lot of noise." Rosemary pinched her red-painted lips. "Well, I shouldn't complain. They're paying students and I must say the turnout was impressive."

Jane leaned forward to peer at the sign-up sheet for *The Nutcracker*. "How many kids are auditioning?"

"Sixty," Rosemary said. In years past, they had a cast of more than one hundred children. "Not terrible, but not as many as I would have hoped. It seems that kids are diversifying. Maybe their parents are limiting the number of activities they can do after school. Whatever the case, it's hard not to feel disappointed."

"Still, it's enough for the show." Jane felt her spirits lift.

"We'll have to double up on some of the dances, but yes, the show will go on." Rosemary flipped open her compact and studied herself in the small, round mirror. "I must say that Henry Birch was looking handsome the other day."

Jane tried to keep her expression neutral. He'd slept on the armchair last night, and she'd woken before him, smiling at the way his arms were crossed around his broad chest, the way his breath was thick and steady, until he opened one eye and cracked a grin across the room, like they shared a special secret. Sophie had come bounding in the room then, demanding breakfast, and happy to see him, and he'd sleepily followed her into the kitchen and let her instruct him on the proper way to dice fruit for the waffles, sparing Jane a wink when he caught her watching.

Jane sighed. "I suppose."

Rosemary plucked the silver cap off her lipstick tube. "I saw you and Sophie leave with him after the festival. I might say he's taken a special interest in you, Jane."

Jane felt herself blush. It had been Henry's idea to give Sophie's waffle a funny face made out of apple slices and raisins. She'd never eat breakfast the same way again. "He's just a friend," Jane stressed.

"So? Remember what I told you and Anna, Jane. The

best relationships start out as friendships. Look at Mark and Anna now! They were best friends before it developed into something more special. Oh, sure they had a little bump in the road, but it smoothed itself out." She gave a mysterious smile. "I knew it would."

Jane laughed under her breath. "You succeeded in bringing Mark and Anna back together, but I really don't feel like being pushed into dating again."

"Who said I'm pushing? I simply mentioned that you can't rule out Henry just because he's your friend. With those dazzling blue eyes and that smile..." She waggled her eyebrows.

"He's not just my friend," Jane said pointedly.

Rosemary's expression fell and she popped the top back on her lipstick. "Love is never easy, is it?" she sighed.

Jane considered her sisters' ups and downs, and shook her head. "No." But then, somehow, how did everyone else seem to be able to find a happy ending?

Rosemary stood and smoothed her skirt. "Time for ballroom. You ready?"

Jane set down her water bottle. "We have six couples registered, and we're open to drop-ins. Grace and Luke are coming."

"Good. They'll need some practice for their first dance. Can you believe the wedding is only six weeks away?" Rosemary beamed. "When I think of it, I don't even worry about the studio. The studio is just a business, and in time it will work itself out, but when it's your children...Well, you understand."

Jane did, and more than Rosemary knew. But unlike Rosemary, her professional concerns were linked to her personal life.

Plucking her angora wrap sweater from the chair, Jane slipped her arms through and carefully tied the pink ribbon at her waist. She exchanged her shorter skirt for a longer one that seemed more appropriate for teaching the waltz and showed a little less leg. There was no one to impress, so why bother drawing attention to herself? She felt a little depressed just thinking of all the happy couples she was about to greet. Couples getting married, couples who wanted to hold each other close, take up a hobby together.

Well, luckily Grace and Luke would be there to cheer her up. She was counting on Luke to be her demonstration partner. Not that he knew that yet, but she doubted he'd have the nerve to say no, not in his mother's studio.

"There you are!" Grace was standing outside the studio entrance, holding Luke's hand, when Jane finally dragged herself out of the office a few minutes later.

Jane's eyes lingered for a beat, allowing one small pang, before she brought her gaze to her sister's. "I hope you don't mind if I steal your fiancé for a bit tonight. It would seem I'm in need of a dance partner."

"Henry can do it," Luke was quick to offer.

Jane frowned. First Rosemary and now her son? From the hopeful gleam in Grace's eye, it seemed everyone was determined to make more of their friendship than was there. Just because an eligible and, okay, handsome man was spending time with her didn't mean he was dating material. Grace of all people should understand why.

"I don't understand why everyone keeps saying things like this. Why would you say that?"

She crossed her arms and stared at Grace and Luke, waiting for them to explain. Finally Luke said, "He's here. I just assumed that meant he was your partner."

Jane felt the blood drain from her face. Henry was here? In the studio? The lobby was so packed and loud that she hadn't even seen him. She shifted her eyes to the left, but a voice in her right ear made her jump. "Hello."

God, he really was cute. That grin, the dimple, that spark of those sky-blue eyes. Jane straightened herself, pinching her lips together. She couldn't even look at Grace or Luke right now, but from the corner of her eye she could see their grins. Nice that they found this so entertaining. If they had any idea what was really going on in her life, she doubted they'd be concerned about the status of her love life. She certainly wasn't. Well, not entirely.

"Are you...taking the class?" Jane tipped her head and held Henry's gaze, trying to understand why she suddenly felt sweaty and nervous and completely flustered. His hair was just as tousled now as it had been this morning, when he'd sat at her kitchen table and regaled her and Sophie with funny stories from his travels, until somehow Briar Creek and all the problems in it didn't exist for a while.

When she'd returned from dropping him back in town, the house had felt quiet, like something was missing, only this time it wasn't the father of her child or the man she had once loved. She'd finally left the house and taken Sophie to the park, just to get away from the reminder, and the wish for something she couldn't have.

She blinked up at him, suddenly hoping he was sticking around for the class, wishing that his time in Briar Creek was more permanent than she knew it would be.

"I thought I'd check it out, if that's okay. It might be something to mention in my article."

"How's that coming along?" Jane asked as they all moved into the studio.

His mouth quirked, revealing a hint of that dimple. "If I'm being honest, Briar Creek does have a little more to offer than I originally gave it credit for."

Jane grinned and led the group into the studio. She stood at the front, her back to the mirror, and scanned the room, recognizing just about everyone in it—classmates from grade school, now married; a few elderly couples, looking nervous; and of course her sister and Luke. *Now, if she could only get Anna and Mark to join . . .* Jane quickly dismissed that thought. They were too busy with the restaurant. Unless—

From the half-open door Jane saw two figures appear in the lobby, barely visible in the shadows. She decided to give them a moment to take off their coats before she got started with the introductions and used the time instead to pop a CD into the stereo, so it would be ready for the first part of the lesson. Behind her, the door creaked open wider. Jane turned, smiling pleasantly, but the grin fell from her face when she saw Adam and Kristy.

Grace shot her a look of alarm, and Jane swallowed hard, clasping her trembling fingers as she tried to remember what she even planned to say to the class. Since when did Adam have an interest in dancing?

She glanced at Henry from the corner of her eye. He gave her a wink.

She drew a deep breath and hoped to God Luke was right about Henry stepping in as her dance partner. Was there anything more humiliating that being the single girl in a room full of happy couples? There was, she deduced.

Being the only single girl when your ex-husband's pregnant fiancée was staring at you with a smug little smile.

Jane hoped her ankles swelled.

Somehow, she made a brief introduction, explaining what they would be working on in the first class, but she couldn't shake the thought that this was a six-week course, and while enrollment was flexible, there was a very real possibility that Adam and Kristy were going to make a weekly habit of this, showing up to torture her, casually coming and going as if they weren't trying to destroy her life. All eyes were fixed expectantly on her as she spoke, and she stopped to clear her throat every few seconds, wishing she was better at public speaking and that her voice didn't quiver. Her cheeks felt warm, with anger, or fear, she didn't know anymore.

She didn't have a choice. "Henry? Would you mind..."

He looked perplexed, but only for a moment. Quickly, he set his notepad and pen on the chair beside him and came to stand next to her. Across the room, Jane noticed Adam frown, and Kristy whisper something to him. Jane looked up at Henry. He was staring back at Adam, his gaze steely.

Her stomach rolled. Maybe she'd overstepped.

"We'll work on the box step first, so if everyone could just take their partner..." She set her arm on Henry's shoulder, feeling the warmth of his body through his cotton shirt. Her breath caught as his hand went to her waist, and not gingerly. Nope, no hesitation there. Henry knew how to hold a woman, how to make her feel with just one touch that he was exactly where he wanted to be. Slowly, she lifted her other hand, and he took it in his, holding it firmly. A wave of exhilaration shot through her as she

looked up to meet his gaze. It bored through hers, but there was a hint of a smile on his lips.

Right. Time to demonstrate. She swallowed hard and tore her gaze from his, looking at Grace, so she wouldn't be tempted to indulge in further masochism by glaring at the man who was single-handedly trying to ruin her life, or meeting Henry's sharp blue eyes and daring to imagine how it might feel if his hand dropped a little lower.

"One, two, three, four." Jane counted out the steps, over and over, and soon all the couples in the room were stepping within their own self-created boxes, many already laughing or whispering to each other.

"We haven't done this in a long time." There was a hint of a smile in Henry's voice.

Jane looked up to find his gaze trained steady on hers, his lips parted in a half smile. Her heart skipped a beat, and she looked down, watching their feet move in perfect unison.

"You've been practicing," she observed now, trying to steer the conversation back to something more professional, but it was no use, not when his eyes were sharp, hooked with hers, refusing to let her go.

Was it just her or did he press himself a little closer?

Her heart flipped with pleasure, and she fought the instinct to pull back, to not let herself get too close. His body felt warm and safe next to hers, and she closed her eyes, listening to the beat of the music, letting herself forget that there was anyone else in the room other than the two of them. His hand slid down her back, looping around her waist, his fingers tracing a pattern on her hip.

The music suddenly stopped and, red-faced, Jane pulled back. For God's sake, she was teaching a class, not enjoying some moonlit waltz!

She marched across the room to the CD player, fumbling to remember the correct buttons to press as her mind spun with emotions. Too much was going on at once, and she couldn't even think straight.

She wondered if Rosemary was still in the building. She'd claim she wasn't feeling well, let her boss stand in her place...

She glanced at Henry, her pulse kicking a notch. He was waiting in the center of the room, and he wasn't waiting for Rosemary, or just anyone. He was waiting, she realized, with a sudden smile, for her.

The music started from the top and the couples began again, improving on their basic steps. Jane averted her gaze from the corner of the room where Adam and Kristy stood, but for some reason she didn't even care in that moment that they were here.

She had her dance partner. And maybe, just maybe, for more than just tonight.

CHAPTER
18

Adam was outside the studio when Henry left Jane chatting with Grace and Luke in the lobby. He tensed, thinking of the confrontation at the Harvest Fest. He needed to get Adam out of here before Jane came outside. It wouldn't help her cause to exchange heated words with him again. But then, maybe that's what Adam was banking on, Henry thought grimly.

"Did you know Jane was teaching the class?" he asked mildly, trying to give his oldest friend the benefit of the doubt, even though it appeared the guy was hell bent on showing Jane no consideration in the slightest.

Adam just shrugged as they reached the parking lot. "You know Kristy and I are getting married in a few weeks. We're practicing for the first dance."

"But you know Jane works here."

"Briar Creek is a small town."

Henry pushed back his temper. "All the more reason to try to give her some space."

"We paid for the class; we didn't cause problems. What are you trying to say?"

Henry kept his gaze steady, but anger coursed his blood through his chest. He tried to keep his tone mild. Tried to reason. "Jane's going through a lot right now. She loves her daughter."

"And I don't?" Adam shook his head, his lip curling with warning. "You're out of line."

He should walk away now, before things got worse, but he couldn't, not this time. Adam's jaw pulsed with thinly controlled rage, but Henry couldn't back down. Not yet. "I'm just suggesting you be a little more considerate of what she's going through, that's all."

Adam gave a low, mirthless chuckle. "Damn, Henry, after everything my family did for you, I expected a little more loyalty."

The fist at Henry's side tightened. Now that was just plain low. In all the years he'd known Adam, payback had never come up. The kindness the Browns had bestowed on him was unspoken. Now, his worst fears were confirmed; the sense of being an outsider, a leech, not a real member of the family. Just a charity case.

"Don't say that," Henry spat. "This isn't about you and me. Jane's my friend, too."

Adam turned to Kristy and handed her the car keys. "Why don't you go ahead and get the heat started?"

With a long, hard glance back at Henry and a flick of long, silky hair, Kristy obliged. Adam waited until the car door had slammed before nailing Henry with a look.

"Is there something going on with you and Jane?" he demanded.

"No. Of course not." Henry tried to keep his tone

casual, but he had the creeping sense he wasn't being honest—with Adam, or himself.

Adam didn't look convinced as he folded his arms across his chest and gave Henry the once over. "My mom said you came to visit her the other day."

Henry nodded, recalling his visit with Patty. "I did. We had a nice chat. You know how fond of your mother I've always been."

Adam stared at him for several, long seconds. "Are we still friends?"

"Of course we're still friends," Henry said quickly. Only he wasn't so sure anymore. He'd overlooked the flirting back when they were still young, but the stakes were higher now, and he wasn't sure he could sit back and say nothing this time.

Adam began walking toward him, a slow, purposeful stride. "I still consider you my friend, Henry, even though we haven't stayed in touch. So do me a favor." He stopped within inches of Henry's face. "Stay away from Jane."

Henry flexed the hand at his side and, before he did something stupid, thrust it deep into his pocket. He took a step back, feeling the blood coursing in his veins as he stared at Adam. "As you said, it's a small town. I don't really see how that can be avoided."

The glint in Adam's eye returned. "You're not in town for long. It shouldn't be that difficult."

Henry stared stonily at his oldest friend, trying to remember the good times they had together, trying to understand how he could have ever grown so close to someone who could be this cold. He hadn't started to see it until well into early adulthood, a good ten years into the friendship, and by then, it was too late. He was part of that

family, and Adam knew it. Worse, he was now using it as leverage.

The two men stood, waiting for the other to break, and no matter how long Adam waited, Henry knew he couldn't agree to what his friend was asking.

"What does it matter if I talk to Jane? You've moved on, you're getting married. Why do you care?"

Adam's eyes snapped open. "Why do *you* care is what I want to know? Why is it so damn important for you to spend time with her? She's my ex-wife for God's sake, Henry!"

"So I'm expected to just cut her out like you did, pretend she doesn't exist?"

Adam's gaze narrowed. "Whose side are you on, Henry?"

"No one's side," Henry said, sighing in exasperation. He should have stayed out of it. No good came from getting messed up in other people's business.

Behind him a door slammed and he turned to see Jane, Grace, and Luke standing on the steps of the dance studio, and from the look in their eyes, they weren't satisfied with his answer any more than Adam was.

What had she expected? Of course Henry wasn't taking her side, why should he?

"What has you most upset?" Grace hedged, as their mother's Victorian house came into view. She'd insisted on riding with Jane instead of Luke, and Jane hadn't argued. Fall garland was draped around the wraparound porch of their childhood home, and a matching wreath hung over the door. It looked warm and inviting, and Jane longed to go inside, flop onto her old twin-sized bed, and

cry into her pillow. It was so much easier to fall apart in the one place you felt most safe.

But she couldn't.

Jane unhooked her seatbelt, but didn't reach for the handle. "I don't know," she replied, but the knot in her gut said otherwise. It was always uncomfortable to see Adam around, especially with Kristy. It took everything in her to be polite and, lately, not physically lunge at him, but it was also a feeling she had slowly learned to live with. The real hurt, she knew, was because of Henry, and because of the way she'd let herself start to feel about him.

"Adam had no business being there. If you ask me, he did it to taunt you."

"You know that Adam hates to dance. It was probably Kristy's idea. She has no shame. Or discretion."

"Anyone who breaks up a family probably doesn't," Grace agreed.

"She only broke it up because Adam let her," Jane said.

"You know," Grace said, her expression turning satisfied, "I bet once they're married and she has that baby, you won't even have to deal with them as much. She'll be way too focused on her own life to bother with you anymore."

Jane's pulse began to race when she thought of everything Grace didn't know. She wanted more than anything to tell her the rest of the story, to explain everything she was going through, but doing so would make her as selfish as Adam. What should have been a fun waltz lesson in preparation for Grace's first dance with her new husband was overshadowed by Jane's problems.

She'd tell Grace everything, but not until after she returned from her honeymoon. By then, Jane realized

with a jolt, everything might already be decided. Her lawyer was already putting their case together, and soon they'd have a scheduled hearing.

Even if she told Grace about Adam's effort to take Sophie across the country, there was nothing her sister could do for her. There were some battles in life she'd just have to fight herself.

"We should get inside," she said, before Grace could talk about it anymore. She didn't want to discuss Henry with her sister—there was nothing to discuss, after all. So he'd been friendly—she didn't need to look for more beyond that. She didn't need a knight in shining armor. She could hold her own.

She held on to that thought as they climbed out of the car and made their way up the winding path to the porch. When she'd mentioned to her lawyer that she could sell her home and move into this one to cut down on costs, he'd advised her against it, and she was happy he had. As much as she loved this old house, it wasn't her home, and she couldn't hide away in it and pretend that she was a child again and that other people could fight her battles and make everything better. The best thing she could do was continue to give Sophie the life she'd always lived and stick with their well-established routine, and that meant staying in the only home Sophie had ever known. Judges didn't like to uproot kids, her attorney reassured her every time doubt crept in, especially ones as young as Sophie.

But did judges overlook financial means and forming bonds with new siblings? She was working on not thinking of everything in terms of catastrophe, on focusing on what was within her control. But late at night, when the house was dark and still, the worried thoughts crept

in. Last night had been the first solid sleep she'd had in a week, thanks to Henry.

She wouldn't be counting on a repeat.

With a sigh, she left her shoes next to Grace's on the front mat and wound her way to the back of the house, where Sophie and their mother were sitting at the kitchen table, eating bowls of ice cream.

"How were the new classes?" Kathleen asked, as Jane bent down to plant a kiss on Sophie's forehead. The little girl didn't look up from her dessert. Sweets were an important matter. They required full attention.

Jane met Grace's eye and shrugged. "We had a good turnout. I haven't seen quite so much hot pink Lycra since the last time I watched a Richard Simmons video."

"You've watched a Richard Simmons video?" Grace retorted.

Jane felt her cheeks flush. "It was after Sophie was born. I was trying to lose the baby weight!"

"You mean you *worked out* to his video! Oh, Jane!"

Her mother and sister laughed, and Jane reluctantly joined them, feeling her mood lift.

"Can you stay for ice cream?" Kathleen asked. "I have chocolate chip."

Jane's favorite. Her spirits rising, she slid into her own childhood seat next to her daughter while her mother fixed her a bowl and Grace began chatting about some last-minute wedding details. "Wouldn't sparklers be gorgeous during the first dance?" she asked, and Sophie clapped her hands in agreement.

Kathleen set Jane's bowl of ice cream in front of her with a smile, then returned to her own seat, patting Jane's hand fondly before lifting her own spoon. Jane ate her des-

sert and listened to her sister and mother talk, and she felt her conviction grow. Adam might have taken her dreams from her, but one thing he couldn't take was her family. It would have been easy to run, to start fresh, but Briar Creek was her home, and she and Sophie both deserved to fight for their place in it.

Forget what he did to her. Forget romance and flowers and all those gestures she'd romanticized and longed for. This kind of love was constant and loyal. And it would have to just be enough.

CHAPTER 19

Main Street Books was bustling when Jane started her shift on Wednesday. The espresso machine hissed, and the entire store smelled of fresh coffee and sweet baked goods. Grace was behind the counter, her chestnut hair pulled back in a ponytail, her cheeks flushed.

"Busy in here," Jane commented, as she tied on an apron. She waved at Rosemary, who sat with her book club at one of the larger tables. This week's selection appeared to be *The Shining*. An appropriate choice for this time of year and a friendly reminder that it was better to be alone than married to the wrong man.

"Rosemary has the club meeting twice a week now," Grace whispered under her breath. "Not that I'm complaining. Let me just finish this order and then I'll duck out. Unless you wanted to cover story time today." Grace blinked rapidly and blew a wisp of hair off her forehead.

Jane gave her a reassuring smile. "You seem like you could use a break. Don't worry, I have it covered."

Grace plated a scone and handed it to the waiting cus-

tomer. "Thanks," she said, untying her apron. "I have to go over our inventory today, and make sure those new releases are on their way. The café should slow down after the book club leaves."

Jane glanced over at the women again, recalling how they had strategized to set both her and Anna up on dates last spring. Things had turned out just fine for one of the Madison sisters. She hoped that would be enough to keep Rosemary and her clan satisfied.

Grace disappeared behind a stack of shelves, but her head poked out a mere second later. "Oh, and I forgot to tell you that Henry stopped in here a little while ago, something about featuring the store in his article. When he saw how busy we were, he said he'd be back. I told him you'd be more than happy to help him out."

Jane felt her heart drop into her stomach. "Oh—"

"Thanks, Jane! You're the best!" Grace smiled and retreated again, and this time, Jane knew she was on her own.

Well, fabulous. She'd vowed to stay clear of Henry since the ballroom class, and now her traitorous heart began to pound at just the thought of seeing him again. She smiled shakily at the next customer and took their order, but her gaze darted to the main door every time it jangled.

"Jane? Yoo-hoo! Jane!" Rosemary wiggled her fingers across the room. "Come sit with us for a bit." Her lips curved into a knowing smile.

Jane shook her head and closed the cash register drawer. "I'm sorry, but I'm too busy at the moment to get away."

"Nonsense. If someone comes in, we'll understand.

And this will only take a minute, I promise." Rosemary stared at her, as if challenging her to refuse.

Jane glanced at the door one more time. Maybe a distraction *would* help.

"I was just telling the gals about the *Nutcracker* auditions," Rosemary said as Jane pulled over a chair.

Oh, good. Ballet talk. She could handle this. What she couldn't tolerate was a heart-to-heart about her nonexistent love life, or a rundown of all the eligible men she should be going out to dinners with. Relaxing against her seat back, she looked around at the other women, but she felt her grin fade as she noticed the eager glint in their eyes. *Oh, sugar.*

"Henry was a real help with our sign-up sheet, wasn't he?" Rosemary pinched her lips and gave her a long, pointed stare.

Jane resisted the urge to roll her eyes. "He was," she said diplomatically. Why, she didn't know, but he had shown a legitimate effort in helping their cause. She could only hope he hadn't suspected how bad off they were, but seeing as no one else outside the studio had picked up on anything being amiss, she had to assume he'd gleaned nothing he could report back to Adam.

"Such a thoughtful young man," Rosemary continued. "Handsome, too."

Jane sighed heavily. "I thought I explained…"

"Pshaw." Rosemary waved off her concerns and reached for her tea. "I was just going over your dilemma with the gals, and we reached a conclusion."

Jane hesitated, realizing they were waiting for a response. "Which is?"

"All is fair in love." Rosemary beamed.

"And war," Jane reminded her. And that's what this was, wasn't it? She and Adam were at war, and Henry, at the end of the day, was not her ally.

"Oh, why turn this negative?"

"Because in my experience, the two are jointly linked," Jane replied, and instantly regretted saying a thing when she saw the women's eyes widen in alarm. One tsked under her breath; two exchanged lingering side-long glances. The others looked at her with naked pity, shaking their heads.

Rosemary just warned, "Don't become cynical, Jane. You'll never find a man with that attitude."

Jane tossed her hands in the air and laughed, "Who said I'm looking for a man? I'm not. I told you I'm not. And even if I was, it most certainly wouldn't be Henry Birch!"

"Oh no?" a deep voice purred behind her.

Jane felt the blood drain from her face as her heart began to pound. She turned with growing dread to see Henry standing behind her, his brow arched in question, his blue eyes gleaming with mischief.

Her cheeks grew hot, and she knew the creamy white turtleneck sweater she was wearing didn't help matters. *Oh my God, another turtleneck!* When would she learn to stop dressing for comfort? "The ladies here were trying to play matchmaker," she explained hastily, pushing back her chair.

"And clearly you didn't agree with their opinion." His dimple quirked, and Jane felt her pulse skip. Why'd he have to be so damn cute? With his brown tousled hair and a day's worth of stubble gracing his jaw, he looked like he'd just rolled out of bed, and now all she could do was

think of him in it. And her with him. And the things he
would do to her.

Stop it, Jane!

"Well, you and I are all wrong for each other, obviously." She bristled at the way his chin tipped on her words.

"Obviously," he said sagely.

She frowned. "I mean, you're only in town for a few
weeks. And we're—" She was going to say *friends*, but
now she wasn't so sure.

With her head held high, she walked on shaking legs
to the counter and stared blankly at the espresso machine,
waiting for the heat to leave her face. Leave it to Rosemary to get her all fired up. She stole a glance in the
direction of the book club's table. All the women were
laughing at something Henry was saying, all beaming up
at him, hanging on his every word, as if he was adorable
or something.

So maybe he was pretty damn handsome. And maybe
he knew how to make a woman feel good. Clearly, she
wasn't the only one who thought so, given the dreamy
quality of Rosemary's gaze.

She ground some fresh coffee beans, whirring out the
sound of his smooth voice, wishing he would just go.

"Hey there."

Jane cursed to herself as her rattled hands nearly
dropped the coffeepot she had just reached for. From the
corner of her eye, she caught a hint of that grin as she set
the pot upright and started the machine.

"What can I get for you?" She smiled pleasantly
as she rounded to face him, keeping her tone brisk and
professional.

"I was actually here to see you."

Jane's eyes widened. "Oh?"

"Grace told me you would be the best one to talk to about Main Street Books. For the article."

Seeing that the bookstore was Grace's pride and joy, her sister really would have been the better person to interview. Jane bit on her thumb, wondering what Grace was up to, and then dismissed her suspicion. Her sister was busy today, Main Street Books had been their father's store, and Jane worked here with her sisters. She was certainly capable of answering a few questions for his article. Surely she wasn't that far gone.

She wished he would stop looking at her like that. It would have been so much easier if he'd just called on the phone.

Jane set a finger to her forehead and gave a small smile, hoping he hadn't detected any misplaced excitement in her earlier reaction. "Of course. She mentioned it. I've just been distracted—"

"By a group of middle-aged women trying to sell me to you?" His eyes flashed. "Don't worry, Jane. You were right. I am the last person on earth you should be getting involved with."

She blinked in surprise. Well, when he said it like that...Jane's shoulders slumped slightly. "Right. Of course. I mean...*obviously*."

"Obviously." Amusement had long since left Henry's eyes, and his jaw tensed now. "So what do you say? Do you have time to go over this with me?"

Jane stared at Henry, a part of her wanting to know exactly what he meant when he agreed that they didn't belong together, but she pushed the urge away immediately. What mattered was that he was right, that he was

not the man for her, even if she did start to wonder what it might feel like to kiss those lips, run her hands through those wavy locks, press her chest against his the way she had the other night at the studio . . . She sucked in a breath, steadying herself, and glanced to the door, where a couple had just entered, heading for the bakery counter. The café's tables were mostly filled and a few patrons were sipping coffees in the English armchairs near the bookshelves. She couldn't fight the pride she felt for everything their family had accomplished.

"It's busy right now," she said, as the door opened yet again.

Henry shrugged. "I can wait."

Of course he could. No matter how much she tried, there was no getting rid of him.

She snorted to herself. Fancy that for a change. The last man in her life ran through the door the second she cut him loose.

"How's the house coming along?" she inquired as she poured him a mug of fresh coffee.

He accepted it and motioned to a pumpkin scone. "Those look delicious."

Anna would be pleased to hear that, Jane noted as she plated one for him. "Do you think you'll be ready to list it soon?" *Are you leaving town soon?* She wasn't sure why she still cared.

"It's hard to say. The place needs more work than I thought. We want to make sure we get as much out of it as we can." He handed over a ten-dollar bill and she reached for it, her fingers so close to his, they nearly touched. She hesitated, admiring the long, tanned fingers, and then all but yanked the money from his hands. That was about enough of that!

She rang up his order and slid his change along the counter, hoping to avoid another chance at physical contact, even though a part of her wanted nothing more than to feel the soft heat of his skin on hers. "Well, I hope it all works out for you. And Ivy," she added, recalling that Ivy was depending on the proceeds from the sale of the house to grow her business.

Henry's smile was warm. "Thanks. I hope everything works out for both of us, Jane." His voice was low and insistent, and entirely too intimate. She pulled back from the counter. "I mean that, Jane."

"Do you?" She couldn't hide the hurt that crept into her tone. "Or are you just saying that because you feel sorry for me?"

Henry frowned. "I feel sorry for what you're going through. I also know you've grown into a strong woman who will find a way to get through this. Look how many hurdles you've already crossed."

When he put it like that... She shook off the kindness in his words. He didn't want to get involved, and she shouldn't be dragging him into this. "I'm working. I can't get into this now."

"I'm not finished with this conversation, Jane," Henry said firmly.

She met his eye. "Well, I am." The couple had reached the counter and she gave them her full attention. "We have some lovely chocolate croissants this morning."

"Jane."

She slid her gaze to Henry's and waited.

"Come sit with me in a minute. Please."

She glanced at the couple and let out a breath. "Fine."

She watched as he retreated and settled at the last

free table near the window. She took her time filling the next few orders and watched the door, willing someone to enter. It would seem the rush was now over. How convenient.

Henry's hooded gaze pulled her attention back to his table. She sighed and decided to face the inevitable. Rosemary's group stopped talking and watched as she swept by them.

"Let's just forget I said anything," she said, dropping into the chair opposite him, happy her back was to the book club. "I don't have very much time, and I promised Grace I would help you with the article."

"That's all you have to say?" he asked, his expression incredulous.

"Well, thank you," she managed. "For featuring the bookstore. It will certainly help business, and I appreciate that."

"I'm not doing this to help you," he replied. He ran a hand over his face. "That came out wrong. I care about you, Jane. And your welfare. "

"My welfare?" she repeated, crossing her arms across her chest. *Figures.* "Pity, then."

His brow knitted. "Jane, you're one of the most capable women I know. You wrestle two jobs, you take care of a child, and you've created a beautiful home, all on your own. And you still make time for your sisters and mother. That's more than most people could say. More than I could say." Something in his eyes fell flat.

Jane studied his face, wondering what had gone wrong in his marriage. It was something they had in common, after all: divorce. Henry didn't seem to want to talk about it, though, and she of all people could respect that.

"You know, I had a bit of a crush on you when we were younger," Henry confessed, his mouth curving into a bashful smile.

Jane felt herself blush, and she laughed to cover her embarrassment. His grin slipped a bit, but his eyes were honest, and all at once her heart started doing jumping jacks. Henry, this man who had started consuming all of her waking fantasies, had at one point in time been attracted to her. Was it possible he still was? "I don't believe you." And she wouldn't. Henry was lean and muscled and smooth and sincere. He was sweet and kind, and he . . . Oh, God.

"I never said anything." He stirred his coffee and set down his spoon. "What point was there? You were crazy about Adam."

She pursed her lips at that. "I was." Why, she couldn't even remember anymore. She supposed it was better that way.

The door jangled and Jane looked up to see a group of women weaving through the book display tables. "I should go attend to them." She stood, remembering. "The article. I'm tied up with class and the *Nutcracker* auditions later today."

"I've got some contractors coming out to the house tomorrow and Friday. How about this weekend?"

The suggestion of a weekend meeting felt somehow personal. "I promised Sophie I'd take her to Old Country Orchard Saturday to pick apples. It's sort of a family tradition." She frowned on her words. *Family* still felt awkward; like it was meant for more than a pair. "Well, a tradition for us."

"Old Country Orchard? Don't they supply cider to the

state?" When Jane nodded, he continued, "Might be good for my article. Mind if I join you?"

Jane fumbled for an excuse and came up blank. "Oh, um."

Henry held up a hand. "It's a family tradition. Sorry. It just sounded fun."

Jane thought of the laughter and warmth she felt the night of the Harvest Fest, when the three of them had gathered around the kitchen table, eating pizza and commenting on the events of the day, focusing only on the positive ones. Sophie had lit up at his presence, or maybe by the way Jane's energy responded to him and his easy smile, his gentle eyes, and that killer smile that made her insides tingle and her mind wander into places it hadn't been in too long.

"Want to meet at the house and drive out together? Say, noon?"

Henry's grin widened. "Noon's perfect."

Jane inhaled a shaky breath as she backed away from the table. If she didn't know better, she'd think she almost just planned a date!

CHAPTER
20

Old Country Orchard was on the outskirts of Briar Creek, about five miles down a winding, tree-lined road, south of town. "Did you ever come here as a kid?" Jane asked Henry as they pulled into the gravel parking lot.

The set of his jaw made her want to snatch back her question. Of course he hadn't.

"We took a school trip here, I think," Henry replied after a pause. "How long have you been coming?"

"For as long as I can remember," Jane said as they made their way up the dirt path to the red barn at the base of the apple trees. She helped Sophie take a small basket and took a larger one for herself. Motioning to a wagon, she said, "We'll probably need one of those, too."

Henry looked at her quizzically. "For Sophie?"

"For the apples," Jane corrected, laughing softly.

Henry's brow drew to a point. "How many do you plan on picking?"

"More than I can carry, that's for sure."

He stared at her. "You're serious."

"That's not a problem, is it? We usually make a day of it and then go home and bake."

His gaze was sharp and unnerving, and Jane held her breath as she waited for him to reply. In the afternoon sun, his eyes were lighter than usual, and his unruly locks glinted with copper highlights. But all she could stare at was that mouth. Those full lips, the dimple that quirked when he grinned. The slight cleft in his chin. "On the contrary. This day is already showing a lot of promise."

Jane felt her breath catch. That it was.

She blinked quickly and turned away before he could see her pleased smile, her stride purposeful as they approached the first row of trees. So he liked this type of thing. That didn't mean she could fall for him. He was probably just gathering information for his article. There were endless reasons why he was the last person in the world she should have a crush on.

A crush—yes, that's all it was. He was a good-looking guy and she was, well, *depraved*, as Grace would probably say. It had been more than a year since she'd been touched in...special places. But a crush was called a crush for a reason, and with Henry, it could only ever end in disappointment.

He used to have a crush on me, she thought with a sudden skip in her heart. She dismissed it just as quickly and yanked an apple from a branch. That was years ago. He'd moved on. They'd both moved on. Both gotten married.

Both gotten divorced.

"How's the article coming along?" she asked, keeping an eye on Sophie as the little girl wandered down the path.

"Better than expected," Henry said. There was a hint of surprise in his tone.

Jane glanced up at him. "If I didn't know better, I'd say Briar Creek is growing on you."

"It has its charms," he said, somewhat reluctantly.

Jane reached up for an apple at the exact time as Henry. She blushed as his hand touched hers, but he just grinned as he snatched it from the branch and handed it to her. "Thanks," she said, falling into step beside him. He grew quiet, and she decided to keep going with their conversation, see if he'd open up a bit more. "Small-town life has its challenges. There were times last year where it seemed I couldn't enter a room without it going silent."

Henry's mouth firmed into a thin line. "Why'd you stick around, then? It couldn't have been easy living in the same town as your ex, not with the way people talk around here."

She chose not to remind him—or herself—that Adam wasn't going to be living in Briar Creek much longer; there was plenty of time to worry about that later. Today was an annual tradition, and she wanted to make the most of it.

"It's been hard at times," Jane admitted with a sigh. She thought of telling him about her pajama days and decided against it. Nothing glamorous about a shut-in. Nothing attractive about flannels and bunny slippers. Besides, there was still the possibility that he would mention it to Adam, and oh, wouldn't that just make her mother of the year? "I've kept to myself more since Adam moved out."

"Sometimes it's easier that way," Henry agreed. "But then, I guess that comes with its own set of sacrifices."

Jane knew about the way people talked about Mrs. Birch, right up until the day the poor woman died last

summer. That couldn't have been easy to deal with, but was it enough to run from?

She glanced at Henry. "It must be nice spending time with your sister."

Henry nodded. "It is. We haven't seen enough of each other in recent years. I hope to change that."

Hope fluttered in her chest. She reached for another apple, waiting for her pulse to settle before speaking again. "You thinking of moving back?"

"No, but it might be easier for her to get away and visit me now."

Jane did her best to push back the heaviness in her heart. It was time to get back to business, the whole reason for him being here at all. "So, Main Street Books. I owe you some information on it."

"Hold on. Let me get out my notebook." Henry sat down in the red metal wagon and grinned up at her, pen poised above the spiral pad. "Hit me with it."

"Well, some of this you probably already know, and really Grace would be the better person to help here." She frowned at that, wondering again why Grace hadn't just handled this herself. Her sister loved to brag about Main Street Books. The store was her life; it had been her favorite hangout growing up, just as the dance studio had been Jane's. "My father left his teaching job to take over the store when I was just a kid. I couldn't have been much older than Sophie at the time."

"And Grace took it over last year?"

Jane nodded. "After my father died..." She swallowed hard. It still hurt to say those words, even now, more than a year and a half later. "She came home to visit last Christmas. The shop was scheduled to be closed, actually.

Anna had her own business, and I was, well, dealing with my own mess." She narrowed her gaze, thinking of how fraught she'd been a year ago at this time.

She felt tired thinking back on it. Almost as tired as she felt now, nearly a year later.

"I asked Grace to come home for the holidays," she continued. "When she learned about the store, she found a way to reinvent it, with Anna's help."

"So, it's become a family effort, then?"

Jane gave a smile. "It has. Grace had been gone for five years. We weren't sure she'd ever come home." She shrugged. "Sometimes tragedy has a way of bringing people together."

"I guess so." Henry's brow furrowed, and Jane realized she'd hit a nerve.

She set a hand on his arm, her stomach tightening at the forwardness of her gesture, but he didn't pull back. If anything, it felt strangely natural. "I'm sorry. You must still be struggling, with your mom. I know it's still painful for me to think about my dad." She felt her frown deepen.

She dropped her arm and resumed picking apples from a low-hanging branch.

"I was hard on my sister," Henry said, catching her off guard. "I wanted her to leave Briar Creek years ago. I couldn't understand why she'd choose to stay."

Jane considered his words. "You have a lot of hard feelings about this town."

"Wouldn't you? I'm sure you know how people talked about us around here. My mother had quite a reputation. Half the time I wondered if it was the reason she drank so much. It's not easy living with that kind of talk."

No, it wasn't. Jane set her basket on the ground. "I'm sorry, Henry."

He shrugged, then stood and slid his notebook back into his pocket. "Nothing to be sorry about. It is what it is. You can dwell or you can move on."

And he'd chosen the latter.

She opened her mouth to say something, but from the set of his jaw and the determination in her eyes, it was clear the conversation was over. Henry was stubborn and proud, and he didn't want anyone's pity. He just wanted to live a quiet life where he didn't have to be reminded of the past.

She could relate.

"Mommy, can I have an apple?"

"Are you still hungry?" Jane remarked. She shared a smile with Henry. They'd just indulged in cider and donuts and split an enormous slice of warm pie. "Wait until we get home, honey. We'll have dinner soon, and you know how I feel about food in the car."

"It's an apple," Henry chided, low enough to ensure Sophie couldn't hear.

Jane pinched her lips and slid her eyes back to the road. "I know, but rules are rules. It's easiest to stick to them."

She considered her own rules, the ones that pertained to dating and romance. The ones that Henry broke. He hardly had long-term potential.

"When I go to school on Monday, I'm going to tell all the kids that I have a loose tooth," Sophie announced from the backseat.

"Oh, really?" Jane smiled. Sophie was already trying to reach new milestones, trying to grow up too quickly.

She glanced at Henry. "I want to tell her to just enjoy her youth, you know?"

"I wouldn't know, actually. I felt like I was born an old man." He chuckled, but there was an edge of hurt in his voice.

"You're a good brother. And son," Jane added after a hesitation.

"I always adored Ivy," Henry remarked, ignoring the rest of her comment.

"I'm going to tell everyone I lost a tooth. Look, Mommy, my tooth came out."

Jane glanced up in the mirror to see Sophie munching an apple, grinning happily. "Sophie! I told you, no eating in the car!"

"Sorry," Sophie mumbled, even though she didn't appear the least bit repentant. She bit into her apple and chewed.

Jane rolled her eyes. The sun was quickly fading, and she hated driving in the dark, especially on these winding back roads with no lighting. She turned on her brights and gripped the steering wheel, trying to tune out Sophie's endless chatter. It was hard to believe there was a time she had waited for Sophie to start talking, wondering if it would ever happen. Now, the chatter filled every silence, and when Sophie was gone, at school or with her dad, the quiet was almost unbearable.

"Are we going to have pizza again for dinner?" Sophie asked now.

"I made a lasagna, honey."

"Oh! Yuck."

Jane squinted into the distance, searching for the next turn. "What do you mean by that? You love my lasagna!"

"Well, I like pizza better," Sophie said grouchily. "And so does Henry."

Henry flashed her a look of chagrin. "Actually, lasagna is one of my favorite meals."

Jane's heart sped up. Was that a hint? She gripped the steering wheel tighter as she considered how to respond. She suddenly wished Grace were here, or even Anna. They'd know how to smoothly reply, how to casually respond in a way that didn't seem too eager, or too uninterested.

Oh, what was she saying? There was nothing to read into at all. So he'd had a crush on her. That was ages ago. He was obviously over it by now. He'd more or less told her so in no uncertain terms. Still... She glanced at him sidelong, catching a hint of those deep-set eyes.

"Well, you're always welcome to join us," she said lightly.

She braced herself, waiting for him to brush off her invitation, to tell her to just bring him back to the inn, but Sophie cut in first: "Yeah! We can have a lasagna party!"

"Is everything a party in your house?" Henry asked, but there was an undercurrent of amusement in his tone.

"We like to, um, celebrate the little things," Jane said. No more pajamas before seven. Never again.

"Like teeth!" Sophie cried. "I can't wait to tell all the kids about my tooth."

Jane gave a tired smile. "Teeth don't just fall out, Sophie. They have to get loose first. Your time will come."

"She wants to fit in with the other kids," Henry remarked. "I used to feel that way, too. Especially when there was a lot going on at home."

Jane frowned, feeling sad to think of Sophie just want-

ing to be like other kids. It was probably why she wanted Henry to join them for dinner: to have some semblance of a full family life again. Some of the older kids at the school came from divorced families, but off the top of her head, Jane couldn't think of any in the kindergarten class.

When had the dream turned into reality? She suddenly felt like she'd failed as a mother.

Sophie chattered all the way home, until Jane finally rounded the car into their driveway. In the backseat, Sophie held the apple core in one hand, a small piece of fruit in the other. "See? My tooth!"

Maybe it was the drive, or maybe it was the stress of everything else coming down on her, but Jane's patience was shot. "Sophie, I told you that I don't like you eating in the car, and I definitely don't like you playing with your food. Now eat that piece of apple, please."

"But Mommy—"

"Eat it, please," she repeated.

"But Mommy—"

Jane stared at the tiny white piece of apple. "Eat it now, Sophie. And I'm not going to say it again."

"But Mommy, it's my tooth!" Sophie burst into tears, and that's when Jane saw it. The small gap where Sophie's lower front tooth used to be.

She screamed, then clasped a hand to her mouth, biting down on the inside of her knuckles.

"You weren't joking!" Sophie shook her head and Jane took the tiny tooth from her daughter's hand. "Oh my goodness, honey, I'm sorry. I thought this was a piece of apple!"

Sophie started giggling through her tears and Jane felt her own eyes began to prickle. She could still remember

when this little tooth had popped through, just six months into Sophie's life. Now it was resting in her palm, its time served. Where had the years gone?

She suddenly felt Henry's gaze on her. His eyes were wide, but his lips twitched.

"You must think I'm crazy," she muttered.

He glanced from crying child to tearful mother and shook his head, but a small smile played at his lips. "I think you both are."

"You know what this means?" Jane said excitedly to Sophie. "The tooth fairy is coming tonight!"

"She is?" Sophie's eyes lit up as she wiggled to get out of her car seat.

Jane laughed and released the clasp, then climbed out of the car. She poked her head back in and met Henry's eyes. "You coming?"

"I wouldn't miss it," Henry replied.

CHAPTER
21

Henry watched as Jane spread a thin layer of children's glue over a dollar bill and sprinkled it with pink glitter. Her fine brow fixed in concentration, she waved it in the air a bit, tapped a finger over the surface, and then, satisfied that it was dry, tucked it into a drawstring jewelry bag.

"Ready?" she asked, grinning.

Henry startled. The loss of Sophie's first tooth was clearly a big event. Big enough to warrant screams and tears and a huge bowl of ice cream for dessert. Big enough to call for three bedtime stories instead of two and a special nightgown Jane quietly admitted she had been saving for Christmas, having purchased it on sale just last week. He hadn't assumed he'd be a part of the ritual, and he wasn't really sure he should be. Sophie was Jane's daughter. Jane's and Adam's, and he was just a bystander. A role he'd played far too often in life.

Jane was already walking down the hall toward the staircase, and he shoved his hands in his pockets, following her uncertainly. The front door was just ahead and

he had a sudden thought to walk right out it. He should go, now, before it was too late, before he became more entrenched in Jane's life than he should be. It was too easy to be lured in by the domestic bliss, to imagine how simple, easy, and fulfilling life could be.

The longer he stayed the more he hated the thought of leaving, returning to his empty hotel bed, eventually moving on to an equally quiet hotel room, and then another. Travel was meant to be shared, and he told himself he was the one sharing it through his words and photos and experiences. Who was he kidding? Not himself. Not anymore.

The first step creaked under Jane's foot and she froze, wincing as she craned her neck in the direction of Sophie's room at the far end of the upstairs hall. Henry realized he was holding his breath, not moving, getting far too invested in this little game than he had any right to.

But damn it if it wasn't sort of fun.

"She's still asleep," Jane whispered, taking the next step.

Henry nodded and crept close behind, allowing himself one sweeping glance at Jane's tight waist, the soft flare of her hips. His heart was beginning to pound as they neared the top hallway and approached the open door. Sophie had been so excited she could barely eat her dinner, and she'd insisted he help her search every toy box and drawer until she found her sparkly pink pen, which she used to write the tooth fairy a note, under his tutelage. Now, Jane carefully pulled it out from under Sophie's pillow, along with the tiny ring box containing her tooth. It read: *Dear Tooth Fairy, Please take good care of my tooth. I might want it back someday.*

Sophie barely stirred as Jane slid the jewelry bag con-

taining the glittery dollar bill under the pillow, but just as Jane was pulling her hand out, Sophie rolled over, causing Jane, then Henry, to drop to the floor.

Her eyes were wide when they met his, and they stared at each other, both breathing heavily. Jane pressed a finger to her lips with the hand that wasn't still wedged under the pillow. A sliver of moonlight peeked through the parted curtains, casting shadows on Jane's face, bringing out the sparkle of her eyes.

He had a sudden urge to lean over and kiss her, to taste her sweet lips, run his hands through her hair, hear his name on her breath. He swallowed hard, easing the tightness in his groin.

Jane pulled her hand free from the pillow and grabbed his arm. "Run!" she whispered, yanking him toward the door by his shirtsleeve. They dashed to it like a pair of robbers fleeing the scene of a crime, down the hall, and straight down the steps. By the time they hit the first floor, they were laughing so hard his ribs hurt.

"I bet you never knew parenting could be so much fun," Jane chided as they walked back into the kitchen. She opened a drawer and set the box containing Sophie's tooth inside.

Henry wasn't sure whether to be alarmed or touched by the gesture. He half wondered if she'd throw it out. That's probably what his mother had done.

But then, the tooth fairy had never visited his house.

He leaned against the counter. "For some, I suppose. You're an excellent mother, Jane."

She dropped her gaze, and her lashes fluttered softly. "Thanks. I just hope the judge agrees."

He hated the defeat in her tone.

"How can he argue with a glittering dollar bill?" Henry said lightly, but his chest pulled tight when he saw the strain in Jane's smile.

"I'm just so thankful this happened tonight and not on a night she was with Adam. If I had missed this..." She shook her head. "I would have been crushed." She let out a long sigh, suddenly looking tired. "That's the hardest part of all this. It's not about not being with Adam. It's about missing out on special things with Sophie. I'm already dreading the holidays. I've been dreading them since last year. Thanksgiving and Christmas used to feel so magical; now I just wish they didn't exist at all."

He felt the same way, for different reasons.

"You know, there was a time when I thought I could stay married to Adam, even though I was unhappy and even though I knew he was..." She met his gaze. *Cheating on her, the bastard.* "I didn't want Sophie to be shuffled across town, split between her parents. I thought I could keep us together, for her sake. Maybe for mine, too." She shrugged. "Eventually, I had to speak up."

This surprised him. All along, he'd assumed Adam had left Jane. He searched her face, noting the resilience in her eyes, the calm smile on her lips. She wasn't the same girl he'd once watched glide down the aisle on her father's arm. She was strong, and maybe even a little jaded. She'd get through this.

He hoped so, at least.

Someday he hoped to come to terms with his own divorce. For now, it was easier to shove it in a box and forget about it. Eventually, though, the truth came out, didn't it? No amount of hiding from the past could deny its existence, the part of you it claimed.

"Well, it was all worth it for one reason and one reason only." Jane smiled. "Sophie."

Henry gritted his teeth, frowning hard. He'd never experienced that kind of relationship with a parent, and he would have done anything to have it. "Do you really think they could take Sophie from you? You're her mother."

"And Adam's her father." Jane looked so sad and fragile that Henry kicked himself for saying anything at all. He wanted to stand up, put his arms around her, and tell her it was all going to work out. But he couldn't promise that. No one could.

He balled a fist, thinking of Adam. Of course he'd want to be close to his daughter, but at what price? It was selfish, and downright cruel. *But hadn't Adam always put himself first when it came to Jane?* he thought, thinking back on the scholarship she'd given up for him.

Jane deserved a man who showed her kindness, who appreciated her strengths and rewarded her for them, not punished her. She deserved someone who was here every day, wanting the simple joys of family life that Jane so clearly treasured.

Adam wasn't that man.

Henry ran a hand over his tense jaw. He wasn't either.

Jane opened the fridge and peered inside. "Can I offer you something to drink? Coffee? Wine? We might have some beer in here."

"Coffee will be great," he said easily.

Jane frowned but said nothing as she started a pot. He forced a breath, telling himself to calm down and not take it to heart, but he couldn't fight the part of him that hated the stigma in this town, the one he couldn't ever seem to shed, no matter how many years he'd been gone.

"I never drink," he offered. His voice was loud and assertive, as if confessing to something he'd been keeping a secret for a very long time. "I saw firsthand what alcohol could do to a person." Henry ran a hand over his jaw. Even the smell of the stuff made him feel like he was ten years old again, and he didn't want to go back to that place.

"I've seen Ivy with an occasional glass of wine—"

"She shouldn't." The words were barked out with such intensity that Jane was startled. Henry held up a hand. "Sorry. I just... I'm sensitive about this, as you can tell. Even though I knew my mom had problems, she was still my mother, and the only parent I ever knew. I hated the things people would say."

"In these small towns, it's hard not to be the subject of gossip at some point or another. It's one of the reasons I haven't told anyone about the custody situation."

Henry frowned. "Not even your family?"

Jane shook her head, and Henry leaned in over the kitchen island, suddenly wishing he was standing closer. She was wearing another soft sweater, but one that scooped down, revealing her collarbone. She was so pretty, so welcoming, so—

He cleared his throat. "But you're so close to your family."

"Exactly," Jane said. She scooped the coffee grounds into the filter and turned to him. "Grace is getting married in a few weeks, and Anna's busy with her new restaurant. Why burden anyone with my problems?"

Henry thought of his sister. Was this the way Ivy felt, too? Why she had waited so long to turn to him?

"Believe me when I say they'd want to know. They'd want to be there for you, Jane."

Jane shook her head with force. "No. I'll handle this on my own. They can't change the outcome anyway."

Her hair slipped down over her face, and Henry reached up and brushed it back. Catching her eye, he dropped his hand quickly.

"The coffee's ready," Jane said, reddening. Her back to him, she flung open a cabinet and grabbed two mugs. Their drinks in hand, he followed her into the living room, happy for the change of scenery. Things were getting too cozy in there, and here he could keep his distance.

He eyed the armchair where he'd slept just a week ago. He should sit there, keep a safe distance. Instead, he settled next to her on the couch.

On the end table was yet another picture of Sophie, this one taken on what appeared to be her first birthday.

"Did you and Adam ever discuss having more children?" Henry asked, and then regretted his words when Jane's brow creased. She blew on her coffee and sipped from her mug.

"Not really. Adam and I didn't talk about much. I was so in love with him when I was younger, I didn't stop to notice how different we were. Adam likes his freedom. He liked things on his terms."

"And taking the scholarship to the dance academy would have messed with his plans." Henry scowled.

Jane met his eye. "Exactly. He wanted to get married and go out and live his life and have a nice sweet woman who sat back and took care of him, no doubt the way his mother did."

Henry stiffened at the mention of Patty. He owed her a phone call. He owed her so much more than that.

"And what did *you* want?" Henry asked.

Jane blinked and stared at the fireplace before sliding him a strange smile. "Do you know, I can't remember the last time anyone asked me that. It's been so long since I've stopped to think of myself, I don't even know how to respond." She paused. "All I want is to keep my daughter with me. That's the only thing that's important."

"Do you want to remarry?"

Jane arched an eyebrow. "Do you?"

Henry pulled back against the throw pillows. "Touché," he said, when what he was really thinking was, *Hell, no.* He'd meant it when he told her he wasn't marriage material.

His mouth thinned. Wasn't family material either.

He suddenly felt prickly and out of place in this carefully decorated living room with the framed photos above the mantel and the baskets of toys in the corner. Jane deserved a man who wanted all this, a man who would come home at the end of the day and pick up the dolls and tuck Sophie into bed, and help Jane with the dinner dishes.

And that wasn't him. As much as he wished it could be, it wasn't.

He'd tried the family thing. Twice. And both times it had ended in disaster.

He set his mug on a coaster and rested his elbows heavily on his knees. He should go. Now. Before he did anything stupid.

He slid her a glance, noticing the way her full lips parted, her gaze steady, her lashes fluttering softly. A lock of hair slipped over her cheek, and without thinking, he reached up and tucked it behind her ear.

She gave a hesitant smile, her eyes widening slightly

as his hand grazed down her neck, his thumb tracing her delicate collarbone, trailing over to her shoulder. Her skin was soft and warm, her breath shallow, and her eyes searching. He lowered his gaze to her mouth, unable to hold back or fight this urge that had built for so long, and brought his lips to hers. He kissed her lightly, once, pausing for her to return the gesture, to show him this was all right, even though he knew it wasn't, even though he didn't want to stop anyway. She smelled like apples and honey, and her hair was so silky, her lips so tender. He tried once more. Hesitantly, she kissed him back, and his groin stirred with desire as he reached his arm around her waist, pulling her close, feeling her breasts against his chest and her hair in his face, lacing it through his fingers, tangled in his palm. He laced her tongue, tasting her mouth and breathing her air, wanting this moment to continue to forever.

Suddenly, Jane pulled back. "Sophie."

Henry felt a wash of shame. "Right. She might walk in—"

"No, she's calling out for me." Jane was quick on her feet, hurrying to the base of the stairs. "She never calls out."

Sure enough, he heard the cries, too, the ear-piercing screeches. "Mommy, Mommy, Mommy!" And there was Jane, on her feet, up the stairs, dropping everything. Even their kiss.

And damn it if that didn't make him want her even more.

"Mommy, mommy, the tooth fairy came! The tooth fairy came!" Sophie was running down the hall, meeting Jane at the top of the stairs, jumping up and down and

showing off her glittering bill. "And she took my tooth! And she left me money!"

"That's wonderful, sweetheart! But it's time to go back to bed, now."

"Can you sing me a song?" Sophie asked.

"Of course—"

"No. Him." Sophie pointed right at Henry, and he felt his stomach uncoil.

"Oh. Um." He turned to Jane for help, but she just shrugged. "Well, okay then."

He walked up the stairs more slowly, past Jane and that funny smirk on her face, and followed Sophie into her room. Ivy would have loved a room like this when she was little, he thought, taking in the pink billowy covers and the matching ruffled curtains. A pretty little doll-house was wedged in the corner, along with a small round table containing a tea set.

"Go on. I'm listening," Sophie said once she was tucked in to bed. She stared up at him, her eyes narrowing. "Sing me a lullaby."

Henry tried to think of a children's song and came up blank. His grandmother had sung to him as a child, but that was so long ago, the best he could do was hum the tune. He looked around the room for inspiration, trying to think of something that would meet a little girl's approval and finally did his very best version of "The Itsy Bitsy Spider." Sophie listened patiently through the entire thing, her little mouth curving into a pleased smile, but when he finally reached the end at long last, she said, "That's not really a bedtime song, but I enjoyed it anyway."

Henry blinked, then chuckled under his breath.

Jane was in the hall when he came through the doorway; no doubt she had been listening the entire time.

"Don't say a word about my singing abilities," he warned, wagging a playful finger at her.

"Actually I was just going to say you did a great job. You'll make an excellent father one day." Her eyes flashed with amusement, but Henry felt his zest for banter fade.

There would be no children in his future, and no wife either.

And it was time to remember that and get the hell out of this house before he ended up making a bigger mess of Jane's already complicated life.

"I should get going," he said, when she came back downstairs.

He looked away when Jane's brow crinkled. "Oh. Okay."

He strode purposefully to the living room, took his mug, and brought it to the sink in the kitchen.

"You don't need to help clean up," Jane said softly. She struggled to meet his eye as she hovered within arm's reach, so close he could kiss her again if he wanted to do, and God, did he. Her lips were red and full and her eyes a notch brighter than they'd been just minutes before, and all at once, Henry knew that something had shifted. They'd gone from a warm friendship to something more. Something dangerous.

"Don't worry about it," he said tightly, managing a smile as he move through the kitchen, his mind beginning to race. He'd crossed a line, lost control for a moment there.

He hesitated at the door as he slipped on his coat, wanting to say something that would take away the questions in her gaze, but wanting even more to kiss the frown from her mouth.

He stiffened. What good would that do for either of them? He could tempt himself, live the fantasy he'd longed for all his life, or he could turn his back, march outside and get back to reality. Move forward, no looking back, that's what he did best. It had worked for him so far, no reason to mess things up now.

No matter how much he wanted to.

CHAPTER
22

Ivy closed the door on her apartment and hurried down the back steps to her shop. Her leg was sore from the injection, but she still felt better than she had in weeks. Not that she'd be admitting this to Henry. He worried too much. It was one of the reasons she hadn't wanted to burden him, though now that she had, she was happy he was back in town.

Now, if only she could get him to stay . . .

Grace was standing outside the shop, peering in the windows, as Ivy came into the storefront. She hurried to the door, unlocked it, and let her friend in.

"You haven't been waiting long, have you?" She shivered against the biting October wind. "I just ran upstairs to . . . grab something to eat."

"I just got here, actually." Grace's green eyes sparkled as she rubbed her hands together. "So, is it ready?"

Ivy pulled in a long breath and let it out slowly. She'd spent most of the afternoon working on the sample centerpiece for Grace and Luke's wedding. Given how wishy-washy Grace had been about what she was looking for,

Ivy could only hope she liked the result, or at least gave a clear direction on what she didn't like about it.

"It's in the back room. I'll go get it."

She hurried away, worrying her bottom lip as she questioned her design. She'd taken liberties—something she tried never to do—but honestly, the situation called for it. Her sanity called for it. Most of the flowers Grace liked didn't go well together, and Ivy knew Grace's style well enough to know what would really make her happy. She hoped so, at least.

The phone rang as she made some last-minute adjustments to the arrangement. "Petals on Main," she answered hurriedly from the office phone. She wedged the receiver into the crook of her neck and tucked a rose stem deeper into the round mercury glass vase.

The woman on the other line began explaining her situation—florist fell through, last-minute wedding, Forest Ridge Country Club, a week from Saturday...Ivy scribbled the information down, but her hand stopped when the woman introduced herself. It was Kristy Richardson. The *other* woman.

Grace had mentioned that Adam was getting remarried soon. Ivy just hadn't realized it would be this soon. No wonder Jane had looked so upset the other day.

Ivy closed the door a crack. Even though Grace wouldn't know who she talking to, she felt suddenly sneaky and disloyal. Jane had been like a kid sister to her growing up, and still was in many ways. How could she show support to the people who had caused her friend so much pain?

"I'm sorry, but I'm unfortunately all tied up for that date," she fibbed.

"I'll pay you double," Kristy offered. "Please, I'm desperate."

Double? Ivy's heart skipped a beat at the thought, but no. She wasn't going to sell her soul or lose a friend over a paycheck. Once the house sold, her situation would be better anyway. She just had to hold on for a few months.

"I have a friend who's an event planner. I'll send them all your business. I happen to know she has four big holiday events coming up and is looking for a florist."

Ivy frowned. Kristy didn't back down easily, but then, was this surprising? She'd swept in on a married man. A married father. "I'm sorry, but perhaps your event planner friend could help you find another florist."

"They're all booked. And I've heard you're the best in a fifty-mile radius."

There were only about half a dozen florists in a fifty-mile radius, but nevertheless, Ivy sat a little straighter.

She checked herself. The woman was a sweet talker. And a bride. And Ivy didn't like working with brides, especially ones who stole her friends' husbands!

"I'm sorry but—"

"Triple. I know exactly what I want. Sahara roses and red berries. Very simple."

Ivy considered this. That was a very simple arrangement. And for triple her usual fee...

"I'm sorry," she said, lifting her chin, "But I'm booked solid through Thanksgiving."

She disconnected the phone with a sigh. She'd allow herself to think about the income for thirty seconds, and then she would banish it from her mind. It was dirty money, she told herself, bad friend money, and she would have felt terrible taking it.

Henry was generous and willing to help, and if things got too tight, she'd just have to take him up on his offer. She'd like to avoid that, though. He'd given her too much for too long. It was why she insisted on covering the arrangements herself, even when she'd hoped to use that money to get a bigger apartment. Why she'd insisted on staying in town, even when Henry begged her to leave. Henry's shift had lasted twenty-three long years. He shouldn't have to shoulder everything himself.

Of course Henry didn't even know the half of how bad things really were, financially speaking. If he did… Well, she didn't even want to think about what he'd do. Probably shut the whole place down. Probably wire the bulk of his savings straight to her doctor, setting up some payment plan to make sure she was taking care of herself.

She *was* taking care of herself. She knew her body, and besides, she'd gotten by on a reduced insulin schedule for a while. If she could just monitor her blood sugar for a few more weeks, until that house sold…

Ivy picked up Grace's sample and sailed into the storefront, holding her breath. Grace's eyes went wide when she saw the colorful display of lilies, tulips, roses, and berries that burst from the antique vase. Ivy set the heavy arrangement on the table and stared at her friend expectantly, waiting for her to say something, and hoping, hoping so much it hurt, that she was pleased. It had been Ivy's idea to tuck in the creamy roses for a touch of elegance, and the Queen Anne's lace as filler. This was her best friend's wedding—a day they had dreamed of since they were little girls sitting in Grace's pink bedroom, flipping through magazines or flopped down on her big, comfy

bed, chatting and giggling long into the night. She wanted this day to be perfect for Grace.

"What are these?" Grace asked, motioning to a small orange flower.

"Button mums," Ivy informed her. She raked her eyes over her friend's face, bracing herself for a reaction.

"I..." Grace inhaled and shook her head. "I love it. It's perfect!" There were tears in her eyes when she locked Ivy's gaze.

"Really?" Ivy reached out and embraced her friend. "I wasn't sure, since you hadn't mentioned roses in a while, and the berries—"

"I mean it, Ivy. It's perfect. I know brides must be especially stressful clients, so thank you."

Ivy couldn't stop herself from smiling. This was what she loved so much about her job—being able to brighten someone's day. As much trouble as wedding orders could be, when they came together, she had to admit they were particularly worthwhile. Especially when it was your oldest friend's special day.

"Oh, well, maybe you've helped change my mind. Maybe I'll start giving a little more input to brides and it will help things go smoother." She glanced at the door to make sure they were alone. "You'll never believe who just tried to hire me. Kristy."

Grace didn't blink. "The nerve! You said no?"

Ivy nodded, deciding not to mention the incentive Kristy was offering. "Of course. There's no way I could do that to Jane!"

Grace shook her head, scowling. "They just can't leave her alone, lately. I know Briar Creek's a small town, but a little consideration would be nice."

Ivy thought back on how Adam and Henry had dined at Rosemary and Thyme. She hoped her brother, at least, would be more sensitive going forward.

"Is Henry going to the wedding?" Grace inquired, and Ivy tipped her head. She hadn't even thought to ask, and now her stomach knotted with dread.

"I don't know," she replied honestly. "He's over at the house today overseeing the painting of the old siding."

She frowned, thinking of how lost Jane had seemed the other day. There was a sadness in her eyes she hadn't seen in nearly a year, and back then, Ivy hadn't a clue what was going on. Jane liked to hide behind smiles.

Ivy knew that look. She wore it herself too many times. Her entire life, it seemed, had been spent with her chin up, teeth bared, trying to focus on the beautiful things in life instead of the ugly ones.

"I'm worried about Jane," Ivy admitted.

Grace looked up from the bouquet she was still admiring, startled. "Jane? Because of the wedding?"

Ivy shook her head. "No... Well, yes, that, too. I'm not sure that's what's bothering her. I've always gotten the impression she was over Adam."

"I think it's more about disappointment at this point," Grace agreed. "He broke up their family and their life. She trusted him and he let her down. I think her feelings for him are much more negative than positive at this point. There's certainly not any longing for reconciliation."

"She just seemed really sad the last time I saw her. Remember that day she stopped in when we were going over the flowers?"

"She did seem a little distracted. She was the same way at the cake tasting." Grace's expression turned to one

of worry. "You don't think my wedding is upsetting her, do you? The timing is just terrible."

"Maybe that's all it is," Ivy said with a shrug, but she wasn't entirely convinced. There was almost a look of fear in Jane's eyes, and she'd left so quickly.

"I'll talk to her about it," Grace said firmly. "I've tried before, but she can be stubborn. I think she'd be happier if she got out more. Dated. Had a little fun." Her brow arched as she homed in on Ivy. "Speaking of…"

"Oh," Ivy laughed nervously under her breath. How could she think about dating right now when the only man she ever wanted was about to come back into her life, even if it was only for a night, and even if he might have a date on his arm?

She balled a hand at her side. She couldn't stand the suspense for another second.

"Maybe there will be some single guys at your wedding. For Jane." She added. Her chest began to pound as Grace mulled this.

"Maybe a few, but I can't say any of them are Jane's type, unfortunately. She knows most of them anyway."

Ivy was nodding far more quickly than natural, her breath catching in her throat as she waited for Grace to just come out with it already. Who was coming alone? Who was coming with a date? And who, God forbid, would the date be? Some equally brilliant surgeon with a Barbie doll figure and a long list of degrees from Ivy League schools?

Oh, who was she kidding? Brett Hastings had never given her the time of day. Why would he fall for her now? The town florist. He was off saving lives, and she was… Trying to save her own, she supposed sadly.

• • •

Henry finished hauling the last of the boxes from the kitchen to the giant Dumpster they'd rented and heaved a sigh. Setting his hands on his hips, he stared at the old house, trying to see it from an impartial view, not one tainted with unhappy memories and years he could never get back. Ivy had told him to be sure not to toss anything worth keeping, but she'd already taken the few photo albums their grandmother had maintained and any other nostalgic items when their mother had died last summer. Now all that remained were old chipped dishes, stained and damaged furniture, and the remnants of a time he wanted to put permanently behind him.

With one foot in front of the other, he forced himself back into the house through the creaking back door, which had half fallen off its hinges, and washed his hands under the kitchen tap. He dried them on his pants and turned, leaning back on the counter, to take in the room. The cupboards were cleared out, and the peeling vinyl floors had been ripped up to reveal a pine subfloor. Still, whoever bought this place would need a sharp imagination and a desire to make it their own. Henry could sink all his savings into a proper renovation, but that would take too much time, and it would be too much of an investment, financially and emotionally. He needed to get this place cleaned up and sold. He needed to see it changed. But he didn't want to be the one changing it. The less energy he put into it, the better.

He rubbed a hand over his jaw, his five o'clock shadow prickling under his palm, and then brought his fingers higher, tracing his cheekbone. They'd been standing here in the kitchen. He must have only been about twelve. His mom

was cooking dinner, a rare change from their usual bowl of store-brand cereal, and he was helping, taking the trash out to the road, doing his best to stay out from underfoot, to keep things calm. He snuck a bottle in the bag, like he tried to do most weeks, unless she was down to just a few and it was too obvious. Then he diluted the clear stuff with water. Anything to keep things from getting too far out of control.

He usually snuck out to the trash once it was dark, once she'd had a few and didn't notice or care what he was up to, or if he was even home, but that night she was standing there, at the stove, and she turned right before he finished sliding the bottle of wine into the bag. She'd snatched it back with one hand, and slapped him across the face with the other. His grandmother's ring, the one she always wore even though it was too big for her and the stone always slid around to her palm, sliced his cheek, and the cool, thin liquid spread fast.

He'd said nothing, just marched to the sink to wash the cut clean; then he took out the trash, taking his time on the long walk back up the drive, staring wistfully at the warm glow emanating from the Browns' house, wishing he could just run over and join them, but he couldn't. Mrs. Brown would see his face, and there would be questions, and he didn't want to have to answer them. Besides, he couldn't leave Ivy alone with their mother when she was like this.

When he came back into the house, the kitchen was empty. The frying pan of eggs was in the sink, facedown, and the burner was still going on the range. Henry flicked it off, grabbed some cereal and the jug of milk, and called out to his sister. When she asked what happened, he told her he'd slipped on the driveway.

He closed his eyes now and then turned on his heel,

letting the back door bounce against the frame as he hurried from the house. He nodded to the workers on his way to the car, and quickly slid inside and shut the door. He cranked the radio, attempting to drown out the sound and images, the memories he'd tried to forget.

The lights were on in the Browns' house, just like always, and before he had any time to reflect, he pulled the car out of his driveway and into theirs.

Mrs. Brown answered the door with a smile full of surprise. "Henry! We were just sitting down to eat."

"I don't mean to intrude," he said, shoving his hands deeper into his pockets.

"Nonsense!" She was already ushering him inside. The smell of chicken stew wafted through the warm air, and he grinned to himself. "I was going to call and invite you over, but you seemed so busy up at the house, I thought I'd better let you keep working." She led him back into the kitchen. "Roger, look who's here! I swear, it's like he could smell the stew and knew to stop by."

Mr. Brown laughed and stood and gave Henry a good hard handshake. His eyes crinkled at the corners, a little more lined than Henry recalled, but just as kind. Henry could still remember sitting at the table as the meal neared its end, while Roger and Adam planned to shoot hoops on the driveway until the sun went down, and later, when Roger paused at the door, looked at him squarely and said, "You coming or what?"

He'd told himself if he ever had a son, he'd play ball with him like that.

He stopped himself. There would be no son. Just like there would be no wife. He was a drifter, always hanging on the sidelines of other families' comfortable rou-

tines. He knew better than to try to make one of his own again.

The taste of Jane's lips was still fresh. Almost as clear as the hurt in her eyes when he'd left so abruptly. He should call her, stop by the bookstore and explain himself. A woman like Jane didn't need a guy like him. He had nothing to offer her.

Mrs. Brown smiled as she brought the pot of stew to the table and encouraged him to take a seat. He chatted with Roger, about work and travel, and football season, trying to banish Jane from his thoughts and the guilt that was gnawing at him with each tick of that grandfather clock in the hall. Photos of Sophie in a ballet costume hung from the fridge by magnets, and he averted his gaze, standing instead to fetch the plates and help set the table.

"You've seen the pictures of our granddaughter," Roger said proudly. "That little girl has me wrapped right around her finger."

"He built her that playhouse in the backyard," Patty added, pointing out the French doors that opened onto the deck. A bright pink life-size dollhouse consumed the base of an oak tree, its roof littered with golden leaves. "Took him four weekends, and that was before Sophie changed her mind from having it be purple to pink."

"I sure do hate the thought of Adam taking that job in Colorado," Roger grumbled, reaching for his fork.

"We're thinking of getting a second home there," Patty volunteered, her eyes turning hopeful once again.

Henry chewed his food, barely able to get it down. They were making plans, plans based on the outcome that Sophie would go to Denver with Adam and Kristy. If Jane knew...

"I imagine it's a difficult situation for everyone," he said.

"I've tried to talk Adam out of it," Patty said. "He said it was too big of an opportunity to pass up." She stared pensively at her fork for a few seconds before eating again.

"Ah, well, enough of the depressing talk." Roger cleared his throat. "It's not every day we have Henry back. I'm sure there are plenty more interesting things to talk about!"

Patty's smile turned shy. "Actually, since you stopped by the other week, I did a little bit of investigating and I found some of our old photo albums. Did you want to look through them after dinner? It might be fun."

She was offering him a glance into a part of his past he hadn't wanted to run from, but one he had somehow pushed aside all the same. "I'd like that very much," he said.

The Browns chatted and told stories through dinner, and soon the earlier tension had passed. It wasn't until the dishes were cleared and coffee was served with a plate of warm cinnamon streusel cake that the unwanted emotions started to emerge once more.

"I just love this one," Patty said, opening the first of several dusty old leather-bound photo albums. She tapped her finger on a picture of Adam and Henry—he couldn't have been more than eight at the time. "This was Halloween, do you remember? You boys went as Indiana Jones. You used jump ropes for lassos." She laughed.

"And look, this was later that year at Thanksgiving. There's you and Ivy." She was careful not to mention his mother, who had spent the day on the couch watching a taped broadcast of the parade. It had been the first

Thanksgiving he and Ivy had had since their grandmother passed—their mother hadn't bothered with holidays. After that year, they never missed Thanksgiving again. Well, until Henry left town.

He stayed late, longer than he intended, looking through old photos with a knot in his stomach, trying to make sense of why he felt so unsettled. He'd tried to make a family of his own, memories he could capture like Patty had, in a neat little album to pull out on a rainy day. He'd failed. Failed his wife. Failed himself. Not to mention his mother and sister.

There couldn't be any more casualties.

Patty stopped him at the door. "We'll see you at the wedding?" She thrust a thick, oversized envelope into his hand. "I suppose Adam's already invited you, but you should have a formal invitation."

Henry gritted his teeth and looked down at the square envelope in his hand. He grazed the pad of his thumb over the cardstock, wishing he could just hand it back, or maybe that he could look forward to going. He wasn't sure anymore.

When Adam had mentioned the wedding, Henry had assumed he'd be gone, back in San Francisco, maybe down in South America or in Europe, gathering research for his next article. Now, he was forced to make a choice. And either way he feared he was going to hurt someone he cared about entirely too much.

CHAPTER
23

Jane crossed one leg over the other and shifted in her chair, hoping to stop her hands from shaking as her attorney skimmed through the thick stack of files spread on his desk. Her palms were sweaty and she was breathing too hard, but she couldn't help it. Her pulse was pounding in her ears. She couldn't take the suspense much longer, even though every new bit of information from her lawyer only filled her with anger and fear.

"It appears that Adam plans to move to Colorado right after the first of the year."

Jane nodded abruptly. That was just over two months away. In two months, her entire world could be ripped out from under her. Again.

"Can the courts really make a decision that quickly?"

"Oh, certainly," Rob replied. He glanced down at his notes again and sighed. "They're asking for a court date of December first. We'll see if the judge agrees."

"Right after Thanksgiving," Jane murmured, feeling her frown deepen. It was Adam's year to have Sophie that

day. She'd gone along with it, thinking that she couldn't bear to have a Christmas without her child so soon after the divorce. But now, she stood to lose so much more than holidays.

"I know this is scary, but he's going to have a hard time proving that Sophie is better off going with him than staying where she is. She has an established routine here, a support system, and judges don't like to uproot children from their homes."

Jane tried to take solace in this but struggled. "What about my income?"

"The courts can't expect you to suddenly earn what Adam does. You were the stay-at-home parent for nearly five years. They understand."

"But you said he's citing his financial stability."

"The courts do take that into consideration, just as they did the first time around. The guardian ad litem will be visiting both you and Adam and meeting with Sophie to determine what is in her best interest."

"It's obviously in Sophie's best interest to leave things as they are. Briar Creek is her home. Her family and friends are here. Her aunts, all her grandparents. I've been with her every day since she was born. She has her routine, her school. Her bedroom with her things." Her voice was growing shrill and panicked just thinking of all the things Sophie stood to lose. All the things Adam wanted to take from her.

"And this is why it's best for you to focus on that. Continue giving her the life she has always known. If she goes to ballet class, take her to ballet. If she has dinner with her grandmother once a week, make sure to keep that up. For a child as young as Sophie, courts frown on big changes."

"What about the family situation?" Jane asked, balling a fist in her lap. "Will it hold any weight that Adam and Kristy are getting married and that Sophie will have a sibling next summer?"

"It will certainly be taken into consideration, I can't deny that."

That was all she needed to hear to feel the familiar burst of panic shoot through her. She sat shaking, legs crossed and hands clamped, every nerve in her body on high alert. Adam had a good job, a new family in the works, and she was just a single mom with nothing to fall back on.

Even if she asked her mother for money, it wouldn't reflect a stable lifestyle, not the way Adam did. Besides, Kathleen worked for herself, decorating homes on a referral basis. She was hardly in a position to share what had been left to her by Jane's father.

She'd just have to sit tight. Go about her day and hope to God it was enough.

"When will the guardian ad litem be visiting?" She dreaded the meeting now as she did last winter, when she'd watched through the window, waiting for the car to pull up and her life to be judged.

"Soon, assuming the courts agree to the hearing date."

Jane nodded and stood. Her neck and shoulders were cramped with tension, but she couldn't relax. The meeting was over, and a strange sense of longing came over her. She didn't know what she'd expected to come from it, but somehow she'd hoped for closure, for finality, for something more than this endless limbo and fear. She was exhausted. Every bone in her body ached, and her head was pounding from lack of sleep. She wanted nothing

more than to go back to her house, crawl into bed, and never get out of it. But she couldn't. She had two classes this afternoon, and for that, she should be grateful.

"Just keep doing what you're doing, Jane. Live your life. Love your daughter. You're doing the best you can. Leave the rest to me. That's what you're paying me for."

Right. That's where all the money she should be spending on Sophie was going—to the lawyer she was forced to hire thanks to stupid Adam.

Tears blurred her vision as she made her way out into the lobby. She managed a watery smile as she passed the receptionist, and somehow made it to her car. Adam was selfish. Always had been. He did what he wanted without any consideration for the casualties. Even his own daughter.

He may be fighting for custody of Sophie, but she was fighting for her daughter's well-being. She had to focus on that.

Despite the attorney's encouraging words, Jane's heart was still heavy by the time she rounded the bend into Briar Creek. She glanced at the clock on the dashboard, deciding she could go home, and no doubt sit by herself and let her mind run wild with disastrous possibilities, or she could visit her mother or one of her sisters. She decided to stop by the bookstore. It wasn't often she had a chance to sit and enjoy a cup of coffee, and she needed an energy boost if she was going to get through her four o'clock class.

Grace was ringing up a tall stack of books and a large coffee to go when Jane entered the shop a few minutes later. Her older sister smiled on instinct, but then jerked

in surprise when she swept her eyes on Jane's attire. Darn it. She should have thought to change first. Black dress pants called for suspicion. As did the matching V-neck sweater. It was a far cry from her usual attire, and Grace knew it, too.

"Look at you!" she cried as Jane grew nearer. "What have you been up to today dressed like that?"

Jane shrugged. "I thought I'd mix things up, dig some old stuff out of the back of my closet..."

Grace arched a brow, and Jane stifled a sigh. She wasn't buying it, and why would she? Jane was stuck in a rut. Even when she'd stopped into a few boutiques on Main Street and treated herself to some new clothes, she knew in her heart she had it all wrong. Those peasant tops, she later learned, weren't meant to be tucked in. She'd only discovered that when, showing up at Anna's, grinning and feeling confident, her sister's eyes had widened, her mouth pinched, and her hands quickly unstuffed the soft cotton material from Jane's waistband. And those jeans she had thought were at the pinnacle of current fashion were, it now seemed, the fashion for the fifty and over crowd, as was the entire shop, which had looked so cute from the window. Apparently back pocket design was important. As was the color of the denim itself. And nothing was supposed to taper, unless it fell under the category of skinny jeans, which just...confused her. Did they really succeed in making you look skinny, or just the opposite?

She knew Grace, having lived in New York for so many years, tolerated all this under a thin veil of impatience, and she would like nothing more than to make Jane over. But Jane liked her yoga pants. And she liked her routine. Wasn't enough being shaken up already?

"My, my, Jane, if I didn't know better, I might think you were making a deliberate effort." Grace's smile was sly. "Are you meeting someone special?"

Jane barked out a laugh, but her face flushed with heat when she considered how close to the mark Grace really was. There was someone special in her life, or there had been. Sort of. When she wasn't consumed with worry about the custody battle, she let her mind wander back to that night with Henry, to the feeling of his lips on hers, the way his skin was warm and smelled of spice.

It had felt good. Better than that: It had felt right. But it wasn't right.

She bit down on her lip, trying not to frown. She hadn't seen Henry since Saturday, when he'd abruptly left, barely even saying goodbye, much less explaining himself. Clearly he was regretting the kiss, just like she should be.

She brought a finger to her lips and just as quickly snatched it away. So he was a good kisser. Lots of men probably were. Men who weren't connected to her ex-husband. Men who weren't just passing through town.

"I had a meeting about Sophie," she explained, hoping to keep things vague and get off the topic of her love life, or lack thereof. Catching the flash of concern that sparked in her sister's eyes, she quickly added, "School stuff. No big deal."

No big deal at all. *Just my louse of an ex trying to take my child halfway across the country.* Nothing she couldn't handle on her own.

Grace filled a mug with coffee and handed it to her. "I'm glad that's all it was. For a minute there, I was worried. Are you sure everything's okay, Jane? I get the feeling something's bothering you."

Jane took her time adding cream and sugar to her coffee at the antique console next to the counter. If she met Grace's eyes, there was a strong chance she wouldn't be able to compose herself any longer, and she couldn't fall apart now. Not in the middle of Main Street Books, for gossip to stir and circle back. Not when Grace kept absentmindedly glancing down at her engagement ring like that.

"I'm just tired is all." She forced a smile. "The coffee helps. I think I'll take a chair over near the window, if you'd care to join me."

The door jangled and Grace let out a heavy sigh. "Keep a spot open for me. I could use a break myself."

Jane moved to the small round table near the window, the very same one Henry had occupied on his visits here. She smiled softly, pushing back the pull in her chest when she thought of the way he'd looked, sitting here, bent over his laptop in concentration, and unbuttoned her coat. Her back was to the room as she positioned it on the back of her chair and slid into her seat, but as she lifted the mug of steaming, rich coffee to her lips, she jolted in surprise. Adam's mother was standing right beside her; she hadn't even seen her come in. The coffee splattered on the table and she frantically began swiping it with the lone napkin she had thought to grab. She fumbled in her handbag, looking for the packet of tissue, and began sopping up the mess.

Patty Brown's hands appeared next to hers, clutching a thick pile of napkins. Jane felt her breath catch as her ex-mother-in-law wiped up the last of the spilled mess, wishing, for once, she didn't have to be kind. It would be so much easier if Adam's family were as terrible as him.

If Patty could have stayed away, the way she'd done since last December, when their separation was announced.

"Thanks," she said a little breathlessly. She took her seat again, her smile frozen on her face.

"I didn't mean to startle you," Patty said gently. She hesitated for a moment. "Can I get you another coffee?"

Jane dismissed the offer with a wave of her hand. "It's fine. Grace is joining me soon. She'll bring me a new cup." She glanced over her shoulder at her sister, who stood with hands on hips, eyes stern, mouth thin, and felt a little better.

"Perhaps I could sit with you until then," Patty hedged.

Jane looked up in alarm, but the weariness in the woman's eyes halted the excuse on her lips before it had time to fully form. She nodded. "Okay."

Patty seemed nervous as she pulled out the chair and slipped into it. She didn't remove her coat, and she clutched her handbag in front of her with both hands. "This shop has never looked better," she mused, glancing around. "I'd heard about the changes you and your sisters had made. I...didn't want to overstep and come in before."

"I'm surprised to see you," Jane admitted.

"I saw you through the window, and...well, I feel bad, Jane. I wanted to reach out to you many times over the past several months, but I didn't know how. I...didn't want to make things worse." She tensed. "I don't think Adam would be happy to know I was here, but I thought, if we just bumped into each other..."

Jane shared a smile with her. "Literally," she joked, hoping to lighten the mood. It was what she did best. She made difficult situations easier for everyone around her. But what about herself? Who was looking out for her?

Grace, she thought, glancing to her left again. And, maybe...Henry.

"I'm sure you know about everything that's going on," she said.

Patty closed her eyes. "As a mother myself, I can't even imagine. It's not easy for Roger or me either. We love having Sophie close by."

Jane didn't like the way she was talking, as if Adam would win, and Sophie would move to Denver. She clung to the lawyer's words, feeling her conviction grow, and took a sip of what remained of her coffee. "Nothing has been determined yet."

"I know I shouldn't get involved, but I haven't been able to stop thinking of you all these months, especially these past few weeks. I figured you might think I didn't like you anymore or that I was mad at you, and I wanted to make sure you knew that wasn't true. You were like the daughter I never had. You might not officially be a part of our family anymore, but that doesn't erase the time we had together. Or our connection through Sophie."

Jane swallowed the knot that had wedged in her throat. "Thank you. That means a lot." And it did, for some reason. It would have been so natural for Patty to side with Adam, to take a firm stance.

Maybe everything wasn't as black-and-white as Jane thought. Maybe things were a lot more muddled. Like Henry.

"Sometimes I think back on the days when you and Henry and Adam would sit around my kitchen. I loved the sounds of your laughter. The house feels so quiet now." Patty smiled sadly. "Henry came to dinner last night," she offered, brightening. "It was almost like old times."

Jane blinked, and waited for her heartbeat to resume at normal speed before she spoke again. "How nice. Yes, I know he's back in town."

Grace came to the table and set a proprietary hand on the back of Jane's chair. "Is everything okay here?"

Patty smiled kindly at her. "Grace, it's good to see you. The store looks lovely. You've done a wonderful job with it."

Grace's expression was tight. "Thank you." She stared at the other woman, and Jane shifted in her chair.

"Well, I should go," Patty said. "It was good seeing you, Jane. I...wish you well, regardless of how everything turns out."

Jane's pulse flickered as Grace turned to her quizzically. "What does that mean?"

"Grace." But her sister wasn't listening, and from the glint of determination in her eye, it looked like she wasn't going to let this drop.

"What do you mean?" she asked Patty.

"Grace, I know you're probably mad at me, and you have every reason to be. You're sticking by your family the same way I have. That's what makes all this so difficult." She glanced at Jane desperately. "I don't wish this on you, Jane. I'm sorry. I truly am."

She glanced from one sister to the other, ducked her chin, and hurried from the store. Jane closed her eyes, feeling the dread sink in, sensing Grace's eyes on her the entire time.

"Jane? Do you have something to tell me?"

She should say no, she should make an excuse, smile brightly, follow Patty's lead, and flee the scene. But she couldn't fight it anymore. "Adam's moving to Denver," she said flatly.

Grace jutted her bottom lip, digesting information. "Oh. Well, I'd think you'd be glad."

"He wants Sophie to come with him."

Grace's gasp was audible. "But you're her mother! He can't do that! Can he?"

"That's for the judge to decide," Jane said miserably.

"Oh my God, Jane. Oh my..." Grace shook her head and reached over, squeezing both of Jane's hands in her own. "How long have you known?"

"A couple weeks," Jane admitted.

"And you didn't tell me." Grace's eyes crinkled with sadness.

"I didn't tell anyone." Well, except Henry, but he already knew from Adam. Her stomach stirred at the thought.

"When are you going to learn that you have to let people in?" Grace reprimanded.

"You're getting married!" Jane cried. "This is a special time! You're my sister—"

"And you're mine," Grace said sternly. "All your life you've been taking care of everyone else. Sometimes it's okay to let people take care of you."

Jane nodded, thinking back on the kindness Henry had shown her with his suggestions for the dance studio, the way Sophie lit up when he gave her attention.

She could do this on her own, but Grace was right. Sometimes it felt good to let someone take care of her for a change.

CHAPTER
24

Saturday mornings at Hastings were always busy, and usually Jane avoided the old diner, opting instead to have breakfast at her home or take an early shift at the bookstore before her classes. This morning, however, she'd been awake since three, waiting for the sky to turn gray, for the first streak of light to peek through her curtains. But as much as she waited for the new day to come, a large part of her dreaded it.

Today was the day her ex-husband was getting remarried. And she, well, she was still sleeping on her side of the bed, clinging to her old routine. Today it stopped.

At five, she flung off the blankets and stuffed her feet into her bunny slippers. She sighed, pausing as she always did when she realized all it took anymore to make her bed was to pull up her side of the covers and toss on the pillow sham.

The house was quiet without Sophie's presence, a haunting reminder of things to come, and Jane struggled to make coffee or engross herself in the early-morning news.

She needed a distraction, and the first place to open in Briar Creek was Hastings.

She dressed in her best clothes—newish jeans, boots Grace had *strongly* encouraged her to buy at a fall sale last month, and a soft open cardigan that landed at her knees. She rarely wore jewelry, but today she slipped on a necklace and earrings, and she applied an extra dab of gloss to her lips, even though it was barely seven.

She was the first person in Hastings, but already the clatter from the kitchen was a welcome opposition from the eerily quiet streets. The lampposts along Main Street still glowed, and Jane sat at the counter, feeling bold.

There would be talk today, no doubt, murmurs about the wedding at the Forest Ridge Country Club, about sweet little Sophie in her navy blue velvet dress, and poor Jane, left on her own for the day, no doubt hiding her pain behind that smile…

She could have stayed inside all day. In her pajamas with the curtains drawn. But that would be letting them win. Letting *him* win. And really, what had she lost? A husband who had consistently put his needs before hers? A man who disregarded her feelings, passions, voice? A person who had betrayed her, lied to her, and then tried to take the one good thing he had ever given her?

Good riddance. Today was the official end of her time with Adam. Tomorrow he was someone else's problem.

She ordered a coffee while she skimmed the menu, deciding to treat herself to a Belgian waffle with chocolate chips, whipped cream, and strawberries. She'd spent far too much of her life shelving her whims. The door behind her opened, and in came the elderly couple from her ballroom class. The wife's eyes went wide when she

spotted Jane, and she muttered something to her husband who, being hard of hearing and clearly grouchy about being whispered to, bristled until his wife said loudly, "Her husband is getting married today! To the woman he was sleeping with! When they were still married! And they have a love child! That's right, the bride's pregnant! It's a shotgun wedding!"

"Where's the reception?" her husband asked.

"Forest Ridge Country Club!"

"Fancy."

Fancy indeed, Jane thought miserably.

The woman looked at Jane, tutted loudly, and shook her head, her eyes brimming with pity as she slid into a booth.

Jane smothered a sigh and turned back to her menu. She'd throw in some chocolate sauce for good measure.

She sipped her coffee and listened to the sounds of the diner. It filled up quickly, mostly couples settling at the tables behind her, and every once in a while there was the slight mention: "There's Jane. Her husband's getting married today." Or sometimes, "Her husband's getting married today to that homewrecker." That made her smile, even though she did start to wonder how she would turn and leave and face the crowd, who were no doubt watching her with pity or sheer curiosity. She told herself their intentions were in the right place, but it didn't make it any easier. Someday she'd like to go back to just being Jane Madison. Not Jane Madison, whose husband had made the town fool out of her.

Sharon Hastings came around through the back and tossed her a big smile. "Well, isn't this a bright spot in my day! Can't say I see you in here much. What's the

occasion?" Her eyes went wide and she clamped a hand to her mouth. "Oh, Jane. Forgive me. I wasn't thinking—"

Jane laughed softly, shaking her head. "It's fine."

"Is it really fine?" a deep, husky voice next to her said.

She turned to see Henry, staring down at her, his blue eyes glimmering with challenge, his brow furrowed. Be still her heart. There it was. That flutter. She couldn't stop it if she tried, and oh, did she want to, almost as much as she wanted to stop staring at the flecks of green around his pupils, and the slight quirk of his full mouth.

"Is this seat taken?" he asked, already sitting down, and Jane quickly tossed her hair over her shoulder.

She caught Sharon's eye just as she realized what she was doing. A wash of embarrassment shot through her. For the love of Pete, she was flirting. Primping. Whatever you called rolling your shoulders and smoothing your hair and running your tongue along your teeth, hoping there wasn't any food caught, and wishing there was still some smidgen of lip gloss left.

Okay, so she was pleased to see him. But she deserved to indulge a little this morning. Her ex-husband was getting remarried to a blonder, chicer woman after all, and no, it hadn't gone unnoticed that despite all her time in the dance studio and her strict diet, Jane was somehow a good five pounds heavier than the pregnant woman, whose wedding dress was no doubt a size two.

"How are you doing?"

Jane shrugged under the heat of his stare. "Fine."

His mouth slid into a lopsided smile that didn't quite meet his eyes. "I'm beginning to think *fine* is your favorite word."

"What do you want me to do? Fall apart? Break down crying?"

"I guess I just want you to feel you can be honest with me," he replied.

Well, he was one to talk. It had been two weeks since their kiss, and he was yet to tell her what it had meant.

"If you must know, I'm beginning to feel like everyone in this room is staring at me or trying to pretend they aren't."

Henry shifted his gaze to the right and then to the left. "Welcome to my childhood," he muttered, glancing down at the menu.

Jane frowned, realizing how it must have felt, to grow up listening to people talk about you, say things about your mother. It was a powerless feeling, and one she didn't enjoy, but it wasn't one she could hide from anymore. Not like Henry.

She glanced at the clock behind him as he placed his order, and her heart skipped a beat when she spotted the time. Six hours to go until the ceremony. She couldn't wait for it to be over with.

"How's Sophie doing?" Henry asked, and Jane hesitated, searching his face for a hint of…something… in connection with that kiss. It seemed he was making a deliberate effort to keep the conversation neutral. She supposed she should be grateful for that. She was already on edge this morning, and potential disappointment was probably better left for another day.

"She's good," she said, deciding not to dwell on her daughter's current whereabouts. Sophie had been so excited for today, and it had taken every ounce of willpower to pretend to match her daughter's enthusiasm.

"No more visits from the tooth fairy?" He grinned, and Jane skirted her gaze from those lips. To think they

had been on her, on her mouth, her neck, her skin...She pinched her lips tight.

"Not yet, but she does have a wiggly one."

"Another to add to your collection," he said, smiling warmly.

"We've—"

"How's class?"

Jane laughed, but Henry seemed saddened somehow, or distracted maybe. He held up a hand. "You first."

She had been going to say they'd missed seeing him around, but something in his eyes, the guarded way he watched her, made her rethink that. He was holding back, and sometimes the unspoken was the most obvious form of communication.

She wanted to ask, *What happened the other night?* "How's the article coming along?" she said instead.

"I've been tied up a lot with the house, but...the article's been a nice distraction. There's a lot to like about this town, I've found."

"Briar Creek has a way of luring people in and keeping them here."

Her grin faltered. Something in the set of Henry's jaw told her nothing could keep him here, or bring him back. Not even Ivy, and probably not her.

Henry shifted in his seat and took a long swig of his coffee. It was easy to fall into the routine small-town life could offer. There were fewer choices about what to eat, where to eat, where to go. Everywhere you turned was a friendly face or, more accurately, someone who knew you. Or thought they knew you.

He bit back on his teeth. He could idealize it all he

wanted, but no amount of wishful thinking could undo the dark side of this town.

Ivy wanted him to stay, of course. She hadn't come out and said it, but she would, in her own subtle way. But just as she was compelled to make a better life for herself here, he was determined to do that elsewhere. He loved her, but it wasn't enough to make him stay.

Nothing could make him stay.

He shifted his eyes over to Jane as she tucked a strand of hair behind her ear. He swallowed hard, fighting against the tightening in his groin at the curve of her lips, the way her lashes fluttered ever so softly when she blinked, the way her eyes came alive and crinkled at the corners when she smiled at him.

He pulled in a breath, ready to come out with the heavy, hard truth of the day, but Sharon Hastings was sliding his toast to him then, and the moment was lost.

"I'm surprised to see you here, actually," Jane said, her smile slipping a notch. "I wasn't sure if you'd be going to Adam's..."

Henry set his fork down before he'd even taken a bite of his omelet. *Here it comes.* He turned to face her square in the eye, feeling a pang rip through his chest at the curve of her mouth, knowing that what he was about to say would steal that smile from her lips. "I am, actually. I thought I'd stop by before I started getting ready."

Jane did a poor job of masking her surprise. "Oh. I see. Of course." She shook her head, a pink blush crawling up her cheeks as she reached for her mug with both hands.

"Jane."

She continued shaking her head as she sipped her coffee, her eyes darting to him before glancing away again.

He set a hand on her arm, but she stiffened under his touch, and he pulled away.

He ran the hand through his hair and heaved a sigh that rolled through his shoulders. Yep. Asshole of the year. Right behind his best buddy Adam, of course. Wasn't this what she'd expected of him? Wasn't this what she'd feared? He'd let her down, just as he knew he would. It was inevitable.

"You're upset," he said, looking at her squarely.

Still she refused to meet his eye. "What? No. Just…" She blinked rapidly as the color in her cheeks rose, and it was then that he noticed the way her eyes shone with tears. But her smile, God help him, her smile was never brighter.

It was that smile that got him every time. That smile that made him want to pull her against his chest and never let her go. That smile that made her impossible to forget. No matter how much he wanted to.

"Jane, please let me explain."

"It's fine. It's fine." She stood, her smile widening against the tears that began to fall, and she furiously wiped them away with the back of her hand, fumbling in her bag for her wallet. She tossed a twenty-dollar bill down on the counter—certainly far too much even with a generous tip—and started shoving her arm into her coat.

"Jane, please. Let's talk."

"There's nothing to talk about," she said, head bowed as she fumbled with the buttons. He tried to see through the curtain of hair that fell over her face, shielding her from him, but she was determined to shut him out. And maybe he should let her.

"Have a nice time at the wedding," she said, her eyes suddenly hard with one last flash on his before she turned

on her heel and marched to the door. Henry watched in dismay as heads at every table swayed to watch her exit and then swiveled back to him. He glowered at them, then quickly slapped another twenty down on the counter, grabbed his jacket off the back of the stool, and hurried after her.

His heart was thundering in his chest, with anger at himself, at this town, at the impossible situation he was put in. The murmurs started as he reached the door, and he swung it open, ready to run out and chase after her, but he turned, one hand on the door, and faced the room first. "The show's over! But please, don't let that stop you from gossiping about it long into the afternoon."

The entire room fell into a hush, but Henry didn't linger for further reaction. Jane was already halfway down the block, her long legs moving at a speed he struggled to match, even at a light jog.

"Jane, wait. Jane!"

She didn't stop until he caught up with her and grabbed her by the arm, forcing her to whirl around and face him head-on. "Leave me alone," she snapped, but the tears streaking her face made him want to do anything but that. She ran a hand over her face, pushing back the strands of hair that whipped in the wind and clung to her wet cheeks. "I'm sure they're all talking about this right now," she said bitterly, jutting her chin to the corner.

Henry shoved his hands in his pockets and gave her a shrug. "Who cares if they do?"

"I thought you cared about stuff like that." Jane sniffed.

"I did," he admitted. "But now I see that I shouldn't have. Let them all think what they will. I'm not going to worry about them. I'm worried about you."

She gave him a long, hard look. "You're worried about me. I told you; I don't want your concern. I don't need you to take care of me."

His eyes roamed her face, noting the way her tears suddenly stopped; her posture straightened just a notch, but noticeably. Her skin was pale in the cool sunlight, and her eyes were electric.

"I don't want to hurt you, Jane," he said, his voice gruff. He cleared his throat and looked away, down the street to the town he'd sworn he'd never come back to, to the town he would soon be leaving again.

He should have kept his distance. Done the right thing from his first day back. Instead he'd let himself dare to believe and hope that this time around it could be different. And maybe it could be, maybe the town had changed, but he hadn't. He was still the same scruffy kid from the rundown house. Still letting people down. Still wishing for things that weren't rightfully his and never would be.

"Do you really want to go to this wedding?" she asked, and his heart skipped a beat at the pain in her voice.

"I think I should go," he said honestly, grinding out the words, struggling to lock her gaze.

She held his eyes for a bit and then lowered hers to the ground, nodding slowly. "The thing about you, Henry, is that you can always be counted on to do the right thing. You're loyal. No one can fault you for that."

Except her, he thought. He opened his mouth to say something and then clamped it shut again. Jane was backing up, walking toward her car, and every nerve in his body was on edge, wanting to run after her, to get in her car and go to her cozy, welcoming home, to sit at her kitchen table and hear her laugh, and stare at the photos

on the wall and wish that he could have been a part of them. To kiss her soft mouth, breathe her sweet scent.

But he wouldn't. Adam was his oldest friend. The Browns were the closest thing to a real family he had ever known, and he was expected there. And he didn't like letting down the people he cared about.

Which was why he never, ever should have kissed Jane Madison.

How are you holding up?"

It was already a week after Adam and Kristy's wedding, and people were still stopping to ask her that question, usually accompanied with prolonged stares of disbelief long after she reassured them she was fine, just fine.

Anna gave a small smile as she waited for Jane to reply, and Jane pushed aside the minor annoyance she had felt at being asked the question. It was a knee-jerk response by now, after a week of hiding in her house. She shouldn't have given such an emotional reaction at the diner last Saturday. It was out of character. Not like her. But she'd been on edge, and Henry had hit a nerve. In one sentence he had confirmed everything she had feared. That she did, in fact, have feelings for him, and that she absolutely shouldn't have let them develop.

"I'm trying to stay focused on my day-to-day routine," Jane told her sister. She took a sip of her sparkling punch and settled back against the couch in her mother's living room. The entire house had been transformed for Grace's

bridal shower, and even though their mother was a professional interior decorator, Jane still couldn't help but be taken by surprise at the thought and care that went into the party.

Bunches of creamy white balloons were hung in each corner, and every surface was anchored with a beautiful arrangement of apricot-colored roses. The dining room table had been turned into a buffet, full of silver trays and tiered stands, with beautiful finger sandwiches, colorful salads, and pastries, cookies, and cakes that looked too pretty to eat. Pink Champagne was flowing, classical music played softly in the background, and all of Grace's closest friends were gathered for the special event.

Anna leaned in closer and lowered her voice. "Has the lawyer said anything more about the hearing?" She looked just as concerned today as she had been when Jane finally came clean with her about the custody battle a few hours after talking to Grace.

"Just that the date has been set for early December." Jane chased away the hard knot in her stomach with another sip of punch. Champagne would probably be a much better solution for her nerves right now, but she needed to stay focused and think straight. She'd made enough foolish decisions in recent weeks.

She glanced at Ivy, who was chatting with Grace, happily sipping her Champagne and munching on one of those gorgeous French macaroons Anna had made. Jane took a particularly pretty lavender one from her plate and nibbled it. Somehow, the taste was good enough to distract her for a few seconds.

"I could strangle that bastard," Anna hissed, and Jane coughed on her cookie.

She set it back on the plate and nailed her sister with a look of warning, but a warm glow filled her. "I won't tell." She smiled, and Anna did, too.

"You still haven't told Mom then?"

Jane shook her head. "I think this wedding is complicated for her. She's happy for Grace, but Dad's absence is too obvious." She paused, thinking that Anna could very likely be getting married soon, too, from the way things were going with Mark. "I feel guilty that Grace won't have Dad there to walk her down the aisle. It doesn't seem right that it was wasted on me."

"Wasted on you!" Anna narrowed her eyes. "You had a beautiful wedding, and Dad was thrilled to be a part of it. It's not your fault the marriage ended."

"No," Jane said sighing. "It wasn't."

She eyed her sister. "You didn't like Adam, did you?"

"Oh, now. Don't say that." Anna picked up a miniature quiche and stuffed it in her mouth in an obvious effort to avoid having this conversation.

"You didn't. It's okay. I understand."

Anna dabbed her mouth with a monogrammed cocktail napkin and met Jane's eyes with a guilty smile. "I'm sorry, Jane. It wasn't that I didn't like him. Maybe... maybe my memory is just tainted based on everything's that happened."

Nice try, Sis, Jane thought, *but I'm not buying it.* "Grace didn't really like him either," Jane said. She suddenly realized that at every family gathering, holiday meal, or social function, Adam had mostly sat silently at her side, not making an effort with any of them, and certainly not trying to form a bond the way she had with his family.

"None of us really knew Adam," Anna eventually said. She peered into the distance, as if trying to make sense of it. "He wasn't very engaging. He was very..."

"Cold?" Jane volunteered.

"I was going to say aloof," Anna said kindly. "He was very quiet and—well, sometimes it bothered me that he just didn't seem very interested in making an effort for you."

"Like taking me to my prom?" Her heart panged when she thought of Henry, standing there on her porch steps, wearing that bashful grin.

"I'm sorry, Jane. You deserve better. You deserve someone who will do those little things, because they're important to you and because, well, because you're important to him."

"Why didn't any of you tell me how you felt?" Jane demanded.

"You were happy, Jane, and so we thought maybe there was something there that we just didn't see. No one really knows what goes on behind closed doors."

Perking up, Anna said, "There's a whole life ahead of you. Look at me! Who'd have ever thought I'd be back together with Mark, and running a restaurant with him, too? Life is full of surprises."

Jane gave a halfhearted shrug. She'd had just about as many surprises as she could handle right now. She didn't need any excitement or thrill. She just wanted security, and comfort, and maybe a guy who did little things for her once in a while.

A guy who would take her dancing, help her out when her business was struggling, maybe even warn her about the huge mistakes she was about to make in life.

But not a guy whose loyalty stopped short.

"Jane, Anna! Come sit with us, we're opening gifts!" Grace was waving them over from across the adjacent living room, where she already sat at in the antique rocking chair passed down from their grandmother. Their mother had stripped and refinished it, bringing back the beauty of its natural grain. Jane hoped to pass it down to Sophie someday. But now, she wondered if it would hold the same meaning. If Sophie went to Denver, her time spent in this big Victorian house would be fleeting, reserved for a few visits a year.

The sisters stood and joined the group, wedging into the sofas and armchairs. Jane winked at Sophie, who sat on Rosemary's lap, happily munching a cookie and ignoring the crumbs that were sprinkling down on her purple smocked dress. As Grace reached for the first gift, Sophie's hazel eyes widened and she leaned forward, soaking it all in.

The first gift was from Anna: a beautiful porcelain cake stand engraved with Grace and Luke's wedding date. Grace fluttered a hand at her chest and grinned at their sister. "It suddenly seems real now. I'm actually getting married in two weeks!"

"Open mine next!" Sophie cried out impatiently, and all the women laughed.

Grace searched through the beautifully wrapped boxes until she found the small one Jane had carried in. She opened it slowly, claiming the pearlescent paper was too pretty to rip, but her hands stilled as she lifted the lid to the box.

"You know the old saying, something old, something new, something borrowed, something blue," Jane offered.

"Something old," Grace said quietly, meeting her eye. "This was Dad's handkerchief. He always had it tucked into his pocket."

"He used it to clean his glasses," Anna chimed in.

A hush fell over the room as they let the significance of the gift set in. Finally, Jane said, "Dad gave it to me on the morning of my wedding. He'd want you to have it on your day."

Grace traced her fingers over the initials embroidered in brown floss at the bottom corner. "Thank you," she managed, her voice barely above a whisper.

Jane looked over to see Kathleen beaming, but tears brimmed in her bright-blue eyes. "I'd forgotten all about that old thing," she said. "He'll be with you every step down that aisle now, Grace."

Across the room, Anna sniffled, and Jane reached into her handbag for her packet of tissues. She plucked one free and handed it to her sister, whose tears turned to laughter.

Soon everyone was joining in, even Jane.

"Oh, Jane. We can always count on you," Anna said, wiping her nose.

"We sure can," Grace said, giving her a long, slow smile. Huffing in a breath, she turned to the pile of presents at her feet. "Which one next? Oh, Ivy, this is from you!"

Ivy, who had been unusually quiet up until now, nodded from her armchair next to Grace. She smiled weakly as Grace playfully shook the box and began popping the tape along the edges. Jane tried to remain engaged as her sister held up the stunning silver vase that elicited gasps of approval from the other women in the room, but she couldn't keep her attention from wandering back to Ivy.

Her eyes were glazed and feverish looking, and there was a high flush in her cheeks despite the rest of her face being an almost ghastly white. She propped her head in her hand, as if supporting herself with the arm of the chair, barely managing a vague smile as Grace thanked her for the gift.

Catching Jane's concerned stare, Ivy abruptly dropped her elbow from the chair and righted herself. "I just need to use the bathroom for a minute," she whispered. She started to stand, almost struggling to do so, and took a step toward the coffee table, fumbling to her left and causing Jane's heart to skip in alarm. Her eyes seemed unfocused, trained on something far away, or not quite there at all—just like the time Jane had fainted once early into her pregnancy She was blacking out, she couldn't see where she was walking, and she was going to smack her head on the edge of the hearth if someone didn't intervene.

A cry went out in the room as Ivy righted herself once more, and after what felt like an interminable pause but was only a split second, crumpled to the ground. Jane, Kara, and Kathleen were closest and managed to bear the brunt of her fall before she slid to the ground.

"She's unconscious!" Rosemary cried, crouching near. In the distance, Sophie began to cry, and Rosemary's youngest daughter, Molly, ushered her into the other room.

Anna quickly called for an ambulance, and Jane reached for her phone, shaking as she scrolled through her call list until she found the number of the man she had silently sworn she would never speak to again.

He answered after the first ring with a hesitant, "Jane?"

"Henry, it's your sister. I'm at my mother's house and

she's collapsed. An ambulance is on its way. They'll take her to Forest Ridge Hospital."

"I'll meet you there," he said quickly. "Ride with her, Jane. Please."

It was the first time he'd ever asked anything of her, she realized, but that wasn't the only thing that made her pause. Henry hadn't seemed the least bit surprised to know that his sister was lying on the floor, unconscious.

"And Jane? Let the paramedics know she's a diabetic."

Henry was already in the lobby of the emergency room when Jane arrived.

"She's awake," she told him. "They took her out of the ambulance and into an exam room. They said they'll come out when you can see her. I managed to keep the others from coming along by insisting Ivy wouldn't want to ruin the shower, as Grace's best friend and all. It wasn't easy, though, I can tell you that."

"Good." His rubbed a hand over his jaw, furrowing his brows over flattened eyes. A shadow fell over his face as he stared through the sliver of glass that lined the double doors to the ER.

"Why don't I get us some coffee while we wait?" Jane didn't wait for a response. The vending machines were against the far wall. She doubted it would taste any good, but it was something to do, and right now she needed to stall, and think of what she was going to say next. Her mind spun with questions—about him and, of course, about Ivy.

Henry had taken a seat with a view of the doors, and Jane handed him the Styrofoam cup gingerly. "It's hot," she warned. "And they only had that powder creamer, so I didn't add any."

"Thanks." He clutched the cup in his hands, showing no signs of drinking it.

Jane took the seat across from him and unwrapped her scarf. "I didn't know Ivy had diabetes," she said. "She never told me."

"She never told anyone." Henry took a slow sip of coffee. He made a face and set the cup down on the table beside his chair, pushing away magazines to make room.

Jane frowned. "Is it recent?"

"Not unless you call first grade recent," Henry said, giving her a long look. "She wanted to keep it to herself, and I honored that wish. Until now." His mouth thinned as he tented his elbows on his knees.

"I don't think anyone heard me tell the paramedics. They asked us to clear the room but I stayed behind to relay what you told me." Jane leaned across the narrow aisle and set her cup next to Henry's. "Why didn't she want anyone to know?"

Henry let out of a long breath. "Ivy and I had a rough time growing up. Our mother wasn't the nurturing type, and everyone knew it. Sometimes we didn't have anything to eat in the house but cereal, because she couldn't be bothered to go to the store. Ivy hated the funny looks kids gave us at lunch when they saw what we brought. They knew we were different. She didn't want to be different. Even something as common as her diabetes made her feel set apart, I guess. It was just one more thing."

Jane tried to picture Ivy back then, not much older than Sophie was now, and felt her heart break a little. "That's why you're so protective of her," she commented.

Henry scowled. "Not enough. I tried...I tried to get her to leave this town when I did. I thought she deserved

a chance to start over, to live somewhere she could feel comfortable being herself, where she'd feel accepted and wouldn't feel the need to...apologize for her past."

"Ivy loves Briar Creek," Jane pointed out.

"I know. I didn't understand that back then, but I'm starting to now."

"I thought you hated Briar Creek." Knowing how hard his life here had been, she supposed she couldn't blame him for wanting to leave.

Not that she particularly wanted him to stay...

"I wish Ivy had known she could trust us with the truth," Jane said, shaking her head. "We wouldn't have judged or thought anything of it. She has so many friends here."

"Now she does, but growing up, she had Grace and I had—" He stopped himself as his eyes flickered to hers and away again.

Adam. Jane felt her heart drop into her stomach. His bond with Adam went deep. Much deeper than any relationship he'd had with her, kiss or no kiss.

"There was a lot of attention on our family, and it only got worse when we reached adolescence. It's hard enough being a teenager without having to stop your mom from making her life harder than it already was." He shook his head, his eyes narrowing. "I hated going to all those town events. Everyone sitting around, having a good time. How could I have a good time when my mother was making a scene, stirring up gossip and trouble?"

"Oh, Henry." Jane tipped her head. "I didn't know it was that bad."

"That's because you didn't pay attention to the rumor mill. You didn't hear all the things they said. The affairs

with married men ... the unpaid tabs at the pub ... My father died before we were born. She was crushed. I don't think she ever really recovered. She wasn't strong like that."

The pain in his eyes was deep, and Jane wanted to reach out, set a hand on his arm, pull him against her. But that wasn't what Henry wanted, even if it was what he probably needed.

What Henry wanted was to be alone. To protect himself from painful memories, and the place that held them.

And what she should do was let him go, not wish he'd stay.

Henry's eyes strayed from hers and Jane looked over her shoulder to see a doctor in scrubs approaching them. "Are you here for Ivy Birch?"

Henry stood. "I'm her brother. How is she?"

"She's stable but we'd like to keep her overnight for observation. You can see her now." The doctor glanced at Jane. "We only allow one visitor at a time in the emergency room, but I can make an exception for your wife—"

Jane blanched and hurriedly said, "Oh. No. I'm..." What was she? Henry's friend? His old friend? Or just some girl he'd kissed? "I'm Ivy's friend," she finished, and the color in her cheeks rose when she stole a glance at Henry, who was watching her with growing intensity.

"In that case, I do need to ask that you wait to see her once she'd been moved upstairs to a room. It shouldn't be long."

"I'll give you time with her and check on her later," Jane told Henry, smiling softly.

He hesitated, and for a moment Jane thought he might ask her to stay. Instead he said, "I'm sure Ivy would like that."

Jane tried to ignore the pang of disappointment that swelled in her chest. She turned and began gathering her bag and the coffee cups, looking for a place to discard them. *Always the mom*, she thought wryly. *Always tidying up, being responsible.*

She stopped when she noticed Henry was still watching her.

"I won't tell anyone," she said, realizing the secret they now shared. "You can count on me."

"I know I can," he said gruffly, and then disappeared behind the swinging doors.

With Sophie tucked into bed and the house quiet, Jane began her usual nighttime routine. She started with the kitchen, where she loaded the dishwasher and wiped down the table and counter, then moved to the family room, where she began gathering discarded toys into a basket. A few crayons had rolled under the coffee table, and she knelt to grab them before tucking them into their box. Sophie had helped with the effort before story time, but there was only so much one could expect from a five-year-old. Still, Jane couldn't ever deny the swell of pride she felt when she watched Sophie straighten her coloring books, softly singing, "Clean-up time! It's clean-up time!" in that sweet little voice.

Tears began to well in her eyes and no amount of blinking could force them back. Jane sniffed and wiped at her face with the back of her hand. There was still hope, she told herself firmly. Still plenty of hope that the custody arrangement would remain in place, and that all she would have to worry about were multiple-week-long summer visits to Colorado, or those awful shared holidays.

She stood, grabbing a basket of toys by the handle, and wound down the front hall to the stairs, nearly screaming when she saw a face staring in at her through the window. Her heart was still thundering when she laughed off her no doubt stricken expression and unlocked the door.

Henry gave a bashful grin that sent a ripple through her insides. "I was about to knock. Sorry I scared you."

"Well, it is almost Halloween." Jane grinned, but the smile started to slip from her face when she considered what else the future held. Something far scarier than masks or pranks. The guardian ad litem was stopping by tomorrow to meet with Sophie, and even though Jane told herself she had already been through this once, she couldn't stop her stomach from gelling with nerves every time she remembered.

"Is Sophie excited for trick-or-treating?" Henry asked as he handed her his coat.

"Of course. She's going to be a tooth fairy." She laughed as she hung his coat on the wrought iron rack. Her fingers lingered on the supple suede that carried his familiar scent. Now this was just getting ridiculous!

Dropping her hands, she glanced at him and gave a tight smile. "I was going to visit Ivy tonight, but I didn't want to interrupt."

"You wouldn't have," Henry said smoothly. That voice . . . She could still hear it, whispering in her ear, right before his mouth met hers . . . "She's being released tomorrow. The doctors and I managed to convince her to take a big step back from the store, though."

"But what will she do?" Grace's wedding was around the corner, and so much had gone into the perfect centerpiece arrangements and bouquets. "She doesn't have any part-time help."

"No, but I intend to find her some, at least through the end of the year. She's let her health slip, and I won't leave town unless she has someone in place."

Jane wavered, not liking the potential result of her solution, but then she thought of the appointment tomorrow. "I can help."

Henry frowned at her. "What about your dance classes?"

Jane shrugged, still not ready to admit the truth. "I have a few classes a week right now, mostly in the late afternoon. My time at the bookstore is flexible, and after Grace's honeymoon she won't need me as much."

Relief flooded Henry's face as his mouth shifted into that easy grin. "Seriously, Jane? You could do it? Twenty hours a week, when Sophie's in school, just through the holiday rush. Ivy insists that after the first of the year she'll work out a new business model on her own, and I have to respect that."

Jane's heart was beginning to race with excitement, and it was taking everything in her not to fling her arms around Henry's neck and weep for joy. All at once, the appointment tomorrow didn't feel so bleak.

"I'll start tomorrow if you'd like."

"How about Monday? I told Ivy the shop was closed tomorrow, no arguments."

Jane arched a brow. "How'd that go over?"

"Not well." Henry grinned.

Their eyes met, and for a moment Jane's breath caught. It was so easy to fall into conversation with Henry, to forget about all the reasons she should avoid him, or maybe even be angry at him. His smile slipped, and for the first time she noticed how tired he looked.

The poor guy had probably been worried sick about his sister.

"Have you eaten?" She knew the answer before she asked, and led him back to the kitchen. "I have some leftovers if you're interested. Nothing special. Just chicken and potatoes."

His mouth tipped into a grin, but his eyes were steady. Jane shifted under the weight of his stare, and her heart began to race with anticipation and she turned from him.

She was grateful her back was to him as she pulled the plastic container of mashed potatoes from the bottom shelf, hoping the cool air would take the heat out of her face before she had to turn around.

Good God, she realized with a jolt. He had a full view of her butt. She whipped around and met his eyes. They were dark and hooded and didn't stray, no matter how much she wished they would.

She shut the door with her elbow and crossed to the counter.

He really needed to stop looking at her like that.

As best she could with somewhat trembling hands, she set the plate in the microwave to cook. "Wine?" she asked, and then covered her mouth. "I'm sorry. I forgot—"

Henry just gave a mild smile and held up a hand. "It's fine. I'll have some water." He watched as she fetched a glass and turned on the tap. He cleared his throat, and Jane's pulse began to drum. Oh God, he was going to say something. What, she didn't know, but whatever it was, she wasn't sure she wanted to hear it. She wasn't sure what would be worse at this point. An apology? An admittance that the kiss had been a mistake?

She had a sudden urge to run down the hall, up the stairs, and lock herself in her room. In her flannel pajamas and bunny slippers. Yep, see, this is why she didn't date. If

you didn't date—or kiss—then you didn't have to worry about awkward little moments like this.

"I wanted to thank you, Jane. For today."

Oh. So that was all. "No need to thank me."

"No, I do." He paused. "I know you were upset with me the last time we saw each other. You had every right to be."

She waved a hand through the air, but a part of her still felt the sting. "Let's not dwell on that. It's over now. I'm over it."

Henry shook his head. "I didn't know what to do. Adam had mentioned the wedding and I didn't even know if I was still going to be in town. But when Patty told me how much she wanted me there..." He held up his hands. "I couldn't say no to her. Not after everything she's done for me."

Jane tipped her head. She knew. The Browns had been like family to Henry. There was no breaking a bond like that.

Silence stretched and the timer on the microwave went off. Jane took the plate out and slid it across the island to where Henry sat on a barstool, but he made no motion to lift his fork.

"Patty and Roger are lovely people," Jane managed. There was no arguing with that.

"Other than Ivy, the Browns are the closest thing to family I've ever had since my grandmother died. I made efforts with my mother, but it wasn't enough. It never changed anything."

"Did she ever try to stop drinking?" Jane inquired delicately.

"No," Henry ground out. His brow furrowed, and he stared beyond her to the wall.

"I can understand why you don't touch the stuff," Jane said, coming to sit next to him.

"I did," he admitted. "Once." He paused, frowning as if considering whether or not to say something. "The night of your wedding. I got drunk and I did something stupid. It was the first and only time I ever touched the stuff. It hit too close. It made me worry I'd end up like her."

"The night of my wedding?" Jane's mind whirled. "What did you do?"

"I grabbed Adam by the collar and chewed him out." Henry gave her a sheepish smile. "It had been brewing for so long. Don't get me wrong, I loved Adam like a brother, but I saw him for what he was. Faults and all. He could be a bit of a...flirt."

Jane pinched her lips tight. Looking back, maybe Adam had been less than an ideal boyfriend.

"By the time the wedding was over, I knew there was nothing I could say anymore, at least not to you. So I had one too many and let him have it. I told him what I'd do to him if he ever hurt you."

Jane became aware she was gaping at Henry this entire time. She closed her mouth and blinked, trying to register what he was saying. All this had been going on while she was no doubt admiring the flowers and the multi-tiered cake. Oblivious.

"But why then?"

Henry hesitated. "Do you remember a blond girl, a friend of Patty's daughter?"

Jane squinted and shook her head. Her wedding had been a blur. "No. Why?" But as soon as she locked onto his hooded gaze, she knew why. Her heart sunk, and she shook her head bitterly. "Once a cheater, always a cheater."

"It was just a bit of flirting," Henry said quietly, and Jane snorted.

If she'd known, what would she have even done? A new bride, on her wedding day? She was grateful in a way that Henry hadn't told her. She wouldn't have known what to do with the information back then. "What did he say?"

"He told me he knew I always had a thing for you, that I always wanted what he had. His family, now his wife. Then he punched me in the face and told me to sober up before I stirred up more gossip than my mother did." He shrugged. "The next day I packed my bags and left town. Adam came to my wedding—out of guilt, maybe, or his own sense of loyalty—but after that I lost touch with the Browns until now. I was a bit lost in general," he added, his expression darkening.

"I don't know what to say," Jane replied. "I guess...I feel like I owe you an apology."

"Me?" He regarded her quizzically. "For what?"

"For giving you such a hard time about going to his wedding. I've had trouble trusting people since everything happened with Adam, and I just assumed..."

"It looked bad," Henry agreed. "It's complicated, Jane. I'm complicated."

"And I'm not?" She laughed, and waved her hand across the room. "I'm a twenty-six-year-old single mom with a string of part-time jobs, barely keeping it together most days."

"You don't give yourself enough credit," he said firmly. "I've seen firsthand the way some single mothers handle the fallout. But you..."

Jane blushed. "Enough with the flattery. I don't take it very well."

"That's because Adam never complimented you enough. You deserve someone who appreciates you more than he ever did. I'm sorry if I'm overstepping, but that's the stone cold truth." He met her eyes, and Jane's pulse flickered. "You deserve a guy who sees everything you have to offer and pushes you to be your best. Someone who tells you how beautiful you are. You deserve a lot of things." He glanced away, his jaw hardening.

It was true, Jane told herself, and deep down she'd known it. Somewhere along the line Adam had stopped telling her he found her attractive, stopped noticing when she made an effort to dress up, stopped caring if they had a night alone out to dinner. It hurt every time, but she'd tried to focus on the bigger picture: the family they had. The life they had built.

But it wasn't enough. Without all those things Henry was describing, the marriage couldn't sustain itself. She couldn't go down that path next time; it would be different.

Her heart began to flutter. She'd never really thought about a next time before, but somehow, being here with Henry, she could almost dare to hope there might be one.

His gaze was roaming her face, his eyes drifting down to her lips the way they had the other night, and Jane held her breath in anticipation, knowing he was going to kiss her and wanting him to. She leaned in as his lips met hers, and slid her hands up around his neck. His kiss was tender, but firmer this time, and she pressed into his chest, feeling his heart beating against hers. His arm was tight at her waist, the other tangled in her hair, pulling her off the stool and closer to him as he deepened his kiss.

He reached down to her hips, shifting back against the counter and swinging her between his legs. Her heart

raced with the thrill of it, her hair brushing his face as his tongue traced her bottom lip, and his hands rose to caress the swell of her breasts.

She tore her mouth from his. "Let's . . ." She jutted her chin to the stairs. They needed to be somewhere private, behind a closed door.

He groaned as she unraveled herself from his grip, limb by limb, but he stayed close behind her, his arms at her waist, and then higher, his breath on her neck, as they ascended the stairs and then firmly closed the door.

He sat down, his lips curving into a slow grin as she stood before him. He set his hands at her hips, lightly tracing his fingers under the hem of her shirt. She shivered, trembling at the softness of his touch, until his mouth was on hers again, his arms squeezing her tighter, his hands unhooking her bra.

She moaned as he lifted the shirt over her head and took her breast in his mouth, and then, rolling on top of her, he brought his lips to the base of her neck and then her mouth. She reached up and fumbled with his belt buckle, needing to be as close to him as she could, to feel his skin against hers.

"Jane," he whispered, as he lowered himself to her. "Are you sure—"

She nodded and closed her eyes to his kiss once more. She'd tried to resist Henry for years, but tonight she was giving in.

CHAPTER 27

Jane knew something was different before she'd even opened her eyes, but it wasn't until she felt the soft rise and fall of Henry's chest against her back that she remembered. She smiled into her pillow and reached down to hold his hand in hers. It had been too long since anyone had held her through the night, and she suddenly realized with terrifying clarity just what she had been missing.

A little voice called out from down the hall, and Jane quickly pulled herself from Henry's grip, hating to part with the warm covers and the heat from his skin. She took her robe from the hook on the back of her bedroom door and belted it tight at her waist. She looked down to see the soft ivory flannel grazing her ankles, and cringed. This wasn't exactly a sexy little number—unless you were living in a nursing home. She hurried to her dresser as she heard the sounds of Sophie's bed covers rustling down the hall and fumbled through her drawers until she found a basic black pair of pajama pants and a slinky long-sleeved T-shirt.

She gathered the robe in her hands, vowing to toss it in the trash immediately and stop buying that kind of junk, stop giving into the defeatist urge, and the strange way her eye always roved to the softest, most man-repellent loungewear available.

She was too young for this.

"What's that blanket in your arms?" Henry mumbled, lazily grinning from the pillow.

Jane glanced down at the enormous ball of plush ivory fabric in her arms. It wasn't even flannel, was it? It was more like an unraveled stuffed animal. "Oh. My, um, grandmother's robe, actually. I was just clearing out the closet and found it."

"You were just clearing out the closet?" Henry's grin turned wicked as he became more alert.

"Oh, I . . . like to get a head start in the mornings, and I was hoping to drop some stuff off at the Goodwill today," she said lamely.

Henry seemed to buy this, but only for a second. "Wasn't that the robe you had hanging on the back of your door?"

Jane felt her face grow hot but then she noticed he was chuckling. "Take off those pajamas and get under the covers with me," he said in a husky voice. "I don't like waking up alone."

This surprised Jane, but she came over to the bed anyway. "But you're alone all the time for work," she began, and then stopped right there. It hadn't even occurred to her, but of course. Henry was handsome, available, and not one to be tied down to one place. Or one person. He might be alone, but who said he slept alone?

"I'm alone too much. Being here with you reminds me

of that." He propped himself on one elbow and reached up to brush her loose hair from her neck. Leaning forward, his lips met hers and Jane felt every nerve in her body melt. She closed her eyes, sinking into the kiss, until the little voice shouted again from down the hall.

She pulled back and gave an apologetic smile. "Sophie's awake."

Henry groaned, but reached for his T-shirt. Jane watched as he shrugged it on, pulling it over the curves of his biceps and the contours of his smooth chest. Was it wrong to wish that this had been Adam's weekend to have Sophie? Very, she knew, but she couldn't help it. She loved her child with all her heart, but her sisters were right. She needed a little romance in her life. Maybe she'd finally found it.

She frowned when she thought about Henry's job, the travel, and his extreme opinions on Briar Creek. If he hadn't even stuck around for Ivy, what made her think he would stick around for her?

Her spirits were just beginning to deflate when Henry crossed the room and slid his arms around her waist, pulling her in one smooth movement against the wall of his chest. She pressed her lips against his warm mouth as he kissed her, softly, but purposefully, and then just as quickly released her. His breath was heavy as he gazed down at her, and his dimple quirked when he grinned.

Sophie called out again. Jane pulled in a long breath. Duty called.

Jane stepped into the hall and frowned. Sophie's door at the end of the hall was ajar, but her daughter's cry was coming from the base of the stairs.

"Sophie?" She hurried down the steps to find Sophie at

the front door, pointing through the windows that flanked either side of it.

"There's someone at the door. Didn't you hear?"

Jane checked her watch. Half past eight. They'd overslept, but who would be here at this hour without calling first? She hurried to the door, craning her neck to see what appeared to be a woman on the stoop, and unlocked the deadbolt. Her breath stopped when she came face-to-face with Joyce Benson. The guardian ad litem.

"Ms. Benson," she said in what she hoped was a pleasant tone, even though her heart was pounding. "I'm sorry, but I thought our appointment wasn't until ten."

"Is there a problem?" The woman narrowed her eyes in suspicion, and Jane shook her head quickly.

"Of course not," she replied with a nervous smile. She opened the door wider, feeling her pulse rush in her ears. "I'm afraid you've caught us in our pajamas. We slept in longer than usual this morning."

"Oh? I saw a car in your driveway. Do you have a guest?"

Jane blinked at the other woman, trying to figure out how best to answer that question, and what excuse she could make for Henry being here. If she was quick, she might be able to run upstairs under the pretense of getting dressed and tell him to hide in the closet. But that wouldn't explain the car. Or the man's coat hanging on the rack for all to see.

"A friend," she said hurriedly, sure to give a breezy smile. "Just a friend."

But Ms. Benson's attention had already strayed. She looked beyond Sophie and Jane to the stairs, her eyebrows arching with what appeared to be overt interest.

Jane cursed inwardly as she turned to face Henry. "Oh, Henry. This is Ms. Benson. The court sent her to meet with Sophie. Ms. Benson, this is our houseguest, Henry Birch."

Henry came around and stuck his hand out, and Ms. Benson took it gingerly, her beady eyes homing in on him with growing suspicion.

"Would you like some coffee?" Jane asked desperately. "I'll go make some."

Not waiting for their response, she hurried to the back of the house and pulled open a cabinet, but she was shaking so hard she was struggling to think straight. Sophie liked cereal in the mornings, but of course they were out. Suddenly she felt panicked. What if Ms. Benson based her judgment on how nutritious Sophie's breakfast was? She should give her homemade oatmeal with fresh fruit, but then Sophie would no doubt announce she never ate this and didn't like it, and oh, wouldn't that be a mark against her?

What was she worrying about? Jane had one thing and one thing only to worry about and it wasn't what Sophie did or didn't eat for breakfast. It was what Henry was doing here for the meal.

She popped a frozen waffle into the toaster and hurried back into the hall, where Ms. Benson was deep in a low conversation with Henry. Jane became aware that she was gritting her teeth so hard her jaw was beginning to ache, and she tried to relax her smile. It was no use.

"I was just telling Ms. Benson about my sister," Henry offered. Turning back to the court-appointed mediator, he said, "Jane was kind enough to ride in the ambulance with her."

"And after that you decided to stop by and spend the night?" Ms. Benson pulled out a small notebook and jotted something down.

Jane's pulse prickled. "Henry's an old friend," she explained. "I've known him for most of my life, and he's in town for a while."

"Oh." Ms. Benson nodded, seeming satisfied with the answer. "So you're staying here while you're visiting then?"

Henry glanced at Jane. "I'm...staying at the hotel in town." His jaw twitched.

Ms. Benson's beady eyes narrowed. "I see." She scribbled something in the notebook and turned to Jane. "And may as I ask if you and Mr. Birch have a romantic relationship?"

Jane knew there was no point in lying. "We're old friends, and we have been spending a bit of time together while Henry is in town."

"And has any of that time involved Sophie?"

Jane resisted the urge to fold her arms across her chest. "We've been helping Henry with an assignment he's writing on Briar Creek."

"And does Sophie enjoy her time with Mr. Birch?"

Jane felt her heart warm when she pictured Sophie at the dinner table, pealing in laughter at the stories Henry told. "She does," she said firmly.

"So it's fair to say that she will miss you quite a bit when you leave town again," Ms. Benson remarked, turning back to Henry.

Jane felt herself blanch. No, no, this couldn't be happening. Her words were being twisted. Something positive and meaningful was being taken out of context.

"Sophie's really enjoying her time with Henry, but I think she understands—"

"Oh, you'd be surprised, Ms. Madison." Ms. Benson gave a condescending smile. "Children hold a lot of emotions inside, especially those who have already lived through so much recent change."

Jane opened her mouth to list all the ways she had tried to *not* disrupt her daughter's life—all the ways she had tried to keep it exactly as it always had been, right down to clinging to a loveless marriage for far too long. She stopped herself. Rattling it all off would only make her look defensive, or worse.

She glanced at Henry. Henry who had made no promises to her. Henry who was hell-bent on leaving this town as soon as he could. Henry, who had told her over and over that he wasn't looking for marriage again.

"Well, let me have a chat with Sophie," Ms. Benson said. "Go ahead about your day like I'm not here," she added, giving a suggestive glance in Henry's direction.

Henry waited until she was out of earshot and whispered, "I'm sorry."

Jane was blinking back tears, shaking so hard she could barely even form a complete thought. Only one thought kept playing over and over.

She might really lose her daughter. And she would have no way of getting her back.

The color had returned to Ivy's cheeks when Henry poked his head into her hospital room. She beamed at him from the stack of pillows supporting her head, but the smile slipped when she caught his expression.

"Stop looking at me like that. I'm fine."

Henry didn't have the heart to tell her that for once, he was worried about more than her. His stomach stirred with fresh guilt as his anxiety kicked up a notch. He'd told himself to stay away from Jane, to keep his distance and let her be, and he hadn't listened to himself. He'd given in, and now Jane was paying the ultimate price.

Her life was complicated enough without him making it worse.

He dragged a hand over his face and entered the sunny room. Someone—presumably a nurse—had pulled back the curtains to reveal a sweeping view of the Berkshires, bursting with fall colors. Soon the leaves would be gone and ski season would start. People always got a laugh when he told them he'd grown up in Vermont and didn't know how to ski.

If he stuck around he'd like to learn...

He jolted. Staying had never been part of the plan. Any more than getting involved with Jane Madison had been.

"The nurse came in a few minutes ago with discharge papers," Ivy said as Henry sat down on the visitor chair near the far wall. His sister eyed him warily. "I know what you're going to say and...don't."

Despite his mood, he couldn't help but smile. "And what is it I'm going to say?"

"That I work too hard, that I don't take care of myself, that I need to stop and eat—properly—and that I shouldn't have had that extra glass of Champagne yesterday and I shouldn't have skipped my insulin, either."

Henry tried to keep his expression neutral, but his mind was beginning to race. "My God, Ivy, this has got to *stop*! Do I have to come over and administer the injections myself like I did when we were children?"

"I knew you'd be mad," Ivy said, narrowing her eyes.

"Damn straight I'm mad. You have me worried sick! How the hell am I supposed to leave town if I can't be sure you're taking care of yourself?"

Ivy shrugged. "Maybe you shouldn't leave then."

Henry flashed her a dangerous look. "Don't say that. Don't say this is all some cry for attention."

"Of course not." Ivy sighed. "What do you think I am, stupid?"

Henry was about to say that, yes, she had been behaving stupidly, recklessly, really, but Ivy continued. "I have to make some changes. Big ones. I don't know how I'll manage, but I don't have a choice."

Henry nodded once. "I've arranged for part-time help starting tomorrow." Something told him Jane wasn't just being altruistic in her services, meaning she would hopefully carry through with her word despite the unexpected turn in the day.

He clenched his jaw. Jane always carried through with her promises. It was a hell of a lot more than he could say for himself.

Henry leaned forward on his elbows and massaged the gap between his eyebrows with his fingers. He'd call her tonight. He'd end it now, before more damage was done. If it wasn't too late.

"Who did you hire?" Ivy asked, tossing the hospital blanket off her legs.

"Jane Madison offered," he said briskly, refusing to mention when or where this discussion occurred.

Ivy's expression turned curious. "She was in the store the other day offering to help...but something told me she was really hinting about a job. Ah, well, see? Something good came from this mess."

"I'll be paying her until the house sells," Henry said in a voice that he knew Ivy wouldn't argue with. "I want to do it. Please just let me."

Ivy stared at him and then gave a resigned nod. Henry sat back in his chair, feeling slightly better. If what Ivy said was true, then by covering Jane's salary he was helping both women.

The nurse came into the room pushing an empty wheelchair and took the signed discharge papers from Ivy. "You're all set to go. We recommend a follow-up appointment with your regular doctor tomorrow."

"Oh, but I work—"

"I'll take her," Henry promised, nailing Ivy with a hard look as he helped her into the wheelchair.

They left the room in silence and stayed that way as Henry pushed his sister to the hospital lobby. "Wait here while I bring the car around," he instructed before jogging out into the cold morning air. He was relieved when she didn't try to resist, and when he spotted her through the window a few minutes later, still dutifully sitting in the wheelchair. Henry helped Ivy into the car, ignoring her protests and sighs, and then slammed his own door shut. He slid the key into the ignition but didn't turn it. Something was weighing on him, and he couldn't proceed until it was off his chest.

He turned to his sister. "How do I know this isn't going to happen anymore?"

A look of guilt took over her soft features. "It won't. I know I said that before, but…this was my wake-up call. I ruined my best friend's bridal shower—I hate to think of other events ending the same way. It reminds me of…" She trailed off and looked away from him, hiding her face

behind a curtain of auburn hair. "It reminds me of Mom. I don't want to be like her," she said, starting to cry.

Henry closed his eyes and then reached over to set a hand on her arm. "You're not like Mom. You have an illness. Maybe she did, too, but she didn't take control of it. You can."

Ivy nodded, but refused to meet his eye. "It's the gossip. The attention. The way people will talk." She suddenly turned to him, her eyes desperate and wet with tears. "I tried so hard to avoid that all my life and now, it's happened."

"And it will soon be forgotten. Trust me. Everyone has enough crap in their own lives to deal with." He offered her a small smile. "Now, if you started passing out at every social event..."

She swatted his arm and then, unexpectedly, leaned over and gave him a hug. "I wish you didn't have to go," she said quietly, pulling back.

Henry started the engine and kept his eyes straight ahead. The way he'd trained himself to many, many years ago.

CHAPTER
28

Jane held the ringing phone in her hands, her heart thundering as she stared at the name on the caller display. Her first instinct was to ignore it, but then she thought of Ivy, and the promise she had made to help out in the flower shop.

"Hello?"

"Jane."

Her heart seized at the sound of Henry's thick, gruff voice. She closed her eyes against the pang of longing. "How's Ivy?"

There was a slight pause on the other end of the line. "She's doing well. I'm staying at her place tonight. The accommodations are a bit tight." His laugh sounded forced, and Jane winced. Clearly, she wasn't the only one finding this difficult. "I told her you'd offered to help in the store. That brightened her spirits."

"Good, good." Jane grew silent. She couldn't bring herself to muster up her earlier enthusiasm or admit to

herself that it might not matter that she now had regular hours through the end of the year. No amount of job stability could make up for an unstable home life, and casual dating was frowned on in family court where young children were involved.

"I was worried about you," Henry said after a long pause. His comment hung there, both of them knowing it couldn't undo the damage.

"What's done is done," Jane said bitterly.

"What does that mean?"

"It means the mediator probably made her decision. Judging from the look on her face when she left, I can only imagine it wasn't in my favor."

She had already put a call in to her attorney, but it was the weekend and she wouldn't be able to meet with him until tomorrow, after her shift at Petals on Main. How she would get through a morning of retail service was beyond comprehension right now. The mere thought of baring a smile and pretending like nothing was wrong exhausted her to the bone, no matter how much practice she had.

"Is there anything I can do?" Henry asked, and Jane closed her eyes.

"No," she said quietly, hating the twinge of hurt that crept into her voice. "There's nothing anyone could do."

Henry said nothing. For several seconds Jane listened to the sound of his breathing, savoring her last connection to him almost as much as she resented it, and then, with a simple press of the button she disconnected the call.

The bright morning sun did little to take the chill out of the air. Frost covered the browning grass along Main Street and left a crystallized sheen on the rooftops. Jane

rubbed her hands together as she glanced through the window of Petals on Main, relieved to see Ivy standing behind the counter and not her brother.

She had tossed and turned all night thinking of Henry, wondering if she had made the right decision, knowing there was no other choice.

With a tired sigh, she entered the shop and gave Ivy a quick hug hello.

"You look pale, Jane. Is everything okay?"

"Says the woman who spent the weekend in the hospital," Jane joked. She didn't feel like getting into her problems right now. It was probably for the best that she was here, able to escape for a bit. "How are you doing?"

"Oh, I'm better. Henry gave me strict instructions not to stay more than fifteen minutes. He said you're already a pro around here."

Jane gave a weak smile and followed her friend into the back room to get brought up to speed. The phone in her handbag began to buzz, and she struggled to listen to what Ivy was saying. She nodded as she stared blindly at the spreadsheet Ivy was referring to, something to do with orders and shipment codes.

The buzzing stopped but her pulse didn't slow. She waited for it. One last alert. The phone beeped. *Voicemail.*

Her entire fate was in that one message, no doubt from her attorney. She checked her watch. Yep, eight-thirty. Her hands began to shake.

"So there you have it. Any questions?" Ivy blinked at her eagerly.

Jane hadn't processed a word Ivy had said, but there was no use asking her to repeat it.

"I'll be upstairs if you need me," Ivy said.

Jane tied on the heavy twill apron Ivy handed her. "Get some rest," she said.

"Not like I have much choice. But yes, I promised Henry I'd take better care of myself, and I intend to." Lowering her voice, Ivy said, "He told me you know... about my diabetes."

Jane tipped her head. "It's nothing to be ashamed of, but...I understand. Sometimes it helps to keep a few things to yourself, so you don't have to always think about what's bothering you." Which was why she didn't intend to tell Ivy what she was going through right now. Her friend would no doubt insist on working, and that would lead to an argument with Henry, and then everything would become a bigger mess than it already was.

No, she was an adult, and this was her problem. She'd created it, and now she'd solve it. Somehow.

She waited until Ivy had gone upstairs to her apartment before pulling the phone from her bag. Her heart sunk when she saw that the call had indeed been from her lawyer.

Unable to bear hearing the news in a voicemail, she dialed him back instead.

"Jane!"

She frowned. He sounded...chipper.

"I suppose you've gotten my messages," she began in a rush. "I need you to call the mediator, or something, anything you can do to explain that nothing was going on with me and Henry. I have a new part-time job through the end of the year, in addition to the dance classes, and there's renewed interest in the winter and spring session. I'm giving Sophie a stable life. You know it. You just need to make Ms. Benson see that!"

There was a long pause. "Didn't you listen to my voicemail?"

Jane gripped the phone tighter. Her entire body had gone cold and she realized she was trembling from head to toe. "No."

"She already knows that, Jane. She put her recommendation through. Adam dropped the petition this morning. The custody agreement will remain intact."

Tears sprung to Jane's eyes as she clapped her hand to her mouth. She swallowed the knot in her throat before finally managing, "But...she seemed so stern yesterday. So...down on me. How—"

"It seems she had a change of heart. Someone came forward with a letter."

"A letter?" Jane frowned. "So you did get my messages yesterday."

"Oh, it wasn't me," her lawyer replied. "Someone wrote a letter on your behalf. Someone with a lot of influence, it would seem."

A chill washed over her arms and she turned to see a shadow in the open doorway to the alley, and all at once, everything became clear.

"Henry."

Jane's eyes glistened with tears, but the joy in her smile made his breath catch. Henry gritted his teeth, tightening his resolve.

"I've just had the most amazing news. I—I can't even believe it. It's Sophie. She's...the custody...Adam dropped it."

Henry stepped farther into the shop, careful to maintain a healthy distance. "That's wonderful news."

Jane's brow furrowed as her smile slipped. "You don't seem surprised. Did you—the lawyer said someone wrote a letter."

He pulled in a long breath. It would be so easy to tell her the truth, but taking credit for it would only make what he had come to say all that much more difficult.

"It sounds like someone was looking out for you." His smile felt frozen on his face, his words stilted. He hated disappointing her again.

Jane looked down at the phone she still clasped in her hands and studied it. When she lifted her eyes to him once more, doubt clouded the space where so much light had just been. "I don't know who it was, but... I'll always be grateful to that person. I hope they know that."

Henry held her stare. "No doubt it was someone who recognized what a good mother you are. Sophie's your world. Anyone could see that."

Jane nodded, seeming uncertain. "I just wish I could thank the person."

"I'm sure seeing you smile is the only payback that person is looking for." He shoved his hands into his pockets. "I actually came in to see you."

"Oh?"

"Ivy will probably find some excuse to come down here, but she needs her rest. I'm sure you understand."

Jane nodded, then tipped her head. "Henry. Are you sure you didn't write the letter?"

"I learned long ago to stay out of people's business. I saw firsthand what happens when people get involved in situations they shouldn't."

"What are you trying to say?" Jane asked, stepping forward.

Henry roved his gaze over her face, taking in the confusion that clouded her eyes. He swallowed hard, knowing what he'd come to do. "I shouldn't have gotten involved with you, Jane. You have enough going on without me coming in and turning your life upside down."

"Last night…" Jane shook her head. "I was upset. I didn't know what else to do."

"You put Sophie first. You did what any good mother would do."

Jane took another step forward, stopping within arm's reach. He let his eyes drift to her lips, remembering the tease of her smile, the way she tasted, and felt…Henry's jaw pulsed, and he cursed to himself, wishing he could stop now but knowing he couldn't. She looked so lost and bewildered, and he hated himself in that moment. Hated himself for taking the joy out of this moment for her. Hated himself for crushing her hopes. But he hated himself more yesterday, when he saw how much he'd almost cost her.

He thrust his hands in his pockets. "I'm heading out this week," he said, his voice gruff and thick. "My editor's got me on a new assignment and I fly out of San Francisco next week."

"Will you be back for the holidays?" Jane inquired after a long pause.

"I'll be on the road, no doubt."

Jane's eyes searched his in confusion. "I just thought…" She gave a sad smile. "I guess I just thought—"

His heart skipped a beat, and he cut in before he could hear what she had to say. Knowing that he'd meant something to her, that she cared, and that she'd want him to be there, after everything, would only make things worse. He started it, and now he needed to end it.

"Jane," he said, his voice softening. "I meant what I said the other day about all those things you deserve. You deserve a man who is home every night for dinner, who tucks Sophie into bed and imagines more children with you. You deserve someone who loves all the things you do, and who makes it his mission every day to make your life a little better. That's not me."

Jane blinked but said nothing.

Henry ground his teeth, forcing himself to go on. "You deserve friendship and love and laughter. And stability."

"But you—"

"I'm none of those things, Jane," he said flatly.

She shook her head. "No," she said firmly. "I don't believe you. Look at all the nice things you've done for me since you've been back. You can't dismiss that."

No, he couldn't. He leaned a hip against the counter, feeling the pull in his chest. "Did you ever wonder why I got a divorce?"

Jane looked confused. "No."

"My wife cheated on me." He dragged out a long sigh, but anger kicked at his pulse. Even now, there was still that sting when he thought back on it.

Her eyes widened slightly in surprise, but otherwise her expression remained steady.

"She wanted all the things you need, Jane. I . . . couldn't give them to her." He shrugged. "I tried." *And failed.*

"But that's no excuse for her to cheat on you," Jane said. "You were the one who told me not to blame myself for Adam's unfaithfulness."

"True, all true. But it doesn't mean I'm any good, Jane. It doesn't mean I can make you happy."

"But you did make me happy."

"And then I nearly cost you your daughter," he reminded her. She opened her mouth to say something, but he held up a hand. "You want to come home to the same house every night, eat dinner, and curl up into bed. You want to walk down Main Street and wave at the people you've known since you were too young to talk. I don't want those things."

"I think you do," Jane insisted.

Henry shook his head. "You're a family person, Jane. You were raised that way, it's natural to you. It's not to me."

"I wouldn't cheat on you, Henry."

"You don't know that for sure," Henry remarked. "And I'm not willing to take that risk. Of hurting you." *Of hurting myself.*

"But Henry—"

"I'm sorry, Jane," he said, backing up to the door. "I'm really, really sorry."

He turned and walked away, through the back door and into the alley, turning his collar against the biting wind. He hurried around the building and followed the streets back to the B&B, stopping to look at no one. In a few days he'd be gone anyway, and this time he wouldn't be coming back. This town was nothing but bad memories. Bad times. Dark reminders. He'd be better once he was on the road, in his routine, putting one foot ahead of the other and never staying in one place long enough to get too close.

It was only here, when he was in Briar Creek, that he dared to think of all he'd once wanted, and all he would never have.

CHAPTER 29

Grace was hunched over the seating charts when Jane came into the kitchen. She pulled out a chair and slunk into it with a sigh. Though she was grateful for the extra work hours, especially with the holidays quickly approaching, she was also bone tired.

Fortunately, their mother was cooking tonight, and from the smells wafting from the oven, Jane could tell her roasted chicken would be ready soon.

"Only a week to go until the big day," Jane said. "Can you believe it?"

Grace's expression lit up. "This all feels like a dream come true, honestly. I keep waiting for something to go wrong."

"Don't say that," Jane said, thinking that she had once worried the same, only with good reason. "Ivy was just unwrapping the vases for the centerpieces today, and you know Anna won't let you down with the cake."

"I wouldn't," Anna unwrapped her scarf as she came

into the kitchen, "if I could finally start the thing." She turned to Grace. "Please tell me you have finally decided on the flavor."

Grace winked at Jane before glancing back at Anna. "Red velvet."

"Of course." Anna tossed her hands up in the air. "I believe that was the very first one I suggested, back when Luke popped the question."

"I needed to be sure," Grace replied.

"Well, so long as you're happy." Anna settled into a chair and tipped her head at Jane. "And speaking of happy... Shouldn't you be beaming from ear to ear?"

Jane forced a smile and forced back the pain in her heart every time she thought of Henry's coldness the last time they'd spoken. "Of course. I'm just still in shock, I guess. I came so close to losing Sophie that it's hard to believe the threat is gone."

"And you still don't know who wrote the letter?"

"No..."

Grace set down her pencil. "I've been wondering, Jane. Do you think Patty wrote it?"

Jane stared at her sister. "Adam's mother?" The thought had never even occurred to her, but now that Grace mentioned it, she could see the possibility. Patty had certainly seemed conflicted the day she'd stopped by the bookstore, and there was the fact that she wouldn't want Sophie so far from her, either.

"Well, whoever it was," Kathleen said, bustling into the room, "it seems like they wanted to remain anonymous. All I know is, had I known—" She gave Jane a stern look. "Had I known, I would have written the letter myself!"

Jane smiled. It had been such a relief to tell her mother

what was going on once the threat had passed. It felt good to deliver good news for a change.

"Maybe it was Patty, then," Jane mused. She chewed on the edge of her thumbnail, replaying the conversation with her ex-mother-in-law. She hadn't seen or spoken to her since, and if it was her, she'd want to thank her. Still, a part of her couldn't shake the feeling that it had been Henry.

"You don't look convinced," Anna pointed out. She stood and filled the kettle with water as their mother opened a tin of cookies, fresh from Anna's kitchen.

"I guess I just hoped it had been Henry," Jane admitted.

Grace raised her eyebrows. "Hoped?"

Jane felt her cheeks flush. "I mean, thought. I *thought* it was Henry." She gritted her teeth, annoyed with her slip. "Stop looking at me like that."

"Like what?" Grace mouth curved into a pleased grin.

"It's okay to have feelings for Henry," Anna said from across the room. "We always wished you'd have picked him instead of Adam anyway—"

Kathleen flashed Anna a stern glance and Anna quickly clamped her mouth shut.

"Is this true?" Jane demanded of her mother.

Kathleen just lifted her hand, sighing. "Henry was always so sweet to you. When I think of the way he showed up on our doorstep to take you to the prom..."

"Because Adam asked him to," Jane pointed out.

Her sisters and mother exchanged glances but no one said anything. Jane frowned, as everything began to come clear. Adam had never even called to tell her he was canceling, and then the doorbell rang, and there was Henry, all dressed up, with that warm smile, and she'd just assumed...

He must have picked up the flowers, too. Pink peonies. *Her favorite.*

Good grief, he'd come on his own. Covering Adam's mistakes, making sure she was taken care of.

Judging from the existence of that letter, he was still doing it.

Even Henry had to admit the old house had never looked better. With the new roof and fresh gray paint covering the dingy white siding, it was almost cheerful. Ivy had hung a fresh pine wreath on the door, secured with a dark orange velvet ribbon. "Curb appeal," she said with a wink. The windows were washed, the yard was picked up, and even the detached garage didn't look so sad anymore.

"I guess we should walk through one last time to make sure we didn't miss anything."

Henry nodded his agreement. The house would be listed Monday. With any luck, they'd find a buyer before the first big snow hit.

He took the steps slowly, knowing this was going to be the last time he ever set foot in the house he'd grown up in, and for some reason, he struggled to accept that. His mother was gone, and soon this house would be, too. There was nothing to hold on to anymore, nothing to blame, nothing to remind him of a time he wanted to forget. In a way, the finality of this saddened him, suddenly seizing him with the notion of all he'd once had here— good or bad—and all he was permanently leaving behind.

The first thing he noticed upon entering the house was the light. Their mother had kept the curtains drawn at all times, but with the heavy drapes gone, the darkness that seemed to bear down on them and fill every day with

dread and despair had vanished. The front hall glowed with morning sunlight that bounced off the freshly painted linen-colored walls. The floors had been sanded and stained, the dark woodwork was painted white, and the banister rail leading up the curved stairs was almost inviting. Henry shifted his eyes to the living room, now empty, and instead of picturing himself and Ivy as young children sitting on the old stained rug, he could imagine other children happily playing, their toys filling the corner, maybe a television above the mantel.

"You'd never know it was the same house," he murmured, turning to Ivy. Even though he'd stopped in to oversee the work, seeing the house in finished form left him awestruck.

"I'm almost sad to let it go," Ivy said. "It wasn't a bad house; it was just…a bad time." She gave a brave smile. "It deserves to have some happier memories."

"We all do," Henry said quietly. He frowned, and turned back into the hall. He'd seen enough, and there was no sense in getting sentimental now. It was a fitting ending to this house and this town, he supposed. Next time he came through, a new family might be calling it home. By then, he wouldn't have any more excuses to look back.

"It seems like you've had a good visit," Ivy commented. "Does any of it have to do with Jane?"

He tried to keep his tone light. "Why would you say that?"

Ivy just shrugged, but a knowing smile played at her mouth. "You spent a lot of time with her, that's all."

"I was always fond of Jane," Henry replied gruffly. He bit back on his teeth and gazed out the window. He still was fond of Jane, and that was all the more reason to put

distance between them. How many times had he seen the hurt in her eyes and tried to take it away? It was different when he was the one causing it. He'd done it once, and he'd be damned if he'd do it again.

And he couldn't trust himself to think there wouldn't be a next time.

He wanted to give Jane everything she deserved and then some. But if he couldn't? The mere thought made his blood run cold.

"Then why'd you go to Adam's wedding?" she countered.

"Why do you think?" he shot back. "Besides, you know I'm not looking for anything serious. I was married once, and it wasn't for me."

"It didn't work out. That doesn't mean it isn't for you. Caroline just wasn't the right person for you."

He couldn't deny the truth in her words. He'd cared about Caroline, maybe even a part of him had loved her, but what he'd loved more than her, he knew, was everything she represented. A stable family life. A good background. But he'd still run from it. Still traveled too much, still invested too little.

He wouldn't be making the same mistake twice.

"Will you come back for Thanksgiving?" Ivy asked hopefully, once they settled into the car. His bags were packed and loaded in the trunk with the intention of dropping her off before he headed to the airport in Burlington.

"Why don't you come out to San Francisco for Thanksgiving?" he asked.

Ivy's expression became tight. "I have some traditions here. Ones I created for myself, I guess you could say. Nothing much—usually a night out with girlfriends after a meal at the Madisons' . . ."

"You've really found your home here," he observed, the bitterness over this fact now gone.

"It's your home, too," Ivy said.

Henry gripped the steering wheel and shifted the car into gear. He stared out the windshield, focused on the winding road straight ahead and not the small house on the hill, growing smaller with each passing second, wishing with everything in him that he could believe that.

CHAPTER
30

The weather in San Francisco was mild this time of year, and Henry lifted the windows in his studio apartment, letting the fresh air filter through the stale room as he went to the small kitchen and flung open the fridge. It was empty, of course, just like the cabinets.

His bags were propped near the front door, and he eyed them steadily, somehow unable to bring himself to unpack. Normally, he didn't bother. He rarely spent more than a few nights each month here, and it showed. Not a single picture hung on the walls. The bedspread was basic, the black leather couch cold and sterile, and no frames rested on the mantel. Nothing to remind him of where he came from, or who he'd left behind.

It was as uninviting as the hotel rooms he spent the majority of his time in. About as generic, too. He'd never put much thought into it, seeing no point in making roots when it was wheels up the next day, but now, having been away for more than a month, he felt a bit depressed to be met with these surroundings. It wasn't a home—a

home was something to come back to. This was just a room. It was functional. It fit his needs. Or it had, until now.

He picked up the phone and dialed his editor, who on occasion was up for dinner when he was in town. They agreed to meet at the steakhouse one block from the office, leaving Henry an hour to read over his article one last time.

He powered up his laptop and set his feet on the glass coffee table. The remote was inches from his fingertips and he flicked on the television. Soon, sounds from a random sitcom filled the room. He glanced up as he opened his document. The usual setup: parents squabbling about something the teenager had done, meddling neighbors popping by at inopportune times, and loud meals where everyone was talking over one another.

He flicked off the television. There was no use pretending anymore. No use filling his life with makeshift families. This was his life, alone, in this sterile little room he'd carved out as his own in the world. This was the life he had chosen for himself. So why was the thought of continuing this way starting to feel unbearable?

He should have had a picture of Ivy out, he realized, staring at his bare mantel with sudden shame. Somehow it was easier not to.

His chest heavy, he turned back to the computer. He just needed to focus, work, clear his head. Eventually the memories would fade and he'd put one foot in front of the other. Eyes in front. He was good at that.

He ran a spell-check of his article and cleaned up some language, then read it over from the beginning one last time, almost imagining himself walking down

Main Street as he read his own description of Rosemary and Thyme, Petals on Main, and, of course, Main Street Books.

He swallowed hard, thinking back on the sounds of the percolating coffee, the smells of scones, and the rain spattering against the window as he sat in the corner, watching Jane from the corner of his eye.

Enough. Briar Creek wasn't where his life was centered anymore.

He hurried through the rest of the article, skimming over the part about the local dance studio that offered drop-in ballroom classes, and chuckling to himself about the chatty proprietor at the Main Street B&B.

After uploading the photos he'd taken, he began scrolling through the shots of the town, robust with bursting fall colors. It was a pretty little town, with the cobblestone streets and quaint storefronts, and looking at it through this lens, it was hard to believe it was the where place he'd grown up. He'd built it up to be a dismal, dark place, but the six weeks he'd spent there hadn't felt that way. Sure, the people were a little nosy, but what was worse? Having people know his business, or not having anyone care enough to do so?

Nick was about the closest thing to a friend he had, and the guy was his editor—he knew nothing personal about him other than a few of his professional habits. Henry had liked it this way, kept it this way, but now... The walls had come down, and he wasn't so sure he could build them up again. Wasn't so sure he wanted to.

For the first time in years his life in San Francisco felt completely empty.

He clicked to the next picture, and his hand froze over the keypad. There, on the screen, smiling back at him, was

Jane. It was the photo he had taken the day of the Harvest Fest—he'd almost forgotten about it. She was sitting at an old knotty picnic table, an enormous, yet-to-be-carved pumpkin in front of her, little Sophie tucked protectively under her arm. Sophie was giggling, her eyes on the pumpkin, but Jane was looking straight at him, her eyes clear and bright, crinkling at the corner, and her smile... Oh, that smile. It was the smile she'd given him when they'd shared a laugh over breakfast, the same smile he'd seen when she told him the good news—when he'd denied having any part of it, denied writing that letter.

It was the last time he'd see that smile, he realized with a jolt. The thought of it suddenly felt impossible.

Henry hadn't realized he was holding his breath until the long sigh escaped him. He closed out of the file quickly and sent the article and a few scenic shots of the town to his editor. Then he stood, flicked off the lights to his apartment, and locked the door behind him.

Nick was already at their usual table when he arrived twenty minutes later. "I read your article. That's one hell of a charming town," he said, reaching for the bread basket.

Henry placed his order with the waitress, knowing Nick would have already put his in, and sipped his water. "It's quaint."

"You said you grew up there?" Nick asked. "Gave it all up for the big city?"

"Something like that," Henry said. He rubbed his hand over his jaw, looking around the room, unsure of what he was looking for, or who. He could keep running, keep bouncing from one hotel to the next, occasionally meeting someone to share a meal or spend the night, but no amount of time would fill the hole in his heart.

Only one person had, and he'd pushed her away. All his life he'd been searching for the one thing Jane could offer him, the one thing he'd found with her. A home. A community. A sense of belonging.

Briar Creek was in his blood, it was a part of his fiber, his being, and all the experiences, good or bad, that had shaped him into the man he was today. He'd married Caroline to run away from his past, just like he landed in a new airport each week.

Before, all he'd wanted was to run. To not get close. But now, all he wanted was to go home. Home to Ivy, to that old ramshackle house that he'd brought back to life. Home to the Browns, who still welcomed him with open arms, and always would.

And home to Jane. If she'd still have him.

Jane stood at the front of the church, clutching her bouquet in both hands, her eyes trained on the open set of doors at the back of the room. The music swelled and the guests stood as Grace appeared in the doorway, her smile visible even through the gauze of her veil. She took the aisle by herself, and Jane experienced only a slight pang at how unfair that was, until she saw her father's handkerchief wrapped around the base of Grace's bouquet. It was as if their father was holding her hand all the way down the rose-scattered carpet.

Grace's green eyes were misty as she took her position next to Luke, and they never strayed from his as she said her vows. Jane thought this moment would be difficult—it was the first wedding she'd been to on her own—but somehow, hearing their promises didn't make her long for her marriage or all that it might have been. It made her

think of Henry, and the things she'd like to have offered him. If he'd given her a chance.

She'd wrestled with anger, hurt, even sadness over his decision, and then ultimately told herself that she had no choice but to accept it. She'd spent how many years loving the wrong man, trying to ignore the warning signs, brushing aside the knowledge that he didn't seem to want the same things as her. Maybe Henry had spared her from that hurt. Maybe he really couldn't give her what she was looking for.

Or maybe he was just a jerk.

She wanted to believe that, and at times she could. After all, if he cared about her as much as he had once seemed to, why sleep with her? Why get involved with her at all if in the end all he ever planned to do was turn his back and walk away?

She pulled in a breath, lifted her bouquet a little higher, and focused her attention on the bride and groom and all the friends and family who had joined them to celebrate this event. She held Sophie's hand as they walked back up the aisle behind the bridal party, admiring her sister, now officially a married woman. She smiled through the photos, and laughed when the Champagne was popped in the back of the limo, and tossed confetti alongside the guests as Grace and Luke entered the reception.

The entire room glowed under chandeliers, and the votives on each table flickered against the gold-rimmed plates. A familiar twinge pressed against Jane's chest as she took her seat for dinner next to Ivy, but Ivy seemed distracted and on edge, and there was a high color in her cheeks.

"Are you feeling okay?" Jane whispered, but Ivy just blinked quickly.

Her smile was radiant, and Jane suddenly realized the gleam in her eye was from excitement, perhaps even joy. "Never better. It seems to me that there are some single men here tonight, after all." She wiggled her eyebrows.

Jane glanced around the room, her spirits deflating quickly. The only bachelors she saw were the usual crowd: Brett Hastings, the sheriff, a few of the other guys from town.

She picked up her fork. May as well enjoy her dinner.

It wasn't until the cake had been cut and the first dance was over that Grace came over to her. "Are you having a good time?"

Jane set her hands in her lap and surveyed the dance floor, where Sophie was twirling in her flower girl dress. "Of course. It's a beautiful wedding, Grace. And it all came together so well!"

Grace swatted her. "I know I wasn't the easiest bride, but you know how it is. I just wanted it to be perfect." She tipped her head as the music turned to a slow number. With bitter irony, Jane realized it was the first song she'd danced to at her prom all those years ago. She'd never forgotten it. "You should get out there on the dance floor."

"Oh…" Jane struggled to maintain her smile. She hardly wished to point out that she had no one to dance with. Well, Sophie, of course.

Her sister frowned as she studied her, and then handed her the small cotton handkerchief.

Jane searched her sister's eyes as she rubbed her finger over the embroidered initials. "But, this doesn't belong to me. It's Dad's, and he'd want you to have it today."

"I have a feeling you'll be needing it back someday." She jutted her chin over Jane's shoulder.

Confused, Jane turned to follow her sister's stare. Her pulse skipped a beat when she saw Henry standing in the open doorway to the reception room, one hand in the pocket of his black suit pants, looking so handsome. Jane felt her breath catch.

He was supposed to be gone, in San Francisco, or wherever else his job took him.

Her heart began to speed up until she realized that none of this changed a damn thing. So he was back in town. He wasn't here for her.

She tried to fight the disappointment that was building up in her chest, tried to focus on her daughter, who was practicing her pirouettes and all but slipping in her new shoes, when an open palm appeared before her.

She looked up, meeting Henry's steady gaze, and felt her heart begin to pound.

"May I have this dance?"

Tears began to prickle the back of her eyes, blurring her vision. She blinked quickly and looked away. "Henry," she sighed. "I . . . don't understand."

"Then let me explain," he said firmly. His voice was strong and thick, and his hand didn't move. She eyed it warily, and then, unsure as to whether she was making the right decision, set hers in it.

His fingers clasped hers tightly as he led her to the dance floor and turned to face her. He set his other hand not on her waist, but around it, holding her tight, making it impossible for her to break away, and oh, did a part of her want to. She looked across the room to where Grace and Anna were watching her with wide eyes, until the weight of Henry's stare pulled her back to him. She looked into his kind blue eyes, and felt a little part of her begin to break.

"I thought you left town," she whispered, skirting her eyes away again.

"I did," he said simply.

"Then why did you come back?" She held her breath, waiting for him to answer, wondering how she would respond when he did. He was here, with his arms around her waist and his chest pulled so close to hers she could feel the beating of his heart under his clothes, and something told her the racing pulse meant he had more on his mind than making amends.

"Because I realized that I could keep running and hiding for the rest of my life, but that was never going to get me where I wanted to be."

Her shoulders rose and fell with each heavy breath as her eyes locked with his. "And where do you want to be?"

"Here," he said simply, but there was a hint of a smile on his lips now, a steadiness in his gaze that made her want to believe that this time, he wouldn't waver.

Still, she had to be sure. "Briar Creek? I thought you hated this town."

He tightened his grip on her and a rush of heat spilled over her body. That scent . . . she hadn't dared to remember it. "Everything I ever wanted was right here, Jane. I just didn't want to believe it. I ran from it instead, put walls up, prepared for the worst. I told you all those things you deserved the other day. It took me a while to realize I deserved them, too."

"You do," Jane agreed, thinking of all he had been through, and all the good he had done. "You've been a good friend to me, Henry."

"I'd like to be more than a friend," he replied smoothly, and all at once, alarm bells went off.

Jane shook her head, pulling back from his grip as panic tightened its grip. She'd trusted the wrong man once before; she'd be damned if she didn't protect her heart this time.

They were standing in the middle of the dance floor, the only couple not moving to the beat of the music, but she didn't care who was watching or what they thought. She needed to think straight, and she couldn't when his hand was slipping down her back, sending every nerve ending on overdrive.

"The last time I saw you, you told me why we couldn't be together. Why you weren't the man for me. It's only been a few days, so what's changed?"

"I have," he said, setting a hand on her arm. "I went back to San Francisco, to that empty shell of a life, and I realized that the only place I wanted to be was in your home, with you, and Sophie. I was happy here, Jane, and if I'm being honest, that scared the crap out of me. It made me think of everything I stood to lose. I missed you, Jane. I missed this town. I missed the way I felt when I was in it. With you. I've been running from myself, but my roots are here. With the people who really know me."

It was too easy. Too easy to believe what he saying. But oh, how she wanted to! She stared into his deep blue eyes, looking for a trace of struggle and finding none. "You... really hurt me the other day."

He shook his head and set another firm grip on her other arm. "I think that's what scared me the most. We spent this great night together and then, just like that, I felt like I shattered your world. All I ever wanted was to make you smile. It...it killed me to know that I could be the reason for you being so upset."

"But then why end it? Why tell me we were better off apart, even after everything had worked out?"

He stepped toward her, and she hesitated, wanting to pull back as much as she longed to walk right into his arms. When he set a hand on her shoulder, a long, slow breath released from her. She was losing the fight, falling all over again. And this was one battle she was hoping to lose.

"I thought you were better off without me, Jane." His eyes were eager, his tone insistent. "But then I realized I wasn't better off without you. You've given me hope again. Hope for this town, for my life, to find everything I always wanted. I want a family, Jane, and I want one with you."

"Henry," she protested, but even as she said his name, she couldn't fight the tears that slowly rolled down her cheeks any more than the ache in her throat. "You wrote the letter, didn't you?"

He hesitated, and then nodded once.

"But why didn't you just tell me?" she cried, lifting her arms as he pulled her against his chest.

"Because then you would have known...Then you would have made it too hard for me to leave."

"What? What would I have known?"

"I love you, Jane. A part of me always has. I love your smile, I love your spirit, and I love the way you care for Sophie." He brushed a tear off her face with the side of his thumb. "I've tried to keep my distance, to float through life on my own, but sometimes in life you have to make a choice and stick with it. And I choose you, Jane."

Jane brought a hand to her lips to stifle the cry that escaped. The tears fell steadily now, but she didn't try to stop them. He'd stood by her, stood up for her, and fought for her and Sophie.

She looked up to smile into the eyes of the man she loved. "I just need you to do one more thing for me."

"Name it."

"Promise to take us on one of your trips someday?"

"Honey, my traveling days are over. I'm here, I'm yours. I'm never leaving again." He leaned in and kissed her mouth softly, and she leaned into him, feeling his warmth and breathing his air and feeling her heart swell with pure joy. "But I will take you on a trip someday. And with any luck, I'll start with our honeymoon."

EPILOGUE

Jane glanced around the table and mentally counted the place settings: Grace and Luke; Anna and Mark; Sharon and Rosemary; Brett; Kara and Molly; Kathleen and Sophie; Ivy; herself, and...Henry. Sophie's construction paper placemats were tucked under each ivory dinner plate, and the centerpiece of blossoming dahlias had been a gift from Ivy.

"You're never going to let me live that down, are you?" Henry smiled into her ear as he wrapped his arms around her waist.

Jane leaned back against his chest and smiled. "Probably not, but in fairness, I only knew what a dahlia was after spotting the description card."

"Hey!" Henry laughed, and Jane joined in.

She hesitated, turning serious for a moment. "How was this morning?"

Henry jutted his lip, his eyes drifting far away for a moment. "It was...what I needed. I needed to say good-bye to my mother, to have my say, I guess. We brought

her a bouquet of flowers, just like Ivy always did when we were younger. I'd like to think it means something to her. Somehow."

"It always did," Jane said, squeezing his hand. "She just might not have had the means to show you that." She lifted her chin to meet his lips, when Sophie's screech interrupted them.

"Yuck! Are you gonna kiss?" A look of disgust crumpled her face. "That's *disgusting.*"

Jane frowned, realizing that her daughter had never witnessed any affection between her mother and father. "We are, Sophie," she smiled.

"Ewww! Why?"

"Because when two people love each other, they like to show it." Jane gave Henry a quick peck and glanced at Sophie. "See?"

Sophie wrinkled her nose, considering this. "I guess that wasn't so bad."

Jane laughed, and reached down to swing Sophie up onto her hip, grunting slightly with the effort. Her little girl was growing up; life was changing, moving forward. A year ago, she'd still been married to Adam, still tossing and turning at night in her empty bed, wondering how she could ever face her fears and confront the cold, harsh truth. She'd dreaded this holiday for a year, unable to bear the thought of not spending it with her daughter, and now, she didn't have to worry.

Thanksgiving was tomorrow, and yes, Sophie would be spending it with Adam and Kristy, but today, Jane was surrounded by the people she loved most. Her sisters and mother, her child...and Henry. She slid into her seat as their friends and family pulled out chairs, already talking

over one another and passing cranberry sauce and potatoes, Rosemary proudly boasting about the success of the adult classes at the studios, and the peak in enrollment for the winter session. She'd even allowed latecomers to join *The Nutcracker*, even if it did mess up the costume orders a bit.

Anna came through the kitchen door carrying a huge silver tray and set the enormous turkey near the head of the table. Dad used to sit there, but now their mother took his place. In her hand, Jane noticed, was the handkerchief.

Anna sat back in her chair next to Mark, but as she did, something shiny reflected on her finger, and Jane gasped. It was a ring. Anna's eyes flashed in alarm and she shook her head softly, then turned to Mark.

He cleared his throat and tapped a spoon against his wineglass, and the table fell quiet.

Jane turned to Henry, who grinned and wrapped an arm over her shoulder, and for the first time in so long she started to believe there was hope to be found for all of them. There was certainly a lot to be thankful for.

When her father's death leaves his beloved bookshop empty, Grace Madison heads home to Briar Creek to help run it...and finds herself face-to-face with Luke Hastings, the tall, dark, and sexy reason she fled years ago. He still heats her up like a shot of whiskey on a cold winter's night, but can they put the past behind them this Christmas and linger under the mistletoe?

See the next page for an excerpt from

Mistletoe on Main Street.

Pretty as a postcard.

As much as she wished to deny it, Grace Madison knew that nothing could top Vermont at Christmastime. Drawing to a stop as the snow-dusted road rounded a bend, she stared at the bridge in the near distance, her lips pursed with displeasure. Snow was falling slow and steady, neatly covering the slanted roof in a white blanket. Someone had hung a wreath complete with a red velvet bow just above the arched opening, and icicles gave a natural picot edging to the red-hued truss.

With a sigh, Grace pressed on the accelerator and drove across the bridge, over the frozen water below, and into her childhood home of Briar Creek. The hand-painted sign to the side of the road welcomed her, boasting of a population the size of her city block in Manhattan.

Make that her *old* city block in Manhattan, she corrected herself.

She continued down the familiar path, turning onto Mountain Road as the sun began to dip over the Green

Mountains. Grace flicked on her windshield wipers and fumbled for her headlights, cursing herself for not having learned the way around her rental car when she'd first picked it up. She scrambled with the gadgets around the steering wheel, smiling in grim satisfaction when the warm yellow glow illuminated the vast stretch of road before her. It was times like this when she remembered why she truly did prefer city life. This was the first time she had driven a car in...well, longer than she should probably admit. She and Derek never kept a car in the city—when they needed to go somewhere, they just hailed a cab.

Derek. No need to think about him now. With thinning lips Grace reached over and snapped off the radio and the depressing reminders of its melodies, but as silence encroached and left her alone with her darkening thoughts she abruptly flipped it back on, desperate to find a station that wasn't bleating Christmas carols with limited interruption. Surely there must be a talk radio station somewhere. Something that wasn't a painful reminder of how lonely this Christmas was going to be for her.

Her windshield wipers were in overdrive, in a vain attempt to keep up with the swiftly falling flurries. Wind swirled the flakes, stirring them up from the road in front of her, blinding her path. She slowed her pace to a near crawl, wrapping her hands tighter around the steering wheel, and squinted through the pellets beating against the windshield.

Her tires skidded on a patch of ice, causing her heart to drop into her stomach, and she eased off the gas, fumbling for control until the car came to an abrupt stop.

Grace opened her eyes and looked around. She was staring at a wall of snow as high as the hood of her car.

The woods around her were eerily quiet, and the only sound to be heard was the thumping of her own heart.

She swore under her breath. She not only had to figure a way to get the car on the road again but, unfortunately, she also still had to continue the drive. As if this trip wasn't bad enough already.

She checked herself quickly. She was not dead, or even injured, save the pinch mark on her arm where she managed to convince herself she really was still here. The impact had been comically soft, leading to nothing but complete aggravation about a trip that was already stressful enough. The ear-piercing scream she had released as the nose of the car collided with the snow pile had obviously been an overreaction—fortunately, no one was around to hear it. That also meant there was no one around to help, either.

The snow had turned heavy and wet, so that the flakes no longer flurried in the wind but instead created a dense blanket on the hood of the car. Gritting her teeth, Grace slid the transmission into reverse and gently pressed the gas pedal. When nothing happened, she gave it a little more force, wincing at the sound of her spinning tires. She clenched her hands around the steering wheel, feeling the panic squeeze her chest, and tried again. Nothing.

Without giving it any thought, Grace whipped off her seat belt and pushed open the car door. The wind howled around her, whipping her long, chestnut-brown hair across her face. The stretch of road before her was depressingly barren. The sun was starting to disappear over the mountains in the distance. It would be dark before long, and this old back road hadn't seen a plow all day. By nightfall, it wouldn't even be granted the light from a streetlamp.

Quickly, Grace walked to the front of the car, pressed her palms against the edge of the hood, and gave it a hard push, grunting at the effort. Four more attempts left her exhausted and upset. It was time to call for help. For not the first time today, she wished that Derek was here. This never would have happened if he had been driving.

Foolishness! She climbed back into the car, turning up the radio for company as she searched for her cell phone. It wasn't that she wanted Derek here—after all, they were over. Finished. She'd given back the ring; they had ended on good, if chilly, terms. No, she didn't want Derek here, not rationally speaking. She just wanted the things that Derek could provide, or at least, once had. Security, stability, safety. Comfort and joy. *Good tidings of comfort and*—Oh, that blasted Christmas carol!

Grace flicked off the radio and kept it that way. The last thing she needed right now was to get worked up. She had promised her mother she would arrive in time for dinner, and the last thing she owed anyone in her family was a frown by way of greeting. It would defeat the whole purpose of coming home at all.

She sighed again as she rummaged through her overstuffed handbag, still in search of her phone. Finding it buried beneath two candy bar wrappers and a receipt for the Christmas gifts tucked into her bags, she scrolled through the list of her family members until she found her youngest sister's number.

"Hello?" Jane's voice was barely audible above the clanking of pots. In the background, Grace could make out her mother's voice, followed by that of her middle sister, Anna. No doubt they were gathered in the warm, cozy kitchen right now, hovering around the big island that

anchored the family home, squabbling over which side dish they should make, or who would cover the dessert. She imagined her little niece, Sophie, watching a classic holiday movie or making out her list for Santa.

Grace hesitated as she considered the gift she had bought Sophie for Christmas. She had no firsthand experience with four-year-olds, and Jane was forever raving about how quickly children changed. The last time Grace had seen her had been in the spring, and the time before that was when Sophie was only a year old when Jane and Adam had visited New York for a long weekend. She had been startled by how different Sophie looked nine months ago, and reminded of how much she had missed by staying away all these years.

Well, all the more reason to chin up and make this Christmas count. It was time to start making up for lost time. Time to stop wallowing in her own sorrow.

"Hey there—"

"Where are you?" Jane hissed through the crackling connection.

Grace frowned. "What kind of greeting is that?" She considered turning the car around right then and there. She could be back in the city by midnight, tucked into her bed with a bowl of her favorite Thai delivery and one of those feel-good Christmas movies that they played by the dozen this time of year. But then she remembered that she wasn't exactly feeling the holiday cheer this year. And that she was stuck in a rental car on a snow embankment on one of Briar Creek's most remote roads. And that she no longer had her own bed or her own apartment to hide in. All of her possessions that weren't locked in a storage unit in Brooklyn, New York, were crammed into four bags in the trunk of this car. *Damn it*.

"Sorry," Jane said. "I didn't mean it like that. I'm just...stressed. You know how it is."

Yes, Grace did. This time of year always brought out a hyper, frenzied side to their mother, who would be fretting for weeks in advance over table arrangements and menus, who would stand twenty feet back from the porch and scrutinize the pine garland with narrowed concentration, until her three daughters would shiver with cold, finally rolling their eyes and retreating inside to the warmth of the fire while their father stood patiently awaiting her suggestions, adjusting the garland to her satisfaction with an amused twitch of his lips.

Kathleen Madison was hailed the "Christmas Queen" of Briar Creek. Their house won the Holiday House contest twelve years in a row, until Kathleen deemed it in poor taste to continue, graciously stepping aside to accept the role of judge. "Let's give another family a chance," she had whispered to the girls, suggesting that no one else in town even stood a chance so long as the Madisons were entered.

A freelance decorator, Kathleen saw Christmas as her biggest opportunity of the year. The interior of the Madison home was always finely detailed with a porcelain Christmas village in the bay window, and an antique train set looping around the spectacular Douglas fir that the family selected together each year at the tree farm. Twice the Madisons' tree had appeared on the front page of the *Briar Creek Gazette*. Their annual cards were each laboriously calligraphied by Kathleen's own hand, and she approached her holiday baking with the rigor typically reserved for army drills. Every neighbor, friend, and teacher looked forward to Kathleen's homemade

gift basket; the annual Christmas bazaar relied on her to deliver. And she always did.

"Are you still coming?" Jane asked, trepidation dripping from her words.

"Of course I'm still coming!" Grace squinted through the falling snow, searching for a sign of headlights.

Seeing nothing, she fell back against the headrest, considering Jane's insinuation. She couldn't blame her sister for being skeptical. With the exception of that painful spring morning nine months ago, Grace had managed to stay clear of her hometown and the memories it held. Five years had passed since she'd first left home—not knowing at the time it would be for good—and each year that stretched successfully distanced her further from her past, until eventually her life was tied to New York, not the sleepy New England town. And definitely not to anyone in it.

"I told you I would be there by dinner," she added, furrowing her brow through the whiteout. She flicked her windshield wipers a notch higher. It was no use.

"I just wanted to be sure..." Jane trailed off as the connection began to crackle. "I didn't know if you had changed your mind at the last minute because of ... well, you know."

"If you're referring to the person we shall not name, you have nothing to worry about. I've avoided him for years, and I plan to avoid him for the next week, too." Grace swallowed hard. It could be done. She'd stay at the house, reading books, baking cookies, and trying not to think about the proximity of her first love. Her first heartbreak. Or everything else she had lost recently. "Besides, I'm not even sure why you're giving this any

thought," she added with more conviction than she felt. "He and I are ancient history."

There was a pause on the other end of the line. "If you say so," Jane said softly.

Grace bit down on her lip, knowing it would be useless to try to defend herself. Jane knew her too well; Grace couldn't hide from her. Everyone in the family knew the reason why she had left Briar Creek and stayed away. It was all because of the man whose name they had promised never to say aloud in her presence. The man who could cause Grace's stomach to twist, her blood to still, and her heart to break all over again, just by mere mention.

She had changed her mind about this trip at least a dozen times, but in the end she knew there was no way around it. There was no telling what would prevail in Briar Creek while she was here. The wounds it would open. The scars it would sear. Her life was crumbling enough as it was—she couldn't risk any more upset.

Things were bleak. She'd managed not to think about it now for, oh—she checked the clock—seventeen minutes. Well, that was two minutes more than the last time she'd stumbled into her darkening thoughts. Her relationship wasn't the only thing that was over. Her career was rapidly unraveling as well.

She firmed her mouth. She couldn't think about any of this right now.

She slammed her foot on the accelerator, whimpering as the wheels ground deeper into the snow.

"Well, before you get here there's something I wanted to talk about—"

Grace almost managed to laugh. Now was hardly the

time to settle in for a long chat. "Can we discuss this later, Jane? I'm sort of stuck in a snowbank here."

"What?" Jane's voice was shrill, and Grace pulled the phone away from her ear, bringing it back in time to hear her sister say, "Should I call the police?"

"Relax," she said, giving the pedal everything she had in her. "I'm fine. I just slid off the road and now I can't get this," she pressed on the gas once more, knowing it was pointless, but still hoping, "stupid car to move!"

"But you're okay?" came Jane's urgent reply, and Grace instantly regretted worrying her. With everything their family had been through in the past year, she knew all of them were feeling sensitive.

"Yes, I'm fine. We've been talking for minutes, haven't we?" Grace put the car in park and trained her eye on the rearview mirror. "I just...I need you to come and get me. I'm going to have to call for a tow." From the distance, Grace thought she detected the sudden glow of a car making its way through the darkness. She perked up, sitting straighter in her seat, watching intently as the headlights grow closer. Sure enough, the SUV slowed and then pulled to a stop in front of her. She bit back a smile as she began gathering her belongings, ready to make a swift getaway.

"Never mind, Jane," she said quickly. "Someone just pulled up."

"Oh, good," Jane gushed. "So you'll be here soon?"

"I'll hitch a ride into town, but I might need you to meet me there." She could wait in her father's bookstore if need be—the thought of it brightened her. There was one silver lining to coming back to Briar Creek, at least. Main Street Books always had a way of making her forget her troubles.

"Okay. If I don't hear from you, I'll assume you're on your way."

Grace disconnected the call, musing over their casual comfort at the mere notion of hitching a ride with a stranger. She would never consider such a thing elsewhere, if the opportunity was even granted. Things were different in these parts, though. If someone saw a car pulled over in Briar Creek, they'd stop and lend a hand. If the same situation happened in New York, they'd just keep on going.

A tapping at her window startled her and she quickly crammed empty coffee cups and evidence from an indulgent stop at a fast-food joint somewhere near the Vermont border into their bags. Smiling apologetically, she shifted to face the window, her breath locking in her chest when she saw Luke Hastings's equally shocked face peering back at her.

She stared at him, not blinking, clutching a grease-stained paper bag to her heaving chest. *This day keeps getting better and better.* She had barely skidded past the town line, and she was already running into the one man she had hoped to avoid. Forever.

The lights from his black Range Rover beamed strong, and Grace noticed with a heaviness in her heart that he hadn't lost his looks since she'd last seen him. If anything, his features had hardened into something more manly and strong. The fine lines around his dark blue eyes gave him character, and their deep-set intensity gave her the same rush it always had. *Damn him.*

Grace held his gaze, knowing she was trapped. She was at his mercy now. He could walk away, refuse to help, drive off and leave her stranded on this unlit mountain

road. In a snowstorm. No man would do that, not even Luke. But oh, she bitterly wished he would.

For not the first time she found miserable irony in the fact that Luke was, and always had been, a gentleman.

Grace rolled down the window with the press of her finger. "What the hell are you doing here?" she demanded.

An inquisitive smirk passed over Luke's rugged features. "Shouldn't I be the one asking you that?"

"I'm here for Christmas," she said tightly.

"Christmas isn't for another week," he said gruffly.

"So, it's still my town."

He lifted an eyebrow. "Is it?"

Grace looked away. "You can be on your way, Luke. I just got off the phone with Jane; she can come and get me." Her face burned as she fumbled in her handbag for her cell phone, blindly reaching for wherever it had landed.

Luke assessed the situation with a frown. "Looks like you've gotten yourself into a bit of a jam." He studied her. "Are you hurt?"

Grace pinched her lips and shifted her gaze from his scrutiny, but her eyes kept flitting back. Despite the winter chill that nipped at her nose and fingers, she felt overheated and stifled. "I'm fine, thank you. Everything is just...fine." And it was, or it would be, when he left. When he turned his back and walked away, like he had all those years ago.

A hint of a smile passed over his lips. "Really."

"Yes, really!" With that, Grace raised the window, feeling a moment of relief for the thin glass that separated her from...from the man whose name was never to be mentioned. She knit her brow and turned to glare at the

steering wheel. Clenching her teeth, she pulled the car into reverse and hit the accelerator at full throttle. The tires spun loudly, but the car didn't move.

Heart pounding, she stared despondently at the dashboard for a few seconds before shifting her eyes to Luke's penetrating gaze. The corner of his mouth twitched, those blue eyes sparked, and Grace dragged a deep sigh, digging her nails into her palms.

He pointed his finger toward the car handle, gesturing for her to unlock it. His intense stare fused with hers, hooded by the point of his brow. His full lips spread thin, giving insight into his displeasure.

Well, the feeling was mutual, Grace thought with a huff. Tearing her attention from him, she unlocked the door. An icy cold wind whipped her in the face as she pushed open the door.

"What were you doing driving on this road in these conditions?" Luke demanded as she climbed out of the car. His dark hair spilled over his forehead, slick with snow. "You should have taken Oak or South Main."

Grace yanked away his half-hearted gesture to help her, and he let his hand fall at his side. She narrowed her eyes at the smirk that curled at those irresistible lips. The lips she had known as well as her own. Every line, every curve, every taste. She squared her shoulders and met his eye stonily. "Well, I took Mountain Road, okay? Besides, I could say the same thing to you!"

Luke tipped his head. "Not really. I live off Mountain Road. And I have four-wheel drive."

Grace bristled. She hadn't even thought to take South Main, even though it would have been a straight shot into town. Somehow, subconsciously, she had driven herself in

the direction of the one person she hoped to avoid. The little part of her that longed for something that could never be had overruled all rational thought. And now, well, she supposed she'd gotten what she'd wanted. She was standing here, staring into the face of the man she hadn't seen, with the exception of that one, fleeting time she'd rather forget, in five years.

"I meant driving in the snow. At...this hour." She motioned to the darkness all around them.

She watched as Luke fought off a smile. A sheen of amusement lit his eyes. He made a show of checking his watch. "It's five o'clock," he said. "And my place is just down that way, as you'll remember." The grin finally got the better of him.

"Well." Grace inhaled sharply, the cold air slicing her lungs, and looked away. The snow was coming down in heavy, thick flakes. The hood of her car had already collected at least an inch, and her hair felt wet and heavy against her gray wool coat. *Perfect snowman weather,* she couldn't help thinking. If she were feeling the Christmas spirit, that is—and she wasn't. She most certainly wasn't.

"What are you doing out here?" he asked.

"I told you. I'm on my way home."

His jaw hardened. "Thought you said you were never coming back to Briar Creek."

She glared at him. That was only half the story, and he knew it. "Jane asked me to come home," she explained. "With everything that's happened recently, I couldn't exactly say no."

Luke nodded slowly. "I suppose not." He looked to the ground, shoving his hands in his pockets. "I didn't know you were coming."

"That's a surprise. Word usually travels fast around here." She folded her arms across her chest defensively, eyeing him through the falling snow.

He narrowed his gaze. After a beat, he murmured, "Yes. Yes, it usually does."

With a sigh he broke her stare and wandered over to inspect the collision site. She waited to see if he would find amusement in her predicament, but he didn't seem to be in the mood for laughs. The realization disappointed her, all at once reminding her of what they once had and no longer did. Standing here with the one person who knew her best, alone in the dark, on this cold mountain road, she had never felt more alone.

"Well," Luke said, bending down to inspect the situation more closely. "It doesn't look like you're going to get it out of this bank on your own."

"I'll call for a tow truck then," she said, rummaging through her bag and inadvertently setting a candy bar wrapper loose. She watched it whip through the wind, somewhere in the direction of the woods, and she could practically see Luke chuckling from her periphery. Finding her phone, she furiously tapped the number for information and waited. Nothing. Her breath caught in her chest as she pulled the phone from her ear and glanced at the screen. Connection lost. Of course.

She eyed Luke furtively, feeling her anger burn as a twinkle of enjoyment flashed through his blue eyes. Was this so easy for him? Did he not feel anything?

"No connection?"

"I had one a minute ago…" She exhaled deeply, and then rolled back her shoulders to fix her gaze on him. A rumble of something dangerous passed through

her stomach as she studied his face. Would he ever not have this effect on her? "If you don't mind going into town for a tow, I'll just wait inside the car." She paused, gritting her teeth as she hesitated on her next words. "Thank you."

He looked at her like she was half crazy. "You think I'm going to go for help and leave you out here?"

She shrugged. "Why not? You've done worse to me."

A flash of exasperation crossed his rugged features. He rubbed a hand over his tense jaw, his eyes sharp as steel. Grace knew that look, knew it all too well. She'd made him angry. *Well, good.*

"Get in my car," he ordered, jutting his chin in the direction of his big black vehicle. "It's freezing out here."

Grace tried to suppress the shiver that was building deep within her. She'd be damned if she let him see how cold she was in her simple wool peacoat. She planted her feet to the ground, but it was no use. She shuddered, then inwardly cursed as Luke's expression softened.

"Here, take my scarf." He started walking toward her, but she reflexively took a step back. He stopped, his shoulders slumping. "Grace. Take the scarf."

Grace lifted her chin, her lips thinning. She glanced at him out of the corner of her eye, and her heart panged. There he was. Her sweet love. Luke Hastings. The love of her life. The man who had chased her through the icy waters of the creek in the heat of summer. The man who had taken her to bed in cool, cotton sheets. The man who had kissed her until she wept, the man who had held her until she couldn't breathe. The man whose smile could warm her heart, and whose frown could stop it. The man who represented every part of her past, and who was

supposed to have held every moment of her future. The man no one since had ever been able to live up to.

"Fine," she muttered, reaching out to take the navy scarf. As she tied it around her neck, she subtly breathed into the fabric, closing her eyes to familiarity of the musky scent. She fingered the fringe at the bottom, knowing she had never seen Luke wear this scarf in all the years they were together.

She wondered when he had gotten it. She wondered if his wife had bought it for him.

"Your bags in the trunk?" Luke asked, and Grace nodded. Without another word, he popped the trunk and pulled out two large bags. He carried them low at his sides to his car and then returned for the second round. "You never did pack light," he grumbled as he brushed past her.

Grace hung back as he loaded her belongings, and glanced despairingly at her rental car, which was obviously not going anywhere on its own. "Should have listened to my gut," she whispered to herself. *Shouldn't have come here at all.*

"You coming or not?" Luke called with obvious impatience.

Grace closed her eyes, shaking her head in the negative even as she began walking toward the glow of his taillights. Each crunch of snow under her boots brought her one step closer to the part of her she had tried to deny since the day she left this town for good. Each inch closer to Luke's world took her further out of the one she had built for herself.

She reached the passenger door and yanked it open. If she stepped inside this car—Luke's car—there would be no going back. She paused, her breath coming in ragged

spurts. She wiped a strand of cold, wet hair from her fore-head. Inside the car, Luke was watching her expectantly, the heat from the vents felt almost suffocating against the crisp evening air.

With one last breath for courage, she climbed inside and left the safety of her world behind with a slam of the door. Like it or not, she was back in Briar Creek. And so far, it was going even worse than expected.

Fall in Love with Forever Romance

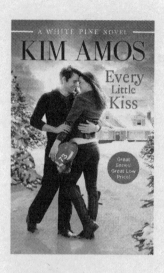

EVERY LITTLE KISS
by Kim Amos

Casey Tanner, eternal good girl, is finally ready to have some fun. Step one: a fling with sexy firefighter Abe Cameron. But can Abe convince her that this fling is forever? Fans of Kristan Higgins, Jill Shalvis, and Lori Wilde will fall for Kim Amos's White Pine series!

HOPE SPRINGS ON MAIN STREET
by Olivia Miles

Now that her cheating ex-husband has proposed to "the other woman," Jane Madison has moved on—to dinners of wine and candy, and to single motherhood. When her ex's sexy best friend Henry Birch comes back to town, their chemistry is undeniable. Can Henry convince Jane to love again? Find out in the latest in Olivia Miles's Briar Creek series!

Fall in Love with Forever Romance

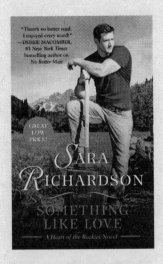

SOMETHING LIKE LOVE
by Sara Richardson

Ben Noble needs to do some damage control. His heart has always been in ranching, but there's no escaping the spotlight on his high-powered political family. The only thing that can restore his reputation is a getaway to the fresh air of Aspen, Colorado. Not to mention that the trip gives Ben a second chance to impress a certain gorgeous mountain guide. But Paige Harper is nothing like the shy girl he remembers...she's so much more.

WALK THROUGH FIRE
by Kristen Ashley

Millie Cross knows what it's like to burn for someone. She was young and wild, and he was fierce and wilder—a Chaos biker who made her heart pound. Twenty years later, Millie's chance run-in with her old flame sparks a desire she just can't ignore...Fans of Lori Foster will love the latest Chaos novel from *New York Times* bestselling author Kristen Ashley!

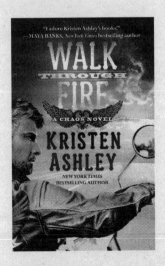

Fall in Love with Forever Romance

"A delightful new voice in historical romance!"
—Tessa Dare, *New York Times* bestselling author

ONE WILD WINTER'S EVE
by Anne Barton

Lady Rose Sherbourne never engages in unseemly behavior—except for the summer she spent in the arms of the handsome stable master Charles Holland years ago. So what's a proper lady to do when Charles, as devoted as ever, walks back into her life? Fans of Elizabeth Hoyt and Sarah MacLean will love this Regency-era romance by Anne Barton.

Also by Olivia Miles:

Mistletoe on Main Street
A Match Made on Main Street

"AND WHAT DID *YOU* WANT?"

Jane blinked and stared at the fireplace before sliding Henry a strange smile. "Do you know, I can't remember the last time anyone asked me that." She paused. "All I want is to keep my daughter with me. That's the only thing that's important."

"Do you want to remarry?"

Jane arched an eyebrow. "Do you?"

Henry pulled back against the couch cushion. "Touché," he said, when what he was really thinking was, *Hell, no.*

He set his mug on a coaster and rested his elbows heavily on his knees. He should go. Now. Before he did anything stupid.

Instead, he turned to her, noticing the way her full lips parted, her gaze steady, her lashes fluttering softly. A lock of hair slipped over her cheek, and without thinking, he reached up and tucked it behind her ear.

She gave a hesitant smile, her eyes widening slightly as his hand grazed down her neck, his thumb tracing her delicate collarbone, trailing over to her shoulder. Her skin was soft and warm, her breath shallow, and her eyes searching. He lowered his gaze to her mouth, unable to hold back or fight this urge that had built for so long, and brought his lips to hers...